the Awkward
Path to
Getting
Lucky

mira

the Awkward Path to Getting Lucky

A NOVEL

Summer Heacock

mira

Recycling programs for this product may not exist in your area.

ISBN-13: 978-0-7783-3085-1

The Awkward Path to Getting Lucky

Copyright © 2017 by Summer Heacock

For questions and comments about the quality of this book, please contact us at CustomerService@Harlequin.com.

www.BookClubbish.com

Printed in U.S.A.

To my dearest mother.

*May this heartfelt dedication persuade you to
ignore the fact that this book is about vaginas.*

*Also, if you read past this page,
I can no longer guarantee direct eye contact.
Love you, Mommy.*

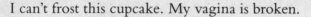

1

I can't frost this cupcake. My vagina is broken.

Get a grip, Kat, I tell myself. *Nothing has changed in the last ten minutes. Nothing.*

Nothing, except I looked at an invoice, saw today's date and realized that in thirty-four days, it will have been exactly two years to the day since I've had sex. Two years. Two whole damn years. I don't even see how that's possible.

I mean, I've been busy! I was starting a business. That takes time. These cupcakes don't decorate themselves.

And this one sure isn't going to if I don't get it together and focus. I've got about six minutes before the customer arrives to pick up his order, and I've got as many cuppies to ice in that time.

"You okay, Kat?" Butter asks, whooshing by me in a flurry of powdered sugar and edible glitter. Butter is all about the edible glitter. "Need some help?"

I shake my head. "Nope! I've got this!" Goddamn straight, I've got this. I'm a professional. I scrape off the shoddily piped chocolate buttercream and carefully squeeze out a perfect topper to the cupcake. I pick it up and set it in the to-go box before tackling the final five.

It's not like I didn't know it had been a while. I knew. But in my head it was maybe less than a year, because letting this go on any longer than that would be absolute madness.

The only reason I know it's been almost two years is that the last time Ryan and I even attempted to have sex was on our second anniversary, and that was an unmitigated disaster.

Things had been stressful at the time. The shop had only been open for just over a year, still in that very manic sink-or-swim phase, and I'd been working nonstop. Then, on the night of our second anniversary, Ryan suggested that we move in together. Thanks to my eighty-hour work weeks, sex had become a sort of secondary thought for a few months leading up to the night, and even when we found the time or the ever-elusive mood, it just wasn't working, physically.

That night, it became flat-out impossible.

Soon after, my gynecologist dropped the bomb: *vaginismus*. A disorder that sounds like a questionable Harry Potter spell, but the diagnosis meant that my jaunty bits had stopped functioning, muscularly speaking. Basically, it made sex really hurty, and it wasn't something I was super in the mood for anyway, what with the promise of excruciating owies in place of sunshine and orgasms.

It made sense not to rush into cohabitation with Ryan while my junk was on the fritz, so we agreed to hold off until my nonfunctioning gal parts were back to behaving properly. Then, on our anniversary last year, he asked me again, but the issue remained, so we tabled the idea once more.

The plan was to try again this year.

This year on the anniversary that is coming up in thirty-four goddamn days.

How have I let this go on for so long? I don't even remember the last time we talked about the issue. I suppose Ryan's been waiting for me to take the lead. That's sort of how our relationship works: I make plans, he rolls with it and fun times are had by all.

Except the whole sex thing, it would seem.

I guess it just sort of fell off my to-do list. There were more pressing issues to be dealt with. Like business plans and fondant sculpting seminars and scrambling with Butter and Shannon to get Cup My Cakes off the ground.

Two years, though.

I need to get laid. Like, yesterday.

I wonder if Ryan is freaking out about this as much as I am. Or, worse, what if he's been freaking out about it for two years like I am right now, but I've had it pushed completely out of my mind? What kind of a hideous girlfriend am I?

I let him believe I'd handle everything, and now here I am—big fat not handling a damn thing.

I pop the last cupcake in the to-go box and seal it up just as the customer walks in. Ben Cleary, a regular who orders two dozen cupcakes every Wednesday for his coworkers. Always half chocolate, half whatever our special is, but prepared in allergen-friendly conditions because his assistant has a tree nut allergy. He's a pretty awesome boss, I assume.

The front entrance opens, and in walk more customers. It's our morning rush, when we get a combination of people coming in for coffee and muffins, and those who pretend they're coming for muffins but are really coming for things covered in frosting.

I wonder if any of these people are dealing with broken bits… I remember my doc saying how common the disorder was, so the odds are good that there are some idle woo-woos in here on a fairly regular basis.

I feel a sudden and overwhelming urge to fix the situation

right this very damn second. Now that it's in my head, it's all I can think about.

I wonder whether Ryan would be willing to give things a test run in the storage room over his lunch break...

Then I remember that today is his quarterly review with his team. The tie-wearing manager comes down from the fourth floor for the meeting and everything. I don't think he could slip away from that, even with the promise of attempted midday delight.

Attempted. Even if I got him over here, or anywhere, for that matter, I don't know if I could physically do it.

Two years.

Twoyearstwoyearstwoyearstwoyearstwoyears.

An urgent sense of panic is engulfing my sanity. There are several men in the mix of people standing in line to order. I start scanning them like I'm a lascivious cyborg. Are any of these specimens potentially sexually compatible?

Butter is handing change over to an older gentleman who comes in twice a week for coffee and a scone. He always wears a bow tie and a bowler hat with a Mr. Rogers cardigan, even if it's ninety degrees out.

Sure, he's probably in his late eighties, but I suppose it's possible he still has some spring in his step. The liver spots on his hands do sort of bring out his eyes.

Stacking up the boxes of cuppies, I give Ben Cleary a good once-over as Butter and Shannon move to greet him at the counter. Hmm, he's a good-looking fella. Very pale skin, blue eyes, dark hair, not too skinny, not overly beefy, kind of quiet. A jawline I could slice my hand open on.

My eyes drift from Ben to survey the front room of our shop. Sky blue walls with trim painted daffodil yellow and a springy green. Designed so that when you walk through the front door, seeing the decor combined with the tasty smells wafting from our kitchen is like stepping into a full-sensory hug.

The innocent decor contrasted with my hyper-focused surge of concentrated frogginess is unsettling at best.

"Uh, Kat?" Shannon says.

"Yes?" I say, my voice sounding detached as my unwholesome gaze shifts to a man who is at least in his sixties. He's wearing a wrinkled lavender button-down shirt tucked into denim shorts and socks with his sandals, but I'm debating his sexual prowess nevertheless.

"Let go of the cupcakes, Kat," she says, and I'm now aware of her attempting to tug the to-go boxes out of my arms. I release my grip and step back, and Shannon gives me a concerned look. "You okay there, Pumpkin?"

I blink at her. Butter is standing at the counter, pouring Ben a cup of coffee, and our new cake decorator, Liz, has come out from the back room to help with customers.

And then there's me. Standing here sexually objectifying senior citizens.

Oh god. What am I doing? I don't want to have sex with geriatrics or random customers. Ryan. I want to have sex with *Ryan*.

He and I are going to have one hell of a chat tonight. And, gods willing, some absurdly long-overdue naked time.

I look up at the kind old man I was just meat-marketing and feel mildly sick to my stomach.

"Uh, Kat?" Shannon nudges me.

"Yep," I lie. "I'm great. I'm awesome. Super awesome."

Shannon narrows her gaze at me, but swings the boxes around to Ben. "Can you finish up with him?" she asks me, her happy customer service expression already back on for the other customers as she moves down the counter.

"Sure." I shake off the criminally unfortunate images that

were just forming in my mind and make my way to the register, where Butter is now showing Ben the Cuppie of the Day.

"White chocolate with a raspberry jam center," she says excitedly. No one loves cupcakes as much as Butter. She's been here with us since day one, and she still gets kid-on-Christmas-morning excited to see these little culinary treats go out the door.

"They look great," he says with a genuine smile. "The hidden truffles last week were a big hit."

I grin. Butter looks like she's going to squee out loud. The hidden truffle cupcakes were all her master plan.

She reaches behind her for a small jar of edible glitter with a brush sitting inside and, in her flustered state, starts dusting the tops of the white chocolate cuppies with reckless abandon.

"That's her way of saying thank you," I offer. "Not just anyone gets extra glitter, you know."

Butter has been known to shower glitter on anyone she thinks needs a boost in their day. Everyone should have a Butter in their lives.

He raises an eyebrow. "I will cherish this honor." He tips his coffee cup to us in a mock salute, takes his boxes and bids us both a good day.

Butter is on cloud nine. I've never seen someone better suited for her job. I love what I do—we all do—but even when we are all exhausted and bitching about the long hours and ungrateful customers who grouse over too much or too little frosting on their kids' birthday cakes (yes, that happens), Butter is always happy to be here.

If I didn't love her so dearly, I'd probably have to hate her.

Mr. Cleary heads out, as do Bowler Hat and Socks with Sandals, and we deal with the rush. I manage to avoid any more wildly inappropriate thoughts about our elderly customers and get my head back in the game.

Okay, so, yes. This is a problem. One that I need to deal with. But right now, I need to focus on getting through this Wednesday and an imminent staff meeting.

After the morning burst, we meet for a little huddle in the back room by the workstations. This routine is partly to gather our wits, and partly so we can stand and drink coffee and catch our breath without any potential customers catching us with our aprons down.

Shannon, Butter and I started Cup My Cakes together three years ago, and we all have our place in the arc of power. Shannon Brimley, tall and tough with a mop of curly blond hair tucked under a tied cake-themed handkerchief most days, is our master organizer. Mika "Butter" Kawai is our culinary genius and a perpetual ball of happiness, with beautiful black hair as thick as her finest buttercream, always pulled back into some sort of braid. Liz Watson, our newest employee, is the teeniest adult I've ever known, all pale skin and even paler hair, and the lord paramount of elegant cake artistry.

And then there's me. The middle child. The resident cupcake decorator and sexless wonder.

"We sold out of the cranberry scones again," Shannon says, taking a sinful sip of coffee. Shannon is the only one of our group who has taken the leap into the big leagues of the adult world. She's been married for a decade and has two tiny little humans she actually created and manages to keep alive and everything.

Of the four of us, I imagine she sleeps the least.

"Should we make more tomorrow?" she asks.

"Maybe a couple?" I shrug. "I'd say no more than six. Then reevaluate."

Butter nods. "I agree." She picks up a chunk of blue fondant off the station and starts rolling it out. "And we definitely need to have another pan of brownies ready to go first thing in the morning from now on. This is the second week straight we've run out well before the end of rush."

"Noted. Liz, how's the Guffman cake coming?" Shannon says, scanning down her little scratch pad to-do list.

Liz makes a face and looks over at the cooling racks, where six layers of cake sit with fondant setting. "I'm about to assemble and then start the second-stage decorations. I kind of hate this cake."

The Guffmans are avid followers of the Green Bay Packers, so for their wedding this coming Saturday, they requested a six-tier cake with a giant Cheesehead thing on it. It's all bright green and yellow and orange colors, and there isn't a single candy pearl to be found anywhere. It is, in fact, Liz's worst nightmare in cake form.

"I can help with it!" Butter volunteers happily. Liz gives a small but appreciative smile.

"Don't you have that fortieth anniversary cake to do next?" I ask Liz. "All covered in intricate stencils and edible rhinestones? Which I honestly had no idea were even a thing until you started working here."

Liz perks right up. "Yes! I forgot about that order."

I raise my mug. "See? There's a light at the end of your Cheesehead tunnel."

Shannon turns to me. "Where are you on the Sadie Hawkins order?"

We were contracted by a local middle school to provide tasty treats for their upcoming dance. Gesturing to the cooling racks in the back, I say, "The first hundred are cooling, I'll start the rest now, and if I go all day, I should have all five hundred decorated long before it's time to head home."

"All right," Shannon says. "Butter, you're going to help Liz, and you'll be working on the triplets' smash cakes, yes?" Butter nods. "Great. And I'll be restocking the front display case and working on the rest of the orders for tomorrow. I'll also be doing a trial run of the personal pies so we can test those out before we launch them next week. Later today I'll go and make our deliveries. Also, the Capuzo order is going out this afternoon, so everyone gird things."

I roll my eyes. Mr. Capuzo is a semi-regular customer who comes in every few months and is either incredibly pleased with our services or pitches a raging holy fit about the weirdest things. Once he bought all the oatmeal raisin cookies in our display case, then came stomping back in five minutes later because he'd thought the raisins were chocolate chips. Never mind the fact that the cookies were clearly labeled—he still considered the raisins to be a "betrayal."

I so would not have sex with Mr. Capuzo.

"Not it!" Butter calls out. "I'm still not over his meltdown from when the strawberry short-cuppies didn't have as much filling as he thought they should. If I have to wait on him, I'll cry."

Shannon grins. "I'll take him."

"The hell you will." I snort. "Last time you dealt with a jerky customer, you flung a cupcake at him."

"It slipped," she says, casually flipping through the papers in her hand.

"It slipped a good five feet and landed with surprising precision on his chest," I correct her. "We had to pay for his dry cleaning. And Mr. Capuzo is too old to have you throw baked goods at his face—or his face through a window—so no, *I* will take the Capuzo when he comes in."

Liz looks moderately terrified. Shannon smiles. "Kat is our Mouth," she explains. "Butter cries, I throw things, Kat keeps us from getting sued." Liz considers this and shrugs with apparent satisfaction. Shannon looks back at her list. "Okay. Is everybody good? Meeting over?"

"Actually, really quick," Butter says, "I was thinking about doing the coconut cuppie with pineapple curd and candied bacon as the headliner tomorrow." She can turn damn near anything edible into a gourmet cuppie. "When you're out on deliveries, could you pick up some supplies?"

"God, yes," Shannon agrees with an enthusiastic nod. "I think that's my favorite of your recipes. Could you make an extra half dozen so I can take them home to Joe and the kids? They love those so much."

Butter beams. "Sure!" she says. I foresee that extra batch getting the royal edible glitter treatment.

Looking around the shop, Shannon asks, "Is that everything?"

Butter and Liz nod. Shannon takes in a deep breath, smiles and sets her pad down. She takes another glorious sip of coffee.

"Oh, hey," I add casually. "There is one thing."

It's very slight, but I swear I see her wince. "What did I forget? Is there another order?" She starts pulling invoices off the stack on her workstation and flipping through them.

I shake my head. "No, it's nothing like that."

Shannon sets the papers down and lets out a gust of air. "Okay, good. What's up?" she asks, lifting her coffee mug to her lips again.

"My vagina is broken and Ryan and I haven't had sex in almost two years and it's really distracting. Help." A strangled, rupturing sound escapes from Shannon, and suddenly it's raining coffee in the kitchen.

2

"Wait…" Butter asks, her eyes aghast. "What do you mean your vagina's broken? How do you break a vagina?"

Liz, looking horrified, leans toward me and whispers, "Did you fall on it or something?"

I blink at her. "No. No, I didn't fall on it." Shaking my head, I answer, "It's a disorder. Well, that's what my doctor said two years ago, anyway."

Shannon stops mopping the spit coffee off her station and points her towel at me. "Is it vulvodynia? Vaginismus? Vaginitis?"

My jaw flops to my chest. "Vaginismus. How could you possibly know that?"

She barely restrains an eye-roll as she resumes wiping down the coffee-splattered counter. "Oh my god, when you said your vagina was broken, I thought it was something like cancer, you dork." She moves down the station and pushes her towel across the coffee-splattered floor. "I went through vaginismus after Heidi was born."

Butter wheels around. "Wait! Your vagina is broken, too?"

"It's been broken for seven years?" A very unfortunate whimper escapes me.

She looks up at us with that semi-irritating mom expression she uses when we push her patience a smidgen too far. "Guys. No. I was having trouble for a few months after I had Heidi, and the doctor said it was vaginismus. So I went to a physical therapist for maybe three months, did the rest of the therapy at home and I haven't really had any issues since."

I'm gaping at her. "How did I not know about this?"

Shannon grins. "Sorry. Next time one of my reproductive parts shorts out, I'll be sure to bring it up at a staff meeting."

I stick my tongue out at her.

"Wait," Butter interrupts. "Physical therapists...for your... vagina?"

"Yes."

"But..." She blinks at me, and then at Shannon. "For your vagina."

Shannon lets out a deep sigh. "Yes."

"They have those?" Liz squeaks. Shannon nods. "Around here?" She nods again.

Butter explodes. "Are you freaking kidding me? We don't have an Olive Garden, but we have vagina therapists? What even is real life?"

Shannon ignores Butter's outrage and focuses on me. "How have you had this for two years? You're with Ryan!"

"We've been in a...dry spell," I say evasively.

"Honey, you guys have gone two years without sex?" Shannon asks, awed. Liz's eyes get wider.

"Technically," I say with a huff, "it'll be two years in thirty-four days. The last time we tried was on our second anniversary."

Clutching her glitter brush like a security raft, Butter looks traumatized. "Tried? As in, you couldn't even do it?"

As I'm trying to think of a way to explain this to her without causing her irreparable mental harm, Shannon moves in front of Butter. "It's like this," she says. Shannon holds up her hand and points a finger at Butter's face. "If I try to poke you in the eye, what happens?" As she moves her hand closer, Butter instinctively slaps it away.

"If you poke me in the eye, I'll punch you in the boob."

I stifle a snort as Shannon continues. "Go with me here. If I move my finger toward your eye, what happens?" She waves her finger past Butter's eye, and thankfully, no one is boob-punched.

"I blink."

"Okay," Shannon says, slowly. "Now, even though you know it's coming, and you know I'm not going to actually poke you in the eye, what happens?" Moving her finger at a glacial pace, Butter's eye still slams shut of its own accord. My knees clench a little.

"That's vaginismus." Shannon says, shrugging.

"Oh my god, you poor things!" Butter says, clutching her heart.

"Hey, I'm fine now," Shannon says, throwing her hands up. "Kat's the one with the broken hoo-ha."

"You know," I say, taking a long pull of my coffee and wishing it was spiked with bourbon, "you're kind of stealing my vagina thunder here."

Shannon goes over to the pot and refills her own mug. "I just can't believe you've gone two years like this. Didn't you do the therapy?"

Liz, sort of looking like she wants to be set on fire, quietly asks, "What does that mean, exactly?"

I shrug. "My doc said it was all about retraining the muscles or something."

"So why didn't you?" Shannon insists. "I mean, two years, hon."

"I did try!" I say, feeling defensive. "Well, *I* tried. It wasn't one of the finer moments of our relationship. She gave me this little packet of things to try with Ryan, and we did for a while, but it was weird, and he seemed really uncomfortable. So I decided I'd figure it out on my own when I had time to focus on it."

Everyone is staring at me. Finally Butter says, "And how'd that work out for you?"

My brows furrow. "I just sort of lost track of time, I guess." If I weren't so annoyed by the look they are all giving me, I'd have to laugh at the perfect unison in which they all started giving it.

Shannon's face looks like she's trying to solve a complicated math problem in her head. "Wait, your second anniversary? Is that why you told him you weren't ready to live together?"

"Could you for once not remember every tiny detail of everything?"

She gasps. "Is that it? I figured you were just being stubborn about commitment!"

"Oh, stop it. It's not that. But when we tried the therapy stuff, it was so goddamn awkward, and I just wanted to be super sure that when we do try again, it actually works. All the failed attempts didn't do wonders for my self-esteem."

Shannon frowns. "I can see that. You need to be comfortable when you go for it."

"See? It's not like I didn't want to get it sorted. I just didn't have the time to invest. Now it's been nearly two years, and Ryan is supposed to ask me to move in together, and I want to say yes, but I can't until I fix this, and I'm five months away from thirty, and I don't want to end this decade with a broken vagina, you guys. I just really don't."

"That's not good decade juju, no," Butter adds as I suck in a lung-piercing breath.

"And you can't just say yes and actually take the damn time to work on it while you're living together?" Shannon asks.

"No!" I yelp, surprising even myself with my vehement tone. "When you move in with someone, it's supposed to be all happy and exciting and horizontally mamboing on every surface of your new place. Not awkwardly sleeping together, wondering when one person is going to get their nethers back on track. I don't want that hanging over us if we do this."

Butter is lightly pulling the bristles of her glitter brush back and forth across the top of her station. "So, you and Ryan aren't doin' it, but you're—I mean, you guys do the other stuff, right?"

For the first time in this conversation of horrors, I blush. "Not exactly," I mutter.

"Kat." Shannon looks astounded.

"It's too weird!" I shriek. "Okay? It's bizarre. We'd kind of hit that comfortable relationship place where there wasn't like, a ton of making out and stuff, so it felt too random to do that stuff knowing how it *wouldn't* end." I realize Ryan and I never discussed it, but somewhere along the line, we definitely stopped doing anything in the sex category in a mutual way. "That's why this is so important! I don't know how it all got so messed up, but I have to fix it. Now. This is not how relationships are supposed to go, and this is on me."

While Shannon and Butter consider my stance, Liz swallows hard. "Is it possible it just…fixed itself?"

I stare at her, dumbfounded that I haven't considered this possibility sooner. "Um. I don't think so? I'm not sure. Can that happen?" A tiny flicker of hope appears.

Butter looks around desperately. "Look, I didn't even know you could break a vagina!"

We all turn to Shannon, who looks perplexed. "Come on," I say. "You're the resident vagina expert, apparently. Can it?"

Shannon closes her eyes and makes a face that I am pretty sure I've seen her give her kids a few times. She calmly pulls her phone out of her apron pocket and starts typing. I know she's hitting Google hard. We all squish over into her station to read over her shoulder.

"Okay," Butter says, reading from medical websites as Shannon scrolls. "It's like you said—there are therapists, and therapies you can do yourself. This is something that is almost one hundred percent treatable. So, wow. Like you said, the muscles just sort of…clenched up there, didn't they?" I close my eyes and take a deep, calming breath as that flicker of hope poofs away, and Butter looks slightly hurt at my expression. "Well, sorry. I'm trying to catch up. And the disorder keeps you from letting anything, ahem, *in*, so that's what the therapy does. You just keep training the muscles until they are used to, erm, the *in* things. It doesn't say anything about it just going away, but I guess the only way to know would be to…check."

"So," Shannon says plainly, "grab Ryan tonight and go for it."

I blink at her. "As much as I am in desperate need of getting some—and I definitely considered the grab-and-go option—I refuse to give it the old college try with him just to have it not work. Again. I can't do that to either of us." I wave my hand at the phone. "I'll just have to go a different route."

"How are you going to do that without your boyfriend?" Liz whispers.

I fight the urge to pat her head while Shannon stares at her. Butter is gaping.

Clearing my throat, I delicately say, "There are boyfriend substitutes, you see."

It takes her a second, but she gets there. Her face turns bright red, and she takes a large drink of her coffee.

"You sweet summer child," Butter says, shaking her head. "So, Kat, you do that, and then you'll know!"

"Unfortunately," I reply, "I'm lacking the appropriate stock for these experiments. That's not exactly my style."

I'm getting the side-eye from Shannon. "Really? You've been boinkless for that long and you don't have any…gear?"

I scoff, "What? I'm more of a right-click-your-mouse than power-up-your-hard-drive kind of gal. So?"

Liz makes a noise, and I'm certain she's going to faint.

"Sweetie," Shannon says, putting her hand on Liz's shoulder, "if you want to leave this conversation, I swear none of us will hold it against you in the slightest."

"No!" Liz insists. "I'm okay! I just…my friends don't normally talk about this stuff. But I'm fine, really! I want to help."

Shannon pats her on the back. "Teamwork. I admire that." She turns back to her phone. "When I was doing my own therapy at home, I had a stash of things I could use that weren't that far off from what one might use to 'power their hard drive,' as you say, so maybe you can kill two birds with one dildo."

Butter snorts into her coffee and starts choking spectacularly.

"You did not just say that." I shake my head.

"Pumpkin, I've got two kids. More people have seen my vagina with a human being coming out of it than I care to admit. I haven't peed alone in nine years. I have no shame. This stuff happens. When I had my gallbladder out last year, you were right there bringing us food and watching the kids and manning the shop and being the best damn friend in the world to me and mine. We don't pick our challenges. You're like family and I love you—you have a problem and I'm here to help. If that help involves dildos, bring it on. I've fucking got this."

This is certainly our liveliest employee meeting to date.

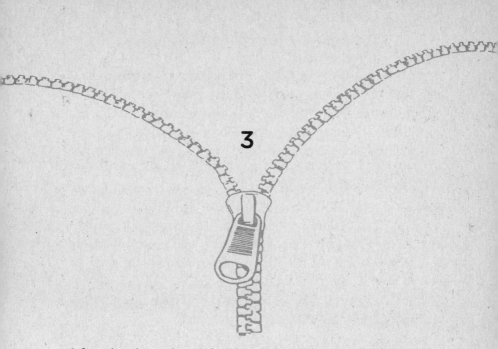

3

After the shop closed for the night, Butter and I hit up the Naughty Market over on Fourth Street. Then I raced home and, with the help of a newly acquired phallic device, made the discovery that my lady bits were indeed still on the fritz.

This did not start my evening with Ryan under an umbrella of joy.

We have standing date nights on Mondays, Wednesdays and Saturdays. If we find some extra free time, we try to meet up more, but working eighty-ish hours a week at the shop doesn't grant me a tremendous amount of time off. Having the together moments scheduled in advance helps make sure I put the piping bag down and remember to have a life. Well, on those three days of the week, anyway.

With a tiny gray storm cloud floating over my head, I carefully stow away all evidence of my experiment in my nightstand before I set to prepping for Ryan's arrival.

I'm feeling uncomfortably electrified about seeing him tonight. For a moment, it reminds me of the jitters from the way back parts of our relationship. When we had a date and I was excited to get ready before he picked me up.

This isn't that. There's an anxiety brewing inside me, knowing it's time to shout until we are both fully aware that the emperor has no clothes and a broken thang.

The more the determination churns in my stomach, the clearer it becomes to me how this has carried on for two years. There's a comfort in our consistency. Our routine may not be dripping with platitudes and romance, but it's ours, and it's soothing.

I toss my flour-covered shirt and jeans into my hamper and change into a nearly identical outfit, sans flour. Taking a look at myself in the mirror, a wave of panic flashes through me.

I quickly yank off my T-shirt and toss it back into a drawer. I have to dig pretty far into the Narnia region of my closet, but I finally find something that's more blouse than T-shirt. At the very least, the cut of the neckline implies I'm aware I have breasts, which is a big step up, really.

Walking up to the mirror in my bathroom, I pull my hair out of my uniform ponytail and grab a brush. Even my hair is efficient. I keep my chocolate-hued locks just long enough that I can whisk them into a ponytail at any height on my head, but not long enough that I have to put in the effort of actually styling them every day.

Plus, when I let my damp hair dry tied back, it finishes all smooth and shiny, if slightly dented. Otherwise I'd have to use blow-dryers and serums, and there'd be frizz to tackle, and I'd just rather spend that twenty minutes sleeping.

As I brush out my hair, a tiny part of my brain wonders when it was that I stopped putting forth any effort in the looks department. I'm expecting some sort of vagina miracle, but I can't even be bothered to make an effort to look nice for our nights together?

Maybe that's what's missing. My vagina misses the joy of getting all dolled up for a night out.

A slightly louder part says it was probably right around the time sex started feeling like a below-the-belt root canal sans anesthetic.

When did Ryan give up?

Did he, though? Is he still putting forth all the best boyfriend maneuvers, but I'm too strung out from work to even notice?

We've fallen into a comfortable groove the last few years. Our date nights are simple, but nice. He brings over takeout, we sit together and talk about our jobs and life and the world that happens around us that I rarely get to take the time to notice. We curl up together on the couch with a couple glasses of wine and watch Netflix or a movie or just keep chatting.

It's nice. These nights are the least stressful parts of my week. I love my time with Ryan, and I can't imagine my life without these moments of Zen with him.

But the more I analyze us, the more I realize there's nothing here that screams "relationship." I could be doing these exact things with Shannon or Butter and have that same feeling of soothing calm.

As much as I'm racking my brain here, I can't find the intimacy in what we've been doing. We have a familiar kiss hello when he arrives, we sit beside each other at the table and on the couch, but we don't cuddle or make out anymore. I'm not even sure we touch each other much.

A wave of sadness washes through my entire body. I miss touching. I miss the feeling of warmth from being physically close to someone. I miss the feeling of skin against mine. Cuddling up next to him used to be one of my favorite things.

I remember when things started tanking in the nookie department, Ryan took a noticeable step back from almost all apparent physical intimacy. When I asked him why, he said he didn't want me to feel like he was pressuring me for sex I couldn't even have.

At the time, I thought that was really sweet, and I appreciated his consideration.

Now I'm just feeling guilty. Like I made him afraid to try to hold my hand. And if I'm being completely honest, I'm also a little resentful, because I really miss that part of our relationship.

I hear my front door open and the familiar sounds of Ryan making his way through my living room to set take-out bags on the counter in the kitchen.

I pull the brush through my hair one more time, set it back down by the sink and head out to greet him.

I peek my head out of my bedroom and watch as he starts setting out containers and cutlery on the counter. He seems right at home.

If I'd agreed to us living together, I wonder if we would have lived here? We never made it that far into the discussion. He'd been hinting at cohabitation for a month or two before our second anniversary, and I liked the idea a lot, but with the onset of trouble in Vagville, I'd always sort of dodged the conversation.

I take a moment and stare at my boyfriend of nearly four years. He's lovely, really. His green eyes are calm and content as he pops the lid off what looks like chicken makhani.

He used to have the sexiest floppy black curls that I loved. It's part of what made me notice him in the first place. Around the time of our first anniversary, Ryan buzzed them off after growing tired of a coworker constantly saying he looked like Sherlock Holmes.

I would have taken this as a high compliment, but Ryan

maintains that Benedict Cumberbatch looks like a bipedal lizard, and the comparison made him self-conscious.

Three years later, it's still cropped short.

The anxious wave hits me again. If I'm longing for the warmth and touching and closeness, I can't even imagine how he feels. Maybe he's been suffering that wave for two years, waiting for me to get it together so he can have it again.

He looks up from the naan he's arranging on a plate and finds me lingering in the doorway.

"Hey, babes," he says with a smile.

"Well, hello there, sir," I say, leaving my place of reflection and heading out to the kitchen. I lean over the bar counter for our welcome kiss.

It's just like every kiss we've had for I don't even know how long, but with everything at the forefront of my mind now, I can't help but overanalyze it. My first thought is it's quick. Perfunctory, even.

It's a takeout-on-Wednesday-nights-at-my-apartment-for-three-years kiss.

Lady bits issues aside, it's alarmingly clear to me now that Ryan and I are way past a simple rut. We've hit a relationship trench, and I've spent the last two years with a shovel in hand, digging us deeper.

And I refuse to hit that two-year drought mark. I just can't let that happen. Which means Ryan and I are going to have to talk about this. It's time. I've put this conversation off for nearly two years for reasons I can't sort out at the moment, but I can't ignore it any longer.

"So," he says, grabbing glasses from my cabinet. "How's life at the office?"

"I think we should see other people," I blurt out, to the astronomical surprise of us both.

4

"Excuse me?" he says, still holding the two glasses.

Putting my hands on the counter for support, I blink awkwardly for a moment, trying to connect the words that just left my mouth to a fleck of sanity in my mind. "I think we should see other people," I repeat, slower this time. "We should take a break."

"Are you breaking up with me?" he asks. He doesn't seem shocked or hurt so much as he seems to want a casual clarification. His lackluster, almost accepting expression makes me suddenly confident I'm doing the right thing, despite the utter lack of forethought I put into this decision.

"No," I say calmly. "I'm saying I think we should take a break, and during that break, you should be free to see other people."

He sets the glasses down, and his face falls into an expression of confusion.

He's still dressed in his work garb. He works for an IT solutions company downtown, where the dress code is polo shirts and jeans at its fanciest. Belts are worn by those who want to put in the extra effort to shine.

I look at Ryan in his half-untucked gray polo and beltless jeans and take a breath.

"Look, I'm just going to address the sexless elephant in the room here." I sigh, throwing up my hands. His eyes go wide. "We haven't had naked time together in almost two years, dude. Did you realize that? In thirty-four days it will have been a full two years."

Ryan's face goes blank, and he tilts his head ever so slightly to the side as he digests the information. "Huh."

"Exactly," I say, crossing my arms. "And I don't know about you, but that seems kind of not great to me."

His confusion returns. "So, because we don't have sex anymore, you want to take a break? A break for what?"

I shrug, feeling electrically charged and sort of sick to my stomach. "I need to get this sorted out, and I honestly can't focus on what I need to do while feeling like the biggest ass in the world for not being able to fulfill my girlfriendly duties."

He rolls his eyes. "If it's been two years, it obviously doesn't matter to me if it takes some time for you to get better. Although it's nice to hear you're thinking about it. I figured you just weren't into sex anymore."

I gape at him. "What?"

"I don't know," he says defensively. "You never bring it up, so I just assumed."

"Well, you never bring it up, either!"

He throws his arms up and says loudly, "Why would I bring it up? It's your problem! What am I supposed to do? Be the jerk who asks for sex you can't have?"

My jaw flops down and I stand up a little taller. "Excuse you," I snap. "*My* problem? If I recall, I tried to get you to work with me on the stuff my doctor told me to do, and you didn't want to because it was *too weird*."

Looking a little embarrassed, he regroups. "Look, I'm sorry, but sex isn't supposed to be that complicated. And you told me she said the therapy was stuff *you* were supposed to do. You said you'd take care of it and let me know when things were okay again."

Now I feel my face burning. "Well, things aren't *okay*." I close my eyes and take a deep breath that is irritatingly shaky. "What I'm saying is, I've gotten so caught up in life and work that I haven't been able to make it a priority, and I want to take the time to focus on everything now."

His eyes shift to the side. His trademark confused look. "That's…good?"

Calmly I continue, "But I *don't* want to feel like I'm keeping you on some sexless leash any longer. That isn't fair to either of us. So let's just call this a break. You go off and do your thing for a few weeks, and I'll be here doing mine, and then we'll regroup and see if we can't get back to where we're supposed to be."

"For how long?"

I square my shoulders. "Until our anniversary."

He stares at me, and I can't tell if he's just contemplating what I'm saying or preparing to argue again. I walk around the counter and close the distance between us. Reaching out, I put my hands on his forearms.

"I love you," I assure him while silently missing his floppy curls all the same. "And I know I told you I didn't want to live together until I got this vaginismus nonsense under control, and I meant that. But you said you'd keep asking on our anniversaries, and I really, really want to be able to say yes this time."

"For the record," he clarifies, "I love you, too. And I've

always been okay with us living together, with or without the sex."

"I know," I say with a smile, "but I'm not. I need to fix this—for myself, and for us. I'm ready to move on to greater things, Ryan. This holding pattern isn't good for anyone anymore."

He looks frustrated, but doesn't pull his arms away. A little calculator in the back of my head announces that this is the longest we have touched in months.

"And you want us to see other people?" he asks.

My eyebrows involuntarily twitch. "Yep. I mean, that's more for you than me, as I'll be involved in independent activities, but yeah. Go out. Get laid. You've waited long enough. And then on our anniversary, we'll meet back up and get to where we should have been this whole time."

Now he does move away from me. I awkwardly let my hands drop to my sides. "You're actually telling me to go have sex with other women. Are you drunk?"

It's my turn to roll my eyes. "No, I'm not. And yes, I *am* serious. I mean, I'd appreciate it if you were careful with protection and didn't, like, actively seek to bang your way up and down the Midwest, but yeah, if you're in a place where an opportunity arises naturally and you want to sleep with someone, I say go for it."

He looks floored. "And you have no problem with that? With the idea of me having sex with someone else?"

I consider this, wanting to be as honest as possible. "It's not my favorite, and I'm not going to go into great thought imagining you in whatever situations may arise, but yeah, I'm okay with it. I can't stand the guilt hanging over me anymore, Ryan. You have needs that I'm not meeting, and it just makes sense to let you live your life while I'm getting my shit together over here."

Ryan gently shakes his head, but seems very calm. He places his hands on the counter by the plates, and his fingers start tapping. Whenever he's deep in thought, they tap out little non-rhythmic signals. He works with computers all day, so I like to imagine he's subconsciously working through things by tapping out binary code or something.

"This is sick."

I give him an encouraging grin. "I like to think it's practical. And it's only thirty-four days."

Ryan stares at me for a long moment, fingers still rapping out a beatless sound, and I can't read his thoughts in the slightest. He looks down at the food he was setting out before I came in and dropped a giant bomb of what-the-fuck.

"I got that veggie korma you like," he says with a sigh, pointing to a tray of yellow sauce. "And the garlic naan."

I'm familiar with this form of acceptance. Ryan is very go-with-the-flow, which is generally a good yin to my yang. Part of me feels a little bad for steamrollering him, but the rest of me knows I'll be able to make it up to him with sweet, sweet lovin' in thirty-four days.

"It smells awesome," I say with a smile.

He seems to easily fall back into our comfortable Wednesday date-night routine as he hands me a plate. "So," he says, spooning rice out onto a plate of his own, "how was work?"

I grab a fork and quietly let out a deep breath. This is going to work. I've totally got this.

Hell, I bet I won't even need all thirty-four days.

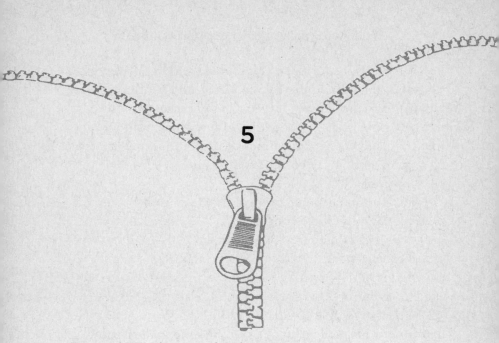

5

"You *what*?" Shannon shrieks at me.

Our morning meeting ended, and I decided to break the news of my master plan to get my vagina back on track.

"I told him to see other people," I repeat, running my finger around the rim of my coffee mug. "We're on a break."

"How the hell is that supposed to help you?" she shouts at me. "You're trying to have sex again, so your plan is to get rid of the guy you could be having that sex with?"

"Will you calm down?" I ask, feeling a bit annoyed at her reaction. "I am going to work on the therapy myself. And I have an appointment with my gynecologist next week. I just want to get things sorted on my end before I jump back into bed with him. I want to make damn sure it all works before we go for it. I'm not putting either of us through another failed roll in the hay, okay?"

Liz looks like I just told her the Earth is actually flat.

Butter looks concerned as she asks, "And how did Ryan take all of this?"

I shrug. "He was okay with it, actually," I answer. "He's a

free agent until our anniversary, and by then, I will bloody well have things in working order, and we'll pick back up again."

I swear I can see smoke rolling out of Shannon's ears. "Part of getting through my therapy had a lot to do with Joe helping me through things, Kat. There was a lot of trial and error!"

"That's you guys," I snap. "You've been together forever and you have kids and it's all kinds of different, okay?"

"Everybody chill out," Butter says, holding up her hands. "There's no reason to get loud with each other."

"But she's being ridiculous!" Shannon argues.

"Lady, calm down," Butter demands, "or I'll hit you with my glitter brush."

Shannon can't help it. The side of her mouth twitches with a hint of a smile. "Well," she says at a far more human volume, "are you going to see other people, too?"

"No. Why would I? That's the whole point. It's a 'Me, Myself and I' kind of therapy."

"Yeah, but the actual having sex thing isn't," she says. "And doing the therapy is very different from sleeping with someone. It's not like you're going to be able to just hop back in that saddle after a few weeks of work and everything goes smoothly, you know? It can take a few tries."

I gasp. "You never told me that!"

Shannon looks around wildly. "When would I have had a chance to tell you? How was I supposed to know you'd run home and break up with Ryan?"

"Glitter brush, guys!" Butter warns.

Shannon takes the kind of breath that I have seen her take many times before when dealing with her children. "I'm just saying that in this case, practice really does make perfect."

"Since he's going to be seeing other people," Butter offers, "why don't you see other people, too? Then you could…uh, practice."

Looking like she's giving this thought way more consideration than it deserves, Shannon says, "That could work, actually."

I look at them like they've each grown three heads. "How am I supposed to date someone new with all this going on? 'So, this is great—however, it's possible I can't have sex with you, but let's go ahead and give that third date a go anyway'?"

Shannon frowns. "Yeah, you'd want to try with someone you were really comfortable with, for sure." With a frown directed squarely at me, she adds, "Which is what I assumed Ryan would be."

I glare at her. "Will you stop? This is hard enough without added guilt from you. He seemed okay with the situation."

I think he was, anyway. And I think I am.

I am, aren't I?

We are all standing here, sipping coffee and contemplating what Shannon has said when the back doorbell dings. Morning deliveries. Shannon sighs and sets down her mug, giving it a longing look before she heads out to sign for everything.

Liz, her white-blond hair pulled back tightly into a chignon today, starts fiddling with a ball of lavender-colored fondant. Butter takes her brush out of her apron pocket and pokes at the inside of a nearly empty glitter pot on her station. Both of them are clearly avoiding my gaze, which is more than a little awkward.

Then Shannon comes running back in with a mischievous smile on her face and a stack of boxes in her arms. She's practically skipping as she sets them down on her station.

"Whatcha doing?" I ask.

"What's up with you?" Butter asks. "You didn't even finish your coffee."

"They came," Shannon says gleefully, bouncing on her toes. Butter gasps. Liz blushes. I glare.

"What came?"

They fly at the boxes, and suddenly it's like Christmas morning, but with powdered sugar dust flying everywhere in lieu of snow. There's a rustling of paper, squealing, a gasp from Liz, and a few seconds later, Shannon and Butter emerge, hands clutching a variety of sex toys.

"Oh. My. God."

"Look what we got!"

I shake my head and rub my temples. "I see what you got. Why did you get them?"

"Well, seeing as you waited two years to take matters into your own hands," Shannon says with an exaggerated wink, "we decided we'd step up and give you some motivation. I remember all the things my doc suggested I use, so we ordered you everything! There are dilators, different kinds of lubes, faux-penises in varying sizes, natural and synthetic materials— all the things a gal could possibly need to stroll her vagina down the road to recovery!"

She and Butter are standing there in our tiny kitchen, a dildo and bottle of lube in each hand, held proudly over their heads in triumph, looks of absolute glee on their faces. Liz's face slowly drops its look of horror as she edges closer to the boxes and peeks inside.

"You guys are the best friends a vagina could have." I smile. "This is also the weirdest thing I've ever been a part of. You had sex toys overnighted to our bakery. Why'd you have them delivered here?"

"Because I couldn't carry all of this on my walk to work," Butter says as she starts loading my arms up with fleshy implements.

Shannon hands me a bottle of all-natural lubricant. "And

if they came to my house, my kids would have thought they were early birthday presents. Back when I was in this scene, they were both too little to notice, but now they wouldn't think twice before tearing the boxes open. And that would be hard to explain to Child Protective Services."

"Fair enough."

"And!" Shannon continues like a demented game show host. "I forgot to tell you, what with the Ryan news, but last night I printed off a whole bunch of instructions on the different techniques for you." She reaches under the prep table and pulls out what can only be described as a home-printed encyclopedia of vaginal information.

I flip through some of the pages. There are diagrams, full-color schematics of anatomy and pages upon pages of different therapy tools, which could also be confused with a sex-toy police lineup. The devices are all assorted by length, girth and so on—and presented in a clinical manner that's both hilarious and a bit unsettling.

"The next time any of you has an even slightly embarrassing condition, you just wait," I say, shaking my head. "It's so on."

"Now we just need to get you a date!" Butter adds.

I drop a dildo. "Excuse me?"

"A date! Come on, we just talked about this! So when your noonie is at full capacity, you've got someone ready to test it out with!"

Shannon jabs a dilator through the air. "I'm coming around on that, actually. Things were definitely easier for me since I had Joe to practice with, so what if we set you up with someone? Because I know this guy Richard from City Planning, and I have always thought he'd be perfect for you."

Butter chokes on a laugh, and her hands, still full of flesh-colored rubber penises, fly to her mouth. I shake my head. "Shannon."

"What?"

"Richard? You want to set me up with a guy named Dick? Come on."

Her face goes still as she processes, and then she doubles over laughing, her ponytail of golden curls flying by my face as she cackles toward the floor. "I swear I didn't think of that," she gasps without looking up. "But, oh my god, that's amazing."

Letting her own guffaw loose, Butter adds, "I knew a Willy in college. I bet he's still single. Want me to give him a call?"

Liz giggles over the boxes. "One of our groomsmen is named Peter."

Jerking up to a standing position, Shannon has tears streaming down her face. "What about Rod who does deliveries on Thursdays? Or, okay, there's a guy who works at the butcher shop by my house, and cross my heart, his name is Lance Johnson."

She flops over onto the prep table, completely taken by hysterics. Butter is making strangled sounds as she tries to pull in air through her laughter, and even Liz has lost it.

"Hardy-har, yes, it's hilarious, they all have names like penises," I say, shaking my head. My coworkers are all in various states of collapse, clutching sex toys, laughing like ten-year-old boys, and while sure, Lance Johnson is actually pretty hilarious, I'm not feeling very chuckly at the moment.

It really has been forever since I've even been out with a guy who wasn't Ryan. Even worse, it's been forever since I've been out with Ryan himself. I can't remember the last time he and I went out on what would be considered a date. We hit that too-comfortable stage even before my giblets went on strike, and half the time we spend together is ordering in and eating from take-out containers on the couch because neither of us wants to bother with dishes later.

We've hit the boring part of being an old married couple without ever doing the marriage bit.

As determined as I am to make this break a short and singular one, there's no love lost for the weird, distant aching that comes from sitting next to someone you love because you've been together forever and wondering if you're maybe just there out of habit.

You order your chow mei fun and routinely ask who wants the last dumpling because you've always done it. And in the early days of being together, you really cared that the other person got that dumpling, because you had all the feelings for them and wanted to see them happy. But after a certain point, you're secretly thinking, "Fuck you, that's my dumpling."

It's never even occurred to me until now that we've reached the "Fuck you, dumpling" phase of our relationship. And I can't help but feel like this is mostly my doing. I don't know what caused my vaginismus, but I do know I haven't made it any sort of priority to fix the situation over the last two years.

It's breaking my heart. Ryan deserves better than someone who hoards her dumplings.

It's only now, standing here with my friends and our hands full of sex toys, that I realize I miss that early stuff in a relationship. Well, not just the early stuff, I suppose. The good stuff.

I want to want to give away my dumplings.

Shit. I feel lonely. And a little pathetic.

Wiping the tears off her cheeks, Shannon tries to regain some adult composure. "Oh, we're just messing with you, Kat," she says. "I promise. We will only set you up with people with non-phallic names, okay?"

I look down at the dildo in my hand and feel unexpectedly sad. "No, you guys are fine," I assure her. "I don't know if the dating thing is a good idea, but I've only got thirty-three days left to make this happen."

"So let us set you up!" Butter insists.

I sigh. "I think you're putting the cart before the horse there, Butter."

"No way! Besides, who cares what comes first, the chicken or the dick!"

From the front of the store comes the muffled sound of a crash, and we all freeze. Like the guilty people we probably are, we scurry around the prep table, through the door, back behind the customer counter. Ben Cleary is standing by the register, biting his lip, fighting a laugh and feverishly attempting to wipe up the coffee we served him no less than fifteen minutes ago.

"I'm so sorry," he says, without looking up, his voice cracking from the laugh he's trying to contain. "I came back because I forgot I needed to change my order for next week. I dropped this. I'm sorry." He finally glances up at us, and all hope for composure is lost. He bursts out laughing—full-on, leaning-on-the-counter, unable-to-breathe laughter.

It's only then that I realize every single one of us has some manner of sex toy in our hands. Some of us multiple. Oh my damn.

Liz screams. She actually screams. She turns tail and flees back into the kitchen, scurrying so fast I can hear her crash into the prep table. Shannon, Butter and I calmly try to fling the contraband behind our heads and back into the kitchen, but someone flings a bit too hard, and there is a spectacular metallic crash as a stack of mixing bowls comes tumbling down. Liz screams again.

Ben Cleary is trying his very hardest to get a grip, but it's just not happening. We all straighten up and try to look as professional as we can, but there's really not a lot we can do to save this. Ben has coffee dripping from his fingers, and there's a puddle spilling over onto our side of the counter. Shannon and Butter are just staring at him, blinking. And just when I think he's got a handle on himself, he splutters into laughter again. I fear he may rupture something.

Motherhood may have robbed Shannon of shame, but I don't think anything could have prepared her for this.

I clap my hands together loudly. Butter and Shannon jump. Ben puts the back of his wrist over his mouth to stifle the sound of his chuckling. There are actual tears in his eyes. "Okay. Shannon, could you go grab a couple of towels and help Mr. Cleary get this spill cleaned up? And, Butter, could you go check on Liz and see if there's anything you can assist her with in the kitchen?"

Butter giggles, and Shannon slaps her across the arm. "Yes, of course," Shannon says, aiming for a professional tone, and they scuttle away.

"And Mr. Cleary," I continue.

"Please," he says, his voice still cracking. He clears his throat. "Call me Ben."

I smile at him. He's being a real sport about the situation, all things considered. The wrist cuff of his shirt has coffee staining the edge. I look closer and see the spatter all over the light blue fabric of the button-up and the gray of his tie. Poor bastard. Came in for a cup of joe, walked in on a cacophony of dick jokes. Didn't stand a chance.

"You said there was an issue with your order next week? If you'll step down here to avoid the mess, I'll be happy to help you with that."

He shakes the coffee off his hand onto the counter and makes his way down to the other end where I'm now standing, holding out a towel for him. "I really am sorry about that," he says, gesturing toward the spill. "It slipped."

I take the towel back from him and give him a little half smile. "I bet it did."

Shannon reappears at the other end of the counter and silently starts mopping up the mess, refusing to look at either one of us, her eyes dancing with a pent-up burst of manic hilarity.

Ben shakes his head and bites down another laugh. "I wasn't listening, I swear," he insists. "I came back in and was about to ring the bell. But when I heard Butter say the thing about the chicken, I laughed, I spilled, and that was it. And then you all came running out with…" He tries to swallow down the guffaw, bless him. His eyes tear up again, and it all comes out as an unfortunate snort.

"I kind of hope you broke a rib just now," I say, grinning.

He clutches the counter. "Oh my god, I'd deserve it. I'm sorry, but that was the best thing I've ever seen in my life."

"We like to keep things fresh here," I say casually. "We are a full-service shop." His eyes pop open, and he makes a small choking sound. Shannon giggles and dives back into the kitchen, and I close my eyes in dismay over what I just uttered. "Oh, shut up. You know what I mean."

"Someone getting married?" he asks, wiping the tears out of his eyes.

"What?"

"The, um, stuff. Bachelorette party?"

I involuntarily squint at him. "Yes. That makes perfect sense. Absolutely. Liz is getting married in October, so yes. That is exactly what those things were for."

"Oh, it's Liz? That's nice. Good for her."

"Ace. Now, you said you needed to change next week's order?" I say, plastering on my best customer service smile. "Well, we're on a roll here, fella, so let's get down to it."

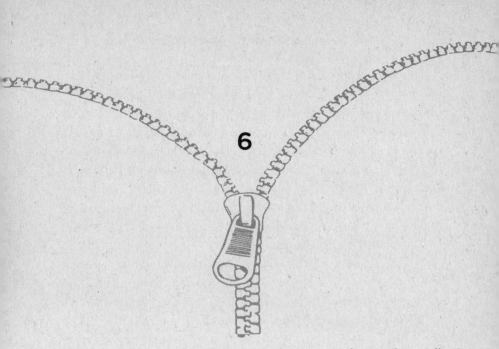

6

"I can't believe you told him those things were for my shower," Liz pouts, stacking a tier of chocolate fudge onto a new platform. "That is so embarrassing."

"Technically, I said they were for your bachelorette party, and he thinks we got them for you. So he probably thinks *we* are the dirty birds, not you," I say with a wink.

The store phone rings and Shannon disappears. Butter adds, "I think this will be good. You'll go home tonight, get your gear going, and soon you'll have a happy vagina. Then we can stop making Liz flinch every time we say *vagina*."

Liz scowls. I give her a sympathetic look. "You really do flinch."

"Did you grow up in a house where you called it something else? Like a cutesy word?" Butter asks. *"Bajingo? Minge? Foo-foo? Vagoo?"*

My eyes narrow at her. "Vagoo? Really? That's…unfortunate."

"I dated a guy last year who called them vagoos. Two dates. I couldn't get past that."

"Nor should you have." I shudder. "It's unforgivable."

Slapping her piping bag onto the table, Liz snaps, "Okay, fine. No, we didn't say *vagina*. We said *special*, okay?"

"Aww, you called it your *special*?" Butter asks.

I consider this. "That's actually kind of genius. I'd grow up thinking my business was like, the key to the universe or something. I wouldn't let just any man near my special, ya know? I like that. My *special*."

"I can't tell if you're making fun of me or…" Liz trails off, biting her lip.

I hold my hands up. "I'm totally not! I'm all for proper term usage, but if you're going to give it an alternate moniker, don't use something lame like *hoo-ha*, call it the fucking *special*. I really like that. Hell, I might start calling mine that."

Butter is looking down at herself. "My special. Okay, you're right. That's got a ring to it."

Liz looks both horrified and oddly accomplished. She picks up her piping bag and sets back in on her cake just as Shannon comes running back in excitedly.

"Guys, oh my god, guess what?"

"We all just voted and we are all calling our vaginas our *specials* from now on," Butter informs her.

Shannon stops midflail and makes an indescribable expression at Butter before remembering that she has news to share. She shakes off her confusion and turns to me and Liz. "Okay, but seriously, guess what?"

"What?" we ask.

"The Coopertown Ravens, the college basketball team? They're looking for an official bakery for their stadium concessions, and they've asked us to audition for them!"

"What?" I trill. "That's amazing!"

"It's a huge contract! They'd sell our cupcakes at every event exclusively! We've got a month to present the designs, and they'll do a tasting and make their selection. Guys, this would be massive for us. The advertising alone would be worth its weight in gold, but the actual contract, plus sales? Hello, big fat bonuses and me taking my kiddos to motherfreaking Walt Disney World!"

"Oh my god, a honeymoon!" Liz squeaks.

"I could fly out to see my Noni!" Butter gasps.

I bounce in place. "I have absolutely no grand aspirations I can think of right now outside of getting laid, but yay!"

"Kat, the art is all you, lady!" Shannon says, her eyes gleaming. "We can work together on the designs, and Butter, I'm counting on you for the recipes. We can do this, guys."

"Who else is in the running?" I ask.

Shannon frowns. "I don't know. But I'd assume The Cakery is, because of course they'd be." The Cakery is a pretentious shop in the city that makes all their frosting out of olive oil and sea salt, and absolutely nothing has gluten. "And probably the usual bridal cake shops? Maybe Odessa."

Butter perks up with a conspiratorial look. "We could scout out the other shops. Go and try their products and make darn sure we'll kick their asses. We could use fake names and wear trench coats! I call Olga for my name."

Squinting at her, I say, "Of all the names you could choose for your secret identity, you pick Olga?"

"What's wrong with Olga?"

Shannon shakes her head. "Let's call that plan B." Looking a bit deflated, Butter fidgets with her glitter brush. "I don't want to know too much and psych ourselves out. It doesn't matter who we're up against or what they make. What matters is that we're going to give Coopertown the best goddamn cupcakes they've ever tasted or seen, right?"

"Right!" the rest of us cheer.

"Let's start researching the team—everything we can find

out to come up with colors, flavor ideas, themes, anything. We've got a month, so let's make it count."

I salute her. "You've got it, Captain." I head over to the teeny desk we have crammed in between the fridge and the wall and open up our shop laptop. A picture of a breast-shaped cake appears. "Uh… Shannon? Why is there an edible tit on the laptop?"

"Oh, yeah. We got an order for a boob-cake for a party. Liz?"

Liz slumps. "I knew today was going too well."

"What's the boob-cake for?" Butter asks.

"It's a breastfeeding support group thing. Their one-year anniversary of meetings or something? Looks doable."

Liz comes up behind me and looks over my shoulder, wincing. "Yeah, I think I can do that with fondant pretty easily."

"Boob-cake." Butter shrugs. "Who knew?"

I sit back in my chair and click open a new browser tab. "I fucking love this job."

I take my phone out and, for a moment, think of texting Ryan to tell him about the hubbub in the shop. Is that something we can do on a break? I never thought to ask how we'd proceed with the nonsexual trappings of coupledom while separated.

Suddenly I realize that he hasn't texted me since we hit the bricks. Is he as conflicted as I am? I don't know what to do with the sad feeling that comes with having to question whether it's proper protocol to message one of the most important people in my life.

I quietly tuck my phone back in my pocket as Shannon, standing at her station scribbling in her notebook, looks up at me. "Okay, this is just a loose estimate here," she begins. "But I'm pretty sure that with the money from this contract, we would be able to hire on another employee."

I whip around. "Seriously? An actual, full-time employee?"

Looking back at her scribbles, she says, "I've been trying to make it work for weeks. I think we're already at the point where we could take on someone part-time right now, but someone full-time would be tight, and I hate to risk it. But with the contract, I think we could absolutely do a full-timer."

"Whoa," Butter says, staring off into the void. "That's the dream, baby."

I lean back in the chair. "What would we even do with ourselves if we could split the schedule with a new person? Life not working eighty hours a week seems like crazy talk."

"I think I'd hire a closer," Shannon says, gazing moonily at me. "And then I could see my kids for longer than an hour every night before they have to go to bed. I could make it to more than one football game each season. I could cook actual dinners like I used to. Or at least be there to order the takeout."

Considering the free-time possibilities, I offer, "I wouldn't have to have only scheduled date nights with Ryan. Plus, I could stop using the whole married-to-my-job notion and maybe not let my special go ignored for two years."

"That there is an important goal," Butter says seriously. "I'd date, too. That's all I'd do with my free time. I'd ask out all the pretty boys and girls. Then maybe my parents would shut up about the horror of me being single."

I frown. "They know you're only twenty-six, right?"

"I don't think logic is crazy important when it comes to familial shame," she says with a flick of her hand.

"Ooh." I turn back to Shannon. "What about a delivery van? We've been looking into that for over a year, man."

She starts poking her notebook with the pen. "We can do a van now, actually. I just hate making the commitment for that kind of expense when we're getting by just fine with what we have."

Butter snorts. "No offense, but your minivan isn't exactly the pinnacle of rides."

"Hey," Shannon scoffs. "It's got a DVD player in the back. Don't hate on my minivan."

I raise an eyebrow. "I'll never get over you driving a beige minivan. If we get a delivery van, you don't get to pick the color."

Rolling her eyes and straightening her apron, Shannon ignores me. "Okay, the presentation is on the twenty-second, so we need to get to work. It's focus time, people."

"Isn't your lady bits deadline on the twenty-seventh?" Butter asks me.

I frown. "Yeah. But that's okay. I can multitask my major life events."

Shannon looks amusingly unconvinced as she tucks her notebook into her apron and goes to wash her hands. Butter winks at me and returns to her cakes.

I turn back to the laptop and stare at fondant and buttercream chesticles of varying quality. There's a surprising number of boob-cake images online. But then, I'm always surprised when we get odd cake requests and discover we aren't the first to tackle them.

The four-foot edible mermaid last year was particularly shocking. To think there could be more than one of those in the world.

Just under a month until the presentation. A month and change until my deadline. I can absolutely handle this.

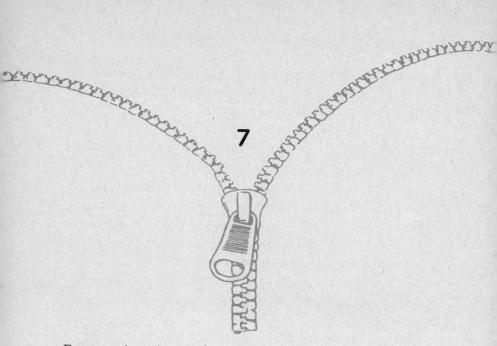

7

Everyone is setting up their stations before the Monday morning rush in silence, as per the usual. No one has had time to let any coffee take effect by this point, so the most we usually muster is a grunt or two in recognition of the other humans in the room.

We've got only a few minutes until the hordes come crashing in, so I am trying to chug as much caffeine as I can while I tie on my apron and get my station in somewhat working order.

"So," Butter says, breaking our unwritten code of silence. "How'd the stuff work over the weekend?"

Liz pops her head up, and Shannon stops in her tracks, holding a tray of brownies she's taking to the display case out front.

I yawn. "Pretty good. I've got some preliminary sketches done. I think I'll come up with some solid ideas for the presentation."

Everyone is looking at me like I'm maybe the stupidest person they've ever encountered. "The stuff," Shannon parrots. "Like, vagina stuff, lady."

I slowly blink at her. "Oh. I didn't get to that. I was working on the Coopertown ideas until really late every night and was too tired. I'll break it all out tonight."

Shannon looks personally offended. "Kat! You have to do it every day! Otherwise it won't work. While I appreciate your dedication to the contract, you can't put therapy off! That's how you got into this whole two-year mess in the first place."

My nature is to be indignant and sassy back to her, but even in my sleep-deprived state, I know she's right. I take another swallow of coffee and say, "Fine. You're right. I promise I'll work on it tonight, okay?"

The front door bell jingles, letting us know our first customer of the day has arrived, and we know a whole gaggle isn't far behind. Shannon races off with her brownies, and I grab a tray of orange muffins with warm cinnamon glaze and follow her.

The rush hits, and Shannon and I are working hard to take care of all the customers while Liz and Butter make sure our display shelves are fully stocked.

An hour or so in, I see a face in line I recognize—a coworker of Ryan's whose name I'm pretty sure is Alice. I smile as she reaches the counter and say, "Hey! Good morning!"

"Hi, Kat!" she says, all sparkling teeth and perkiness, despite it being so early. "How are you?"

"I'm great," I say, keeping my customer service face on, despite the caffeine in my system being severely underwhelming to combat her level of cheer. "What can I get for you, Alice?"

She points at the blueberry muffins and says, "One of those, and a large drip coffee to go."

I grab a to-go cup and start pouring her coffee. I find most customers like to get that to their lips as fast as possible. Hell, I've known people to finish their cups before they even get to the cash register. I admire that kind of dedication.

"How're things?" I ask Alice as I pop a lid on her drink.

"So good!" she says, taking the coffee from me. I reach down to bag up the muffin when she adds, "I was sorry to hear about you and Ryan!"

My head snaps up, muffin clutched in my hand. "What? What about me and Ryan?"

I notice that she holds her coffee with a raised pinky. Who does that?

"That you guys split up," she says, eyeing the other confectionary offerings behind the glass.

"Oh," I say, fighting to keep that professional smile intact. "Right, that is true."

He's telling people we split up? It's been less than five days. And did we really split up? Is that what I should be telling people while we're on this break?

"I know this sounds weird," Alice continues, "but I wanted to come and make sure you were okay with everything before our date. I didn't want to step on any toes, or get involved in something that's still messy, you know?"

My hand clenches on the muffin, and it crumbles into chunks on the floor around my feet. "You're...you're going on a date with Ryan?"

Shannon's head whips up from a few feet away. She can sense danger the way police dogs can sniff out weed in an old station wagon.

Alice looks at her mangled muffin. "Yeah," she says cautiously. "When he said you'd broken up last week, I asked him out to dinner. I hope that's okay?"

Shannon is hovering in her spot, waiting to see if she needs to tackle me to the floor before handing her customer a scone.

I blink wildly at Alice for a few seemingly endless seconds. "Oh, sure!" I trill. "I mean, totally! How great for you both!" I reach down into the case and pull up another muffin, carefully placing it in a bag. Handing it across the counter to her,

I say, "Really, that sounds awesome. I hope you both have a great time!"

Shannon comes over, puts her hand on my shoulder, and in her most friendly-sounding tone, says, "Hey, Pumpkin, can you go trade places with Butter and finish up those cookies for the next round of rush? And have her bring up another tray of the coconut cuppies?"

I smile benevolently at her. "Absolutely." I turn to Alice and keep the look alive. "It was so nice to see you again," I say, moving out of Shannon's way. "Have a great time on your date!"

I scurry into the back room and relay the cupcake message to Butter, who rushes out with a tray in hand.

Flopping down on the stool at my station, I stare off into the void for a moment. Five days. It's been less than five days. How in the damn hell did he find someone to go out with in less than five days?

"Are you okay?" Liz asks, cutting another batch of scone dough. "You look a little pale."

I look up and feel a blank expression plastered on my face. In the background, the sounds of a busy morning rush register in the one part of my brain that's not sitting here repeating the *Five days?* mantra.

"I'm fine!" I say, willing it to be true. I grab my mug and quickly dump the now-cold coffee in the sink, reaching over and filling it again with the pot we keep back by our stations. "I just needed another little jolt to keep me conscious."

She takes this as a suitable response and gets back to her scones, now loading them on a sheet tray for baking.

Shannon sticks her head back through the door. "All right?" she asks me as I chug coffee that's only half a degree below molten lava in temperature.

Liz looks up at me again, suspicious now.

"Super!" I say, raising my mug. "Just super!"

I take another sip and head back out into the front room. The line isn't any shorter.

"You can take some time," Shannon whispers beside me. "Seriously, I've got it under control up here."

I shake my head. "I'm good, really."

And I have to mean that. This was my idea. I told him to go date other people. I'm not sure what I initially thought that would entail, but I can't fault him for doing the exact thing I insisted he do.

Admittedly I didn't assume he'd make progress this soon. He's a pretty quiet dude, and I don't think I pictured him out there getting his mack on, bringing home a caravan of eligible concubines.

Then I remember that Alice said *she* asked *him* out. Was Alice standing around lusting after my boyfriend all these years?

While that thought should probably make me want to punch Alice in the face, all I can focus on is—Why haven't *I* been lusting after him for years?

It took Alice five days to ask him out. It's taken me nearly two years even to attempt to have sex with him again.

Wait. She said when he told her about us splitting up last week. That means she probably asked him on Thursday or Friday.

Less than forty-eight hours and he found a date.

My cheeks feel numb.

"Good morning," a voice says in front of me.

I look up. It's Ben Cleary, holding a to-go cup and wearing a friendly smile.

The last time I saw Ben, he was splattered with coffee, red in the face from laughing to tears, and being a really good sport about an absurdly awkward situation.

His teeth are very white. But not, like, too white. I hate when they're too white.

I'm not sure why it hits me, really. Maybe it's just the reaction to hearing about Ryan moving on in the world. Maybe it's because I've known Ben for so many months as a customer. Maybe it's because I accidentally sexually objectified his admittedly impressive jawline the other day. Maybe it's because he should have looked a little pitiful all splattered with coffee, but he managed to appear endearing.

Whatever the reason, I find myself struck with the urge to offer Ben Cleary my last dumpling.

I mentally jump away from the thought as if it's physically burned me. I can't ask Ben out. I shouldn't even be *thinking* about asking someone out.

Just because Ryan is going out with someone, maybe several someones, doesn't mean I should. The whole point of this is to fight my way back into the relationship I let myself be too busy to tend.

But if that's the point, maybe Shannon and Butter are right. Maybe I really do need to know for damn diggity sure that my equipment works properly before I go back to Ryan.

How's it going to look on our anniversary—after I've assured him I'll fix all the ills—if it's another false start?

I don't think I could handle that. I honestly think it would break my brain or my soul or what little shred of dignity I've got left.

I can't fail. I refuse to.

"You know," I say, sounding a thousand times more confident than I feel, "I still feel really bad about the ambush yesterday." I tilt my head back toward the kitchen of chicken entendre and rubber penises. "I was wondering if I could take you out for a drink to make it up to you?"

The words are out of my mouth before I've had time to properly consider them, and I have to pinch my wrist underneath the counter to keep from exploding with hysterical, nervous laughter.

His eyebrows shoot up. "Really?" He looks down at his shirt and pulls on his tie. "Um, that's not necessary."

Ouch. Wow. I'm on a fucking roll. I force a smile anyway. "At the very least, this week's order is on the house."

"No, wait! I mean, I'd love to go for a drink with you. I just don't want you to feel like you have to out of responsibility."

"What?"

He frowns at me and shifts uncomfortably. "I'm sorry. What?"

I press my forefinger into the squishy spot between my eyebrows and wiggle it around for a second. "Dropping the subtleties, I was trying to casually ask you out for a drink using the pretense of yesterday's embarrassing coffee and sex toy kerfuffle. But really I'm just asking you out. In case that isn't translating."

He stares at me and pulls on his tie again. "I'm...accepting?"

"Are you sure?"

"Yes."

"Neat. Ernesto's, tonight, say sevenish?"

"Okay."

"Awesome."

I'm only slightly aware of the throng of people standing around the two of us. Butter is statue-still at the register, holding someone's twenty over the cash tray. Shannon is standing beside me, grinning as she stuffs some cookies into a bag.

The older man she's prepping that bag for points at Ben and me and announces with a grin, "I'll take one of what he's getting."

Ben turns a bit pink and scoots down toward the register. I arch an eyebrow and smile at the old man. "Sorry, sir. We just sold out."

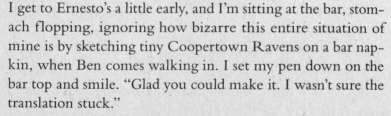

8

I get to Ernesto's a little early, and I'm sitting at the bar, stomach flopping, ignoring how bizarre this entire situation of mine is by sketching tiny Coopertown Ravens on a bar napkin, when Ben comes walking in. I set my pen down on the bar top and smile. "Glad you could make it. I wasn't sure the translation stuck."

He grins and rolls his eyes as he takes the seat next to me. "In my defense, I find your shop a very difficult place to keep any wits at hand."

"Fair enough," I concede. The bartender comes by and Ben casually orders the same beer I'm drinking. My curiosity is piqued, so I channel my skin-twitching anxieties into Q and A. "Did you order that because it's what I'm drinking, or is this what you usually drink?"

"Excuse me?"

"The beer. Is that your usual drink?"

His eyes narrow slightly at me, considering. "No, it's not. And yes, I ordered it because it's what you had, and it was easier. I didn't really think about it."

"If you'd gotten here first, what would you have ordered?"

His lip twitches. "Why do you ask?"

"The drink of choice can say a lot about a person," I suggest, morphing my nerves into theories. "It's not an exact science, but I think there's something to it. Like, if you ordered a whiskey, but made a sour face with each drink, I'd say you were trying to impress me with your manliness. If you ordered a martini, I'd wonder more about what kind of business you do. If you ordered a *fancy* martini with lots of specifics, I'd say you might be a little pretentious. If you had a beer like this on your own, I'd say you were laid-back. But see, you ordered it because I had it, so now I don't know much at all."

Somewhere in my mind, a voice reminds me that Ryan always orders whatever's on tap.

Ben laughs and rubs his hand over his forehead. "You get all of that from a drink order?"

I take a sip of my beer and try not to imagine how Ryan's date with Alice will go as the bartender sets Ben's glass down in front of him. Ben stares at the drink and chuckles to himself. He twists a bit in his chair, and I point to his chest, exclaiming, "Hey! You changed your shirt!"

He looks down, then back up at me. "Yes?"

"Did you change your shirt because we were having drinks, Ben?"

He laughs loudly and rubs his hands roughly over both eyes this time. Reaching over, he grabs his glass and takes a very long drink.

"You are…" He sets his beer back down and stares at me, grinning as he searches for the appropriate word. "Very intimidating. Do you know that? I honestly can't tell if this is your personality and I should be really intrigued, or I'm being punished for the other morning."

I sit straight up, mortified. "What? No! I'm not punishing you! Why would you think that?"

He leans forward and puts one hand on the bar. "You're just really forward. Not that it's a bad thing," he clarifies. "I just kind of feel like I'm making a poor showing, you know?"

Running a hand through my hair, I huff. "I'm sorry. I think I'm so used to being Little Miss Sassypants with everyone at the shop, I don't know when to shut it off. But I swear this isn't a deliberate thing." A horrible calculation of the sheer volume of time I've been with Ryan pops into my head. "And... um. Wow. This is probably an overshare, but I just realized it's been an age since I've been on a date, so it's possible the etiquette has escaped me. Really, I'm sorry if I offended you."

He smiles kindly and leans back in his chair. "You didn't. I just wanted to make sure I wasn't reading you wrong. And how long is an age?"

I do the math in my head and try not to visibly shudder. I don't have the stones to say I haven't been on an actual date in probably three years. Nor do I have the stones to say that technically I'm only on a break from the person I went on those last dates with.

I'm an asshole.

I finally say, "Longer than a while, less than an eon?"

He studies me for a moment. "I get that. This is actually my first night out in a good minute."

"Life, am I right?"

"I will *cheers* to that with my questionable drink choice," he says with a wink.

"Aww." I laugh. "I really am a jerk. I'm sorry. I just think it's interesting! Really, what would you have ordered if you'd gotten here first?"

He thinks about it for a moment. "Let's see. I have to be in the mood for a martini, but when I am, I order it dirty and with gin. Garner whatever information from that you can. Also, I'm a dreadful Irishman, and my father is forever disappointed, but I don't generally care for whiskey, so my manliness will have to remain in question. So if I'd ordered first? Probably a Guinness or a gin and tonic. Those are my regulars."

I giggle into my glass. "Those are good regulars. Guinness will be my next order if we make it to drink two, just FYI."

"If?"

"Well, it's all very up in the air, isn't it? I've managed to intimidate you, we have translation issues and I'm kind of a dick. I mean, the cards are stacked against us, Mr. Cleary."

"See, now we have to make it. It's a challenge. We must conquer this mountain."

I take in a dramatic, shuddering breath. Reaching out, I take his wrist and squeeze it defiantly. "You're right. We can do this. Success will be ours." Thankfully he laughs, so I let him go and take a drink. "We need to keep our momentum going."

"It's crucial," he says with a wink and takes another sip of his beer. "Tell me something fantastic you did today."

My hands feel suddenly hot as I remember Alice and her info-bomb. She's very pretty. Red hair, freckles, a perkiness I don't possess. I wonder if Ryan has told her about our situation. Maybe they're going out fully knowing the endgame is sex.

I gulp my beer and push the images out of my head.

I think about telling Ben that the most fantastic thing I did today was ask him out because my business hasn't had company in two straight years, and at the moment, the prospect of a trial run is starting to seem very appealing, but that seems slightly inappropriate. Slightly.

I sigh. "I feel like I'm letting down our cause to say all I really did today was plot how to make ravens out of fondant.

Although, on Friday, I got to design a boob-cake. That was a highlight."

Ben splutters on his beer. "Boob-cake?"

"It's a cake shaped like a breast."

"Your job is obviously better than mine."

I consider this as I take a long sip. "Probably fact."

Reaching up and loosening his tie a bit, he asks, "So, how did you get into the business of boob-cakes to begin with? If I'd been given that pitch on career day in high school, I don't think I could have resisted the lure."

"The boob-cake siren song is a mighty one," I agree. "And it just sort of happened. Shannon and I went to State together. She was a business major, and I was dicking around in communications with an art minor solely because my mother refused to have a child planning to base her life off an art degree.

"Shannon graduated and got married, had her son, and I met Butter during my senior year on campus. She was part of this bake sale that was trying to raise money for the culinary arts majors to take a trip to France, and she sold me the best goddamn cupcake I'd ever had in my life. To this day, nothing has ever tasted as good as that crème brûlée cupcake.

"We became pals, and after we'd all graduated, we tried our hands at various crap jobs. A few years ago, Shannon had a moment where she realized that she hated watching her degree gathering dust but couldn't see herself schlepping in an office somewhere. I was working as the lowest level assistant possible at a horrible radio station that aired nothing but aggressive talk radio, and I had exactly no desire to move up the ranks. One night we were ranting about adulthood, and Butter brought cupcakes. Lightning struck, and that was it. Cup My Cakes was born."

"Butter's kind of the lynchpin, then?"

I nod. "Indeed. We owe all our baking know-how to her.

Well, and her Noni back in Hawaii, who taught Butter everything she knows."

"I feel like I need to send her a fruit basket or something." He laughs. "My team is obsessed with those cupcakes. And to think it all started because you ladies realized how much adulting truly sucks."

I take another drink. "I'm pretty sure that's how Charlie's Angels formed."

Before I can turn the conversation to the fantastic parts of his day, he turns in his stool to face me, leaning one elbow on the bar. "Kat, in the interest of keeping this second drink dream alive, I'm going for gold here. I have a confession."

I make my eyes go wide. "Oh, my. Okay." Turning dramatically in my seat, I place my hands in my lap. "I'm ready."

"Yes, I did change my shirt because I was meeting you for drinks. And I actually let myself fret about it for a while, too. So when you noticed, I almost fell out of my chair. And I ordered what you were drinking when I came in because I was so nervous, I honestly in that moment forgot what it is I normally drink. And, Kat, I have been buying from your shop for five months, and every week for five months, I've thought about how I might someday work up to asking you out. When you said someone was getting married at the shop the other day, for a second I thought maybe it was you and I'd missed my window." He grins at me, and I take special notice of his white-but-not-too-white teeth. "Now, I'm not saying I'd ever anticipated those particular circumstances bringing this date about, but I'm glad they did." He holds his hands up in front of him. "Our glasses are almost empty. So. That's my Hail Mary for a second drink."

I tilt my head to the side as he takes the last sip from his glass, setting it back down on his napkin with an ominous *clink*.

This is wrong. Ben isn't here because he's emotionally confused by his significant other dating someone new. He's not here because he's debating whether or not to try practice sex with me. He's not here on the whim of a bad mood and a semi-joking idea.

Here's here because he likes me. Because he has been thinking for some time of being here with me.

I feel genuinely sick to my stomach with guilt at the thought of what's unfolded in this bar. I want to come clean with him about the reality of my current romantic entanglements—but more than that, selfishly, cowardly, I want to keep feeling what it's like to be on a first date with Ben Cleary.

"That was a pretty solid Hail Mary," I offer.

"I went for it," he says. "Although, to sweeten the pot, I will say, were there to be a second drink, I would also be willing to throw in dinner, because I'm a gentleman like that. And because I'm hungry." He narrows his eyes at me. "Wait. Unless...you don't study people about their food the way you do with their drinks, do you?"

I shake my head. "God, no. That's not okay. Drinks are drinks. Food is for eating and magic and shutting the hell up. You don't mess with food."

"See, now I know we can be friends."

I gesture to the bartender, and Ben's lip twitches ever so slightly. I take a breath and say, "We'll take two Guinnesses."

All in all, this was a weird day.

Back in my apartment, I set the two ridiculously large boxes of sexual therapy devices on my coffee table.

It's incredibly late, and I have to be up at dawn to be at the shop, but I've got only twenty-nine days to beat this deadline. Shannon's right; this is never going to work if I keep finding reasons to put it off. It's my deadline, and I need to bloody well stick with it.

I open the boxes and start laying out the bounty. Damn, the gals really spared no expense. I think they've overestimated the actual number of vaginas I have.

Flipping through the Encyclopedia Vaginica Shannon printed off for me, I realize that I remember most of these instructions from my doctor. Start slowly, be gentle, go small, work your way up. The vagina is a muscle, I need to retrain it, yada yada.

Okay, so this isn't so bad. Shannon managed to get through this in three months, and that was with two tiny humans at home demanding all her attention, so I can totally do this in four weeks. It's like if I tore my rotator cuff or something. I'd have to do all these stretching exercises to get it back into fighting shape. Not that I want my special to be fighting anyone.

Special. Damn it, Liz.

"Make this a calm and relaxing experience. Play soothing music, burn scented candles, take calming breaths."

I don't have any scented candles, and I wonder if Netflix would count in place of calming music?

I take a deep breath. I can do this. It says this should be a twice-daily routine, but I'm wondering if I can work it in at bedtime and before work. Brush teeth, wash face, train special.

I grab an armful of the therapy gear from the boxes and walk them into my bedroom. Tossing them on my bed, I start changing for sleep.

I had a good time with Ben. While I feel like an absolute monster of a person for not being more open about the realities of my life right now, I've justified the omissions by reminding myself that most people don't unload their entire life stories on the first date.

Jammies on, I head to the bathroom to scrub my face and teeth. I think back to Ben's smile. He really does have nice teeth. And that jaw, though. Seriously. It's criminally defined.

As I give my molars a good once-over, I can't help but wonder what I've been thinking by ignoring such a huge part of my life for two years. While it's great that my militant drive to succeed has gotten the shop into pretty solid shape, doing so at the complete expense of my romantic life seems a little extreme.

I don't remember the last time Ryan and I went out for drinks just to go. Sometimes we go for dinner out, and maybe even a movie on Saturdays, but for the most part, we have been in stuck in the deepest rut ever. Like, natural sunlight can't reach the depths of this rut.

And it's been nearly four years. Two of which have been wonky as hell and entirely without physical intimacy. Four years in a relationship is an eternity in your twenties.

But I'm about to dance out of my twenties. And two years of special solitude is more than long enough, damn it. So I'm getting my nethers in line, and then things will get back to awesome with Ryan, and we are about to land a high-check contract. I'm going to be one of those women who has it all.

But right now, all I want is some *Doctor Who*—and to figure out what the hell a dilator actually is, so I can go to sleep.

Okay. This thing says five to ten minutes—depending on my comfort level—lots of lubricant, then yay sleep.

I'm trying really hard to not think about how odd this all is. But it's medicinal. Medicinal sex toys. That's something I could totally explain to my landlady if she came strolling in.

The thing I bought at the shop with Butter was too, uh, sizable, so I'll have to start smaller. Looking at the pile of items, I feel like I'm in the middle of a hidden camera show. Any minute now, my mom will come bursting in with a camera crew and the pope.

Those must be the calming thoughts the instructions talked about.

Relaxing environment. I grab my remote and queue up an episode of the Tenth Doctor. I shut the lights off and take a deep breath, pushing all thoughts of Ryan and Alice and contracts out of my mind. I ignore the fact that I'm pawing at the protective wrap on a bottle of water-based lubricant my oldest friend and coworkers had overnight delivered to our bakery.

I choose the smallest rubber device, which is innocuously flesh-colored, and take a breath. Here we go.

This isn't so bad. The papers said to try thirty seconds at first. I start counting in my head.

I'm not a prude by any means, but something about this feels impossibly awkward with the good Doctor allons-y-ing across my TV.

I don't think I made it to thirty seconds, but I go ahead and stop anyway. I put the suddenly less innocuous-looking thing on a tissue on my nightstand and shut off my TV. So, maybe no Netflix. Quiet therapy. Time alone with some Zen-like thoughts. That will be good. I can focus more.

And that was pretty easy, so maybe I'll try something a little larger in scale.

This one is inexplicably purple and sparkly. I'm not sure if it's supposed to represent something or if it's just supposed to be festive, but, hey, whatever floats your special.

I take another deep breath.

This isn't working quite as well. I'm startled to meet instant resistance, and my mind flashes with the image of an eyelid slamming shut at the sight of a giant purple glittering finger poking at it.

Ow. OW.

"Fucking ouch!" As a reflex, my hand jerks away from my body, and the sparkly purple faux-penis goes flying across my bedroom. I regret it immediately. "What the hell? It wasn't that much bigger!" I say this to no one, and I really super hope the pope isn't coming.

I look down at my bed, comforter covered in naughty implements, and a feeling of dread settles in.

I'm never having sex again.

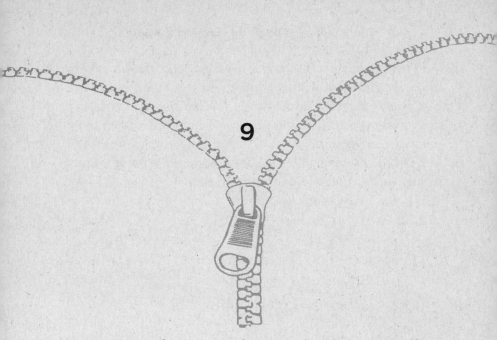

9

Any morning that starts with me in a backless gown and my bare ass on a tissue-paper-covered exam table is not a good day.

I don't know what I was thinking. Well, yes, I do. I thought I'd dive right into therapy, and it would be all rainbows and lollipops, and my vagina and I would go skipping off into the sunset together.

Instead, the therapy was kind of awful. It was actually quite painful, but I kept trying, and I was up half the night battling my lady bits. Now I'm exhausted and my goddamn special hurts.

And I'll admit, I'm panicking a little.

I just *had* to go and give Ryan this stupid deadline. I thought for sure I'd stroll through this whole thing and be ready for nookie and anniversaries with weeks to spare.

Add in the pressure of getting things ready for our presentation to the Coopertown Ravens concessions committee, and I am about two seconds from completely flipping my shit on everything.

There's a knock at the door, and I say, "Come in!" in an

annoyingly happy voice. Why is it so hard to sound normal when you're not wearing pants?

Dr. Snow comes in and gives me a friendly hello. "Kat, it's been a long time. How are you?"

"I've had better days," I say, shifting my weight and regretting it as the tissue paper crinkles loudly under my ass. "Look Doc, I'm going to level with you here. My junk is broken, and I need you to fix it, okay?"

She freezes halfway through sitting down on her rolling doctor's chair. "I'm sorry?"

"Two years ago, you told me I had vaginismus. Well, I still have it. There has to be a pill by now, right? They have, like, fifty different kinds of Viagra. Tell me someone has stepped up to help ladykind out on this one."

Dr. Snow finally sits all the way down and looks down at her high-tech tablet medical chart. "Okay, give me a minute to catch up here."

She starts scrolling through my medical history, and I swing my legs nervously on the exam table. I look around the room, desperate for a distraction. On the wall is a large full-color poster of a uterus with a full-term baby lodged inside. I'm probably overreacting, but I feel like that baby is judging me a little bit.

"Okay," she says finally. "Yes, two years ago I diagnosed you with secondary vaginismus. And—"

"Wait, secondary? I don't remember that. Is there a first kind of vaginismus?"

Dr. Snow squints at me as though she's not sure if I'm being serious. I put my hands in my lap and try to look composed. "Secondary means you haven't always had the condition. You, at one time, were able to have sex without pain. This was something that developed." She crosses her legs at the knees and balances the tablet on her leg. "Patients with primary vaginismus have never been able to have intercourse without pain, or possibly at all. Some aren't even able to have pelvic exams or wear tampons, depending on the severity of their condition."

I involuntarily clench my knees together. That sounds horrible. Here I am, making a screaming fuss over two years, and there are women out there dealing with a significantly more hard-core scenario than me.

This isn't my finest moment.

"Can people with primary... I mean, can they fix it?"

She nods, and my knees unclench. "The treatment is the same, and in most cases, a full recovery is possible. As is my expectation with you."

I exhale sharply. "Okay, yes. Say more things like that, please."

Looking at me sternly, Dr. Snow continues, "So, that was two years ago. You're telling me you've been unable to have sex this entire time?"

"Sort of," I say, smoothing my gown down over my legs. "I kinda just forgot to deal with it."

She blinks at me. "You forgot?"

"I was busy! I was getting a new business off the ground, so it wasn't a big priority, and the whole intimacy thing with my boyfriend sort of took a back seat. Then I realized it had been almost two whole freaking years, and oh my god, that's a really long time. So I tried to do the therapy like you told me, and it's not working very well, and I would just really like to get past this and have sex so I can move on, please. I need your help here."

She's still blinking at me. "You...forgot to have sex."

"It slipped my mind," I say, sighing. "But seriously, though! Tell me what to do."

She shakes her head a little. "When you say the therapy isn't working very well, what do you mean?"

"Well, it hurt really bad, for starters. And at first I was able to do it, but then I couldn't get anything in there at all. I don't know what I'm doing wrong. I have a bunch of printouts. I'm following all the directions. We got all the things, like it said on the website."

"'We'? You and your boyfriend?"

My stomach flip-flops a little at the word *boyfriend*, and it makes me all the more uncomfortable. "No, me and my friends. It's been a group effort. Well, I mean, I'm doing the therapy alone, obviously. But they're cheering me on. One of them actually went through this herself years back, and she's been giving me advice. The whole 'two years' thing hasn't gone over well for anyone."

"You seem really focused on the 'two years' aspect of this."

"Because it's been *two years*, Doc."

"That's a lot of pressure to put on yourself," Dr. Snow says calmly. "How long have you been doing the therapy?"

"Well. *Technically*, I started last night," I admit. Then, a little defensively, "Why do you keep blinking at me?"

"Kat," she says, setting her tablet down on the counter beside her. "This is a process. If you sprained your ankle, I wouldn't expect you to have full motor function in a day. It takes time. You can't rush it."

"I do know that," I insist, feeling really pitiful. "I do, but you can't blame me for being a tad impatient, okay? Look, is there anything I can do to, like, speed things up a little?"

"I don't recommend speeding anything up beyond what your body is telling you it is ready for," she says in a measured tone. "If anything, it will make the situation worse. And honestly, it doesn't sound like you're approaching your therapy with a calm demeanor, which might explain why you're having trouble."

"You're telling me I should have committed to the soothing music and scented candles, aren't you?"

"They wouldn't hurt. This is about retraining your muscles, yes, but it involves your mental state just as much. If you're anxious, your vagina will be, too."

Reflexively I pout. "Okay, yeah, that makes sense."

"Are you sexually active with your boyfriend or anyone else at the moment?"

I narrow my eyes and use every ounce of will I have to push the burning feeling that's creeping up my neck back below the paper gown. "Not exactly."

"What does that mean?"

I sit up a little straighter. "Well, I'm not yet, but I'd like to be, and I sort of have plans to get, um, active."

"I'm actually afraid to ask, Kat."

"I just mean I'd like to give things another shot in bed with my boyfriend without it ending in a car crash of flaming vaginas."

"That's...very colorful imagery."

"Thanks, Doc."

She waves her hand in front of her. "That's a great goal. Of course, I urge you to practice safe sex, and I'd like to discuss birth control options with you before we finish, as I see you aren't currently taking anything."

"Okay."

"Most important, you need to take this very, very slowly. This isn't a race. I understand your desire to take control of the situation, but if you try to push this beyond what you're ready for, you'll make things worse, Kat. Your partner will need to understand that, as well."

I nod, ignoring the screaming voice in my head that keeps chanting *twenty-eight days left.* "Okay. Got it."

"Did the two of you have any luck with the techniques I gave you on your last visit?"

My eyes glaze over a little, remembering how impossibly awkward attempting the couples section of the therapy pamphlets with Ryan was back when this started. He seemed so put out and uncomfortable with everything.

Ryan's a very nice guy, and he'd give anyone the shirt off his back, but at the same time, he's got a selfish streak in him. Sex was easy for him, and he didn't seem to understand that there were circumstances outside my control that he could have assisted with to make that situation a little easier.

It wasn't a high point in our relationship.

"Not particularly," I answer honestly. "Which is why I'm very focused on what I need to be doing first."

"I can understand that," Dr. Snow agrees, much to my surprise. "It's something that needs to be handled in whatever way works best for each individual."

"Yep." I nod and try to look like a person whose personal life isn't a raging case of fuckery.

"And I'd like to refer you to one of the physical therapists over at the hospital. Even if you don't want them to do the actual therapy, they'll be able to walk you through the techniques and help you through this process."

I shake my head. "I think I've got it, Doc."

"There's no shame in accepting help," she says, and I feel scolded. "This is a common disorder, and you're certainly not the first woman to need this treatment."

"It's not an embarrassment thing," I reply, feeling indignant. "I just mean that I know I can figure it out on my own. If I can't, I'll take the referral, okay?"

She eyes me suspiciously. "I would feel a lot better about things if you'd at least go talk with one of the therapists," she says. "You could have an appointment just to discuss applications of the therapy techniques and get support. In fact, you could meet weekly with the therapists just to check in without having them involved in the actual therapy at all. And if, at any time, you feel like you might benefit from their help, you'd already be in the system, and they'd be familiar with your situation."

I can almost hear Shannon's commentary on this conversation. Better safe than sorry, she went to an actual therapist, and la-di-da, it all worked out for her in three short months.

I sigh again in defeat. "Fine. I'll do one appointment, just to talk to them."

She smiles kindly at me. "You're pooling all your resources," she says. "It can't hurt to have a second line of offense ready if you need it."

I cross my legs at the ankles and swing them awkwardly. "So, where did we land on a pill, by the way?"

Dr. Snow takes in a slow breath, and I think I can hear her whisper-counting to ten. "Actually, I'm inclined to prescribe you an antianxiety medication to take as needed."

"I'm not anxious."

"Are you kidding?"

I frown at her. "Rude."

"You are a ball of tension right now, Kat."

I throw my arms up. "I'm not wearing any underwear. My ass is stuck to tissue paper. I've got this big assignment at work, and if I don't figure out how to make perfect little ravens out of frosting, then Butter can't go see her Noni in Hawaii, Shannon can't take her kids to meet Mickey Mouse, and Liz can't go on a honeymoon. And because I don't think you are fully grasping the severity of the situation—*two years*, Doc. I don't need an anxiety pill, I need to get *laid*."

"Kat."

"Fine, I'm anxious."

"If you're anxious, so's your vagina."

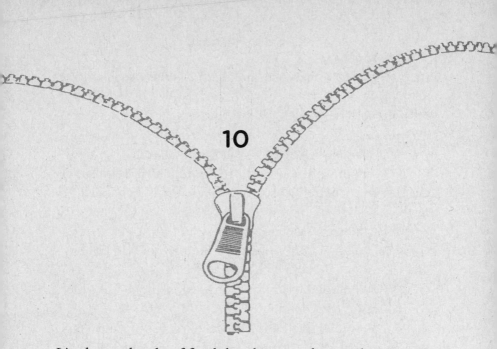

10

Liz slams a bottle of food dye down on her workstation. "I can't get the coloring right!" she snaps. It's not a typical Thursday morning in the shop until someone has a meltdown over food dye. We haven't even hit the morning rush yet, so we're meeting our quota early.

"On what?" Shannon asks. Butter is paused with her glitter brush hanging in midair. It's not often Liz's voice reaches a decibel above gentle breeze.

"The boob-cake," Liz whines. "The…well, the parts."

I bite the inside of my cheek, trying not to laugh. "The nipple?"

Her face flushes a hot pink. "Yes, fine. And the other parts. Who am I modeling this after? Whose boob does this need to look like? I only know what mine look like!"

Butter shrugs, sending a dusting of glitter across the table. "Make it look like mine. I've got nice boobs."

"You do have fantastic boobs," I agree.

Shannon makes a face. "I never thought about that. Should

it look like the woman who ordered it? Is there such a thing as a basic boob?"

"You see?" Liz squeals. "I don't want to offend someone!"

I'm sitting at the desk working on sketches for the Coopertown Ravens, so I fire up the laptop. "Should I...Google boobs?" My mind floods with the potential search results, and I frown. "Actually, I see no way that could end well, so maybe not."

Shannon frowns. "We are a business run entirely by women. We have a plethora of boobs right here. Googling boobs is beneath us."

"Okay, who did the lady who ordered the boob-cake look like the most?" Butter asks.

Shannon studies us all with one hand on her hip and a piping bag in the other. "I guess Kat? Same kind of pale skin, darkish hair. She was taller and had smaller boobs, though."

"Thanks."

Butter waves her hand casually, throwing more glitter around. "So just make a boob like Kat's. There ya go."

"I don't know what her boobs look like, Butter," Liz huffs.

"Show her your boobs, Kat."

"Butter." Shannon sighs.

"Oh, for crying out loud," I say. I stand up, pull my shirt away from my chest and give my ladies a good once-over. I do have to wiggle a little to get the proper lighting. With my hands deep in my neckline and ladies hoisted out of my bra, I hear the front entrance open and scowl. "So help me Odin, if that's Ben coming in, I'm going to burn this place to the ground."

Shannon pokes her head around the door and lets out a whoosh of air. "Nope, just customers." She scurries into the front to handle them, and I get back to my boobs.

"I don't think he'd dare come back in here when it's quiet

without setting off some sirens before he opens the door," Butter says, getting back to her glitter-dusting.

"He'd better not," I grumble. I tuck my dirigibles back into my bra and go to wash my hands. "Even my lack of poise has its limits." I dry my hands off and join Liz at her station. "Okay, here." I grab the dye and start whipping up a color of fondant that is as close to the color of my own nipples as I can get. Which is easily the weirdest thing I've done this week, cake-wise.

"When I went to culinary school," Liz says pitifully, "I never thought I'd be trying to match the color of my friends' boobs."

"It's a proud day for us all," I say, rolling out the fondant. "You can use this for the areola and nipple, I'd think." Liz makes a horrified squeak. "We're all adults here, baby. We can say *areola*. It's fine."

"Maybe I should have been a dentist like my mom wanted," Liz whines and starts shaping the nipple. "It's not too late to go back to school, right?"

Butter pops her head back up. "It's funny," she says, pointing at Liz. "You can't say *vagina*, but you're out having all kinds of about-to-be-newlywed sex with your fiancé, and then there's Kat, who isn't bothered by anything anywhere, and she's the one with the broken special. There's some unbalanced universe for you."

She goes back to decorating her cake, and Liz and I stare at each other awkwardly for a moment. Shannon comes back in and asks, "Did we get it sorted? What boob are we going with?"

"Kat's," Butter says. "I've still got the best boobs, though."

"She's not wrong," I agree. I curtsy and head back over to the sketch pad on my desk. I've got a small pile of royal icing next to it that I'm crafting tiny ravens out of. "Shannon, check these out." I hold up a tiny bird. "I'm not sure how practical they are, but they sure look cool."

"Ooh," Shannon coos. "These are amazing!"

"I don't think I could swing a thousand of them per game, though. They're stupidly intricate." I rub my hand over my forehead. "But they'd certainly make us look more badass than the other shops."

"Maybe they could be for big events? Like for homecoming or playoffs or something."

I shrug. "Could be." I take the little candy raven back from her and set him on the desk. He is pretty boss. I'd likely go blind or succumb to arthritis in my thirties if I tried to make them on the regular, though.

But we really need this contract.

The idea of costing my team this deal kills me. It won't be the flavors or the cake that does it—we rule on taste. Our online reviews always trump the other shops. My assumption is the only other shop that counts as true competition is The Cakery, but this is a college basketball team. Pretention isn't going to get them as far as bitchin' little candied ravens would.

The art is going to make the real impression, so I need to get it right. Every free moment I've had at the shop that isn't dedicated to staring at my own tits has been set aside to perfecting the toppings to these cakes. Butter and Shannon are whipping up batch after batch of potential flavor combinations.

I know they'll nail it. So I can't screw this up.

"You nervous about therapy today, Pumpkin?" Shannon asks casually as she slices through a tray of brownies.

"No," I say, turning my attention back to my notebook. "Why do you ask?"

"Because your face is all squinched up."

I snort. "I'm thinking about ravens. And besides, the appointment is just for intake. I'm not doing the therapy there."

Though Dr. Snow wasn't super impressed with my refusal even to consider doing an official appointment or two, I left her office armed with new birth control pills and anxiety meds for my special, a stack of brightly colored pamphlets discussing the disorder and how to conquer it, and a new determination to get this shit done.

I might have missed the moral of her pep talk, but in my mind, if I can just get past this, things will calm down.

Shannon sighs. "I know you want to do all of it on your own, but it's really not that bad with the therapist. It's kind of like a half-hour Pap smear."

"That's what hell is," Butter says, pointing her glitter brush at Shannon. "Hell is an infinite Pap smear. That's not how you talk someone into going to physical therapy, girl."

"I'm with Butter." I shudder. "And I can handle it on my own. But I'll keep the endless Pap smear on the back burner."

Shannon glares at us both, but I turn back to the desk and resume working on my ravens.

"It's okay to ask for help, you know," she mutters into her mug of coffee.

"I do," I say, narrowing my eyes at the majestic candy bird resting on my notebook. "I'm asking the universe to help this raven not take seventeen minutes to make, but still look this awesome."

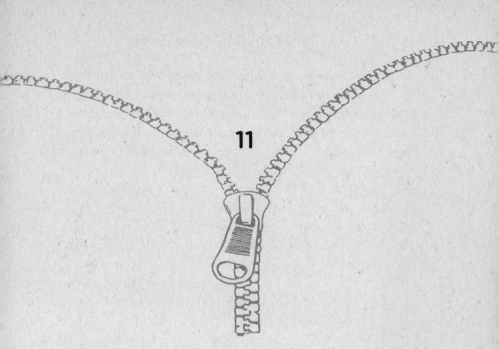

11

I'm still wearing my pants, and my ass isn't stuck to tissue paper, but there's a backless gown on a tray a few feet away that's not instilling hope in me.

The physical therapy pavilion is nothing like what I expected. It's the size of a gymnasium, but with carpeted floors and equipment everywhere. When I walked in, I saw the whole gamut of those in need. A little old lady pulling what looked like giant rubber bands away from the wall. A small child with braces on his knees walking between parallel bars. A businessman doing awkward-looking stretches on a table.

Earlier, in the waiting room, I couldn't help but wonder how many women there were waiting for special therapy.

Now, I'm wondering if there's a comparable therapy for men.

If so, I imagine it would involve…lifting, somehow.

This line of thinking is making me question my own sanity in a big way.

I'm in one of the private rooms off to the side, as I'm assuming vagina therapy isn't something they'd want to parade in front of the elderly and small children.

On the other hand, as the owner of a broken vagina, I'm not sure how comfortable I am with there being only a cloth curtain serving as a door to this little room.

Perhaps something with a dead bolt would be better suited.

The curtain whisks back, and a man appears. "Hi, Miss Carmichael," he says with a smile. All I can think about is how mortified I would have been if I'd had my feet up in the stirrups, on display for everyone to see. He didn't even knock!

"I'm David, and I'll be getting you started here."

"Are you the intake guy?"

He sits on a rolling stool a few feet away. I see the therapy table over there, but I'm not budging from this chair. "No, I'm your PT. Now, let's look at your chart."

I blink at him for a moment. "I don't mean to be rude, but you're the vagina therapist?"

His eyes dart up to me, and he squirms on his stool a little. "Well, I mean, I'm a physical therapist, and that's one of the types of therapy I do, yes. Although if you'd be more comfortable with a female therapist, we can absolutely reassign you."

I shrug. "It's not that. I was just wondering what would make a guy want to grow up and be a vagina therapist." Some frightening mental imagery hits me and I mutter, "Actually, never mind. I have an idea of the appeal."

He lets out an affronted laugh. "Like I said, I'm a physical therapist. This is only part of what I do. It's something I was trained in, just like I was trained in all sorts of other therapies."

I suddenly realize exactly how rude I'm being and feel a flush of embarrassment. I've got to get my nerves under control or someone is definitely going to slap me.

He adds, "One of our other therapists, Constance, is a

woman, but she's our reigning champ of groin injuries, so it's not really about the equipment."

There it is. Penis therapy. I'm tempted to hunt Constance down and inquire about the specifics.

Sighing, I offer, "I'm sorry. That was horribly impolite. I'm feeling a bit twitchy about all of this."

"Understandable," he says kindly. "Give me just a minute to get caught up on your chart, and we can get started."

I tap my toes to the beat of some unidentifiable pop song I heard on the bus ride over, and he reads silently. He seems like a nice enough guy. A bit dude-bro, to be honest. The sleeves of his oxford are rolled up, his tie is too loose and he's wearing cargo pants. He's buff enough for me to assume that he spends his time between patients using all the equipment in the pit to get in extra workouts.

"So," he says when he finishes reading, "this has been going on for about two years? Can you tell me a little bit about what was happening in your life then?"

I frown at him. "Why?"

"Because," he explains slowly, "if I know what might have triggered the disorder, it can help me customize your treatment."

My face forms into an awkward smile. "Uh, well. I was going through a really busy time, starting up a business, and so, well, you know, it'd been a while for my boyfriend and me, intimacy-wise, and when we tried, it didn't work. A few weeks later I went to the doc, she said vaginismus, and here we are."

He starts writing notes in my file and casually asks, "What's your business?"

"Oh, um, it's a bakery? A cupcake shop. Cup My Cakes."

His eyes light up. "Is that the shop Shannon Brimley owns?"

"Yes!" I reply, excited to be talking about something that isn't my vagina. "We started it together. She's my best friend."

A horrid thought pops into my head. "Wait. Are you...were you her vagina therapist, too? Because I know she went to one when she had vaginismus. And I'm sorry, while she and I are the best of pals and share everything, I don't think I can share vagina therapists with her."

David makes a little popping noise as his mouth falls slightly open. "No. No, I wasn't her therapist. Our kids go to the same school. She always brings awesome snacks for the PTA meetings. And you guys have really good cupcakes."

I slap my hand over my mouth. "Jesus. So I just outed my friend for having broken junk to the PTA?"

His eyes go wide as he focuses on my file again. "It's totally fine. So, after your diagnosis—"

"Her vagina isn't broken anymore!" I insist. "That was like, seven years ago. As far as I know, her bits are in tip-top shape now."

He doesn't look up from the folder, but takes a deep breath. "I'm very glad to hear that." Closing his eyes, he repeats, "After your diagnosis, what kinds of treatments did you try?"

Shannon is going to flat-out kill me dead. "Uh, well, nothing, really. Dr. Snow gave me some pamphlets and stuff I could try by myself and with my boyfriend, but things didn't go particularly well, and I never got around to the rest of the therapies."

Now he looks up. "Never got around to them?"

My brain is preoccupied with images of Shannon shoving my head into a preheated oven. "Yeah, you know. Things were super stressful with the shop, and our relationship was already a bit strained. Plus it was all so...awkward. Ryan offered to help at first, do the exercises and whatnot, but it all felt too bizarre to him, I guess." My foot starts involuntarily tapping the pop song again as I push images of Shannon with a chef's knife out of my head. "I feel really bad, though. You know, this kind of thing can be really hard on a relationship. Especially one that's not going great to begin with."

My stomach fills with the heavy sense of guilt, mixed with a hint of vulnerability, and resentment I don't understand. "I even told Ryan he could sleep with other people until the problem sorted itself out, but I don't know if he is. I mean, I know he's got a date, but maybe they won't actually sleep together. That could happen, right?"

David looks rather stunned. "This is...this is not really the kind of information I need to design a treatment plan for you."

Feeling exposed, and wondering why in the good goddamn I just shared all that with him in the first place, I indignantly say, "But you're a therapist!"

"I'm not that kind of therapist."

This is going really well.

I clench my hands into fists and release them a few times. "Look, I'm sorry. This is all very uncomfortable for me."

He sighs. "Why don't we get the exam out of the way now? I can let you get changed and be back in a minute—"

"I knew it!" I yelp, pointing at the gown on the tray. "Can I not keep my pants on for one doctor's visit!?"

"I'm not a doctor."

"Oh, who asked you?" I snap. I've lost any grip on social constructs, and I know I'm being an ass-wagon, but I can't reel the humiliation in enough to stop. Every horrible thing that flies from my mouth just fuels the panic. "Look, I did the exam with Dr. Snow. I'm sure she wrote notes. I'm not doing another one."

He drops his head back and lets out an exasperated sigh. "I need to assess the severity of your condition so I can give you a proper treatment plan."

"Well, you can assess it with my pants on." I sit up straight. There is nothing I want more in the world than to flee from this room immediately. "And it's vaginismus. It's like blinking involuntarily when something gets too close to your eye."

He gives up and sets the file down on the little table by the curtain. "I... I know what the disorder is, Miss Carmichael." He leans forward and puts his fingers on his temples. "Okay, how about this? Let's go over equipment and we can discuss techniques. I'll try to do a generalized plan that you can alter to fit your needs, okay?"

I cross my legs at the knees and exhale with a haughty sound. I don't think I've ever made a haughty noise in my life. What the hell is wrong with me?

"That would be fine," I say.

My brain is now flashing with images of Shannon and David taking turns chasing me with brûlée torches.

He shakes his head ever so slightly and walks over to the tray. Carefully removing the backless gown and setting it on the exam table, he wheels the tray over near me.

If I were to walk into a dungeon made explicitly for torture, I can say with absolute certainty that this tray would be in there.

It looks like a larger, more horrifying version of what sits next to you at the dentist's office. Everything is sitting on a large piece of blue gauze lined with plastic. Dilators of varying sizes, clinical-looking bottles of lubricant, and very scary silver devices.

There's not a sparkling purple item in the lot, and it all smells of chemical disinfectants.

My legs pop up of their own accord, and I bump into the tray as I stand. A dilator goes flying and lands with a loud metallic crash.

"I'm sorry," I say, smoothing down my shirt, silently begging my heart to stop trying to beat out of my chest. "Cramp in my leg. Sorry."

David bends down to get the fallen implement, and looks like he's definitely had enough of me. "It's fine. Now, this is what you'll need to buy for your own use, or we can loan things out as needed."

"Nope!" I trill. "I'm good. Got it all. Totally set. In fact, I think we're good here."

"But we haven't discussed a treatment plan!"

I grab my purse off the back of my chair. "And see, I think you were so efficient, I've got a handle on things from here. I'll check in again if there are any problems. Thank you so much for your time."

Before he can say anything else, I scuttle past him and yank the curtain open. I'm stopped dead in my desperate retreat by a sight I am almost certain I'm hallucinating.

Walking through the therapy pavilion, not ten feet away, is Ben freaking Cleary.

I fight several instincts at once. To dive back behind the curtain. To drop to the floor and army-crawl my way out of here. To run like the coward I am.

"Kat?" he calls. Too late. I've been spotted.

"Oh, hey!" I say, managing to keep the shrillness out of my voice far better than I expected. "How's it going?"

Ben smiles, seeming a little confused, and walks over, a boy of maybe fourteen in tow. "What are you doing here?"

"What?" I ask, trying to think of an appropriate excuse. I notice his tie has tiny Spider-Mans slinging webs all over it. "I was just in the area." I grab my phone and pretend to read something terribly important. "And actually, I'm running late, so I'll see you later!"

He looks more confused than ever. "In the area... Wait... Were you looking for me?"

I lower my phone and stare at him. "Why would I be looking for you here?"

Speaking very slowly, he says, "Because I work here."

My eyes go from Ben to the teen, who is now looking at his own phone, clearly bored as hell. I flash back to our date and rewind to the conversation we had about jobs. We talked about *my* job, but we got distracted by Ben's Hail Mary before I could ask about his job. And though he's been coming into the shop for months to get cupcakes for his coworkers, it never occurred to me to ask him what he and those coworkers do.

Oh my god. David mentioned our cupcakes. What if Ben is the one who brings him those cakes?

"You're…" I try to swallow, but there's no moisture in my throat. "You're a physical therapist?"

The curtain whooshes open farther behind me, and David appears. "Miss Carmichael, you should take these notes with you. They give you some treatment options and some guides to different resources you can find online to assist with the process. Of course, if you need anything, you can give us a call. I, or maybe one of the other therapists, will help however you'll let us."

I bite my lower lip as hard as I can and turn to face him. "David. You have absolutely no chill."

I yank the stack of papers out of his hand, turn back to Ben, plaster on the most horrifying smile I've ever mustered and say, "Well. This has been fun. Nice seeing you, Ben, but I have to get out of here immediately."

Before anyone can say anything else, I turn and haul ass out of the gymnasium, leaving my dignity behind.

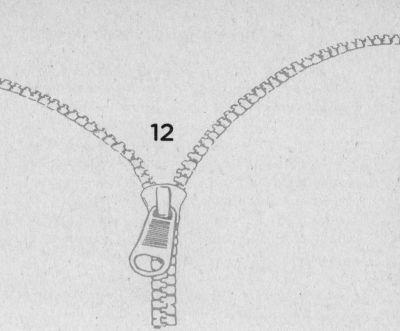

12

"You look like hell," Butter says as I stuff my bag under the desk and tie on my apron.

"Great, that's helpful," I grumble. "Cheers."

"You all right there, Pumpkin?" Shannon inquires delicately. "How was the appointment?"

"It was fan-fucking-tastic," I say, pulling the strings a little too tight. I take a deep breath, undo the knots and start over. "For example, did you guys know Ben Cleary is a physical therapist?"

The echoing gasps that burst through our kitchen are the only acceptable response.

"Shut up," Butter says, looking like she doesn't know whether to sob or laugh or both. "Was…was he yours?"

"No," I say, finally getting my apron on straight. "If Ben had been my therapist, all you'd see is a Kat-shaped pile of ashes here. No, as I was leaving the appointment from hell, I ran into him."

"Did he know why you were there?"

I shrug. "I don't think so? But he probably figured it out.

I was in one of the little side rooms where I assume they put all the broken vaginas."

"Oh my god," Shannon wheezes. "Is he a vagina therapist?"

I freeze in place. "Holy shit. Is he? I mean, the guy I saw did say that kind of therapy is something they're trained for."

Shannon tucks a rag into the pocket of her apron. "Well, if you're going to start dating a guy and your special is broken, you can't do much better than a vagina therapist."

I stare at Shannon for a minute and gulp. "Uh, by the way. My therapist knows you. His name is David, and he says he's on the PTA with you."

Shannon perks up. "Oh, David Larson? You must have gone over to Community North. That's fun. Tell him I said hi next time."

I'm gaping at her. "There won't be a next time. I'm not going back there!"

"Why not?"

"Because aside from the basic fact that I don't need his help, there's the tiny issue of my accidentally telling him you also had to go to a special therapist…"

Butter literally almost falls over. She grabs onto her station for support. Liz resumes manically piping buttercream on a large pink cake.

"You told David Larson I had to see a vagina therapist?"

I casually look for escape routes. "It just sort of…happened."

All of us are frozen, waiting for Shannon to react.

But she doesn't. She barely shrugs and says, "Eh. No biggie. It's not like it's a secret I have a vagina."

"Wow," I marvel. "You really don't have any shame left, do you?"

"Not a drop."

I walk over to wash up, thankful I won't be dying at Shannon's hands today.

"So, what did Ben say?" Butter asks, diving right back in.

"Gah!" I snap, surprising even myself. "What about *that* even? What am I supposed to do about him? What about Ryan? What about the dates he's going on? What was I thinking, asking Ben out in the first place? I mean, I can't go out with him again, right? But you know what? I want to." Until this very second, I haven't even realized how true that is. I want to see Ben again. I want to feel what I felt on that first date. My thoughts come out in a real-time ramble. "Oh god, I want to. I want to throw him down on this workstation and do very inappropriate things to his jawline, because have you seen that damn thing?"

"So…do that? Although, not in here. Health codes," Shannon offers.

"I can't do that!" I shout, walking over to my station and plopping down on my rickety old stool. "I'm supposed to be having sex with *Ryan*, not Ben, and I can't even do *that*! Hell, I can't even handle the weird purple glittery thing yet! How am I supposed to have actual sex?"

"I picked that one out," Butter says proudly.

Shannon chimes in. "Well, if Ryan is out sleeping with other people, so can you. And if you start dating Ben, you can explain it to him. I'm sure he would understand. You can have, like…therapy sex with him. I mean, physical therapist Ben would probably know exactly what to do, you know?"

"Yes, there's a conversation I'd just love to have on our second date. 'Do you feel like Chinese food or maybe Thai? Oh, and by the way, I was at your place of business because the warranty on my vagina expired, and it's currently out of order, but would you mind using some of your professional expertise to walk my lady bits down the yellow brick road, so I can have sex with my currently estranged long-term boyfriend and we can get back together?'" I slump down on my stool as the reality hits me. "And besides, I wouldn't want to have therapy sex with Ben. I'd want to have sex sex with Ben. Like wild, monkey, jawline-biting, holy-fuck-I-haven't-been-laid-in-two-years sex with Ben. Therapy sex is not the romp I'm wanting to have, okay?"

From our front room, a pitiful little *ding* rings out. My entire body freezes. I reflexively check my hands to make sure there are no dildos clutched within them.

Butter bends backward to look out through the door and slaps her hand over her mouth. She looks back at me with panic in her eyes. Shannon runs for the front room. Liz stands frozen in place, her trauma from the day of dildo deliveries all too fresh.

"Oh, hi there, Ben Cleary!" Shannon shouts from the counter.

My head drops onto my chest. "No way," I mutter into my boobs. "There's just no way. Butter, tell me there's no possible way he's standing out there, because I'm about to cry some real Jesus tears right here."

"Jesus has left this shop, baby."

I pull in a deep breath, lift my head high and walk through the door.

Shannon is standing at the display case, wiping down the already pristine glass with the fervor of a madwoman. Ben is staring at a red velvet cupcake in the display like it's the Holy Grail of cuppies and avoiding my gaze.

"Are you fucking kidding me right now, Cleary?" I ask.

Shannon scrubs the window harder. Ben looks up, eyes wide. His words come out in a torrent. "I'm so sorry. I was going to ask you to dinner this morning when I came for coffee, but you weren't in and they said you'd be back before lunch, and then I was confused by seeing you at the hospital, so I thought I'd come back to ask you now, and I figured it would be ironic and you'd think it was funny. I swear to you I will never again come back into this shop after I come for coffee, not ever, not for any reason, not even if I leave my wallet or my dying mother in here, I promise."

"Why would your dying mother be in our cupcake shop, Ben?"

"I have no fucking clue."

"Is your mother really dying?"

"No."

I wave at the air. "Well, there's a silver lining to the day. Good for your mom."

He looks desperately from me to Shannon and back again. "I don't know what to say right now."

I shake my head, and my hands land on my hips. "Shannon?" She freezes mid-scrub.

"Yeah?"

"I've got this."

She says nothing, but scuttles out in a blur of curly blond hair, apron strings and muttered swear words. I can actually hear the flailing and gasping and panicking in the back room.

"At least they have the good damn sense to whisper," I say, smacking myself in the forehead.

Ben looks down uncomfortably at his Spider-Man tie and pulls at it. "I don't know what to do here," he says. "Should I apologize again? Because I can do that."

I flop my hands into my apron pockets. "Do you know what I like about you, Ben?"

His eyes dart sideways and then up at me. "No?"

I give him a half smile. "I like that you keep getting into these wildly uncomfortable situations, and you don't run. A lesser man might've bolted out that door, but you rang the bell. That's impressive. It's brave."

"Or stupid."

"Let's focus on the positives here, dude. You staying was honest. That's good."

"Really, Kat, I am so sorry, I thought it would be—"

"Stop apologizing." I sigh. "You didn't do anything wrong. Although you maybe could've dinged that bell a little sooner."

He raises his eyebrows. "Probably."

Frowning, I ask, "Ben, exactly what is your job?"

"I'm a pediatric physical therapist. I didn't realize we hadn't discussed it."

"Apparently there are a few things we missed in conversation," I say, with a staggering sense of guilt barreling through my chest. I pull in a breath and let it out slowly. "So. How much did you hear?"

His gaze sort of travels against his will back to the cupcakes. "A lot."

"Sex? Boyfriends? Jawlines? Vaginas? All of it?"

"More or less."

I huff. "In my defense, you do have a really stellar jaw, though. I mean, gosh."

"Thank you."

"And I'm assuming you've now figured out why I was at the hospital this morning?"

"I've got a general idea, yeah."

I shift my weight from foot to foot, because I don't know what else to do with my body at the moment. Finally I shrug and slap my hands down on the counter, and he jumps a little. "Sorry. Okay, here's what I'm thinking. This is really awkward."

"A bit."

"So, I figure we have two options. First, we pretend this never happened. We carry on like none of this hideousness ever existed. You are Ben Cleary the customer. I am Kat Carmichael the cupcake wizard. We smile, we say hi, we never

93

speak of this again. Thus ends our venture into whatever it was we were doing. And I won't hold that against you in the slightest, Ben, seriously. No judgment, no animosity on my end. Although I may likely beg you to forgive me for my lack of openness the other night in regard to what I'm dealing with right now."

"What's option two?" he asks.

"Option two? We chat it out. You came here to ask me to dinner? We go on a proper date. Like, not right after work—a Saturday night, restaurant, real date. I'll wear date clothes and everything. If I still own that sort of thing. And we can talk about the not-at-all-embarrassing things you just heard me shouting about. And Saturday night, because that'll give you plenty of time to realize how bizarre all of this is and panic yourself out of it.

"Really, you can take the first option. It's okay. I'll understand completely."

He pulls at his tie again. I'm recognizing it's a nervous habit of his. I'm also realizing that it's probably a bad sign how often he tugs the damn thing around me. Goodbye, jawline. I hardly knew ye.

"Give me your phone," he says, quite unexpectedly.

"Excuse me?"

"Your phone," he repeats. "Can I have it for a moment?"

I'm so surprised, I reflexively reach into my apron pocket and grab my phone without thinking. Before I know it, I've handed it over the counter to him. He takes it and starts calmly poking at it. I'm both slightly annoyed and burning with curiosity. A second later, his pocket beeps and he hands my phone back to me.

"There," he says, checking his own phone. "Now you have my number, and I have yours. That gives you the chance to panic out of it, too." He pockets his phone and looks up at me. "Saturday. Is eight okay?"

I stare at him. "Sure."

"I'll text you details. See you tomorrow morning." Without another word, he turns and walks right the hell out of the shop. I'm left standing here, still holding my phone, at a complete loss for words.

There's a clattering sound, and through the kitchen door come crashing my coworkers, all three trying to pop through at the same time. Shannon is grasping the front counter for support; Liz is covering her mouth with both hands, eyes wide like she just saw the Dark Lord himself; and Butter is legitimately breathing into a small white paper bag.

"So," I say, looking around the shop. "I think that went really well."

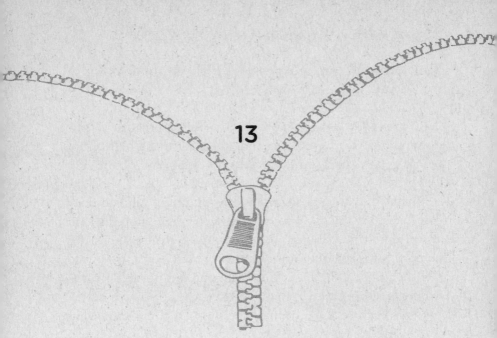

13

Maybe I'm a little nervous.

It's a lot easier to be nonchalant about things when I'm wearing jeans and my apron and a fine layer of flour. It's an armor of sorts. Plus, it's easier to make a quick getaway in sneakers than it is in these little floofy ballet-flat-looking shoes I've currently got on.

According to the lady at the store, they are all the rage for casual elegance, but all I can think is they are trying to murder me by slowly severing my Achilles tendon.

I didn't realize how out of date my closet was. I also didn't realize I didn't own anything that isn't meant to be worn with jeans in some capacity.

In the back of my closet, I found this dress, which was very unfortunately purchased as a funeral dress. I kept it just in case another somber occasion popped up. I wore it only to the one funeral approximately four years ago, though, so I don't think "funeral dress" counts as a running thing. Oh, I did wear it to an engagement party for a coworker of Ryan's nearly three years back! There's some balance there, surely.

Maybe this outing can change the vibe and officially make this my little black dress.

Oh god. The last time I wore this was on a date with Ryan.

Why, oh, why didn't I buy a new dress when I went shopping for these obnoxious little flats after realizing I don't own any footwear that isn't boots or covered in splatters of dried frosting?

Maybe I'm a little nervous. But I promised Ben date clothes, and this dress technically qualifies…right?

I'm standing on the sidewalk in front of Poisson, pretending to check my phone and feeling not at all like running home for my jammies and a blanket fort. As promised, Ben texted directions, and here I stand, waiting for him to appear, wondering why on Earth I ever thought this was a good idea.

"Glad you could make it," he says from behind me, and I damn near drop my phone. I whirl around and plaster a smile on.

"I'm not going to lie, I'm impressed you showed up."

He smiles back. "I don't run, remember? I hear it's endearing."

I roll my eyes. "This is cheating, by the way. You look like you're dressed for work. I'm wearing uncomfortable shoes. I thought we had a deal."

"Hey," he says, straightening his tie. "It's Saturday. It takes an act of God or Congress to get one of these things on me on a Saturday. You should be terribly impressed right now."

I stare at him. "You know, I've known you for months, and I've never not seen you in a suit. I can't even picture you in regular clothes. That's weird."

"I assure you I wasn't born in a suit. I don't even particularly like them." I keep staring at him. "Are you trying to picture me in a T-shirt or something?"

"I literally can't do it."

He laughs. "See? This is good. Neither of us have run screaming in the opposite direction. I think we might just survive dinner. Shall we?"

I giggle in spite of myself. I can appreciate his effort to rise above the hideous awkwardness—and to his credit, he's doing a fabulous job—but at some point, we are going to have to rip this bandage off.

We head into the restaurant, and he's got reservations made and everything. Our table is ready, and we're seated straight away.

I've lived here for years, but this is my first visit to Poisson. It's all white tablecloths and stemware and comfortable elegance. Not overly pretentious or filled with waiters in tuxedos and violin music, but definitely a step higher than Ernesto's.

As soon as the waiter comes to take our drink order, Ben pipes up and goes first. Gin and tonic, with a wink to me. He's going for gold. I order the same with a grin, and our waiter heads off.

"Now, see?" Ben says, opening up his menu. "Think of all the things I won't have a chance to learn about you now." He clicks his tongue.

"Ha-ha," I fake-laugh at him. "You're in top form tonight. But look, there's a giant elephant on this table, so maybe we should chat about—"

"No, wait," he says quite seriously, and sets his menu down. "Hear me out."

I frown. "What?"

"Okay, so, yes, we've got this thing." He holds his hands up, almost as if he's preemptively surrendering. "And yeah, it's awkward, and we agreed we would talk about it, and I think we should, but I was hoping we could have our date first."

"What does that mean?"

His mouth pulls up in a hopeful half smile, and he puts his

hands down. "I came to the shop to ask you out to dinner, and then weirdness happened. So let's just follow that order. Let's sit, eat dinner, have what I assume will be a wonderful time. And after, we can talk about all the awkward things. But by then we will have the presumably wonderful meal under our belts, you know?"

I'm trying to fight a grin, but losing. "And just have it hanging over the presumably wonderful meal?"

"It doesn't have to hang there," he says with a shrug. "We'll get to it. I want to talk about it. Especially the bit about you wanting to have crazy, wild sex with me. I liked that part." I choke on air, and he laughs. "I'm kidding. Mostly. But we will talk about everything, I promise. I made a deal, and I'll keep it. I don't want you to think I'm sitting here dwelling on it. I just wanted to have a nice night with you so we have that to fall back on when we do open that can of worms."

I take a not-at-all-dignified drink of my water in an attempt to clear my throat. "That was mean."

"Sorry," he says. He doesn't look even the slightest bit contrite.

I sit back in my seat and cross my arms and am mildly delighted by the flash of worry that hits his eyes. "I'm curious. Why all the trouble? This seems like a lot of work for a date, fella."

Now he looks penitent. And a little embarrassed. "Well, I…" He pulls on his tie, and I feel sort of bad. I uncross my arms and lean back toward the table to show I'm listening. "Honestly?"

"Honestly is good, yeah."

"I find you very confusing. And a little scary. And intimidating."

"Those…those aren't good adjectives, Cleary."

"You are, though! But I also think you're very charming, and clever, and assertive, and I like you. So."

"You like me."

He looks down at his tie again and grins. "Hey, you like me, too. I heard that, you know."

I smile. "Yes, you did."

Our waiter comes back and deposits our drinks on the table. "Are we ready to order?" he asks.

Ben looks at me cautiously. It's a carefully weighted look. He's not applying pressure, but he's also not letting his hopefulness go unnoticed. I'm impressed.

It's also not at all in my nature to just throw pressing issues on the back burner and deal with them at a later time. And it's not like my relationship with Ryan is just going to magically disappear over appetizers and make this a normal date. Traditionally, I'd rather just get it out of the way so it's done and we can move on.

But then again, with my track record, my vagina would probably beg to differ, and I've only got twenty-four days left, so maybe I could try rolling with things just this once.

I pick up my menu and smile again. "I think we need a few minutes."

14

"Two years?" Ben whispers across the table. "Seriously?"

I pinch the bridge of my nose between my fingers. "Yes. Two years. Well, almost two years. But, god, why does everyone focus on that?"

He sits back awkwardly. "I'm sorry. I didn't mean to make you uncomfortable."

"There is nothing about this that isn't uncomfortable, Ben."

I'm not overselling. I've laid it all out there. The vaginismus, Ryan, Alice, the therapy, everything. The news of my broken special is hanging in the air like a giant neon unusable vagina.

A flash of understanding crosses his face. "Therapy sex. Okay, I get that now."

I close my eyes and take a deep breath. "This is wonderful."

"No, I'm sorry," he says, and almost reaches across the table for my hand. Thinking better of the idea, he yanks it back right quick. I'm relieved. I don't think I could handle any physical contact without bursting into flames. "I just meant I didn't understand that at all before."

I drain half my drink. "In my defense, I hadn't planned

to drop that on you until the third date, so don't hold it against me."

His eyebrows shoot straight up. "Really?"

"No, not really. I don't know when that information would have come around—I didn't think I'd be dating, to be honest." I force a smile. "Aren't you super glad we have that lovely dinner to fall back on now?"

"Yes, actually," he says seriously, and I feel like a big jerk.

"I'm sorry. This is just...astonishingly uncomfortable."

"So, what..." He pauses, clearly wondering how to phrase this delicately. "What can you do about it? You're doing therapy yourself, you said. And you're seeing Dave."

I hold my hands up. "No. No, I am not seeing Dave. My doctor made me do the intake appointment, but I can do the therapy on my own."

He looks confused, but says, "Well, Dave is really good at his job. And there are several others who are just as good, if you'd rather see someone else."

Shaking my head, I take a deep drink. "No. Why is everyone so fixated on me having a therapist? Aside from the fact I think Dave super hates me after that appointment, I can do the therapy myself. It's not the therapy that's the problem."

"So what is?"

Fighting the urge to shove my dessert fork in my eye, I reply, "It's after therapy. *After.*"

"The actual...sex?"

"Give the man a prize," I say, feeling sad. "I have no idea. I assume at some point I will have to bite the bullet and give it a shot, or just accept my life as a sexless wonder. I just really, really, really don't want to try again with Ryan and have it end in failure. Aside from not wanting to go through the physical pain of it not working—which, let's be honest, that's a big motivator—I don't think I could face him if I put us through that. Again."

He looks at me for a moment, carefully opening his mouth and then closing it, words forming and disappearing before he can get them out.

"Spit it out, sir."

"Is there anything… I mean…" He breathes out slowly and pulls his hands through his hair. "I have no idea how to say this appropriately, so please don't throw a drink at me or something if I get it wrong. But is there anything I can do to help?"

I bite the inside of my lip to keep from smiling. "Are you offering to have sex with me, Ben Cleary?"

He laces his fingers together and fidgets. "You know, I went to a Catholic school my entire childhood, and this conversation has me waiting for a nun to come up and slap me on the back of the head with a ruler, I swear."

"You are sweating a little."

He reflexively wipes at his forehead with the back of his hand. "I'm serious, though," he insists. "You said you've only got twenty-four days left, so is there anything I can do?"

I give him a genuine and kind smile. "Look, I'm taking this as you are legitimately offering to help and not just trying to get laid, but this isn't a simple situation."

"I'm not even going to dignify that 'get laid' part, just so you know," he says and shakes his head. "And yes, this is odd, and I'd definitely feel more comfortable if you went to one of the therapists instead, but if therapy isn't for you, I get that. I don't know, a friend in need. If I can help, I want to."

I sit back in my chair and tilt my head. "Are we friends, Ben?"

"Aren't we?"

My brows pull together. "How do you know as an adult? It's not like when you're five and you meet someone on the playground, and you both like the swings, and suddenly they're your new bestie."

"I still like the swings."

"Me, too."

He leans forward and puts his hands flat on the table. "Okay, how about this. If I called you in the middle of the night and needed your help with something, would you help me?"

"What kind of help?"

He thinks for a moment. "Maybe my car broke down and I needed a ride. Or my apartment was flooding. Or I needed to hide a body. The usual. Would you come?"

I consider this. "You know, I think I would."

"And if you called me, I'd be there. I think that's how adults determine friendship."

I smile. "That's a pretty solid barometer. I like that." He sits back in his chair, pleased. "So, okay. We're friends. Wanna find some swings?"

"I really do love the swings. I'll knock a kid right out of the way."

"No, you wouldn't."

"Okay, I wouldn't," he concedes. "I'd wait very impatiently for my turn."

"Just for the record," I say, "Mr. Very Nice Guy, you don't have to feel obligated to help me or my lady bits out of this jam we're in. This is a lot to take on. I don't want to cock things up for everyone."

"Should we set up some ground rules, or something?"

"As in, Rule One, we won't let this cock things up?"

He laughs. "Yes, that can be our official first rule."

The waiter comes by, and I motion for another round of drinks. "Might as well be good and drunk for this," I say. "Okay, what else?"

He holds his hands up. "This is your show, Kat. You get to make the rules."

Pointing at him, I ask, "Just so we're clear, you're not that kind of therapist, right?"

He shakes his head. "No, not at all. I mean, I know of the treatments, and I learned some techniques in college, but I've never done it." For a moment, he manages to look even twitchier than he has all night. "But I don't feel comfortable doing...that. If you want the actual physical therapy, I can't do it. I could lose my license."

My body involuntarily shudders. "No, no, I don't want that kind of therapy from you. Really, really no." I frown a little. "But I don't want you to get into trouble. Can you even do any of this?"

He considers this. "Well, I can't date my patients. And I can't perform physical therapy on anyone outside the hospital for insurance reasons. But you aren't a patient, and this is definitely not sanctioned physical therapy."

"This is..."

"Unofficial therapy sex?"

I stifle a giggle. "I feel like we're living outside the law."

Laughing, he says, "I'm a rebel." I look at the rebel's tie a little closer and realize the print is of stylized dinosaurs. Definitely a rebel. He adds, "So, legally, I'm okay. Let's just think of this like I'm not Ben the pediatric physical therapist—I'm Ben, your friend, doing what I can to help out. But what about you? Are you all right with this? How do you even want to go about any of it?"

I rock back and forth in my seat for a moment. "Well. If this is therapy sex, and not, like, we're dating sex, shouldn't it be, um..."

"Therapeutic?"

I frown. "I was thinking more *perfunctory*. But that doesn't sound right."

He stares at the table. "So, not—" he motions with his hands, as if he can grab the right words if he just tries hard enough "—romantic? Emotional? What do you mean?"

I'm still frowning. "Yeah, I think. Okay. That."

"Are you sure?"

I straighten up. "Yes. I mean, this is a means to an end, right? So, the romance, and foreplay, all of that, seems kind of misplaced."

"I'm just curious," he says carefully, "but wouldn't things like foreplay maybe help?"

I stare at him. "Damned if I know. I have no idea what I'm doing."

He stares back. "I don't have a clue, either."

"This is probably a terrible plan."

The waiter comes back with our drinks and we both grab and start guzzling before he can even set them on the table.

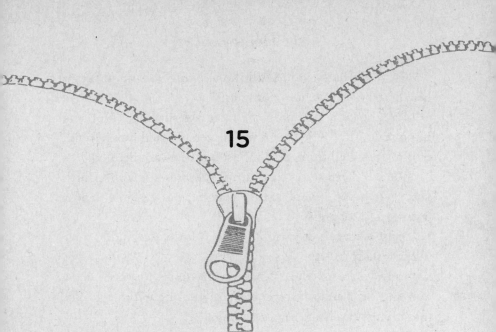

15

"Fuck this fucking raven!"

I grab the now-unusable fondant and throw it across the kitchen. Butter and Liz both freeze mid-decoration. I take a deep breath, pick up my X-ACTO knife and lean back over my station.

"You, uh, you okay, sweetie?" Butter asks gently.

"I'm fine," I mutter, focusing on cutting the wings as carefully as I can.

Shannon comes walking back into the prep area and straightens her apron. "Why do we hate ravens?"

"Kat is having a moment," Liz says. Out of the corner of my eye, I can see her gesturing to me with her eyes wide.

"Could we not point at me, please?"

"What's going on, Pumpkin?" Shannon asks, standing next to me at my station. "You look a little…manic."

"I'm fine," I say, accidentally cutting the head off this bird. "Fuck." I stab the damn thing with my knife out of spite, move on to a fresh patch and start cutting a new one.

"Okay, seriously, stop with the fondant," Shannon says in her mom voice. "What's going on?"

I slap the knife down on the table and snap up. "Nothing. I'm okay, really," I lie. I run my fingers through my hair and pull my ponytail tighter. "I'm just a little overwhelmed."

"We still have two weeks until the presentation," Butter says. "We haven't even finalized the recipes yet, hon. You're putting a lot of pressure on yourself."

"I just want to get it right!" I say a little too loudly, sucking in a sharp breath.

"Lady, you're on edge. What is happening with you?" Shannon puts her hand on my shoulder, and I honestly feel like I might burst out laughing or crying.

"I'm supposed to have sex with Ben tonight," I whimper.

The three of them—all three, simultaneously—drop their jaws open.

"Okay, honey, if that's your reaction to sleeping with someone, I'm pretty sure you're doing it wrong," Butter offers.

"Oh, shut up!" I snap. "This is serious! What if it doesn't work? Which it won't. Of course it won't."

"So don't do it yet," Shannon says. "If you're not ready."

"Oh my god, I'm ready," I say, and I can feel my hands clenching into sweaty grips at my sides. "Me? I'm ready. I'm so ready. You bring Ryan or Ben in here, and I'll go right the hell now, okay? It's not me I'm worried about. It's my goddamn special that's going to mess this up."

"Kat, you are losing it," Butter says, bringing me a bottle of water. "Calm down."

I take the water and chug until the ringing in my ears stops. "My doctor gave me anxiety medication for my vagina," I sigh. "That's my life right now. My junk is strung out."

"I'm getting tense just watching you," Shannon says. "My

doc gave me those pills, too. They were helpful. But what did your doctor say about everything?"

I shrug. "Take it slow, don't rush, blah, blah."

"That doesn't sound 'blah, blah,'" Liz scolds.

I hold the bottle to my forehead. "I know, okay? I do. I know I'm being stupid about this. I just..." I slump down onto one of the stools by the sink. "I just want to get past all of this, you know? I don't want this to be my thing anymore. It's all I can think about lately. I feel broken."

"But you're not," Butter says.

"I am, though!" I insist. "And it's not like I have to wait for a bone to grow back. It's something I can fix. It's driving me crazy."

"Because you're a control freak, you dork," Shannon says with a smile and pokes me in the arm. "But you can't force this. And if you really like Ben, I don't think rushing into doomed sex is a great idea."

"It's not about that. This is therapy sex," I clarify. "We talked about it."

Butter gapes. "Seriously? You're doing that?"

I shrug. "He wanted to help. I want to have sex. It seemed like a good plan."

Shannon appears to be blatantly judging me. "What does therapy sex entail, exactly?"

"Well, Shannon," I say in my best fake announcer voice, "I'm glad you asked. The plan is that this is in no way a dating venture, nor a romantic endeavor, but merely one friend helping another with physical assistance. It's not about kissing and swooning. It's about seeing what works and what doesn't."

Shannon rubs her temples. "I see no way this can end horribly. None at all."

"Look, when you were going through this, you had Joe. And you had all that comfort and trust, and it worked. But I don't have the luxury of time to form a marital bond, okay? Ryan and I aren't in a place where we can do that, and I refuse to go all trial and error with him again. Joe was there to test your progress out on, so that's kind of what Ben is. He's my...tester."

I can see her forcing her eyes not to roll. "This deadline is your choice. Why don't you back the pressure off yourself and take this slower?"

"I'm with Shannon," Liz offers in a quiet voice. "This doesn't seem to be helping you much."

"Because I'm terrified if I don't do it now, I'll find some reason to push it off like I did before," I shout, feeling an acidic burn of tears behind my eyes. "And two years from now, we'll all be sitting here having this same conversation. Ryan and I will be in the same miserable place, except he'll be off sleeping with other people because that seemed like a good idea at the time, and our rut will be so deep we'll have reached Earth's core levels. And you know what? My vagina can't handle another two years on the shelf, okay? It's not a fine wine. It will not get better with age, stored in a dark cellar. It needs to be uncorked right the fuck now."

Butter frowns at me but delicately asks, "You're going to have sex with Ben, but it's not going to be while dating? How does that even work?"

"This is just, I don't know, business. He knows all about Ryan and our arrangement, and he gets it."

The room is filling up with their judgment and doubts. It's okay. It's not like I don't already have everything they are likely thinking dancing around in my head anyway.

It hits me that until a couple of weeks ago, if there'd been something stressing me out this much, I would have been sending shouty or whiny texts to Ryan during the day. For four years, he's been my not-Shannon/Butter/etc. outlet.

Is that even a thing I could do now?

Is that even a thing I *want* to do now?

Furthermore, I know I gave Ryan permission—nay, blatantly ordered him—to sleep with other people, but we never really agreed to me doing the same.

And what if this all fails horribly and Ryan and I split up? Because I damn well won't keep him tied up in a relationship if our future is going to be like the last two years.

I'm definitely going to die sexless and alone.

"Okay," Shannon says, clapping her hands together, making me jump. "Kat. This is your thing, and yes, what you've got going on right now is a little…strange, but this is your issue. If this is how you feel like you need to deal with it, well, then we support you, don't we?"

"Of course we do," Butter says. Liz nods.

Shannon continues, "We know how important it is to you to not surpass that two-year mark, so that makes it important to us, right ladies?"

Butter cheers an enthusiastic, "Right!" while Liz's nodding accelerates.

"Is there anything you need from us? Is there anything we can do to help?"

I look at her, and I feel the burning in the back of my eyes again. "Am I being an idiot?" I rub my hands roughly on my apron. "This is the best option I can think of right now, but is it horrible? Am I being stupid?"

Shannon stares at me and considers everything. "Did you discuss everything with Ben?" I nod. "And you told him about all of it? Like, the honest truth?"

I nod harder. "I did. And he didn't run away screaming or anything. And I've known him for five months, what with him coming to the shop every day, and we all know he's a nice guy, right? He just doesn't seem like the kind of guy who

111

would be pushy about sex in general. Like, I need someone who will let me do this in my own time, and I think he will. He was definitely there for everything when we talked about all of this. And plus, he's a therapist, so I feel like he'll get what I need and at least understand what's working and what isn't, you know?"

"Those are all excellent points," Shannon offers.

A pitiful squeak emanates from my throat. "This scares me to death. Aside from all the Ryan stuff, I really like Ben. I like having him in my life as a friend. What if I'm screwing everything up with therapy sex?"

Butter comes over and gives me a hug. "I dunno," she says. "I think if he was willing to hang around with all that, he's probably not one to scare easy. I mean, he came back after dildo day, girl."

Liz makes a whining noise. "Oh god, you're going to end up being best friends, and I'll have to see him forever and re-member that, aren't you?"

"That's now my main goal in life," I say, clinging to Butter. "Second only to getting laid, of course."

Dr. Snow says I need to relax, so I'm going to relax, damn it.

I've got two hours until Ben shows up at my apartment, but I'm certainly not feeling relaxed. I've got a tiny bottle of antianxiety medication for my special rattling around in my purse, but I can't bring myself to take that leap. Not that I'm against medication or anything, but it feels a little early in the game to be calling in a pinch hitter.

I can relax.

I stare at my phone, the GPS leading me to a spa that is apparently located a mere ten blocks from my apartment. I haven't had the time or desire to waste an afternoon at a spa since my mom gave me a gift card to one for my twenty-third birthday. I think I've probably passed this place several times, but it's never registered in my mind before.

If I can't deep-breathe my way into a calmer state, I'm going to pay someone to help.

I get why everyone says I'm pushing myself a little too hard right now, but I didn't plan on the Coopertown deal lining up with my special epiphany. And quite frankly, all this below-the-belt nonsense is making it a little hard to focus. If I could just get a better grip on the situation, I'd be free to give those damn sugar ravens my full attention.

When I was in school, I would do projects when they were assigned. Shannon and my other friends would wait until the last minute, or spread the work out over a few days or weeks. Not me. I would sit down the night we were given the work and settle in until it was done. I didn't like the responsibility hanging over my head. I wanted it done and out of the way so I could look toward anything else that might come my way.

I'd much rather get this particular homework knocked out and off my to-do list instead of waiting until the moment it's due. A moment when it's important and I'm emotionally invested and it would be devastating in one way or another for it all to go south.

I come upon Eden's Tranquility and tuck my phone back in my pocket. I open the door and am greeted by a tinkling bell sound from somewhere. There's woodwind music playing from overhead speakers, and a heady combination of aromatherapy smells that I'm assuming have been mixed up during the day.

The lights are low. There's bamboo everywhere. So, a spa.

A calm-looking woman behind the front counter smiles at me. "Welcome to Eden's Tranquility," she says. "Do you have an appointment with us this evening?"

I walk up to join her and experience a slight fear of catching my hair on fire. I can't imagine they really need so many candles at the hostess station.

"Um, no," I explain. "Your website said you accept walk-ins. I was wondering if you have anything available for right now?"

"What kind of service are you looking for?"

I look at her hopefully. "Well, I need something relaxing. And—" I say, glancing up at the clock on the wall "—something that has me in and out in an hour."

She smiles serenely. "All of our services are meant to soothe and relax."

Pursing my lips together for a beat, I take a breath and say, "Okay, great. Then I need something that will relax me up right nice in an hour. And it's pretty important."

Giving me a somewhat questionable look, she starts typing on her computer. "We can certainly try. Most of our therapists are booked for the evening, but it looks like Tamara has an opening right now. Would you like to book a massage?"

I consider this. Massage, relaxed muscles, bingo. "Sign me up."

The hostess, whose name is Brittany, according to her name tag, sits me down in a squashy armchair surrounded by ferns and bamboo with a stack of paperwork to fill out. Truly, they are asking for more information than I have to give at a doctor's visit.

I don't know why they need to know how much alcohol my grandmother drank per day, but I go ahead and scribble out that Grams liked a tipple of sherry on Sundays.

After a small chunk of time, a woman with naturally bright red hair comes out to greet me. "Hello, Kat," she says, shaking my hand. "I'm Tamara. I'll be your massage therapist this evening. Let me take those."

"Hi," I greet her, handing over the freaking ten-page essay

worth of answers I've just written out and wondering why I can't get away from therapists. "Thanks for fitting me in."

"Of course," she says, flipping through the papers. I can tell her soothing voice is something that's been rehearsed. I wonder if it's a job requirement here. "Follow me, please, and we'll get started." She leads the way through the lobby, and we head through a narrow hallway to the individual treatment rooms. "Now, I'm told you are hoping for a relaxing experience? Did you have a particular need you want met, or were you more looking for a night off?"

We reach an empty room, and she motions me inside. The walls are painted a soothing sage green, and it's all accented with dark wood. The only lights are very dim wall sconces and candles lit on a table by the door. A massage table stands in the middle of the room.

"Erm," I reply. "I have um, a date, yeah, a date tonight, and I was hoping to go into it nice and Zen, you know?"

Tamara smiles at me. "Yes, of course. First I'll have you get changed, and then we can get started. Brittany mentioned you're on a schedule, so I'll make sure to have you out of here on time." She motions to an empty basket on a chair next to some hooks on the wall. "You can place your clothing and personal belongings in the basket and on the hooks, and then lie facedown under the sheet. I'll give you a few minutes to get changed."

In a flash of red locks, she's out the door, and I'm left wondering how long a few minutes is. Is this like a leisurely time when I can undress at a mellow pace, or more like eating in prison, when I've got about sixty seconds to get done what needs to get done before the door bursts back open and the riots break out?

Best not to risk it. I don't think getting caught by a stranger with my pants around my ankles would be particularly conducive to a calming atmosphere.

I peel off my clothes and quickly fold them in the basket. I tuck my bra inside my T-shirt, because it's a thing women do. I'm not even sure where I learned this trick, but everyone I know does it. There's got to be a science there.

Quickly, I climb under the sheet and wait patiently for Tamara to return. It's odd to me that this is the first of two people I am intending to get purposefully naked for today, thus breaking my streak of being naked for no one in a very, very long time.

I'm on a damn roll.

My stomach flops a little at the thought of my evening plans, so I quickly change my mental subject. I'm supposed to be centering or something. Deep breathing.

A gentle knock on the door sounds out and I say, "Come in."

Tamara enters the room, and thanks to my lying mostly naked on a table under a sheet, I can't really see much of her as she moves around the room. Some tinkling music starts playing from the general direction of the cabinet by the door and I hear the gentle clatter of plastic bottles moving around.

Tamara walks over and holds a bottle close to my face. "How is this scent?" she asks. "If you'd prefer something more citrusy, I have other options."

I smell lavender and something else, which I assume is perfectly fine, so I say, "It's great." I figure if it's not, I can always take a super fast shower before Ben gets to my place.

Tamara squeezes some goo into her hands and rubs them together to warm it up. "Before I begin, are there any muscle areas you'd like me to pay special attention to, or anywhere you're having pain or trouble with?"

Completely without meaning to, I snort. "Yeah, my special," I say.

"Your...your what?"

I freeze on the table and look up at her awkwardly. I didn't mean to say that out loud. I really did not. "Um. My uh, well...that's what I call my lady bits."

Tamara's hands go right to her hips, one eyebrow cocked up, and she looks more like an annoyed lunch lady than a massage therapist all of a sudden. "Sweetie, we aren't that kind of place." Gone are her dulcet and soothing tones. "If you want that kind of rubdown, try the Golden Hands on Cathedral."

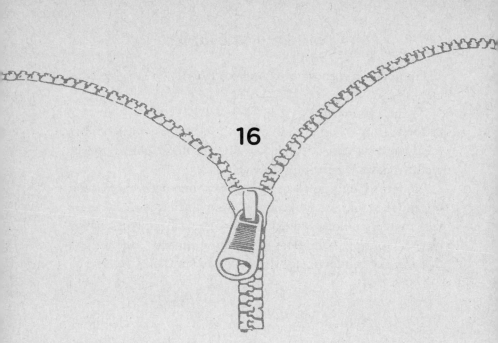

16

"You've got a nice place," Ben says, surveying my living room.

"Thanks," I say. I swing my arms in front of me and press my lips together tightly. "Thanks for, you know, um, coming over. And stuff."

"Not a problem," he says, pulling at his tie. "Thanks for inviting me."

We are standing near my front door, just at the entrance of my living room, and we can't seem to move beyond this point. I could give him a tour. I could offer him a seat on the couch. I could take him back to the bedroom and ravage him.

I could do a million different things, but no, I'm standing at my front damn door more awkwardly than anyone has ever stood anywhere ever.

I didn't know how to prep for this evening. If it had been a date thing, I would have spit shined the joint up, put out a few candles maybe, turned on some music.

But this is a therapy session. So I made sure there weren't any dishes in the sink, no errant bits of laundry on my bedroom floor, and my prep ended there.

"It's a really nice night," I offer.

He nods. "Yep. It's getting really warm out."

"Yes, it is. Oh, can I take your jacket? Wait, do people do that? You don't take suit jackets, do you? Or do you if it's hot out? Why do I not know that? I have absolutely no idea what proper etiquette is regarding suits."

He sort of squints at me and pushes his tongue against the back of his teeth. "I... I don't know."

I lean back on my heels and stare at the carpet. He puts his hands into his pockets and looks around the room silently. This is miserable.

"Drinks!" I yelp suddenly, startling us both.

"What?"

"Drinks! I'm offering to make us drinks! I should have opened with that."

He presses his thumb into his temple. "God, yes, drinks. Drinks are awesome. Let's have drinks."

I ditch him by the door and flee for my kitchen. It's only about ten feet away, but I take the retreat anyway. "Wine. I have wine. How about wine?"

"Wine is great," he says, joining me by the counter.

I grab a bottle of white out of the fridge. "Can you get glasses out of that cabinet?" I ask, pointing to the door by his head. He does as instructed and reaches inside, pulling out glasses as I fetch a corkscrew from the drawer. "See? This is fine. We have wine. Can't go wrong with wine."

Okay, I definitely have to stop saying *wine*.

I yank the foil off the top and get the corkscrew in. Then, for the life of me, I can't get the cork out. I pull as hard as I can, but the damn thing isn't budging.

"Can I help?" Ben asks.

"I've got it," I lie. What the fuck is with this bottle? I take the very classy approach and put it between my knees and give it everything I've got, but it's not moving at all. The cork is starting to deteriorate.

I'm about to throw this bottle across the apartment.

I'm pretty sure Ben senses the danger. "Here," he says, "you hold it." He positions the bottle in the crook of my arm like a football, grabs the neck with one hand and the corkscrew with the other, and says, "Okay, pull."

It takes a minute, and we really struggle with it, but finally the blasted thing pops out and sloshes us both with wine.

We stand there, me holding the bottle, him holding the corkscrew, staring at the cork, wine dripping off the sleeve of his suit.

"This is going really well," I say, panting slightly.

"Maybe pour," he suggests breathlessly.

I do, and we drink. This is a nightmare. I wasn't nearly this nervous the night I lost my virginity. It was my freshman year of college, there were some tepid wine coolers involved, and I'd known the guy for only a few weeks. But he lived in my dorm and he was nice and I'd made the decision to not spend one more week as a virgin. At the time, I hadn't met anyone I was interested in spending the rest of my life with as of yet, and it was time.

Okay, so the parallels are a little more real than I'd like to admit.

"Did…" I look at my empty glass. "Did we just chug our glasses?"

He's staring at his own empty glass with the same look of confusion. He looks up at me with a flash of desperation. "Pour faster?"

And I do.

Within ten minutes, we have a second bottle opened and poured, and we haven't even moved out of the kitchen.

"I feel like we are making really good choices here," I say after another lengthy swig.

"Me, too," he says, wincing down another gulp. "I think the fact that we just swallowed down a bottle and a half of wine in three drinks isn't a bad sign at all."

I serve out the rest of the second bottle. "Totally," I say, raising my glass. "My doctor did say relaxing would help, so. There ya go."

He pauses mid-drink. "You're talking to your doctor about this?"

I swallow hard. My stomach is not impressed with the last ten minutes. "Yes? Why?"

He shakes his head quickly. "No, that's good! I mean, I was actually a little worried you were maybe rushing into things. But if you've got your doctor in on it, that makes me feel better."

I scoff, "Excuse me, Cleary, but I'm a grown-ass woman, and I don't need you or my doctor to give me permission to do anything."

He blinks really hard. "That's not what I meant, Kat. I'm sorry. I didn't mean to offend you. I was just worried I wouldn't be doing things the right way. I've never actually heard of therapy sex, and I don't want to make things worse, you know?"

"I…" I sway slightly and realize the room is spinning a bit. "I think we should sit down now."

Like a child clutching a security blanket, I grab another bottle of wine and carry it to the couch with me. I don't even bring my glass. I flop down on one end, and Ben drops down beside me.

Was Ryan this nervous on his date with Alice? Did he have to get stumbling drunk to make it through the conversation?

Or did he glide through it and go on to more dates?

It's been over two weeks. He could have had a new date every day for all I know.

We haven't sent so much as a single text message since we started the break.

My head feels sloshy, but even still, while the thought of Ryan on a conveyor belt of hookups doesn't make me feel warm and fuzzy, it doesn't bother me nearly as much as I feel like it should.

"That was really stupid," Ben says, rubbing his eyes with the backs of his hands.

"I regret that, yes," I say, already fiddling with the cork on the third bottle.

He slowly starts pulling off his jacket, as if he finally realized the sleeve was wet. He gets it peeled off and flings it onto the chair adjacent to the couch. "You seem really, really nervous," he observes.

"Shut up," I say, popping the cork. "So do you."

"Of course I'm nervous!" he says, waving his arm around as though my apartment as a whole serves as evidence. "I'm terrified. I have no idea what I'm doing. And it's almost guaranteed I will say something completely wrong and piss you off. I've never seen you so not-composed. It's very unsettling."

"We all have off days," I say with a shrug, and take a sip of wine. Smaller this time. I hand him the bottle and he takes a drink. In my defense, I'd intended to be extra relaxed for this, and instead, I think I narrowly missed being arrested for solicitation. That really threw a wrench in my soothing game.

"Kat, what are we doing?"

"We are preparing to have medicinal sex. By getting blind drunk, apparently."

"And you're sure you want to do this?" He passes the bottle back to me.

"Yes, I am very sure I want to have sex, yes."

"And the rules?"

"Those still apply, right?"

"Do you want them to?"

I nod. "Yes. Because I am hoping what's happening right now will in no way be a reflection of either of us for our friendship and whatnot. I think you're very nice." I take another drink and realize I'm now drinking red wine. I didn't even know I had red wine.

He smiles. "I think you're very nice, too. And we made a deal. This is therapy…stuff. This is weird therapy. Definitely not what I do at the office."

I give him the bottle again. "Okay. So. Rules."

"I can't remember them all."

I close one eye. I don't know why. "No smooshy kissy stuff. No foreplay. No romancey things. Just…stuff. Sex stuff."

He frowns. "I kind of feel like a prostitute. I'm not allowed to kiss you?"

"You're not getting paid, so that's not accurate. And since this isn't official therapy, I don't think my insurance would cover it. As for the kissing, we talked about that, remember?"

He takes another drink and closes his eyes. "Oh, right. That was a good point. That's not how I'd want our first kiss to go."

"See? Rules. Rules are good."

He takes another drink and nods. "Rules *are* very good. That's a good rule." He tips the bottle my way and looks at me with sleepy eyes. "But I really do want to kiss you, you know. Very much."

My stomach does a little flippy move, and I take a nervous sip of wine. "I'd let you."

Realizing what I just said, I clap a hand over my traitorous mouth. He grins at me, and it's all I can do not to pounce on him and devour him from the jawline down. "There you are," he says. "I wondered where you'd gone."

I'm determined to avoid another slip like that, so it's time to get back to business. I lean forward and set the bottle of wine on the coffee table. Then I very carefully move closer to him on the couch until I'm right up next to him, sitting on my knees, looking down over him. "Should we..." I begin tentatively "...get started?"

He looks up at me with heavy eyes, the edges of his mouth still pulled up in a smile, but his brows pull together. He closes his eyes and drags his hands roughly over his face before looking up at me again.

"Kat, I'm not sure if I can do this."

I almost flinch, I'm so surprised. "What? What's wrong? Did I say something?"

He reaches out and puts his hand on my arm as quickly as he can in his wobbly state. "No! God, no! It's not that! You're... great. It's just..."

"What?"

He shakes his head and gives me a very sheepish smile. "I mean, I don't think I can *physically* do it. That was a lot of wine. Like, a lot."

I stare at him, blinking for a moment. Then I get it. "Oh. Ohh!" I drag the sound out far too long as I flop back against the cushions.

"I didn't plan that well," he says, his words slurring a bit around the edges. "I didn't even eat dinner before I came over. I was too nervous. I'm all but certain I'd fall over if I tried to stand up right now."

A snort-laugh falls out of me. "Oh man, I didn't eat, either. Wow, we really did make awesome choices."

"The best."

"This is the second time tonight I've failed at getting naked with someone. These are spectacularly bad stats."

He blinks slowly at me. "I don't understand what that means."

I sigh and pat him on the shoulder. "Long story. Are you going to be okay? Do we need to have your stomach pumped?"

"I think I'll live. I just need to maybe not move for a few minutes."

I nod and kick my feet out onto the coffee table. He wraps his arm around my shoulder and drops his head back onto the couch. Poor bastard. Though I don't think I'm far behind him.

"Want to order a pizza?" I suggest. "I've got Netflix."

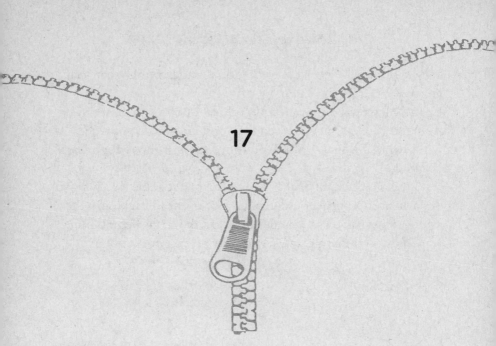

17

The blaring sound of a bullhorn erupts in my apartment.

At least, I think I'm in my apartment.

I flail around, trying to get upright, and realize I'm not alone. Then I also realize I'm on my couch.

Quite suddenly, I'm not on my couch anymore.

I'm on the floor, and the bullhorn is my phone, ringing from my end table. Oh god, the vibration against the wood is going to kill me. It's echoing through my brain.

Ben lurches forward and clutches his head. "Christ," he mutters. "What is that?"

I unpeel my tongue from the roof of my mouth. "My phone," I gasp. "It's over there." I point to the table by him and immediately put my hands back to my forehead, pressing as hard as I can to keep everything from throbbing out.

He reaches over, fumbling and uncoordinated, and grabs the blasted, screaming device. He hands it to me, and I answer. "Hello?" My voice sounds like dirt tastes.

"Kat? Where are you? Are you okay?" Shannon says, her most worried mom-voice blasting through the speaker.

I struggle to keep my eyelids open. "I'm fine. Why are you calling me?"

There's an uncomfortable pause. "You were supposed to be here an hour and a half ago, Pumpkin."

I yank the phone away from my ear and look at the time, struck by a wave of panicky guilt. At least, I think it's panicky guilt. It's either that or I'm about to spew on my phone. "Fuck!" I shout. "Shannon, I am so sorry! I will be right there. Give me twenty minutes. I'll be right there."

I hang up on her before she can hit me with more questions and fly up off the floor. I regret this immediately as I tumble to the side and nearly fall over onto Ben, who only sort of catches me. He's not looking much better than I feel.

"Do you seriously have to go to work?"

"I'm late," I say, trying to rub the hangover out of my eyes. I look around the living room. The TV is still on, there's a pizza box on the coffee table, and the third bottle of wine appears to be empty. "Oh god," I groan.

He's still squeezing his forehead with both hands. "Don't worry. We didn't do anything. Although all of our other choices were problematic, at best."

"I..." I struggle to form thoughts, let alone words. "I have to get dressed."

Stumbling away to my bedroom, I yank my clothes off as soon as I'm through the door. Obviously there isn't time for a shower, which is possibly the only thing that could save my life at this point. I smell like a winery. A winery and desperation. And a little bit like pizza.

I throw on a fresh T-shirt and jeans and race back into the living room with sneakers in hand. Ben is trying to tidy up by taking trash into the kitchen.

"It's fine," I say. "Just leave it. I can get it later."

"It's seven in the morning," he says, squinting at me. "Do

you normally have to go in at seven on Saturdays? Because it's seriously Saturday."

"Buck up, sir," I say with a grin. "I was supposed to be in at five thirty."

"This makes my wearing a tie for you last Saturday less impressive, doesn't it?"

"You're actually still wearing your tie, you know."

He looks down and seems genuinely surprised. "So you're saying we're even?"

I chuckle. "Yeah, that's totally the same."

Looking a bit unsteady on his feet, he says, "I called a cab, by the way."

I frown. "You didn't have to do that. I usually take the bus in."

He seems both apologetic and frustrated. "I figured we could split it. I'm too hungover for anything but a cab home. Or possibly still drunk. I'm not actually sure. And since we're going in the same direction, I thought I'd be gentlemanly and share the cab. I figure it's the least I can do, since I get to go home and die while you have to go and be a productive member of society."

I stop stuffing things in my purse and give him a once-over. He looks adorably horrible. His hair is smooshed at odd angles, his eyes are barely open and the sleeve of his shirt has a lovely stain from the first bottle of wine. His tie is loose and hanging all askew.

And if his head is pounding a beat anywhere near as viciously as mine, he deserves a medal for staying upright.

"Yeah, you're right. It's the least you can do." I give him a wink, pick up my bag and head for the door.

He grabs his jacket off the chair and follows me. Just as I'm locking up, the cab pulls up to the curb. Stepping out from the cover of the awning and into the sunlight might be the most painful thing I've ever experienced. A wounded squeak escapes me, and a groaning hiss leaves Ben.

We climb into the car. I give the driver the address and collapse into the seat, closing my eyes tight against the brutal rays of the morning sun.

"I will say," I offer up as we pull away from the curb, "as terrible as I feel—and make no mistake, I might possibly be dying—there's some comfort in you going down with me, Cleary. Misery loving company, and all that."

"I'll be sure to feel extra guilty when I go home and go right back to sleep. Because I'm gonna. All damn day. I'm thirty-two. I'm too old to get that smashed." We ride in mutually nauseated silence for most of the trip, but as we hit the inner part of the city, he blinks against the hateful sun and looks at me. "How late do you have to work today?"

My expression turns into a reflexive sad face. "Six."

"That's cruel." He shakes his head. "Just unfair."

We pull up to the shop. "I brought this on myself." I sigh. "Go. Sleep for those of us who cannot."

"I'll willingly make this sacrifice."

I open the door and step out. "And uh, thanks for the, well, hideous drunken awkwardness that was last night?"

He smiles, then winces, pressing his palm to his forehead. "Anytime, Kat."

I shut the door, flinching when the loud sound ricochets through what I assume are the now hollow places in my head where my brain used to be. I turn and run for the shop. Normally I come in through the back entrance reserved for employees, but today is special and I'm late as hell, so it's a matter of getting in the damn door as quickly as possible.

We're still in the middle of our morning rush, and there are dozens of customers lined up for coffee and pastries. Shannon, Butter and Liz all give gasps and looks of shock when they see my appearance, but thankfully they are too busy dealing with the crowd to stop and demand an explanation.

I race past them into the back room, stow my bag on the desk, grab my apron, throw it on, wash my hands at warp speed and head out front.

I'm going to fake it until I make it. If I can survive the rush without vomiting on a customer, I am going to treat myself later by crawling inside a cup of coffee and drowning.

Saturdays are always surprisingly busy, with people coming and going from the moment we open until right after the usual breakfast hours. Not that I'm a particularly lazy person, but I can't imagine getting up at dawn on a Saturday unless I was required to by job or law.

We keep our shop closed on Sundays to give the staff one promised day off a week, and I'm always grateful for it. Sundays are for Zen time, I don't care who you are. You don't get up at dawn on Sunday. It's unnatural. If I had to be up serving people cupcakes with the sun on a Sunday, I don't think I'd have very good customer service skills to go with them.

See? This is good. By ignoring the pounding in my head, the horrible gurgling in my stomach and the weird furry sensation on my teeth, and focusing on making sure each person I talk to has a pleasant experience, I am almost certain I'm not going to fall over dead or anything. This is good.

"Are you okay?" Shannon hisses in my ear as she reaches around me for a chocolate fudge with strawberry compote.

"Mistakes were made," I whisper back. "Too much wine."

"You look like death," Butter says as she walks by. "Literal death."

I shake my head. "Thank you, Butter. You mean figurative, but thanks. That's super helpful."

Butter shrugs and hands a bag of muffins across the display case to a customer with a smile.

Liz pops up beside me and starts filling the coffee machine with fresh grounds. She asks in a barely audible voice, "So, did you...you know? With Ben? Did it work?"

Shannon and Butter are both with customers, but I can see them both listening, as well.

I huff. "Guys, we can talk about that later, okay? Maybe when there aren't twenty customers waiting for our attention?"

Liz puts her head down and stares at the coffee machine with way too much focus as she fills it, Shannon raises an eyebrow at me, and Butter puts a hand on her hip.

"I can help the next customer," I say with more cheer than I thought was physically possible in my current state.

A woman I know I've seen in here before comes up looking annoyed. This can't be good.

"I'd like to speak to a manager," she says tersely.

"How can I help you?" I ask, taking in a soothing breath.

The woman straightens up and stares me down. She looks very polished, very prim. Her hair is smooth and shiny and pulled back in a low ponytail. Her clothing is pressed and perfectly tailored. She is a sharp contrast to my unbrushed hair and teeth and 30-proof breath, and I'm pretty sure she knows it, too.

"Last week I ordered two hundred cupcakes for my son's fifth birthday, and I found them to be unsatisfactory. I would like a refund, please."

She slaps her receipt down on the counter in front of me, and I pick it up.

"Oh, I remember this order. I actually made these cupcakes. What was the problem?"

"When I placed the order, I specifically requested that each cupcake needed to have at least one hundred sprinkles, and I'm not convinced they all did. At the party yesterday, while the cupcakes where on the table, I saw that some of the cupcakes had more sprinkles than the others, and it looked horribly uneven." She pulls her phone out, and I can't help but note the Burberry case on it as she opens the screen to a photo of a child's birthday party. Sure enough, there are the two hundred cupcakes I'd spent a good chunk of Thursday making, looking perfectly sprinkly. "I took two of the cupcakes, and I counted. One had eighty-seven sprinkles, and the other had one hundred forty-three." She swipes her phone, and there is a picture of a napkin with two piles of sprinkles. My jaw flops open. "This is unacceptable. When I placed the order with her—" she points to Shannon "—I was assured this would be handled. It ruined the ambience of the entire party, and I would like a refund for my order."

I stare at her. I just stare. I can't even blink. I feel everyone within earshot staring, as well. I look down at her receipt. I look over at Shannon, who is trying to bag a scone up for someone else while the wheels are spinning in her head. Butter is pouring a coffee beside me and stiffening up. Liz is at the register and shrinking down to appear as invisible as possible.

"Are...are you serious?" I finally say. "You want a full refund on an entire cupcake order, which I am assuming was eaten, because of a two-cupcake quality control sprinkle test? In real life, you want that to happen?"

The woman bristles. "Yes! What kind of customer service is this? I made a very specific order request, and it wasn't met! My son's birthday was ruined!"

My mouth drops open again, and I can feel a torrent of profanity building on my tongue. I look back to Shannon, who is either having a stroke or blinking out a message in Morse code. The other customers, most of whom are regulars, are watching with a dedicated rubbernecking fascination.

I know what I want to say, and there is a poetic combination of swear words heard only within the confines of a lumberjack convention within that speech. And I would, too. Fuck this woman. But in my head are the potential online reviews that would hit just as we are set to present to the Coopertown Ravens, and I picture Shannon's tots as they see their dreams of hugging Mickey Mouse whisked away. Butter resigning herself to Skyping with her Noni. Liz spending her honeymoon at the motel off Route 15 instead of somewhere tropical or Parisian.

But really, though, fuck this lady.

"Ma'am," I say quietly. I take in another deep, calming breath, swallowing down any four-letter words with it. "I apologize for any inconvenience my inadequate sprinkle-counting skills may have caused on your son's special day. However, you did examine the order with our other manager when you picked them up—I was there for said inspection—and at that time, you gave your approval for the cupcakes and the number of sprinkles contained upon said cupcakes, and because you did, in fact, use all the cupcakes for their intended purpose, I'm afraid I am unable to refund your entire order."

"This is ridiculous!" the woman shrieks. The sound feels like barbed wire in my ears. "Do you know who you're talking to?"

"No." I stop her, holding up a finger. "No, I don't, nor do I care. And what's ridiculous is you expecting me to refund you literally hundreds of dollars for a product you used. What's ridiculous is that I'm standing here with a raging hangover, and somehow that's less painful than the idea of you sitting at your son's birthday party counting out sprinkles on cupcakes. Because I'm sorry, lady, that's freaking weird.

"But I respect that this was important to you. And I'm sorry you were unhappy with your experience. Although mostly, I'm hoping to end this so I can go find some aspirin and silence. So how about we jump away from the absurd notion that a small business is going to essentially pay for your kid's party because you think the customer should always be right, and I offer to refund twenty-five percent of the costs for the sprinkle suffering we have caused? Deal?"

The front room of the shop has gone completely silent. The woman glares at me. "This is appalling customer service, and this is not the last you'll hear from me. I'll not be shopping here again."

"That's fine," I say with a shrug. "Try The Cakery. They seem more your type."

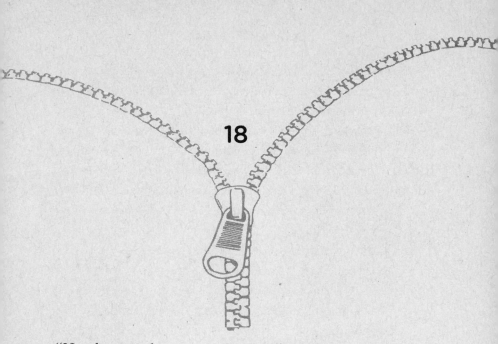

18

"Has she posted a nasty review yet?" I ask again as I stack up clean mixing bowls.

Shannon rolls her eyes. "Will you stop asking? Who cares? That woman was horrible."

"And if she does," Butter says, rinsing off her piping tips, "I'll just go in and post what really happened. The damn troll."

Liz shrugs as she closes the storage door after putting away the fancy wedding cake she's currently decorating. "I think you handled that really well. I would have cried."

"I would have punched her," Shannon mutters.

Butter ponders this for a moment. "I think I would have done both."

"I believe you," I say and rub my forehead. "I just don't want us having any bad press right now. Ugh, that awful woman. Her 'this isn't the last you'll hear from me' crap. You know she's just sitting somewhere counting the sprinkles in those photos as she polishes a three thousand–word Yelp review."

Butter waves her hand, dismissing the wench. "She was just trying to get a free meal. Forget her. Let's talk about you."

I drop my head. "Let's not."

Shannon wheels around in the chair at the desk where she's been tallying up the day's invoices. "No, let's. You've been stalling all day. You show up late for work looking like you got hit by a vodka truck, and that's after a massive breakdown yesterday saying you were going to give Mr. Cleary the special tour. Spill, woman."

I drop onto the stool by my station and want to cry, I'm so tired. "For starters, it wasn't vodka, it was wine. A hell of a lot of wine. And there was no special tour, thanks to excessive wine. That's it, really. It was the most awkward, embarrassing encounter that has ever happened—we drank three bottles of wine in about fifteen minutes and got pass-out drunk. Woke up on the couch when you called. All in all, a tremendous and humiliating failure."

"So, no sex?" Butter asks sadly.

I shake my head. "Alas. I'm starting to think it's not meant to be. I'm never going to have sex. And if I'm making a list, I don't think drinking is in my future, either. And spas. I don't think I'll be frequenting spas anytime soon."

Butter comes over to me, a pot of edible glitter in her hand, and calmly dumps some on my head.

"Butter. What…just what the fuck?"

She tilts her head, stares at me for a second and gives her shoulders a quick shrug. "I don't know. You looked like you needed it."

"I looked like I needed you to dump sugar on me?"

Shannon chokes on giggles over at the desk, and Liz is staring with her mouth open. Butter is unrepentant. "Think of me as your Glitter Godmother. It's like a fairy godmother, but more sparkly. You're looking pretty dreary today. I thought you needed the shine."

I shake my hair and watch as the glitter comes cascading down. "This is what my life has been reduced to. I'm so without hope that people resort to throwing garnishes at me."

"You do look a little more optimistic with the sparkles," Liz offers.

I nod. "I'll keep this in mind for emergencies."

"So, what happened with Ben? Are you guys okay?" Shannon asks, staring at the glitter pile on the floor at my feet.

"I think so? He was pretty destroyed this morning, so he went home to sleep. The lucky bastard." My phone buzzes in my apron pocket, and I reach for it, desperate for this conversation to be over.

"When are you going to see him again? I mean, it sounds like you guys have a lot to talk about."

My eyes go wider than they've been capable of being all day, and I make a little strangling sound. "Um. Apparently, right now." I read the text I just received out loud. *As promised, I'm not entering, but I do happen to be on the sidewalk if you have a moment.* Crap."

"Why crap?" Liz asks.

Shannon pokes her head out the door and makes a squealing noise. "I see him. Can I let him in?"

I sigh. "Crap because I just spent the day sweating and oozing out pinot and not showering. But yeah, you can let him in." Shannon flees to the front room, and I hear her unlocking the door.

"On the plus side, you're very glittery now," Butter points out. "So, that's a big improvement."

"True."

A moment later, Shannon comes awkward-dancing back

into the kitchen alone, and we all stare at the door, waiting for him to appear. "You can come back here," she calls to Ben.

His head sort of floats into view. "Are you sure? I don't want to intrude."

"It's really fine," I say, and wave him in. "Welcome to where the cupcake magic happens. And not that I'm unhappy to give you this very detailed tour, but what are you doing here?"

He hands me a giant to-go cup from one of the fancy coffee shops over on Bleeker. It smells so good, I could weep. "I felt bad that I got to spend the day nursing myself back to functionality, so I thought I'd bring you this and check to see if you lived."

"See, now, that's just considerate," Butter says with a giant smile. Ben flushes a bit, but returns the grin.

"Thank you," I say, taking it from him. "How're you feeling, by the way?"

"Better. You?"

"Worse."

He tries not to laugh, but I see it dancing in his eyes. "I'm sorry. I didn't realize you had to work today. I really do feel bad. Can I make it up to you?"

"You're forgiven, really," I say, holding up the coffee as evidence.

"Actually," Shannon says, stepping forward, "you barely had time to eat today. And nothing fixes a hangover like something greasy and delicious, right?"

"Is that a thing?" I ask. "I don't think that's a thing."

Shannon elbows Butter in the ribs. "Oh, yeah. It's a thing. Yep. Food. You should go have food. Together."

"We can finish clearing up!" Liz trills in a bizarre, strangled voice.

"You guys suck," I say, taking a drink of my coffee. "And

you're not even kind of subtle." Ben snorts and looks down at his feet. "I don't know what you're laughing at," I say. "You should be terrified standing in here. You know what we talk about in this room, man."

His head pops up, and he looks from woman to woman. The panic hits their faces, as well. Liz squeaks and hides her face behind a mixer. Butter starts whistling, and Shannon tries to smooth out her apron.

I smile. "Okay, that was fun." I wink at Shannon. "All right, I'll see you ladies Monday." Walking over to the desk, I grab my bag and make my way past Ben through the door to the front room. I look back at him. "Are you coming?"

He looks around. "Am I?" I stare at him. "I am." He turns back to the kitchen. "Um, it was nice to see you ladies. Thanks for the shop tour."

I head to the door and hear him close behind me. The gals all call good-nights behind us.

"Exactly how much do you enjoy watching me squirm?" he asks with a hint of a grin. "Just so I can know for reference. Is it a lot, or more of a casual, occasional thing?"

"I'd like to say casual," I say and take a drink. "But it's just so easy to do, and hard to reel it in sometimes."

"A true hazard."

"Indeed."

He walks over to a dark blue sedan at the curb and opens the passenger door. "Come on," he says. "Dinner. Let's see if we can't detoxify you some."

"Aww, see? Here I am being a jerk while you brought me coffee *and* you're driving me to dinner? That's not fair."

He grins as I head for the car. "It's fine. I just have to figure out what makes you squirm."

Just as I'm about to climb in the car, I get a good look at him and gasp. "Oh my god! You're dressed like a normal person!"

He looks down at himself. "I...yes?"

I point at him. I can't not point. "You're not wearing a suit. I don't know how to process this." He's wearing a pair of worn-in looking jeans, sneakers that have seen a mile or two and a black T-shirt with—oh my damn. "Is that a *Firefly* shirt? You're a Browncoat?"

He stares at me. "It's Saturday."

I'm genuinely caught off guard by how different he looks. He always looks very handsome in his suits, and while it's a little bizarre seeing him sans tie, he somehow looks more Ben-like dressed this way.

I lean against his car and narrow my eyes. "So. You show up here all dressed like a regular person, and I find out you're a geek, too? I don't know what to make of this, Ben."

"Okay, if you have a problem with *Firefly*, I'm not sure we can be friends," he says, the edges of his mouth pulling up.

"Heck no," I scoff. "That shirt makes me like you all the more. But still. You don't have a tie or a jacket or anything. It's weird."

He chuckles and shakes his head. "So, the squirming thing," he says, walking around to his side of the car. "I guess we've established it's 'a lot' then, right?"

We go out for Mexican food, sans margaritas. It is a surprisingly effective helper for my physical state. Not that I ever intend to beer bong three bottles of wine again, but if I ever do, I'm immediately following it up with enchiladas.

After dinner, we decide to walk back to my apartment, since it's only a few blocks away. The evening air is warm and comfortable, and the company is quite nice.

As we approach my place, he says, "So, last night didn't go particularly well."

"It wasn't the best. Maybe next time we shouldn't get black-out drunk first."

He chuckles. "That's a solid plan. And I suppose that implies you do want a next time?"

I stretch my neck out. "Sure. If you're up for it, I am."

"I'm in," he says and nods.

We reach my door and I turn to him. "Thank you for a very nice dinner fresh on the heels of one of the weirdest nights of my life, Mr. Cleary."

"Back at ya," he says and smiles. He stops and squints at my neck. "Did you know you're covered in glitter? I didn't notice it until just now, but the awning light is making you look like a disco ball. It's all over your neck."

I laugh. "Yes, actually. Butter thought I needed sparkling up earlier, so she doused me with edible glitter. I can't get it to wipe off, so I'll have to shower. Not that I'm not in desperate need of a shower anyway." Ben grins and then purses his lips together, trying to hide it. "What? What's wrong?"

"Nothing," he says, still grinning, looking down at the ground.

"Tell me," I demand.

Rubbing the back of his head, he says, "Well, it's…" He shrugs. "I mean, it's just I can think of so many more fantastic ways to remove edible glitter from someone's neck."

At first I feel a mischievous smile pull at my lips, but in an instant it's gone. The potential delight is replaced by a wave of sadness I didn't expect.

He sees it playing out on my face. "I'm sorry," he says, shifting gears immediately. "That was inappropriate. I didn't mean—"

"No," I interrupt him. "That was fine." I reach out and put my hand on his arm to reassure him. "You are totally fine."

"What happened? You just shifted really fast."

I shake my head a little. "I'm sorry, actually. I just…" I take a breath and wonder if this is wildly tasteless, but roll with it anyway. "I've been with Ryan four years. Four whole years with the same guy. And I didn't realize it until you just said it, but in those four years, I don't think we've ever once looked for the *fantastic* way of dealing with something. I guess I didn't realize we don't have that kind of spark, you know? It just made me feel kind of sad."

He pulls at his shirt where his tie would normally be. "I didn't mean to make you sad."

I smile at him. "*You* didn't. And I'm glad you said it. It's nice to know there are *fantastic* things out there. Something to aspire to."

His mouth pulls up in a very kind half smile. "I mean, I'm not an expert or anything, but I'd certainly know what to do in this particular glittery situation."

"What would you do?" The words are out of my mouth before I even know I'm saying them. But I want to know.

He swallows hard. "Um, I. Well, I think it would be hard to explain."

I smile. "Show me?"

I don't know what I'm doing. The hangover has me in what I assume is physically gross territory, I probably still smell like the inside of a bottle of wine, I'm covered with sugar glitter and I'm wearing my work clothes that are likely saturated with a thin layer of flour and flop sweat.

Never mind the rules I've set up for us, Ryan included. This will likely break them all.

But I don't care.

"What about the rules?" Ben asks, echoing my thoughts.

"This can be a free pass?" I suggest, grinning as I move closer to him. "It doesn't have to be related to anything. Not the therapy, not relationships. Not anything. This can just be because you said you had an idea, and because I really, really need you to show me something fantastic, Ben."

His eyes have gone dark and he's breathing a little too hard, but he steps closer to me, lifts a hand up near my face, then hesitates. "Can I..." he whispers. "I mean, can I touch you?"

"It's a free pass," I say, the grin still playing at the edges of my mouth. "Make it count."

His hand comes back up, finding a home with my skin. His long fingers stretch from my cheekbone all the way down to my neck. His other hand appears, gently positioned under my jaw on the right.

I'm having every possible emotion at once. It feels like it's been at least one million years since I've been in this position, and I want to shriek like a tween and go text Shannon and Butter about what to do next. I want to take control of the situation and kiss him. I want to call Ryan and ask if he feels this way when he kisses Alice or any of the other potential women. I want to stop this and go back to the security of my rules, because I have no idea what I'm even doing here.

But I don't. Because more than any of those things, I want to feel something *fantastic*.

Ben in conversation is a casual, tie-fidgeting, easygoing person.

Ben in this moment is none of those things.

His lips move directly to mine, perfectly controlled, no nervousness to be found. I close my eyes and let him kiss me. My arms are stuck at my sides, my hands clenched into tight fists. I don't know if I could control myself if I reached out and touched him. But damn, do I want to touch him.

His left hand moves carefully down my throat, across my shoulder, his fingers gingerly tugging the collar of my shirt aside. He takes his mouth from mine and brushes it along my jaw slowly, his other hand guiding my head ever so slightly to the side. I squeeze my eyes shut and hold my breath as his lips pull down the side of my neck. My knees feel shaky.

His mouth moves across my neck with soft kisses, each placed slowly, deliberately, and I pull in a broken gasp of air. He starts back at zero, the base of my neck, but this time, the tip of his tongue trails just behind my collarbone, his teeth lightly dragging against the front side.

"Jesus," I gasp, and my arms jump without permission, grabbing his chest, unable to decide whether to push him away or pull him closer. One hand wants to stop this, because I laid out rules, and they are important rules and what I am feeling is so not covered under the scope of those rules.

The other hand wants to pull him into my apartment and dump glitter over my entire body just to see if he'll rise to the challenge.

My brain is at a loss, but I can't seem to let go of him. I clench one hand into a fist on his chest, gripping his shirt tightly, and my other hand—I'm assuming the one that wanted to yank him in through that door—jumps up to his jaw and stays there.

His forehead drops to mine, and we just stand there, me still clinging to him for reasons I can't quite explain, breathing a little too hard. He's got one hand still wrapped around the back of my neck, his fingers resting in my hair, and the other arm around my back.

Finally, after what seems like forever, he speaks.

"That's what I'd do," he says.

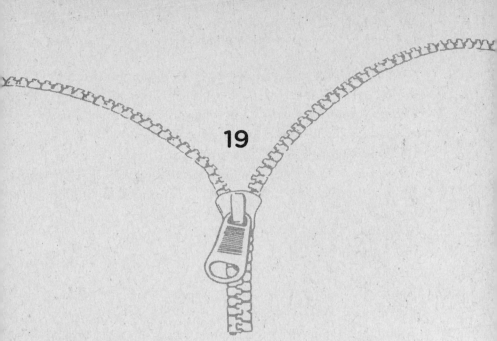

19

"And you have a fabulous day, Mr. Montgomery," I say, handing my customer his tiny pie box and coffee. He gives me a big smile and heads on his way.

"Seriously," Shannon hisses at me as she wipes off the counter beside me. "That's the third person you've told to have a fabulous day. It's a Monday morning. What the hell has gotten into you?"

"Nothing," I say, and give her a look. "I'm just in a good mood."

"Wait!" Butter yelps, scaring Mrs. Tottle, who is trying to pick a tea. "Did you...did you and Ben?"

I roll my eyes. "No, we did not. And we can discuss things after the rush, okay?"

Shannon gasps. "So there are things to discuss?"

I fight a grin and shake my head. "Come on, we've got customers."

Liz scurries behind me on her way to refill the coffee machine and whispers, "Speaking of..."

Ben walks in the entrance for his morning cup of joe, and

I smile. Then he smiles. And then so do Shannon, Butter and Liz.

"I hate you people," I mutter as I head over to the register. Ben stands in line patiently, poking away at his phone like a good be-suited grown-up. I'm starting to wonder if glittery times Ben in a T-shirt was a hungover hallucination.

I'm not sure I'd care if it was. It was a pretty damn good hallucination.

When it's finally his turn, I get him his regular order of coffee and say, "Hi there."

"Hey."

Butter, Shannon and Liz have all stopped working and are staring at us.

"Oh my god, will you guys go help these people?"

Ben laughs. "I bet it's never boring working here."

"It's a hoot," I say and hand him his coffee. "Did you have a nice weekend?"

He takes a sip and thinks for a moment. "It was okay. I had a boring Sunday full of errands and laundry. My Saturday night was pretty awesome, though. You?"

I bite the inside of my cheek to keep from smiling. "About the same." He grins, looking very proud of himself. Part of me is tempted to knock him down a peg, but the other parts of me think he doesn't look nearly proud enough. "See you tomorrow morning?"

"Yep," he says, handing me money for the coffee. "And are we still a go for tomorrow night?"

Now I can't fight the smile, cheek-biting or not. "Sure." I pass him his change.

He gives me his very best crooked smile. "Until then." He turns to my coworkers and says, "Have a good day, ladies."

"Bye!" they call out in unison.

We finish up the morning surge, and after we get the front situated, we head back into the kitchen for the morning meeting.

"Okay," Shannon says, tapping her pencil against her notepad. "As much as I want to know what's put the giddyup in Kat's get-along, first we've got business to attend to."

"Shoot," I say, taking a sip of coffee.

"First, Liz has three wedding cakes going out this weekend, so we are all going to have to pitch in on those. Also, Liz has tomorrow afternoon off because she has a dress appointment, right?"

Liz flushes. "I am so sorry," she says. "I tried to reschedule, but this was the only time they could get me in."

Shannon smiles. "It's totally fine, hon. We've got this. And it's your wedding! That trumps everything else." Liz beams.

"Butter," Shannon continues, "I need your final recipes for the Coopertown menu by next Monday at the latest so Kat has plenty of time to get all the art and decorations perfected. We've got a week and a half until the presentation. It's just about go time. How are you guys feeling about things?"

"I feel good," Butter says with purpose. "This will be my best work. You just wait."

"I'm on it," I say and nod. "We're going to get it, Shannon."

"Okay, we've got two big orders for cuppies, one due late Wednesday, one due Saturday morning, plus our regular orders. Kat, those are all you. We have five birthdays this week. I'm going to split those with Butter, and I'll take the deliveries as they come."

We all nod and make our own notes.

"Now," Shannon says, shifting her gaze to me. "This is a big one. Kat, I got an email this morning from Channel 7. Next Wednesday, they want our shop to come on their morning show to do a cupcake demonstration. This one is all you, baby."

"Whoa!" Butter says, clapping her hand to her chest.

"Seriously?" I say.

"And they'll be promoting it for a few days before, which means it'll be free advertising leading up to the Coopertown presentation. The TV spot happens the morning before, so if all goes well, we'll have every possible chance with this."

"Holy shit, Shannon," I gasp. "That's huge! How did you even swing that?"

"I whored myself out in every possible way, not gonna lie. So we need to make this count."

"Why am I doing it? Shouldn't you go? You're a bit more dazzling than I am, hon."

"One of the anchors has a toddler who has a birthday coming up, and they wanted to do a live thing about decorating for a birthday party. You're better at on the spot art than I am. I thought you could go and show them how to do a few easy cuppie decorations, but suggest in the end that buying from us is the best option, naturally."

"Obvs." I wink at her.

"Can you do it?" Her voice is weighed down with the desperation of just how important the Coopertown contract really is. "I have total faith in you. You know that, right?"

"I've got this. I won't let you down, I promise. I'm The Mouth anyway, right?"

"Yeah, you are," Butter says, and waves her glitter brush through the air. I'm reminded of her Glittery Godmother magic.

I walk right over, grab Butter by the face and kiss her right on the lips. "Thank you, by the way."

I release her and head back to my stool as she splutters and flails her brush around, causing a little glitter tornado to form.

"What did I do?"

"Are we all done with business?" I ask Shannon.

"Is this about you and Ben?" she asks. I nod. "Then yes, ma'am, we are."

I launch into a fairly detailed account of my Saturday night.

As soon as I'm done, Butter comes over and resolutely flings edible glitter at my cleavage.

"Goddamn it, Butter."

"If that's what he did to glitter on your neck, you'll thank me for that later," she explains.

"So, you really didn't sleep together?" Shannon asks.

"Not yet," I say. "What can I say? I'm a simple gal. It was a good kiss. And!" I raise an eyebrow. "My therapy has been going spectacularly well since Saturday night. Like, magically well. I don't know if I'm more relaxed, or if it's all finally paying off, but whatever it is, it's going great. So we've got plans to try again tomorrow."

"Without wine this time?" Shannon asks with a grin.

I tap my nose. "There ya go."

"You're killing it," Butter says proudly. "Your special is all happy with fifteen days to spare, you've got a very talented new friend, you'll get past all the weird with Ryan, you're going to be on TV and we're going to kick this contract's ass. All before summertime comes."

I sit back and admire the situation.

Things are looking up.

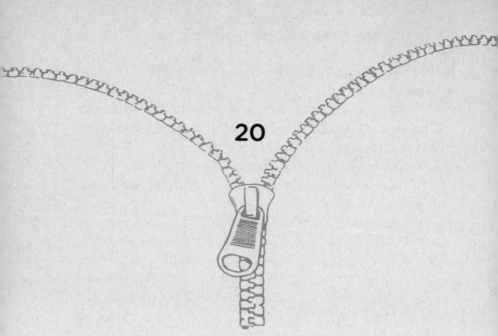

20

Normally I thrive under pressure, but right now, there's a part of my brain that's inclined to feel overwhelmed with everything happening all at once. I'm trying to ignore it—I just need a little organization and compartmentalization. Situations like this are when my type A personality shines. I assume it has to be useful at some point, as opposed to just annoying everyone all the time.

Standing at my station, I'm quietly making mental lists and swirling fudge buttercream over a box of devil's food cuppies for an order that's going out first thing in the morning. Butter and Liz are working on a wedding cake that's meant to look like it has intricate beading draped down the five tiers.

Whenever cakes like this come in, all I can think is that I hope I'm not quite so fussy when I get married. On the one hand, I'm very grateful for all the orders we get. But on the other, who the hell spends time thinking, 'Gee, I wish I had a cake that takes twenty-two man-hours to make and looks like it has actual pearls and lace on it'?

This is why I don't decorate the big cakes. I don't have the patience.

The back door opens, and suddenly the kitchen is filled with all sorts of chatter. Shannon's husband, Joe, walks in with their two kids, Brandon and Heidi.

Shannon pops her head up from the desk where she's been sitting doing paperwork for the last half hour. "Hey, guys! What are you doing here?"

Little Heidi is still young enough that she can embrace her enthusiasm without caring what anyone thinks. She runs over to the desk squealing, "Mommy!" and throws her arms around Shannon's neck.

Brandon, fully ensconced in the rules of being a pre-tween and too cool for that sort of thing, stands awkwardly by his dad and shoves his hands into his pockets. "Hey, Mom."

Joe smiles. "I figured we'd come and steal you away for the night. Go get dinner as a family," he says. "I know you've been crazed, so we're staging a mom-napping."

"Aww," Butter says. "I want to be you guys when I grow up."

Shannon lifts an eyebrow. "Did you just call us old?"

Liz freezes mid-placement of an edible pearl. Butter presses her lips together. "Uh." She looks over at Joe. "So! Where are you crazy folks going tonight?"

Shannon is still staring at her with an eyebrow to the sky. Joe snorts.

"Hey, kids," I interrupt. "How's school?"

Brandon manages to stuff his hands deeper into his pockets. "Fine."

I wait patiently for more information, but that's all I'm getting. "Super. Good talk, sir." I turn to Heidi. "How about you, kidlet? What's new in the first grade?"

She bounces over to my station and peers intently at the

cupcakes I'm working on. "It's good. I like math, but my teacher keeps making us read chapter books."

"What's wrong with chapter books?"

"I like the science books. She says they don't count as chapter books."

"Lame."

"Aunt Kat? Why did you not put as much frosting on that cupcake as you put on those cupcakes? Is it a special cupcake?"

I look down, and sure enough, her little finger is pointing at a slightly under-frosted cuppie.

Heidi is the kind of kid who demands accountability from her adults. If she's required to give full disclosure as a youngling, she wants that courtesy in return. But being wee, she can't exactly come out and ask for it. So she does this.

Last December, I was watching the kids for an hour on a Sunday when Joe was down with the flu and Shannon had an errand to run. The three of us were in the front yard building snow forts when Shannon pulled in the driveway in a rush. She'd sort of missed the edge of the pavement and driven over a small sliver of lawn, creating a slushy, muddy mess.

"Mommy, why did you drive on the grass?" Heidi had asked.

It was obvious it had been a mistake. She just wanted to hear her mother say the words, "I did something wrong."

I like this about Heidi. It's her way of deriving a shred of power in a powerless world. It's impressive to me.

Then again, she's not my kid, and I don't have to live with a tiny person calling out every single error I make all the time, so I could see where the charm might wear off for her parents after a while.

I give her an enchanted grin. "You know what? I messed up. I didn't even notice. Thanks for pointing it out, hon."

Heidi looks incredibly satisfied with herself. Shannon leans back in her chair and gives me a look that says her daughter will now be intolerably smug for the rest of the night, thankyouverymuch.

Joe says, "Butter, why don't you take the kids up front and spoil their dinner before Shannon shreds you for calling her old?"

Heidi hollers, "Yay!" and even Brandon looks excited. Butter abandons her bowl of pearls and happily scurries out of the kitchen with the kids trailing behind her like sugar-seeking ducklings.

"By the way, you're not old," I offer, still redoing the subpar cuppie pointed out by Heidi. "Regular spring chickens, you are. And hi, Joe."

"Hey, Kat," he says, leaning against the fridge. "How's the sex quest going?"

My hand slips across the piping bag and I squirt frosting all over my station top. Joe snorts again. Liz gasps. I gape. Turning to glare at Shannon, I shriek, "You told Joe?"

Shannon drops her head into her hands. "Thanks for that, Joe." She wheels around and pleads with me. "He's my husband! I had to! I didn't want him to find the charge for the stuff we ordered you and have him wonder what it was about. And besides, we don't have secrets! We share everything!"

I shake my head. "Could you maybe not share the details of my special with him?"

Joe laughs. "I forgot about that. Special. That's awesome."

"Shannon!" Liz yelps.

"You are never having sex again, ever," Shannon declares to her husband, slapping her hand on the desk.

Joe puts his hands up. "Oh, come on! I'm just teasing! I'm rooting for you, Kat. I remember how it was for Shannon, but she got through it. I know you'll be back on the horse in no time."

Taking a deep breath, I count to five in my head. "Great. Thanks, Joe."

"You know, I was thinking," Joe says, "if you're so worried about not ever getting any, why don't you just find a guy and get on with it?"

I like Joe. He's a great guy. I've known him since I was eighteen, when he and Shannon met at college and became attached at the hip forevermore. From literally anyone else in the world, this line of questioning would be met with a punch to the groin. With Joe, I know it's coming from a place of caring, a decade-plus of friendship and that weird blurry line of overfamiliarity from being married to my best friend and thinking he's as invested in my life as she is.

"I'm working on it," I mutter, scraping globs of buttercream off my equipment.

"You know, my friend Barry has always wanted to ask you out. He's a pretty okay guy. I bet he'd be up for it."

I try to remember Barry. "Doesn't he work with you at the bank? The one with the goatee?"

"Yep. You guys could have a night, be done with it. Sex quest vanquished." He pokes at a bowl of sprinkles on Shannon's station. "Don't get me wrong, I hope it all sorts out with you and Ryan, but if it ain't workin', I've got your back."

Joe's known Ryan pretty much as long as I have, and I always sort of hoped that when I paired off, my guy would be BFFs with Joe just so it could bring my chick flick friendship with Shannon into higher resolution. But while Ryan and Joe get along fine, their personalities are so different. Ryan tends to be a bit of an introvert, whereas Joe has never met a stranger in his life and will find any excuse to throw a shindig, usually just so he can show off his grilling skills.

Shannon makes a noise. "I am going to end you when we get home. Just so we're clear."

Joe shrugs. "Only trying to help."

I put my focus into wiping the frosting off all my gear, but the thought is in my head. My big concern with Ben is that a failed sex attempt would tarnish whatever we might have going on in the friendship sphere, so maybe there's some merit to Joe's idea.

"Oh, Jesus," Shannon snaps. "Please tell me you aren't even sort of considering what he just said."

I wave a buttercream-covered hand at her. "No, not really. For starters, Barry is kind of a slimy dude, so really no. Sorry, Joe. But I was just thinking in general. I don't want to mess things up with Ben, you know? Maybe fixing the issue and then going back to Ryan and keeping Ben strictly as a pal isn't a terrible idea."

"It's a horrible idea!" Liz squeals.

Joe looks affronted. "I don't know if it's horrible…"

"No," Liz cuts him off. I've never seen her so forceful, let alone to her boss's husband. It's amazing. "It's the worst idea I've ever heard! I don't know how all of what she's doing with Ryan and Ben is going to work out, but the answer to everything is definitely not going out and having a one-night stand with some other guy."

Shannon looks proud. "Liz, if we get the Coopertown contract, you are so getting a raise. That was glorious."

I shake my head. "No. God. Right. That's an awful plan." I shudder.

Crossing his arms and pouting, Joe mumbles, "It was just an idea."

I roll my eyes. "Thanks for the input. But I'm figuring it out."

Shannon huffs and stuffs her stack of paperwork back into a folder in the desk drawer. "We're leaving," she says apologetically to Liz and me. "I'll see you ladies in the morning."

I can hear her muttering outrage and profanity to Joe until they hit the front room, when her voice comes out in enthusiastic mommy tones.

I call out as cheerful a farewell as I can muster before I turn my attention back to the task at hand. I really need to finish frosting this batch of cakes, but my mind is distracted.

It's not just the awfulness of Joe's plan that has me in my head. I'm trying not to think about the fact that I needed a good nudge to *see* the awfulness of Joe's plan. But what's really got me unsettled is that I considered what it would be like—sleeping with someone else—and the thought felt unwelcome. Intrusive.

Because, I realized, I don't want to sleep with anyone else. And even though my aim here is being able to have sex with Ryan again, it would seem that right now, I want to have sex only with Ben Cleary.

Huh.

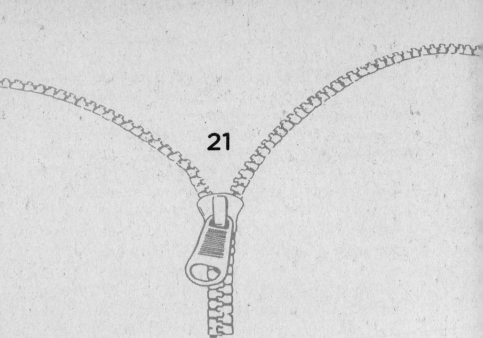

21

I've got seventeen million cupcakes on a cooling rack and at least forty-two million more in the oven. I officially hate cupcakes today.

I set my timer, sit back at the desk and go over my instructions for the Channel 7 show. The anchor wants to throw a zoo-themed party for his son, so I'm looking into what animals would be the cutest and easiest to show someone else how to create. I figure it will be good to show off a little and whip something out that's best left to the professionals, but then fall back on something basic that even a novice can do. And judging by the video I found on YouTube of the anchors' highly flammable performances with the local hibachi chef from a show last week, *basic* is a generous concept

Plus, I'm still trying to perfect a royal icing raven that can be assembled quickly for a thousand cupcakes per basketball game if need be.

Basically, it's all cuppies, all the time right now.

Except for those glorious moments when my mind wanders

back to Saturday night, and I think of lips and tongues and—sweet baby Jesus—what Ben did with his teeth.

And how maybe, by the end of tonight, I'll crash through the boundaries of therapy sex, and I can finally get back into the land where I get to kiss and be kissed and fling sexy-times glitter like it's my job.

"Oh my gosh," Liz says, coming in through the back door, mid-panic.

"What's wrong, sweets?" I ask, hopping up from the desk.

"My mom can't make it up for my appointment!"

"I'm sorry," I say sincerely. "Is everything okay?"

"No!" she snaps at me. I flinch. I don't think I've ever heard her bark before, outside her outburst at Joe. She's a new woman. "Mom's got a stomach bug and can't make the drive, but what will I do without her? She's the one who is supposed to keep me from walking out with a bad dress, or from paying twice as much as I should!"

"So, she's like your bodyguard?"

Liz nods desperately. "I'm not good at saying no to people. I just assume everyone is being nice and don't realize I'm getting taken advantage of. What am I going to do? I already tried to reschedule the appointment and couldn't!"

I shrug. "I'll go with you. I love telling people no."

Liz's eyes go huge. "But the shop! We're so busy!"

"Shannon," I call out. Shannon's head magically appears from the front room. "Liz's mom can't make her dress appointment, and she needs a bossy mouth to make sure she doesn't get screwed. Can you and Butter hold down the fort so I can ride shotgun?"

"No problem." Shannon's head disappears.

Liz scrambles after her. "Are you sure? I don't want to be an inconvenience!"

Shannon's face pops back into view, and she looks like she

wants to pat Liz on the head. "Honey, this is for your wedding. Of course I'm sure. Kat, take the laptop. You can work while you're there if you get a minute. What do you have going?"

"There's eleventy billion cuppies in the oven on timer. Set them out to cool and frost if you get a moment. I'll decorate in the morning. The invoice is on my station."

"Got it," says Butter as she restocks the front display cases.

"Are you really sure?" Liz asks, wringing her hands.

I roll my eyes. "Yes, we are sure. Come on, or I'll start saying no to *you*."

I prance through the kitchen, grab the laptop and my sketch pad, and watch as Liz frantically grabs her purse and hangs up her apron, bouncing around to make sure she hasn't forgotten anything. Then we head out the back door.

Twenty minutes and two buses later, we are across town at La Bella, a swanky bridal shop just bursting with dress options. As the ladies at the shop start fawning over Liz, I feel really sad that her mom isn't here for this moment. Liz is super close with her family, and I know she'd love to be sharing it with her mom. I can tell it's bothering Liz, too, but she's holding it back as much as she's able. Her eyes are a little watery, her eyebrows cinched, her hands twisting over each other.

It's hard for me to picture what she could be feeling here. To me, marriage has never been that big a thing. I mean, I guess I've assumed that Ryan and I will eventually get married. It's the way we're headed, I suppose. But I've never been one of those gals who dreams about her big day or spends hours thinking about the perfect dress or floral arrangements.

I will definitely not be someone with a five-tier waterfall cake.

I just can't see myself getting that jazzed about the pomp and ceremony. It's a day. A party. An expensive party, no less. I get the significance, but I also know that I'd much rather have a savings account than a bunch of pictures of me wearing a five-thousand-dollar dress for six hours.

But then there are people like Liz. This is obviously off-the-charts important to her. I'd bet actual money Liz spent part of her childhood with a pillowcase hanging off her head, pretending to be a bride.

In the very deepest part of my brain, the place I try very hard to ignore, there's a feeling of regret. A feeling that wishes I knew what child-Liz felt like.

Liz is whisked off by the sales associates, who hand her a glass of champagne and a carefully crafted monologue about big days and special moments and thanking her for letting them be a part of it. I grab a seat right outside the bridal display area, a big round room that's 90 percent mirrors with squashy couches for an audience to view the fashion show.

Liz seems to know what she's looking for, generally speaking. The associates try to talk her into trying on giant poufy numbers, but Liz, in her shy little voice, insists she's looking for something more clean and basic.

One of the salesladies comes out with this enormous Cinderella-looking contraption, and Liz shoots me a look of horror.

"Really, no. She wants a simpler style, thank you."

The associate levels a needling stare at me but carts the lacy monstrosity away. Liz gives me a smile. I wink.

She comes out in various dresses, and I take notes in my sketch pad, depending on what she likes and doesn't about each one. I use Liz's phone to take a picture of her in each dress and text them to her mom, who sends replies that are in all caps. She even calls a couple of times, until she realizes she can't hear us while she's looking at the pictures. I try to set her up on Skype on the laptop, but she doesn't understand a word of me walking her through the install, so I abandon ship. Our dress search is an involved process, but Liz is happy to have her mom there in some capacity.

She looks just lovely. When she's left to her own devices, she's confident and fine. She knows what she likes. It's when the salesladies try to barge in with their opinions on the matter that Liz gets flustered.

"Can we have a few minutes?" I suggest when I see Liz looking particularly nervous. The associates raise their eyebrows at me but shuffle away, leaving us alone in the giant mirror room.

"They are so pushy," Liz whispers.

"Commissions, baby," I say, then add, "You look really pretty."

She straightens up and looks at herself in the mirror. "This one is very nice."

"Are you scared?"

"Of picking the wrong dress?"

I blink at her. "No...of getting married."

She giggles. "Oh, sorry. No! Why would I be scared?"

I'm aware that I'm gawking at her, but I can't seem to stop. "I don't know. Aren't most people?"

She shrugs. "I'm just excited. Paul and I already live together, so that won't change. And we've been dating for three years, so it's not like we're rushing into it. I'm just looking forward to saying 'husband' from that day on. That will be the fun part."

"Oh my god, you're one of those happy couples, aren't you?"

She laughs at me. "Aren't you part of a happy couple?"

I put my hands up. "Slow down there, killer. I don't think I qualify as part of normal coupledom right now."

She turns to face me. "You and Ryan have been together for a long time, right?"

"Ages."

"I mean, I know you're going through a thing right now, but wasn't it good at some point? You guys are together for a reason, right?"

I sit back down on the smooshy couch. "I don't know, actually. Sometimes I feel like we're together just because we're supposed to be. Like, we get along, we're a good fit, we like each other, so why not? We've never really had that oh-my-god, let's-rip-our-clothes-off, hot-and-heavy, super romantic stuff side."

Liz makes a disappointed face. "That sounds depressing."

"Right?" I slump down. "In my defense, I didn't realize it was like that until all this deadline stuff popped up. I just sort of thought that's how everyone did it."

"What about in college? High school?"

I shrug again. "I've never been the 'follow your feelings' type. I just sort of think about what makes sense and then roll with it. If I dated a guy, it was because I thought we'd get along, not because he gave me tinglies. I always assumed if someone gave you the floppy stomach feels, it meant you were destined for dramatics, and honestly, who has time for that?"

She's gaping at me. "Who taught you that?"

I frown. "I guess I didn't realize I'd been taught. I just sort of thought that's what I knew. Now that I think about it, probably my aunt, actually. She babysat me a lot while my mom was at work, and she was very strict. Hated Disney princesses, and love was about structure, not feelings, that sort of thing."

Liz gasps like I just told her Santa wasn't real. "That's terrible! All the crazy emotions are the best part of being with someone! Are you seriously telling me you've actively avoided tingly love your entire life? That you're going through all this with Ryan, and you don't have tingling love feelings for him!?"

I blanch and sit up straighter. "Well, it's not like it was a conscious plan or anything! But I guess so. What's so bad about that, anyway? It's sensible."

"Kat!"

"Oh, come on! It can't be that big a deal! It's just less romantic and maybe a little more boring, but that's not horrible. And okay, I'm kind of a control freak, but it's not the end of the universe, right?"

Liz shakes her head at me, the expression on her face one reserved for people who publicly admit they hate puppies and happiness. "You're dead inside."

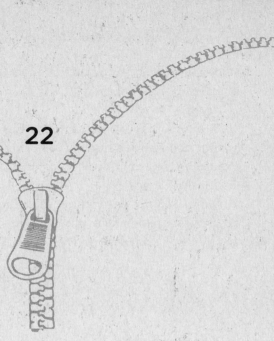

22

"Well," Ben says, calmly, "we've made it into the bedroom, and your apartment isn't spinning, so I'd say this is progress."

I giggle. "Yes, we are leaps and bounds ahead of last week."

He looks around my room. "Is it okay to say I still feel very awkward?"

"I'd be concerned if you didn't," I say in agreement. "I do."

"Great." He claps his hands together. "Okay. Kat. This is your rodeo here, so you lead the way. I don't want to over-step my boundaries."

"Yeah…it's the lead-up that's got me stumped," I confess. "Normally there's an order of operations, so to speak."

"Fair point."

"Like, do we just…get…naked?"

He smiles and pulls at his tie. "That's rarely a bad thing for a woman to say, in case you were wondering."

"It's just…this is therapy stuff. So it's for science. How do you get naked for science? There's no protocol for this."

"So I'm the Igor to your Frankenstein?" he asks, and then shakes his head quickly. "No, ugh. I'm sorry. That's awful.

That was the only scientist and assistant combination I could think of."

I snort. "That was hilarious. Go with it."

He gives his tie a solid yank. "Okay. Naked for science. That sounds easy enough."

"Right," I agree. "Let's just rip the Band-Aid off. Wait, no. Band-Aids hurt. That's a horrible analogy. No Band-Aids. Forget I said that."

"Naked science analogies are hard," he says. "We can mark that in the minutes later."

I stare at him. He stares at me. "Okay." I say. "So." I lean back on my heels and stuff my hands into my pockets.

The muscles in his jaw stand out. "Would it…will it help if I, uh, start?"

"Start getting naked for science?"

"Yeah."

I purse my lips together to keep from giggling like a maniac. "Sure."

The edge of his mouth pulls up in a nervous grin, and I match his expression. "You know," he says, pulling his suit jacket off, "I'm sure I've done stranger things in the name of science before. I can't think of any at the moment, but I'm sure there's something." He tosses his jacket on the chair by the window and starts loosening his tie.

His tie joins his jacket, and he's got the second button on his shirt undone when I yelp, "Stop!"

He freezes completely still. "What's wrong?"

I feel like I'm going to be sick. I don't know what it is about his hand on that button, but I don't want to see what's behind it. Not like this.

"I can't… I can't do this."

He raises his hands calmly. "Okay. That's fine. Are you all right?"

My eyes feel like they're vibrating. My stomach is collapsing upon itself. My chest is aching. I think I'm having a panic attack. Maybe. I've never had a panic attack before.

I turn tail and bolt for my bathroom, slamming the door and locking it behind me. Ben calls my name as I run, but I ignore him and sink to the floor, fighting for a breath.

What the hell am I doing?

I struggle to pull in deeper breaths. This is surreal.

"Kat," Ben's voice says from the other side of the door. "Are you all right?"

I drop my face into my hands and then pull away like my palms are on fire when I feel tears. I'm crying. Why am I crying?

"Kat."

"I'm fine," I call out in a wobbly, thick voice I don't even recognize as mine.

His voice comes out near me through the door. He's on the floor now, too. "Kat, you are legitimately scaring the hell out of me. Please open the door."

I can't think of anything in the world I want to do less than open that door. But I can't think of anything more ridiculous and childish than making him sit on the other side, not knowing what's going on.

Although I'm pretty in the dark on the facts right now, too.

Reaching behind me, I turn the lock. Quickly wiping the tears from my eyes, I scoot out of the way, leaning against the sink cabinet, and let the door slowly swing open.

"I'm sorry," I say with a shrug and a pathetic attempt at brevity. "I don't know why."

Kneeling in the doorway, Ben looks like he's doing everything he can to not combust from barely contained panic right here in front of me. He rubs his hands roughly across his pants.

"Kat, I swear I'm not trying to make this about me or anything, but did I do something wrong? What just happened?"

"No, you didn't do anything." I shake my head and flap my hand unconvincingly through the air. "And come on. Isn't this how all precoital rituals go?"

"Kat, I'm really confused, and a little scared. I don't have a clue what's happening right now."

My shoulders slump. "We have that in common."

"All right," he says slowly. "I'm just going to sit, then. Is that okay?" He curls himself into the doorframe so that he's facing me, pulling his knees up and wedging his feet against the opposite side of the frame. "And then, when you're ready to talk, I'll be here."

I nod, but my brain is stuck on an out-of-control hamster wheel of emotions I don't understand. Fifteen minutes ago, I was all systems ready for launch. Things have been great the last few days. Therapy has been going perfectly. This was supposed to be a good night. I'm not saying it was going to go off without a hitch, but this certainly wasn't what I had planned.

I'm obviously attracted to Ben. Saturday night and every single wildly inappropriate fantasy I've had about him and his jaw and his delightfully long fingers prove that. I'm attracted to him as a person, as well. He's kind, he's awkwardly charming, he's funny. Why the hell did that second button cause me to lose my shit? That should've been cause for celebration.

Through my lashes, I look up at Ben. He's kindly not sitting there staring at me. He could probably teach me a thing or two about tact. The muscles in his lovely jaw are locked up tight, and his eyes are worried. He's also fidgeting with the band of his watch, strapping it and unstrapping it over and over.

"Ben," I say after a moment. "Tell me a flaw."

"I'm sorry?"

I drop my head against the sink cabinet, and it makes a

little *thud* sound. "I mean, I'm over here all freaking out on the bathroom floor, and you've got all my gory details. Crap relationship, sexless forever, broken lady bits, all the things. And then there's you—all sensible and grown-up and wearing ties and whatnot. So I was thinking, if you have a flaw, I'd really like to hear it."

He thinks for a moment. "Well, I'm a pretty solid computer geek in my off time. I play games online with a group of guys from the hospital. This also explains my general lack of opportunities to meet women."

I sniffle and shake my head. Smiling, I say, "That's not a flaw. In fact, that's kind of adorable."

"Hmm. Okay. How about this?" he says, and the edge of his mouth twitches. "I'm divorced."

My mouth drops open, and I just can't help saying, "Shut up. Are you really?"

"Really."

A connection clicks in my head. "Oh! You said you hadn't dated in a while, too. Huh. I keep forgetting people our age actually get married." I grin at him. "I'm not going to lie. I didn't see that coming."

He grins right back. "I haven't dated in a few months because I don't generally go anywhere I'd meet anyone to date. And believe it or not, I can be a little shy about asking someone out."

I snort. "I'd never have guessed. So, did you guys split up a few years ago?" He laughs, and I feel compelled to ask him for those tact lessons sooner rather than later. "Crap, is this rude? Do you not want to talk about it?"

"It's fine," he says, still smiling. "I've made all my peace with that part of my life. It's been eleven years, after all."

My eyes involuntarily squint at him as my brain calculates. "Eleven years…but that would mean…" I say, triple checking the math in my head. "Holy crap, you got divorced at twenty-one?"

He chuckles and brushes his hands over the legs of his pants. "Yes, I did."

"How the hell old were you when you got married?"

"Eighteen."

I'm gawking at him. I can't even blink. "You. *You* got married at eighteen."

He starts working on his watchband again but keeps a light tone when he says, "A little less judgment would be nice."

I'm a dick. "I am so sorry," I say, flailing my hands in front of my face. "I swear I'm not judging. I'm just... I'm really shocked!"

He leans his head against the door frame and has a relaxed expression on his face as he explains, "Jessica and I were together all through high school. It was a stupidly small town. It's just what people did. The fact that we graduated and didn't already have kids was some kind of scandal, actually. Our parents were truly kind of disappointed that we hadn't already spawned a herd of grandchildren." He shrugs. "We both wanted to go to college, but our families were insistent that we not go off living in sin, or risk being tempted by what I assume they thought were lines of people waiting to break up a couple of high school sweethearts.

"So, the summer before we went off to school, we got married. And we stayed married until the summer I graduated. We divorced. I went to grad school. That was it."

"That was it?" I ask. "I feel like you left out a few steps." Quickly I add, "Which, if you don't want to talk about it, that's totally fine, of course."

He grins. "No judgment?"

"Not a drop."

"Really, that *was* kind of it. We didn't know who we were

yet—there was no way to be in a marriage like that. We got married because we thought we were supposed to, because everyone expected us to. That's just what people did. And because our families really pushed it. We loved each other, sure, but it wasn't really a grand romantic choice. We were definitely in love, but we were also scared to death. The fact that our parents were so insistent made us feel like it had to be the right decision. So we did it.

"And away from that town, away from our families, out of high school, it was just the two of us. I always wanted to do the right thing. Be a good person. But I wanted to finish school, have a career, do things. She wasn't quite sure. One week she wanted to have kids right then. The next she wanted to travel. The next she wanted to party. One time she actually tried to drop out of school to start selling these water purification systems.

"We just didn't know who we were," he repeats. "The longer we stayed in it, the more cornered she felt, and the more helpless I felt. So we ended things and were both worlds better for it." He looks up at me and smiles. "Although at first, I was kind of shunned from our church for being a filthy sinner, and my grandmother wouldn't talk to me for two years."

"That's a little harsh."

He shrugs. "Catholics. They all dealt with it eventually. I think there was a lot of guilt on their end. Again, it's been over a decade. We've had time to process." The corner of his mouth pulls up and he looks at me, assessing. "And that's my flaw. Well, I have more, but that's my big one."

I scooch over and tap his foot with mine. "That's not a flaw. That's life stuff. It happens."

He taps me back. "You could probably say that to yourself."

I scoff, "Touché."

And here I thought I had problems. I can't imagine someone pressuring me to get married at eighteen. I was still a kid. Hell, I still feel like a kid half the time. Poor Ben.

Through my whole relationship with Ryan, I've always assumed we'd get married for similar reasons, though. It's just what people do. People get married. We've been together for years, so marriage is supposed to happen. Sure, I'm not tingly head over heels, but I do love him.

Ben fidgets with his watch again and frowns. "I have a question," he says. "Which you don't have to answer, because it's none of my business. But I'm curious."

"Hit me."

"When you first told me about all of this, I kind of looked stuff up on the disorder at the hospital, to brush up. I'd heard about it in school, and I know several people at work who specialize in it, but I wanted to be better versed." He stares down at the floor, and I've never seen him look so sheepish.

"That's totally fine," I say as kindly as I can. "I would have, too."

I think his cheeks are flushing a little. "My question," he continues, "is do you know what brought it all on? Did something happen?"

"Happen?"

He twists his watch band uncomfortably. "I read that it can come about after a trauma, or, um, abuse. I didn't want to pry, but I didn't know if something happened with your ex, or—"

"Oh, god, no," I say, shaking my head. "Really, it was nothing like that. My doctor said it was probably all the constant stress from opening the shop. Things were in a weird place with Ryan, but definitely not the scary kind."

He lets out a breath I didn't realize he was holding, and his shoulders relax some. "I'm sorry. I probably shouldn't have asked that. I just worried that I might be ignoring a serious aspect of things, and didn't want to step on any bad memories, or say something wrong."

I smile and reach out to squeeze the hand that's fidgeting with the watch. "I'm glad you asked. And I'm glad you worry about things like that. Pretty sure it makes you a good person, Ben." I give his hand another squeeze and lean back against the cabinet again. "Ryan's not a bad guy. There was no dramatic thing that caused everything to shut down. It just sort of happened, and we didn't know what to do once it was there. It's like we stopped being in a romantic relationship with each other without either of us acknowledging it."

"I can definitely understand that," he says, smoothing his watchband down.

I lean my head back and think back to my life with Ryan when this all started. When the disorder sprang up and any chance of sex came to a screaming halt, he was supportive about fixing everything, but he didn't seem overly invested in helping. It was really hard for me to show him the exercises the doc gave me that we were supposed to do together. I don't like asking for help, ever. So when he went into it half-heartedly, and abandoned the therapy ship due to the awkwardness of it all, I didn't really want his help after that.

If I had managed to get a handle on things myself, he would have been on board. He just wasn't overly enthused about the conquering of that mountain. He was supportive, but neither of us possessed the devotion to think about working through it as a team.

That's why I encouraged him to sleep with someone else. I wanted him to have that physical connection with someone that I can't give. But also, I wanted to relieve some of the guilt I feel. There's a pang of insecurity that my body, this disorder, is hurting him, as well. I feel like sex with someone else would be just that: sex.

Sometimes I think maybe he's just lazy. That he'd be happy to have sex again with me if I'm able, but he isn't willing to dive in with dedication to repair the cause.

But it isn't just him. I'm not really willing to ask him. With the memory of how things went last time, I'm not sure I could take the assistance even if he offered. And I'm honestly afraid that maybe we're lacking the level of intimacy needed to overcome the situation.

Ryan and I have never had passion so much as we have a comfortable consistency. It never once occurred to me during the course of our four years together that this is a problem.

"I'm dead inside," I blurt out suddenly, and my eyes flood again.

"I'm sorry?" He sits up straighter, stunned by my mood shift.

I wipe the tears away with the back of my hands. "Liz says I'm dead inside because I grew up thinking Disney princesses were flighty and impractical."

Ben blinks. "That's very specific."

"Why are you here, Ben?" I look up at him with puffy, tear-stained eyes and determination.

He meets my gaze with confusion. "Because we're talking?"

I close my eyes and huff. "No, not right this second. I mean in general. Why are you doing this? Any of this. This is *bizarre*. By any standards, this is completely absurd."

He leans his head back against the door frame. "We talked about this. You're confusing and intriguing and amazing and intimidating and I like you. Remember? Lots of adjectives."

I sniffle pitifully. "Would you like me if you found out I could never have sex again, ever?"

He sighs. "Kat, yes. I don't think that's going to happen, but if it did, I genuinely wouldn't care. There are plenty of other things you could do, you know. And I'm committed to letting you call the shots here, but I do think you're overlooking some of those things in your therapy, honestly. From what I've read, some of it seems pretty important to the process."

Another giant tear drops down my cheek. "I just don't want to mix everything up. It helps me to compartmentalize things, you know?"

"Does it, though?"

I shrug. "I think so."

He doesn't push me. "We'll do whatever you're comfortable with, okay? This is for you, so you decide."

"I'm sorry this keeps going so horribly."

"I just don't like seeing you upset," he says, his expression pained. "And I'd like to formally request putting therapy and science aside for a few minutes and reinstating friendship status, because I really, really want to hug you right now."

A laugh escapes me. "Permission granted."

"Oh, thank god," he says, and scrambles across the floor toward me. He leans against the sink beside me and wraps both his arms around me tight. "You scared the shit out of me, you know."

"I'm sorry. This is all a bit unnerving for me, too."

He drops his chin down into my hair and pulls in a breath. "I don't think you're dead inside. I think you just see things differently than Disney princesses. And that's not a bad thing."

I tilt my head against his chest. "Ben?"

"Yeah?"

"Can I ask you something now?"

"Shoot."

"Do you ever feel tingly feelings?"

He kisses the top of my head. "Exclusively."

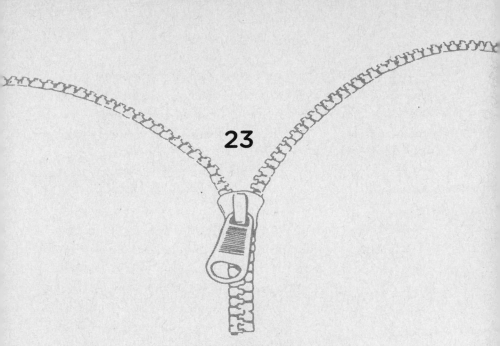

23

"All right," Shannon says, calling our emergency employee dinner meeting to order. "Shit's getting real, Kat's only got thirteen days left and it's time to go big."

The shop was crazed today. My eleventy billion cupcakes had to be frosted and decorated, we all had to pitch in on the wedding cakes, the first few of the birthday cakes had to go out—and that was in addition to our usual orders. Plus I was practicing my on-the-spot zoo animal cuppie art. There wasn't time to properly address my current situation apparently.

Which I would have been fine with.

I wasn't even going to bring anything up—beyond saying things didn't get far last night, sexy times–wise—but then Ben came in for his morning coffee and to pick up his office cupcakes, I got weird, and he asked if I was feeling better. Shannon overheard and pounced. Butter overheard that, and now here we are, holding an after-hours emergency employee dinner meeting at Ernesto's.

"So you freaked out because he was taking his shirt off?" Liz asks delicately.

"Yes." I drop my head onto the table with a loud *thud*. "I'm dead inside." Liz makes a terrified squeaking sound. "It's fine, hon," I say, not lifting my head. "I'm glad I know now."

Butter pokes me. "You're not dead inside. If you were, you wouldn't have been hyperventilating in your bathroom."

"Thank you for conjuring that imagery."

Shannon asks, "But why did it bother you? I don't understand."

I throw my hands up. "I don't know! I don't. Trust me, I'm very pleased at the thought of seeing Ben naked."

I've played that moment in my head a hundred times since last night. Every mental run-through ends with me on the edge of my damn seat waiting to see what's behind that shirt.

"Here's what I don't get," Butter says. "Why do you want to keep everything separate? Who cares if you kiss or whatever during the therapy?"

"I do. I care."

"Why, though? If Ryan's out sleeping with people, you can be damn sure he's kissing."

I sigh. "Because that's not what I'm doing with Ben. I don't want to date him for a few weeks and then ditch him to go back to Ryan. That would hurt him. This way, it's all sectioned off."

Shannon reaches over and takes my hand. "Honey, you know I love you. But that is truly the stupidest thing I've ever heard."

"Thanks," I say drily.

"I'm serious. Doing intimate things with someone over and over, it's going to bleed into the friendship. And maybe keeping it all sectioned off is what's freaking you out."

"You say that like you've had the feels for every guy you've slept with. Those concepts aren't mutually exclusive for me, okay?"

Shannon gives me her mom face. "Maybe the problem is you've got the feels this time, and trying to ignore them is screwing with you."

"I can't have the feels for Ben, okay? That's completely against the rules. I like what I've got with him on the friend-ship side of things, but I've got four years with Ryan waiting for me to get my shit together. I don't want to lose any of this."

Butter shakes her head. "Relationships aren't handed out with warranties, kitten. You're juggling too damn many things. You're a raw nerve right now."

I lay my head down on the table. "He made me feel... *fantastic.*"

The gals all look between each other. "That sounds like a very special term," Shannon says. "Care to elaborate?"

I snap up. "Okay, look, when you had a broken vagina, you got to pick how you wanted to deal with it. This is how I am comfortable with handling things right now, yeah? No, I don't know if it's working, I don't know if it's a good idea, I don't even really know what I'm doing, and yes, chances are solid I'm going to cock this all up spectacularly. But for right now, this is what I've got."

The waitress brings us a basket of breadsticks and another pitcher of beer. Shannon, ever the mom of the group, takes over pouring for us all. I slump down in my seat and let a wave of defeat wash over me. Things shouldn't be this hard. I'm not saying life should be a cakewalk, but this seems excessive.

I'm not asking for a lot. I'm not begging the universe for a lottery win or anything. I just want regular life stuff that I'm working hard for. There should be a little give somewhere.

Ernesto's is feeling the dinner rush, and the tables around us are all full of families and couples and people fresh off work, tucking into plates of baked ziti and salad.

According to the statistics in my printouts, at least a few

of the other women in this restaurant probably have vaginas on the fritz. Even with me and Shannon taking up two slots in those odds, there's probably a handful of women dreading the thought of therapeutic dilators and dildos while they wait for their appetizers. There's some depressing comfort in that thought. Misery and company and all that.

I could put up an ad and form a support group. We could meet here over breadsticks and beer for Broken Specials Anonymous. We'd get together and discuss therapy techniques, how we're all progressing, and just be there to sympathize that no one else can possibly understand how messed up all of this is unless their own junk stopped working. No matter how much their friends love them and want to help—even the ones who've been through the Broken Special club before.

Across the table, Liz perks up in her seat, and a smile breaks across her face. I follow her gaze to the front of the restaurant and see the source of her lifted mood.

Her fiancé is headed our way. He's got the same moony grin on his face, and his eyes are focused only on her as he makes his way past the tables and diners. Somehow, without breaking eye contact with Liz, he manages to avoid tripping over the three-year-old two tables over who is playing spaceship with a breadstick in the walking space.

We don't get to see much of Paul. He works as a nurse in the neonatal wing of the hospital across town, which keeps him on a pretty crazy schedule. Whereas Shannon's husband is a behemoth covered in intimidating tattoos under his suit jacket, Paul is walking toward us wearing scrubs covered with cartoon puppies wearing superhero capes.

He's a very skinny fella, but when he's next to Liz, it's barely noticeable. She's decidedly fun-sized. He's got lovely brown skin and a mop of shaggy pitch-black hair. I can never tell if that's a specific look he's going for, or if he's just too busy to get a trim.

I think we've seen him a grand total of three times since Liz started working at Cup My Cakes, but he seems like a very nice guy, always polite and smiling. I get the impression he's just as shy as Liz is, though, so we try to go easy on him.

Meaning we won't be waving sex toys in his face during this visit. I save that for the guys I'm having medical sex with, it would seem.

"Hi, honey," Liz says as he nears our table. She's positively glowing.

"Hey, baby," he says, beaming back at her.

"Paul," Shannon says and gives him a wave. Butter and I say polite hellos as Shannon asks, "How the heck are you?"

He finally looks away from Liz just long enough to answer, "I'm good. Hi, Shannon." He nods at Butter and me. "Hello, ladies." Turning back to Liz, he says, "You forgot your keys this morning, babe." He holds out a set of keys, and Liz makes a slightly embarrassed face that's quickly drowned out by gushing adoration.

"Oh my gosh, thank you," she says, taking the keys and standing up to hug him. "Do you have time to stay for a little while, or do you have to get back to the hospital?"

Looking genuinely disappointed, he says, "I have to get back. I just didn't want you to be locked out later, or have to stop by the hospital to get mine before you head home."

She's grinning like a little kid who just found the Easter Bunny standing in her living room. She turns back to the table and addresses all of us. "I'm going to walk Paul out, but I'll be right back, okay?"

"You guys are so damn cute," Butter says with affection.

"It was nice to see you again," I say as Liz leads her fella back out of the restaurant.

I admit that the cynic in me wants to mock this interaction somehow. They can't possibly be that happy, can they? There has to be a flaw somewhere.

Even watching them walk away feels like I'm intruding on an intimate moment. To anyone else, it's just a couple holding hands as they walk by. But looking closer, I can see how lovingly she's laced her fingers through his. How he smiles as he kisses the top of her head.

I'm surprised by the pang of jealousy that twinges in my stomach.

"Why do you want to have sex?" Shannon asks, jolting me out of my inane ponderings.

I take a sip of beer and regain focus. "The same reason balloons need air, sweetie."

"No, I have a very real reason for asking this one."

I shake my head. "I don't know. People have sex. It's what we do. We're supposed to have sex."

Butter gapes at me. "Honey, you are *so* doing sex wrong."

"I believe that's been established, yes."

Liz comes back to the table, her face all swoony until she takes her seat. Her expression is replaced with one of awkward tension and concentration. This is the effect I have on people now.

Shannon continues. "Kat, even back in college, you never fell in love with a guy and went through that gooey honeymoon phase where you just couldn't stop sleeping with each other. Remember me and Joe?"

I make a face. "Oh, god, yeah. You guys were ridiculous. I had to sleep in the common room half that semester. Jerks."

"I've known you for eleven years, and I have never seen you act like that. Not even with Ryan."

"So? Sex is awesome. I dig having sex. Don't get me wrong. But it's for a purpose, right? You feel an urge, you have sex.

If there's no one to have sex with, you satisfy your urge on your own. I've just never been the consumed-with-lust-for-a-particular-someone type."

"You are doing sex so wrong!" Butter yells.

"I'm going to throw my drink at you, I swear to everything!"

"Kat told me she had a really uptight aunt who said love wasn't about feelings!" Liz blurts out.

Butter's and Shannon's eyes bounce over to Liz. "What?"

I raise an eyebrow. "Liz. Dude."

"I'm sorry," she pleads. "But it's kind of weird the way you act like you can completely separate feelings from a relationship! I don't even understand how that would work! Maybe that's part of what has you so conflicted right now and why things with Ryan are so weird. And you said you never really felt sparkly feelings in relationships before, so maybe we can help with that."

"Traitor."

"No, this is good!" Shannon interjects. "Tell us about the aunt."

I sit back in my seat and make a petulant sound. "My aunt Julie. She took care of me a lot when my mom was working. She was super religious and rigid. She was nuts. But I knew she was nuts! Come on."

"How was she nuts?" Butter asks.

"I don't know. She'd say things like women were there for their husbands only, sex was a sin unless it was for procreating, God would punish us for disobeying our menfolk, and you got married to take care of your husband and make babies, not for love. See? Crazy. I mean, I was like ten, but dude, even I knew that was goat-balls loony."

"But you said she told you all that stuff about how you love and feelings and stuff. And princesses. You said *princesses*," Liz says emphatically.

I try to remember. "Okay, yes, she told me that you shouldn't trust the gooey feelings you get over boys because that's the kind of thing that gets you into trouble. Relationships are about establishing a connection to structure a family around. And she said that Disney princesses are stupid because they meet a guy and follow the feels and then end up poisoned by an apple or something, and let that be a lesson to us all."

Butter pipes up. "Hon, that sounds like you a little."

I scoff, "No, it doesn't! Rude."

"No, not the crazy stuff, but you've got to admit, you're all about the practicality. I don't think I've ever seen you roll with your feelings on something. Everything is about control and thinking things through and what's the most sensible choice."

"Because I don't like to be irresponsible, you're saying I'm bad at love?"

"No one is saying that!" Shannon exclaims.

Butter clears her throat. "I'm saying that a little."

Glaring at Butter, but speaking to me, Shannon continues, "But maybe you picked up a little more from her than you thought you did."

While I can differentiate in my adult mind that Aunt Julie was a bag of dicks, I'm sure my child brain had a harder time. She was a grown-up, and I was a kid. My mom loved her sister, but even she didn't prance around oozing respect for Julie, despite Mom's ability to treat everyone with kindness and consideration. There were a few flecks of exasperation or contempt in my mom's comments every now and then, and I clung to those. They were the life jackets that buoyed me through the flood of Julie's ramblings.

I was scared of God for a while. I didn't necessarily believe what my aunt had said, but the seed had been planted, and the possibility haunted me.

And there were drops of truth sprinkled in with Aunt Julie's zealotry. She wasn't just constantly spouting the evils of sex and feminism and death to Snow White every hour of every day. She taught me how to bake pies, trim green beans and hem my own skirts. There was good in her, knowledge in her.

It sometimes made the wrong stuff harder to spot.

I frown. "She used to drag me to church with her when my mom had to work late. It was awful. I remember this one time when I was maybe twelve, the pastor was saying how masturbation was a sin, and if you touched yourself, you'd burn in hell forever. A month later, I woke up in the middle of a steamy dream and, hand to heart, I burst into tears and thought God was going to smite me in my bed."

My friends are all staring at me.

"Well," Butter says calmly. "That's fucked up."

"Jesus," Shannon whispers. "What the hell kind of church was this? And what is wrong with your aunt? No wonder your vagina hit the bricks."

"Well," I half snap, "why did your vagina check out?"

Shannon looks at me with an exasperated eyebrow raise. "Because I'd just pushed a nine-pound human being out of it, and the recovery and stress of a newborn and a toddler and life made it a bit skittish."

"I'm sorry, but why didn't you ever tell any of us about it? I didn't know any of that was happening at all." I can feel my ears burning with annoyance.

"Because I was handling it," she answers with a shrug. "It wasn't that big a deal at the time."

"So you're saying I'm being overdramatic?"

"Ladies!" Butter interjects. "This isn't a vagina competition." She turns to me and wiggles her index finger at me as

Shannon picks up a breadstick. "And stop trying to change the subject by picking fights. Back to your aunt."

Liz looks horrified but determined. "You know all that stuff your aunt said was crap," she says. I'm impressed she said *crap*. "But as a twelve-year-old, you probably had a hard time letting that go. I bet your subconscious held on to a lot of it."

"I don't have the energy to fight my subconscious, you guys, and my insurance doesn't cover that kind of therapy. Plus the twenty-seventh is coming up. I'm starting to panic a little here. What the hell am I going to do?"

Shannon chuckles. "Calm down. Man, you actually have been kind of overdramatic the last few weeks. But maybe you could, I don't know, confront your demons or something."

"Yes! That's a good idea!" Butter agrees.

"What does that mean?" I ask, trying hard not to scowl.

"You've been reluctant to roll with feelings? Let's dive into feelings. You tend to stray away from embracing lusty experiences? Let's get knee-deep in some lust."

I hang my head. "Guys, this is stupid. I'm going to be fine."

"Maybe," Shannon says and leans forward to get my attention. "But you're cracking, and you're my best friend, and I don't like watching this. On a more selfish note, we've got a lot riding on the next few weeks, and I need all of us on our A game. You've got just thirteen days left, so if getting you all up in your lust demons will help, then by god, we're hunting down some motherfucking lust demons."

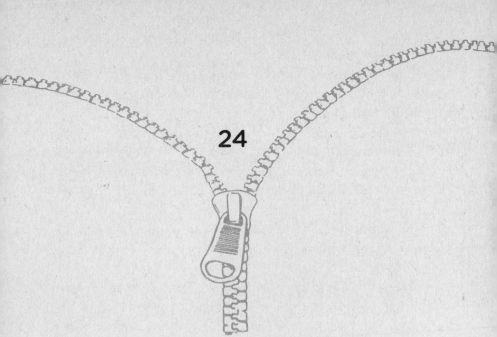

24

I don't see how this many people need cupcakes on a Thursday morning. We've got two orders going out today, I'm boxing up one of the birthday cakes to hand over to the customer on the other side of the counter, I've got a wedding cake comprised of three hundred cuppies to make, and there's a line ten people deep just waiting to order.

This shouldn't bother me, I'm sure. Yay, business. But oh my damn, I haven't even had a proper dose of coffee yet.

I look at my list of invoices. "Shit," I hiss. "Shannon, I've got to finish an order. They're due any minute."

She closes the lid on a small box of muffins she's packing up. "Gotcha covered, baby."

Butter rushes behind me with two cups of coffee and a to-go bag of something and heads to the register to check someone out. Liz is in the back making the occasional strangled sound as she tries to finish what is proving to be a hideously difficult wedding cake.

Whoever decided they wanted a cake that looked as if it had a peacock with full plumage draped down the tiers is a lunatic.

I run into the back room and grab a piping bag. "How're you holding up, sweets?" I ask as she places vibrant layers of fondant feathers down a silver cake.

"I hate this cake!" she cries. "It's taking forever!"

"After the burst I will come back and help, okay? I've got two cuppie orders today, and I'm doing some trial batches of the Ravens cakes with Shannon and Butter, but I think we can get it done."

She whimpers. "Thank you. This is going to take hours. I can help you with your wedding order later."

"Deal."

I start shoveling chocolate frosting into the bag and twist it off. I prefer working back in the kitchen, but Shannon thinks it's good for business to show off a little during the busy times if we can swing it. The customers love to see the product come together, and even though a swirl of icing is tantamount to blinking for us, it tends to make people say, "Ooh."

Out in the front, I set the unfrosted chocolate cupcakes directly into the carrying box. Efficiency is my goal today. Just as I start squeezing, I see Ben walk in out of the corner of my eye. I give him a busy and apologetic smile as he queues up. With a grin, he nods his head and disappears into his phone, trying his best to not get knocked over by people coming up to view our display case.

"Butter, can you grab more raspberry scones from the back?" Shannon calls out.

"Yes, ma'am!" Butter says, saluting with one hand and handing a customer change with the other. She scurries into the kitchen and Shannon takes her spot at the register. I pipe faster.

"Okay," I say, setting the bag down and closing the lid. "I'll box up the other dozen and then they're ready to go."

"Perfect," Shannon replies. Quite suddenly, her hand shoots

out behind the counter, invisible to the customers, and grabs my hip in a death grip. I yelp.

"What?" I squeak.

Her face has morphed into a terrifying, frozen customer service smile. She speaks through clenched teeth. "Oh, holy Jesus, Kat. That guy who just walked in? The one behind Ben? Oh, fuck. He's on the Coopertown committee. As in he's actually one of the people who will be making the decision about whether or not we get this contract."

I can feel my eyes bulging, but I look away from him. "Fuckity hell. What is he doing here?"

Shannon's cheeks look painfully lodged in the smiling position. "I have no clue. But keep moving, goddamm it. Go warn Butter and Liz, and then finish packing up your order. There will be no screwing this up, do you hear me?"

I nod and carefully pry her fingers off of my hip.

I calmly set the order I'm working on off to the side, smile a friendly smile at all the customers in line and walk with grace and purpose back into the kitchen.

"Guys!" I whisper-scream while trying to straighten my apron. "All hands on deck. Game faces. The big-shot Coopertown dude is queued up in the lobby." Liz looks like she might faint. Butter stands up straight, and it kind of looks like she's sticking out her boobs. It's so distracting, it pulls me out of my panic. "What...what the hell are you doing?"

She looks from me to Liz and back again. "What?"

I point at her chest. "Those."

"I'm standing at attention?"

"Okay, but you look like you just loaded your tit-cannons and are going into battle."

She raises an eyebrow, and her hands fly to her hips. "Aren't we?"

Liz looks down at her own boobs, and I have to physically stop myself from doing the same.

"Touché," I agree. "But look, holster those bad girls, Sarge." Resuming focus and, with that, panic, I say, "Look, I don't know what he's doing here, but we need to wow this bastard, okay? We've got a full house out there. Let's utilize it. And no pressure, but if we screw this up, Shannon will legitimately kill us all. Like, scratch our eyes right the hell out, okay?" They both nod, and I'm a little worried Liz might be sick. "Butter, get those scones out. Liz, go help Shannon ring people up. I'm right behind you."

They scuttle to the door and I grab another to-go box, carefully but quickly placing a dozen vanilla with blueberry jam filling and blueberry buttercream inside for the rest of my order.

When I return to the front, I see the line hasn't gotten any shorter, but the Coopertown fellow is getting closer. Shannon still has her robo-smile plastered on, Liz looks like we are about to be invaded by ninja cupcake warriors and Butter is taking an order while fidgeting with the glitter brush sticking out of her apron pocket like it's a security blanket.

Ben looks up from his phone and gives me a confused look. I try to smile as I run over to set the box I'm holding with the rest of the order I've been pulling.

"Can you pack up a half-dozen red velvets?" Shannon asks in an ethereal voice, waiting on a customer.

"Of course!" I say with what feels like too much enthusiasm. I bend down behind the display case and start boxing up cakes. My phone buzzes in my pocket, and I dare to look. It's a message from Ben. *You okay?*

With one hand and a death wish, I quickly type out, Big client behind you. O_O

I tuck my phone into my apron and get back to boxing.

Shannon looks down, still smiling, but her expression has now passed right into creepy territory. Her eyes look desperate. "It's okay," I whisper up to her. "We're doing fine." I hand her the cupcakes and stand up.

"Thank you," she says in the same weird voice.

We keep up the show-dog level of customer service and make our way through the line. Ben gets up to the register and Butter gives me a wink as she wiggles out of the way.

"Hey," he says quietly over the counter. "So, big fish, eh?"

"Shannon is going to lose it," I whisper back. I reach behind me and pour his usual coffee order. "Sorry it's so busy today. I feel like we're ignoring our best customer."

He smiles at me, and it stretches all the way up to his eyes. "I'm your best customer?"

Out of the corner of my eye, I see the Coopertown guy reach the counter. Shannon has made her way over to him, smile still frozen in place. Her cheeks are going to be sore tomorrow.

I turn back to Ben and grin. "You're the best lots of things, Mr. Cleary."

His hand reflexively moves to his tie, and I don't know whether to giggle or reach across the counter and bite his jaw.

"Kat?" Shannon calls over, and I jump a little.

"Yeah?" I side-eye Ben. "Excuse me for a second." Walking over to Shannon, I slap on my own crazy smile and say, "What's up, Shannon?"

"Kat, this is Mr. Peterson from the Coopertown Ravens." She gestures awkwardly toward him, and I want to pat her head and see if I can get her to calm down and take a breath. I reach across the counter and shake his hand.

"Pleasure to meet you," I say.

"And you," Mr. Peterson says. He sort of looks like Colonel Sanders without the mustache. He's wearing a beige linen suit, has gray hair that's almost white, and looks like a kindly old grandfather who would probably give you a pound of chocolate before dinner without realizing it was driving your mom bonkers to do so. "I was in the neighborhood and I realized I've never been in this store before. I thought I'd drop by and get a feel for things before the official tasting next week."

Shannon just keeps smiling. I sigh inwardly. The Mouth to the rescue.

"That's great!" I say. "We're glad to have you. Is there anything I can interest you in? Our chocolate with peanut butter is particularly delicious today, if I do say so myself."

He chuckles. "I think I'll take you up on that. Actually, while I'm here, I was hoping to get a peek at some of what you're working on for your presentation! I know it's not until next week, but I'm so interested in the process."

I blink at him. Shannon's hands clench into fists behind the counter where Mr. Peterson can't see them. Butter is over at the register checking out other customers, and Ben has moved off to the side and is rubbernecking the scene with an uncomfortable fascination while pretending to drink coffee. Liz is frozen in place by the espresso machine.

"I'm… I'm sorry?" I look to Shannon and then back to him. "We don't have any of the cakes we'll be presenting ready right now, unfortunately. Although we will be doing a trial run later today."

Mr. Peterson's face falls. "Oh, I was just hoping to see some kind of premise. I do so enjoy the artistic side of it all."

Shannon kicks me behind the counter. Hard.

"Uh, well," I stutter. "I do…oh! I do have my sketch pad. I've been working on drawings and stuff. And I've got, erm, some ravens made out of fondant. I'm not set on them yet, but I've been tinkering with the concepts."

His eyes light up. "Wonderful!"

"Great!" I say, feeling nothing of the sort. "Excellent. Shannon, why don't you tell Mr. Peterson about some of our most popular flavors and I'll go get…what I've got."

"Absolutely!" Ethereal Shannon says.

I head to the kitchen and cast a desperate look back toward Butter, Liz and Ben so that Peterson can't see. Once in the back room, I flail my arms around helplessly. *Shit, shit, shit.* Grabbing my book off the desk, I tear it open and try to find any pages that have anything that would be considered showable to someone in a professional capacity. I find exactly nothing.

I spew out a string of profanities, head over to my station and look through my pile of defunct ravens to find something I can show the man. Jesus, why did I ever think any of these were ever a good idea? I come across my little royal icing ravens, which looked amazing two weeks ago when I first made them, but are now looking a tad weathered. It's still the best I've got.

Oh god, Shannon is going to have a stroke right there at the counter when I come out there with this.

This isn't how this is supposed to happen. We are supposed to have all our recipes perfected and the art looking spectacular and Shannon will whisk it into the presentation and wow everyone with our mastery.

Not me stumbling out there with my failed fondant and absentminded scribbles.

An image of me abandoning the pile of ravens and scuttling out the back door like a coward flashes through my head. It's a pretty damn tempting idea.

But no. I woman up, grab the least disappointing-looking ravens in the group, pat my notebook in my pocket, say a prayer to the universe, mutter a few more curses and head back into the front room.

Butter is tending to customers, watching carefully out of the corner of her eye. Liz has started moving again and is assisting as best she can. Ben is pretending to look at his phone. I say *pretending* because I can see the screen, and it's not even on.

"All right, Mr. Peterson," I say in my best fake-confident voice. "I apologize for not having more to impress you with at the moment, but it's a taste, at least." I give him what I mean to be a friendly smile, but I think I overcompensate, and I'm pretty sure it's coming off as flirty. I carefully line up the royal icing and fondant ravens on the glass countertop in front of him. "I've been tinkering with different ways to get a powerful statement raven piece onto the cakes and it's been tricky, I don't mind saying." I give Mr. Peterson a wink, and now I *know* I'm coming off flirty. Dial it back, Mouth. "This isn't quite what I'm hoping to go with, but it gives you a general idea." I pull my pad out of my pocket and set it up next to the birds and start flipping quickly so he can't focus on how not-spectacular most of the pictures are. "Visually, the raven presents a perfect focal point for a wow factor, but of course it's equally about the flavors and the overall quality, I think you'll agree?"

He nods and smiles, but doesn't look terribly blown away by what he sees. "Of course."

I'm losing him. I can see sweat forming on Shannon's übertense brow. I slap my notebook shut. "Mr. Peterson," I say firmly but with a pleasant voice. "I assure you, what we provide for the presentation, and what we hope we will get to provide to your fans as your official cupcake concessions seller, will be far superior to anything you are seeing sketched out in my little book here—or, quite frankly, anything you're going to find anywhere. We'll give you a product that not only represents who we are as a shop but also matches the quality and performance of your university and your team. You will not be disappointed with us, sir."

Mr. Peterson looks up at me, and for a moment, his expression is unreadable. Shannon is beside me holding her breath. Butter, Liz and Ben are all perfectly motionless at the other end of the counter. Hell, even I've stopped blinking.

Finally Peterson smiles and lets loose a small laugh. Looking down at our display case, he says, "Well, I will say your selection is impressive, and everything looks absolutely delicious. What flavors you've used!"

I exhale just a bit. "Why don't you let me send you off with a little sample pack? The cupcakes we're bringing you next week will be absolutely magnificent, but unfortunately, our blueberry doesn't match up with your team colors, and I'd hate for you to miss out."

Shannon finds her voice. "Yes, let me box you up some of our favorites." She wriggles past me to the display case and I step out of the way, all the while smiling at the old man.

"Thank you, yes," he says. "That sounds wonderful. And I look forward to seeing your presentation materials next week. I'm confident you'll have something worth showing."

My eyebrows shoot up, but I try not to take his comment in the insulting way it sounded, but in the spirit of the kind smile with which he delivered it. Shannon hits her flow and starts describing our tasty treats, then quickly says, "Oh, Kat, could you check on that cake in the back for me?"

What cake? She gives me a pointed look. Oh! She's giving me a chance to flee.

"It was wonderful to meet you, Mr. Peterson," I say with a serene smile. "I hope you enjoyed our little shop here."

"The pleasure was mine, dear."

Faux-serenity in place, I smoothly walk from behind the counter and into the kitchen, where I quickly lose all feeling in my legs. I lean against my workstation and pull in a shaky breath. This is fine. This is so super fine.

I can still hear Shannon sweet-talking. The shop is nearly empty now, as the rush has finally dwindled down.

Butter comes walking briskly through the door with… Ben?

I pop my head up. "What…what are you doing here?"

He puts his hands up. "I have no idea. She made me come." He points to his tie, which is gripped tightly in Butter's hand.

"Butter, what in the hell?"

"Are you okay?" she asks, eyes wide, still gripping the tie.

"I'm fine," I say slowly. "Now let go of Ben."

She looks down at her hand and seems surprised at its contents. "Oh," she says. "Sorry."

Smoothing down his shirt, Ben looks at me awkwardly. "It's okay."

I motion at him. "Why did you drag him back here, anyway?"

Butter shrugs. "I don't know. He was there. You said all hands on deck. I panicked."

I reach up and pinch the bridge of my nose. "Sure. Okay." Looking back up at Ben, I say, "Actually, why were you still out there?"

He tugs at his tie. "I, uh, well. I'm not really sure. It looked like a big deal, and you seemed nervous, and it felt wrong to just leave in the middle of it. Oh, and I was going to ask if you wanted to get pizza tonight, but things got weird and I forgot. So."

"Aww," Butter says, stepping back. "That's so sweet!"

Shannon and Liz come rushing through the kitchen door. "That went horri— Ben!" Shannon trills.

Ben winces and looks up at the ceiling. "Hi."

Under any other circumstances, I'd be laughing hysterically. I manage a faint grin. "Pizza sounds great. And you can absolutely run away now," I say.

Letting out a whoosh of air, he says, "Thank you." He turns for the door, but stops short. "You're okay, though?"

"Aww," Butter says again. I roll my eyes at her.

I give him the most reassuring smile I can muster. "I'm fine. Lively day at the office. You know how it goes."

His lip twitches a bit. "Right." He looks awkwardly at everyone, raises his eyebrows and says, "Yeah, so. Nice to see you all. I'm gonna just…" He points at the door and quickly disappears.

Liz is pressed up against the blast-chiller, eyes wide, gaze bouncing between me and Shannon. Butter has her glitter brush out and is rolling it around in her hands, looking at it as though the secrets of the universe lie hidden in the bristles.

Shannon is looking straight at me with one hand on the counter for support and the other on her hip. She looks somehow crestfallen and determined and exhausted all at once. She takes in a deep breath and lets it out slowly.

"Fuck," she says.

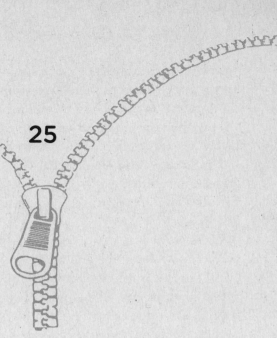

25

Shannon has worn a trench behind the display counter from her constant pacing today. We finally had to kick her out of the kitchen when her infinite looping kept taking her past our stations and she'd bump into us as we worked.

"Goodbye new employee, goodbye ever seeing my kids before bedtime. Goodbye Walt Disney World. Goodbye sanity," she mutters to herself.

"You're maybe overreacting a little," I offer.

She gives me a look of malicious intent, and her phasers are definitely not set to stun.

So, okay, the interaction with Mr. Peterson didn't go particularly well. But it could have gone a lot worse. Maybe.

We could have set him directly on fire or he could have punched us all in the face one by one.

Butter and Liz are in the kitchen wrapping things up for the night, and Shannon is behind the counter, finally done with the pacing, putting the last of the register takings away. I'm mopping the front room so we can go the hell home.

"It's going to be fine," I say to Shannon, dragging my mop

across the floor in even swirls. "We are going to get everything sorted out perfectly before the big day and knock his damn socks off. This set a nice low bar for what he expects from us. Now when we go in all guns blazing, he won't know what hit him."

"So you're saying it's a good thing we completely flopped this morning?"

I pause to consider this. "You have to *really* want to see that as a potential silver lining, but sure. Let's go with that."

Shannon doesn't seem convinced, but I think there's something to the theory. I resume mopping, my head swimming with thoughts of tiny ravens and buttercream nightmares when the sound of a gentle tapping on the glass of the front door rings out.

I look up and see Ben standing on the other side. Smiling, I prop the mop against one of the armchairs in the seating area and go to unlock the door for him.

"Hey," I say, letting him through. "How was your day?"

"Considerably more dull after I left here," he replies with a wink. He waves a hello to Shannon at the register, who silently nods back, not to be disturbed whilst counting money. "But then, it always is. Butter isn't going to drag me around by the tie again, is she?"

Staring ominously toward the kitchen, I answer, "Anything can happen here, Cleary. Never let your guard down."

He straightens his tie and plasters a dramatic expression on his face. "I'll never surrender."

Giggling, I grab my mop again. "Give me just a second to finish, and then we can go. I'm sure you're very impressed by this glamorous view of me right now."

He cocks his head and studies me as I work. "You do make mopping far more enticing than I ever thought possible."

I don't know whether to blush or roll my eyes, so I shake my head and keep working.

"All right, Kat," Shannon says, coming out from behind the counter. "I'm going to pack everything up and go take the deposits to the bank. Then I'm off. Butter'll lock things down tonight. You good up here?"

I swipe the mop across the last patch of floor and plop it back in the bucket. "Yes, ma'am. All clear. See you in the morning."

Shannon squints at the windows and says, "Wait, is that…?"

Following her gaze, I see our front door opening again. In walks a sort of familiar-looking guy in his mid-thirties, wearing a rumpled suit. He's got very dark hair piled back with way too much product, and he's sporting a goatee.

"Barry?" Shannon says. "What are you doing here? Are you supposed to meet Joe? I don't think he's planning on stopping in tonight."

Oh my god, Barry the Goatee. Definitely not going to him for therapy sex.

"Hiya, Shannon," Barry says with a toothy grin. "Actually, I am here to see this one." He points at me, and an unfortunate expression freezes on my face.

"Me? Why?"

Shannon's face passes through several emotions very quickly. She goes from her customer service smile to confusion to I'm-going-to-murder-my-husband-with-my-bare-hands in a blink. She rips her phone out of her apron and starts furiously punching buttons. I'm assuming Joe is on the receiving end of those clicks.

"I heard from a little birdy," Barry explains, his teeth gleaming, "that you're in the market for a relationship that isn't too serious. I meant to get your number at that Labor Day party last year, but I thought you were with that one guy. When Joe said you were looking for a casual thing, I knew I—"

"Shannon!" I shriek.

She has her phone to her ear and is screaming into it. "Joe!"

"Uh…" Ben says from behind me.

I whip around. "Wait, no. No, no, no. Really no, Ben. This is so not what it looks like."

Barry stands up a little straighter. "Who's this guy?"

Butter and Liz come running out of the back room and stand behind the counter. "What's up, everyone?" Butter asks cautiously.

Whirling around to face Barry the Goatee, I insist, "Look, I don't care what you heard, but I am not looking for anything, least of all from you. Aside from that being the most offensive attempt at asking someone out I've ever heard, I'm just flat-out not interested."

"So…that's a no?"

"Hard pass, Barry. Hard pass. Not now. Not ever."

Barry grins again. "Feeling a little shy because I asked you in front of all these people? We could go get a drink and—"

"Get the hell out of this store, or I swear to god I will bury you in the same shallow grave my husband is destined for tonight, you creepy little grease stain!" Shannon shouts, shoving her phone back into her apron.

Bristling, he attempts to straighten his wrinkled jacket. "There's no need to get personal about it. I'm just making sure she understands the offer on the table here. Don't be bringing your marital troubles in and making things more complicated."

Oh shit.

A sound I'm pretty sure I've heard on Animal Planet right before an antelope dies erupts from Shannon as she lunges at Barry. It's absolute chaos from there. I grab for Shannon. Ben grabs for us both. Butter and Liz run from behind the counter. I can't tell if Shannon is trying to strangle Barry or just get him out the door, but I'm trying to pry her off him, and I think Ben is trying to separate the lot of us. Butter joins the mix, and then there are just arms and shouting sounds and bedlam everywhere.

I don't feel my feet hit it, but one of us knocks into the mop bucket and over it goes. A new wave of screaming echoes through the shop as the warm soapy water soaks most of us from the knees down.

In a flash of long black hair, Butter slips on the now deathly slick linoleum and hits the floor with a thud. Liz stands a few feet away yelping, "Stop!"

My foot hits what I have to assume is pure soap, and my left leg juts out independent from the rest of my body. Ben gets an arm around my waist as I fall, but the momentum is too much, or the floor is too slippery, because he goes right down with me.

The sound of tires screeching to a halt outside causes us all to freeze. Did someone call the police?

I glance up and see Joe climbing out of his car looking angrier than I've ever seen him—or anyone else—look.

He stomps across the sidewalk, throws open the shop door so hard I'm genuinely surprised the glass doesn't shatter and, without saying a word, grabs Barry by the scruff of his neck. Joe turns, dragging Barry behind him, and is right back out the door.

Shannon stands panting, her fingers still curled into claws. Liz is behind us, her hands clasped over her face in horror. Butter, Ben and I are all lying motionless in the puddle on the floor.

We watch as Joe jerks Barry to the sidewalk and releases him, getting right up in his face, jabbing a finger under his nose. Joe might work in a bank, but by the look of him, he'd be better suited as the bouncer of a nightclub. I don't think I've ever appreciated how exactly how enormous the man truly is. He's well over six feet tall with a shaved head and a beard that probably makes him look terrifying to other people.

I've known him forever, so under normal circumstances, while I've always been aware he's a big dude, it's hard to find him menacing when I've seen him playing princess tea party with his daughter.

But watching him shred into Barry, I can't see how I ever missed his essence of ferociousness. Rabid bears would be less frightening.

A moment later, tail lodged firmly between his legs, Barry turns and flees. Joe stretches out his neck, tugs down the sleeves of his suit jacket and calmly makes his way back into the store.

The little bells that tinkle when the door opens sound wildly inappropriate in this context.

"Everybody all right?" he says, looking down at the bunch of us on the floor. Butter is closest, so he reaches down and carefully helps her up. Her feet dart out a few times, but she manages to hold steady.

He comes over as Ben and I try wriggling ourselves up.

"You're Ben, right?" Joe asks.

Ben, eyes comically wide, says, "I'm—yeah?" as if he's suddenly unsure.

"I'm Joe. Shannon's husband. Nice to meet you. I've heard really great things. Sorry about all of this." He sticks his hand out, and Ben looks to both me and Shannon with blatant confusion before shaking it.

"It's, um, yeah. Great to meet you, too."

Joe takes me by the elbow and helps me the rest of the way up. I latch onto one of the armchairs to maintain my balance, and Ben clings to my wrist for good measure.

"Kat," Joe continues. "I'm really sorry about this, and I'll take care of it. I promise I will find a way to make that up to you. It really was a misunderstanding, but I'll have to call you later and explain." He turns to address Shannon. "I've got to go get the kids from the sitter, and I'll grab dinner on the way home and meet you there. You can kill me after the kids go to bed. Kat can come, too, if she wants. Do we still need milk? I can pick it up."

"Goddamn right you'll pick up the milk," Shannon mutters.

He walks over, bends down and gives her a quick kiss on the lips, which she reciprocates, and quickly walks back out of the shop. We all watch in silence as he climbs into his car, starts the engine and drives away.

The only sounds around us are the surreal splats of water droplets from our clothes hitting the floor.

"Guys," Ben says finally, "what the hell just happened?"

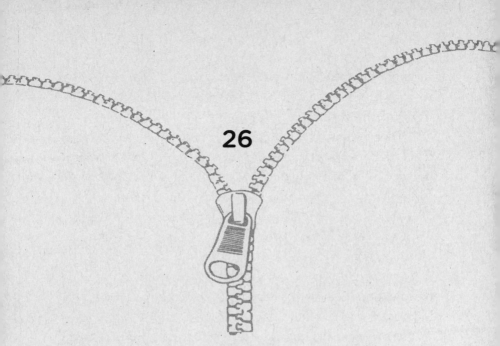

26

"Thanks for driving me," I say, awkwardly poking at Ben's dashboard. "I'm not sure they would have let me on the bus with soap dripping from my jeans."

"It's no problem," he says, his eyes a little too focused on the road.

I can't handle the tension and blurt out, "Okay, so how mad are you right now?"

Keeping one hand on the wheel, he uses the other to rub his forehead. "I'm not mad, Kat. Just a little confused."

"I am absolutely not looking to date Barry," I say with a shudder. "And I know that looked really weird, but I swear I had nothing to do with him being there."

Ben shakes his head. "It's fine, Kat. We've never had a discussion of… I don't even know what to call it. Sex therapy exclusivity? It's none of my business."

"You *are* mad!" I yelp. "I'm not out there recruiting dudes by the dozen, Ben! I don't understand what happened with Barry the Goatee just now, but that wasn't my call, man."

Taking in a slow breath, he says, "You really don't have

to explain yourself. I know how important your deadline is to you. I mean, you're down to twelve days, and I know we haven't had much success. It's not—"

A frustrated, guttural noise escapes me. "Ben. Oh my god. That was not an act of therapy desperation! I do not want to do therapy with Barry the freaking Goatee. I'm not looking to do therapy with anyone else, thank you very much."

Ben brakes for a stoplight and turns to stare at me. "Really?"

I awkwardly brush at my jeans. "Yes. Really. I like you. Shut up."

One corner of his mouth pulls up, seemingly without his permission, and he turns his attention back to the road as the light turns green. "Oh."

We drive in silence, and he appears to be contemplating the situation at hand.

While he deliberates, I'll just be over here dying of acute mortification.

I'm going to kill Joe. I don't know what he did, but I think I will be justified in his murder, assuming Shannon doesn't get to him first.

My dry spell has reached the point where spouses are diving in to throw solutions at it.

Icky solutions, but the point stands.

And my deadline is inching closer every minute. Twelve days. Twelve tiny days to slay the dragon. I make an unfortunate squeaking sound.

"What was that?" Ben asks as we enter my neighborhood.

I twist in my seat, and my hands clench the seat belt across my chest. "Let's try again tonight. Third time's the charm?"

Making a moderately exasperated noise, he replies, "Kat, come on. That's not what I meant. You don't have to prove anything to me. I would never want that."

"I know that. It's just...*twelve days*," I whimper. "I've only got twelve days left! Where the hell did the last few weeks go?"

His hand flies back to his forehead. "Are you sure you're even in a place to try tonight?"

"Absolutely. Why wouldn't I be?"

He gives me a side-eyed look. "Well, I don't know about you, but I'm still wearing mop-water clothes that are becoming surprisingly stiff as they dry."

Hearing him say that out loud makes the discomfort fly right into focus. He's not wrong. My jeans are starting to feel a bit cardboard-like. And the soap is making my skin sticky and unpleasantly itchy.

"Okay, fair point," I say. "What about this? We kind of screwed up dinner plans, and yes, we are both a little gross right now. How about we break for an hour or so, get cleaned up and then pretend the last half hour never happened?"

We pull up to my apartment complex, getting an impressively good parking spot on the street. He puts the car in Park and stares at me silently for a moment. He takes in a long, controlled breath and lets it out just as slowly. I'm all but bouncing with anticipation in my seat.

"You really want to try tonight?"

"Very much. Yep."

I swear I see him shake his head ever so slightly, but he says, "If that's what you want to do, we can give it a shot."

"Great!" I trill, and clap him on the arm. "All right, I'm going to go shower because seriously, mop water, ew. And I'll call you in about an hour when we're both ready to meet up again?"

He nods once. "Sounds good."

Emboldened by the new goal, I hop out of the car and wave a gleeful goodbye as I prance down the sidewalk to my building.

Before I can even get my key in the lobby door, my phone rings in my pocket. I pull it out and answer without looking at the screen as I struggle to get the door open. "Hello?"

It's Joe. "Hey, Kat," he says.

"You are dead to me, I hope you know."

I can hear his contrition through the phone even before he speaks. "I'm so sorry," he says. "I swear I didn't tell him anything about what you've got going on right now."

"Then how did this little scenario in the shop come about, Joe?"

"I was talking to him the other day about how you might be looking for a casual relationship right now. A no commitment kind of thing. I knew he was into you from that barbecue we had last year, and I wasn't thinking. Then Shannon told me about you and that Ben guy, and I didn't think to say anything to Barry about it. But in my defense, I didn't think he was going to do *that*."

I get to my apartment and fling the door open. "While I appreciate your attempt at laying such sophisticated groundwork, you do realize you essentially offered me up as a concubine to Barry, right?"

The line is silent for a few uncomfortable beats. "Now I do."

"There ya go." I slam my door shut and start stripping off my unfortunately soapy shoes and socks.

"Hey, Ben isn't upset, is he?" Joe asks. "I promise I didn't mean for that to happen. I feel really bad about everything."

"Good. You should," I say with a huff. "And I think he's okay? If he's not, I'm turning Shannon loose on you."

He groans. "I don't expect to survive the night as it is, man."

"Also good."

"I really am sorry. If you need me to explain to him that

it was all my fault, I'm on it. Same with Ryan. I'll gladly call him and explain. I don't want him pissed at me."

I freeze completely still, standing partially stripped and sticky in my living room, and it hits me: I didn't think about Ryan once during the Goatee fiasco.

Plus, I haven't heard from him in nearly three weeks. I don't think this should be our first topic of conversation.

"Uh, no," I mutter, resuming peeling off my soapy gear. "I've got it. He'll understand. It's fine."

"The offers stand," he maintains. "And I swear you will never hear from Barry again, trust me."

"I believe you," I say. "And, Joe?"

"Yeah?"

"Don't ever poke your nose in my love life again unless you get my express written permission beforehand, okay?"

He sighs. "Got it."

"I've got to go shower the mop crud off of me," I say. "I hope Shannon doesn't kill you too hard. Or maybe I do. Not quite over it yet."

"It could go either way. Have a good night, Kat."

"Night, Joe."

I end the call and get back to pulling my disgustingly damp jeans off.

Twelve days. Twelve fleeting days between me and my deadline.

I can do this. Therapy has been going well on my own, even if it has gone unfathomably bad with Ben thus far.

In all fairness, we haven't even made it to the actual act of therapy sex yet, so I've got hope that we can make it work if I can get past my random bursts of hideous awkwardness leading up to things.

I need tonight to go well. I need to shatter this deadline into a million little pieces and knock it out of my head. And if things work out the way I hope they will over the next few hours, I could move on from all this nonsense and focus on a million more important things.

Like my upcoming TV debut. And the Coopertown presentation.

My last attempts at preparation didn't go my way, so obviously wine and another spa visit are out.

What I need to do here is be completely ready by the time Ben makes his way back. All systems go, a paragon of relaxation.

I look over at my kitchen counter and see the bottle of pills Dr. Snow prescribed me. *If I'm anxious, so's my vagina.*

I run over, now sans pants, and grab the bottle. "Take ½–1 pill as needed for anxiety," the directions read.

At this point, I will genuinely take all the help I can get.

I pop the lid off, throw a whole pill in my mouth and quickly grab a glass of water to wash it down.

I recap the medicine, set it back on the counter and head to my bedroom. Hopefully the medicine will kick in before I call Ben back, and after I shower, I'll take extra time to do my own therapy before he gets here. I should be relaxed and ready to go.

Running to my bathroom, I start the shower and while I wait for the water to heat up, I head back into my room and start pulling items out of my nightstand. I set a bottle of lubricant on the stand and the rest of my therapy items on my comforter. I am nothing if not prepared tonight.

This is going to work, I can just feel it.

I blink myself awake and feel alarmingly incoherent.

Squinting into the darkness, I try to gather my thoughts. I sit up, my knees bumping into a variety of faux-penises on my bed. I'm still wearing a bath towel, and my hair feels oddly crumpled.

The clock on my nightstand, the LED glinting through the bottle of lube, reads 3:07.

Oh my god. Ohmygodohmygod.

I had taken my sweet time in the shower, scrubbing up, shaving my legs, determined to take my prep to a hospital-grade level of cleanliness. I started to feel the medicine kicking in, which definitely helped on the relaxation front.

When I was out of the shower, I meant to lie down and do my therapy before I called Ben. But I was like, really relaxed. Too relaxed.

Retucking my towel, I fling myself off my bed and regret it immediately. I'm feeling a bit wobbly still.

I run out to the living room and grab my phone off the edge of the kitchen counter. I push the button and see I've got multiple missed texts and two missed calls from Ben.

Shit, shit, shit.

I don't even bother to read them before I hit Call Back.

After five long rings, his sleepy voice answers. "Hello?"

"Ben," I groan. "I am so sorry."

"Hey, are you okay? What happened?"

"I fell asleep!" I slap my hand to my forehead. "I took this pill my doctor gave me to help me relax and I passed out right after my shower. Ben, I am so, so sorry. I didn't mean to leave you hanging."

I can hear him rubbing his eyes. "It's fine," he says through a yawn. "I was worried about you, though. I didn't know if you'd panicked or if the Goatee guy came around or something. You're all right?"

I scoff, "The Goatee wouldn't dare come around here. I'm pretty sure Joe had him put down. And yeah, I'm fine. I'm sorry I made you worry."

"I'm just glad you're okay."

Still clutching my towel, I drag my toe across the carpet. "I'm guessing the plan for tonight is off the table now, right?"

He chuckles. "Since I have to get up for work in a few hours, I'm going to say it's probably not the best idea, no."

I can feel disappointment manifesting as a pout. "Yeah, no, I totally understand. I really am sorry. About everything today. Erm, yesterday."

He yawns again. "Maybe we can talk tomorrow?"

"Sure. Go back to sleep."

"You too," he says. "G'night, Kat."

"Night."

My spirits sink as he ends the call. I look down at my phone and see the texts. There are three from Ben, asking if I'm okay and checking in. One from Shannon apologizing again for Joe and Barry.

And one from Ryan.

Drove by the shop today, realized I hadn't said hey in a while, so I figured I should! Hey!

I blink at the screen.

That's it? Three weeks of no talking, and I get a "should" and a "Hey!"?

Nothing about this evening went well. Not a damn thing.

And now it's the middle of the night, I'm starving, no sex was had and my bed is covered in dildos.

It's officially a new day. Eleven days left.

While I was hoping the third time would be the charm, I'm trying really hard to not think about what's supposed to happen when you've gotten three strikes.

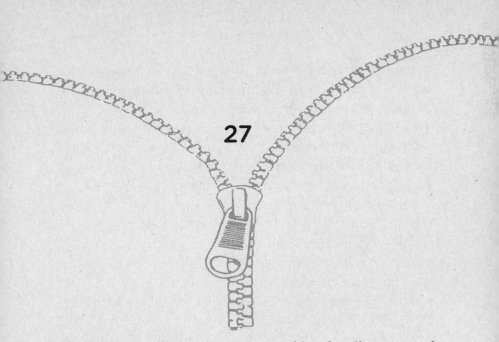

27

There isn't enough coffee in the world to handle my mood this morning.

I slog into the back room, dropping a gym bag under the desk and waving a feeble hello to Butter, who is yawning over at her station.

"What the hell is that?" she asks, pointing at the bag. "You working out now?"

"Not exactly," I say, tying my apron on. "How're you today?"

She yawns again. "Well, I went home and panicked about all the recipes for the stupid Coopertown thing, so I was up until two in the damn morning testing them all out again. My kitchen looks like the shop dropped by for a booty call."

"That's some disturbing imagery." I shudder. "Did you make any progress?"

She deflates a little. "I don't even know. I feel like I've made so many new versions of these cakes, I don't even know what tastes good anymore. I wrote it all down, so I'll whip them up for you guys later today."

Empathy is pouring out of every part of me. "You're doing amazing, Butter. Seriously, no one masters cakes like you, baby. I've got every confidence in you."

She looks down at her station and grabs her glitter brush, rolling it across the flattop. "Do you feel like we will sort of be ruining everyone's lives if we screw this up? Because I absolutely feel like I'll be destroying some lives."

I walk over and wrap my arms around her shoulders, giving her a squeeze. "You, my dear, will not be screwing up anything for anyone. Seriously. Even on your worst day, your stuff is the best I've ever tasted. You've got this, Butter." I step away and give her a little pat on the ass for good measure, which makes her giggle. "But I do feel you on the pressure. I'll be glad when this is all over."

"How about you? You're looking a little twitchy yourself."

"I'm swell," I lie, picking up today's invoice list. "Not at all overwhelmed and agitated. Maybe it was Mr. Peterson and his judgment. Or maybe it was Barry the Goatee and his kamikaze visit to the store. Or the fact that I had plans with Ben last night that fell spectacularly to pieces. I've got a laundry list at this point."

Butter winces. "That was such a mess. I thought Shannon was going to kill that greasy little sleaze." She shudders. "How did Ben take all of it?"

I sigh. "He's fine now, I think. I eventually convinced him I'm not really sending out carrier pigeons to recruit one-night stands. Although things didn't exactly improve after we got the Barry stuff sorted out."

"Oh, lord."

"I know, right?" Shaking my head, I slap my invoices down on the workstation. "We were supposed to try therapy sex again, and I went and drugged myself up to the point of unconsciousness instead." I hold my hand up to stop the horrified expression building on her face. "I'm fine. I just didn't think the medicine my doc gave me would knock me out. I slept right through calling Ben back, and by the time I woke up, it was halfway to dawn."

"That's not what you want."

"Not so much. But by then, I couldn't get back to sleep, so I figured I'd do therapy on my own, but it wasn't working very well. I thought, okay, I'm stressed, the medicine has worn off, I've only got eleven stupid days until my deadline, things suck. Then I looked at the printouts, and they said this stuff about relaxing environments with scented candles and shit. So I went to the bodega on the corner in my jammies like an adult at three thirty in the damn morning and was looking for the scented candles."

Butter blinks at me. "How'd that go?"

I lean against my workstation. "Not great. They had one that said it smelled like a shooting star, and I'm telling you, man, nothing has ever pissed me off more than the idea of a candle smelling like a shooting star pissed me off."

Pursing her lips, she says, "Um. Why?"

"Because what the fuck does a shooting star smell like, Butter? Like, please enlighten me on where someone got the comparative scents to make this creation!" I am suddenly shouting. "I mean, come on! Of all the things to make a candle smell like, some genius sat down and thought, *shooting star*! There's something a house should smell like! That's a perfectly identifiable scent that makes absolute sense and isn't at all ridiculous!"

Butter snorts. "I'm sorry." She tries to compose herself. "So, I'm guessing you didn't get a candle?"

I wave a hand without much feeling. "No, I did. I'd gone all the way down there. I wasn't about to leave without a candle, you know?"

"Probably not Shooting Star?"

213

"No. Satsuma Dawn. Surprisingly nice and refreshing, actually."

Butter shakes her head. "Sweetie, you need to get laid."

"You freaking think?"

Shannon and Liz come walking in through the back door. "Good morning," Shannon grunts into a to-go coffee cup. Liz looks surprisingly normal. She's the only one of us who hasn't fallen victim to the Coopertown hysterics. I assume she's never been happier to be the wedding cake expert than she is this week.

"Although," Butter continues, looking optimistic, "with all the therapy you're doing, you're probably rolling in orgasms, right? That's gotta cut the tension a little."

A bursting laugh rips out of me so hard I think I've collapsed a lung. "God, no. Really no. There is nothing sexual about the therapy at all, Butter. It's not like I'm sitting around jilling off twice a day, every day. Orgasms aren't part of the deal."

Shannon sets her bag down on the desk and turns to face me, eyes still heavy. "Wait. You mean you are doing all that stuff to yourself, and you're not crossing a finish line?"

"No."

"Not ever?"

I glare at her. "This is kind of the point of the therapy, dude. To get to a point where I can finish that line."

Liz starts setting up her station, but looks confused. "What's jilling off?"

Reaching over to pat her on the head, Butter explains, "Guys have jacking off, ladies have jilling."

Shaking her head, Liz says, "Why do I ask questions? I never want to know."

Shannon ignores them, but looks at me like she just heard someone insist all our world leaders are actually potatoes.

"Honey, no wonder you're so damn tense. You could use a good jilling."

"So," Butter interrupts. "Did the candle help?"

I scoff, "Not as such. But by then, I had an hour until my alarm was set to go off and it's possible a thread of insanity had settled in, so I pulled at it."

Shannon, still standing over at the desk unloading her things, freezes. "Wait, what did you do?"

I smooth out the pockets on my apron. "I was feeling a little down about having lost my mojo, you know? So I started thinking about the last time I felt good and confident and sexy, and I honestly couldn't remember."

It's true. Aside from my funeral/date dress, I couldn't find a single thing in my closet that made me feel like anything other than a full-time baker. All my shirts have a fine residue of flour on them, and I was disheartened to discover I don't even own any cute underwear anymore. Everything is practical and sensible and convenient, with the exception of the shoes I bought to wear on my date with Ben.

And even those were bought with the notion that they'd be comfortable.

As much as I like to embrace responsibility, the lack of anything lacy or pretty or enticing anywhere in my apartment bummed me out pretty damn hard.

They're all staring at me. "So...?" Butter says.

The words come out in a torrent. "I hopped online and came across this ad, and I signed up for a burlesque class tonight after work at the theater over on Fifteenth." I sigh and throw my hands in the air. "I don't know. In the pictures they were all wearing corsets and sequins and had their boobs all propped up. My boobs haven't been propped up in eons, guys. Everything is stressful and my special is broken and I feel like shaking my ass for a few hours."

Shannon stands up straight. "That's…a great idea. It sounds awesome. I've always wanted to do that."

"Me, too!" Butter says, swaying provocatively in place. "I don't even need a broken hoo-ha for that. I just like to shimmy." Then she stops and points at my gym bag. "That's what you're doing! I knew you weren't going to the gym!"

Rolling my eyes, I say, "Thanks."

Liz pipes up. "That sounds fun. I thought about looking into that place for my bachelorette party, but my friends were all too shy for it."

My eyebrows lift. "Wait, your friends are shier than you?" She flushes, and I instantly feel bad. "Oh, hon, I'm sorry. I didn't mean that. I just didn't figure you for the burlesque type."

She almost frowns at me. "Just because I'm not as open with talking about things as you guys doesn't mean I don't want to do fun stuff." Her voice gets quiet, and she starts poking at the cutting board on her station. "Shy people want to do things, too, you know."

Genuine guilt sets in. Sometimes I forget how being The Mouth comes easily to me. I stuff my hands in my apron pockets. "Um, do you want to come with me tonight? There are plenty of open spots in the class. It looks really fun."

"I want to go!" Butter yelps, throwing her hand in the air.

"Me, too!" Shannon announces.

I look around at them. "Really?"

Shannon slaps her hand down on the metal worktop. "Hell yes, I do. This week has been horrible. This is exactly what we all need. A girls' night out, shaking all our jiggly bits, embracing our lust demons? It can be a team-building exercise or something. Maybe I can write it off as a business expense!"

"Easy, Tiger," I say with a grin. I turn back to Liz. "What

do you say? You in? I think it'll be a blast. I'm told they have costumes. I'm very into this idea."

Liz fights back a smile and keeps poking at her board. "Okay. I guess so. It really does sound fun."

"Yay!" squeals Butter. "I knew I shaved my legs for a reason this morning!"

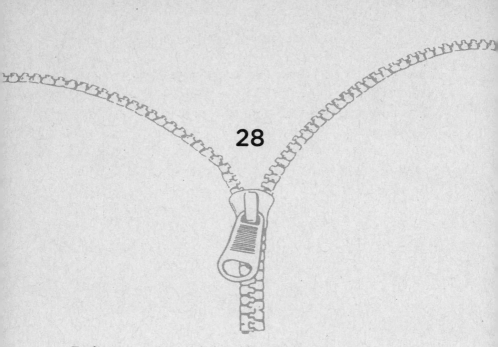

28

Feeling very "reward thyself," we all decided it was a group lunch from the deli down the street kind of day. With all the pressure we've put on ourselves to fill regular orders on top of trying out the new Coopertown recipes, we deserved a treat.

When you spend all day surrounded by baked goods and confectionary delights, a treat comes in the form of corned beef and kettle chips.

Butter and I have ventured forth together to retrieve the noms to bring back to the crew, and it's nice to get away from the shop together.

The crazy hours we work don't leave a tremendous amount of free time to hang out in a non-baking capacity, and the moments I get with my best friends outside our professional bindings are rare.

The mid-spring weather is glorious, even if some of the weird flowering trees lining the sidewalks do smell a bit like underwear that's been left at the bottom of the hamper for a few months.

Not really sure what the thought was behind peppering our town with that stench once a year, but they sure do look pretty.

"I'm really excited about the class tonight," Butter says, bouncing a little as she walks. "I can't remember the last time we had a real girls' night out."

"And this will be our first official non-work or vagina panic frolic with Liz," I offer. "If we don't scare the poor thing off tonight, I think it's safe to say she's officially in it for the long haul."

"I think she's gonna make it," Butter offers, ever the optimist.

"Agreed. She's tougher than she looks." We stroll in silence for half a block when I decide to make the most of our quality time. "So, Butter, my love. Tell me what's going on. I feel like all conversations lately have been very vagina heavy." A prim-looking woman in a gray blazer passes by just as I say "vagina heavy" and stumbles. I give her a toothy smile as she rubbernecks us, regaining her footing. "Tell me what's new in your life? How're things?"

She smiles, happy to be the center of the attention she normally pushes onto others. "Things are okay!" she says. "The Coopertown stuff is definitely getting to me, and I can't wait until it's over and we're strutting around town with that contract, but otherwise, things are good."

I bump into her with my elbow. "Oh, come on. Nothing not bakery-related to share? Have our lives become that boring?"

She ponders. "Well, I went out on a date with a guy I met at my dry cleaner's a few weeks ago. He was really dull. He ordered his dressing on the side of his salad and only drank water at dinner."

I shrug. "Maybe he doesn't drink?"

"Nope, I asked. He drinks."

"Or he is super conscientious about drunk driving?"

"Nope. He took a cab both ways."

"Mormon?" I suggest. "Oh, wait, no, you said he drinks. I got nothin'."

"He just said he was in the mood for water," she says, looking confused, even still. "Which, I dunno. Combined with the dressing thing, and the conversation over dinner, I wasn't feeling it."

I can't help but wonder what he could have possibly said that would turn Butter, a sparkling unicorn personified, off. "What conversation?"

She looks at me, cocks an eyebrow and one side of her mouth lifts. "The drinking topic was the most interesting part."

I make a face. "Eek. Fair point. You can do way better."

"Damn right, I can." She smiles to herself and adds, "There's a really sweet gal I've been flirting with for a few months at the Greek restaurant by my apartment. After the Coopertown stuff is done, I'm gonna go for it."

I pat her shoulder. "Atta girl. Do me proud."

Butter looks up, closes her eyes and basks in the glow of the sun upon her face. Which is a bit dangerous, considering we're still walking. I loop my arm through hers to guide her as she savors the sunshine.

I'm feeling very "stop and smell the roses" on this walk, and it's a welcome vibe. I haven't had a moment of peaceful thought in weeks. Even keeping Butter from walking into a parking meter seems like a relaxing event.

"Can I ask a question?" Butter says, finally opening her eyes as I carefully steer her away from a phone pole.

"Always," I answer, keeping my arm wrapped with hers.

"Do you know what caused your special to close up shop?"

I grin at her use of *special*. "Kind of, but not really," I say, my mind pulled from the bliss of our walk and back into the land of rebellious nethers.

"It's just such an awful thing to have happen," she says, looking awed. "Even worse when you don't know why. Like, it's just this thing happening to you for no reason. Luck of the draw, and all that."

I consider this as we make our way through a crosswalk. Part of it was the pressure of the shop, I'm sure. I think back to what life was like for Ryan and me when things went south down south.

We were definitely in that comfortable rut, that I remember. We'd already assumed the position of takeout for date night and whatever was on cable or Netflix as our entertainment. Part of me was thrilled with the arrangement, as I didn't have time to put a lot of extra energy into the trappings of a high-maintenance relationship.

But I also remember feeling sad sometimes that we didn't do anything exciting for each other. There were no flowers or cards or surprises just to thrill the other person.

The old married couple vibe and all.

"You know what," I say, a forgotten moment coming back into vivid focus, "I actually do remember a thing that happened that made things weird."

Butter perks up. She loves getting the good dirt. "What was it?"

I stare off into the distance as I sort through the events, and now it's Butter guiding me around the sidewalk.

"It was the stupidest thing, really," I begin. "It was one of our date nights, and we'd been sitting there watching a bunch of episodes of some show, a sitcom, I think, and I realized it had been a few weeks since we'd gotten down to business, you know?

"So, I brought up the dry spell, and I was joking around

and suggested we try some role-play. I said he could be Captain America and I'd be Peggy Carter and we could save the world all naked-like."

"I am so here for this," Butter says. "I don't know which of those two I lust more for."

"Right?" I say with a laugh. "And I know I was definitely kidding, *not kidding*, but it was supposed to, like, segue into actual lovemaking."

Butter's brow furrows. "Didn't it?"

I frown. "No, actually. He went on kind of a tangent saying he thought role-playing was stupid and he didn't see the point. That sex was fine as it was, and people who needed to dress up or whatever were weird."

"Well," Butter scoffs, "that's rude as fuck."

"I never really thought about it," I continue, "because I mostly started off joking, but honestly, I thought it sounded like fun. Even just talking about it was fine with me, but I felt really judged by him."

We make our way through another crosswalk and Butter says, "I would have, too! That was dickish of him."

I shrug as we step onto a new block. "He wasn't trying to be a prick. He was just being honest. But at the same time, it bothered me that his honest reaction was to be so harsh about things. It was like, if he didn't need something, it was lame. And sex was easy for him. It never took much to get him started, or long to get him finished, if I'm being frank, and so he never stopped to think that other people—like me—might want to do other things."

"That's half the fun, is all I'm saying."

I grin. "Agreed."

"Did you ever tell him he made you feel like shit? Because that was a rotten thing for him to say."

I shake my head. "No, I didn't see the point. I didn't want

to shame him for telling his truth." My eyes glaze over as I remember how awkward I felt at the time. "We didn't do anything that night, but the next time we tried, maybe a week later, I remember now...that was the first time sex was difficult.

"It just got worse after that. And I knew he was gearing up to ask me to move in with him, which made me feel kind of twitchy with things the way they were. Over the next two months, each time got more and more uncomfortable until finally, on our anniversary, it didn't work at all."

"Ugh," Butter groans. "That's terrible. That would have upset me, too."

There's so much about those few months with Ryan that I haven't let myself think about. I don't know if I was purposely avoiding them or meant to get to them eventually, but it's all rushing back now.

"When I came to him with the stuff Dr. Snow told me to do, like the couple parts of the therapy, he read over the pamphlets and said it looked like stuff I could mostly do myself. He just wasn't into it at all.

"Then, when I insisted that we were supposed to do it together, we made it a few minutes into one exercise and he was just...done. I know he was uncomfortable and embarrassed— I sure as shit know I was—but he was not into *any* of it. He just didn't get why he had to be involved, I guess."

"I'm trying really hard not to hate him here, Kat," Butter says darkly.

I smile at my feisty pal. "I know it sounds like it, but I swear he's not an ass. Not really. It's just hard for him to put himself in other people's positions. Honestly, I can't say I wouldn't have been just as weirded out if things had been reversed.

"But I think that's why it's so important for me to know for absolute certain that things down there are on the up and up before we try. I seriously don't want to put either of us through that kind of mortification again."

Butter looks incredibly annoyed on my behalf. "I'm sorry, but he should be there for you, broken special or not. And it's all well and good for him that his dick is functional, but it's not fair to put all that pressure on you."

Out of the corner of my eye, I see a very businessy-looking man do a double take when Butter snaps the word "dick" at top volume.

"It's me putting the pressure on myself," I assure her. "I don't think it would shock anyone to hear that my toughest critic and worst enemy is myself."

She considers this. "Well, I am here for you no matter what, and you do you, but I don't think you should have that much hanging on your shoulders."

I give her arm a tight, loving squeeze. "Well, right now, I want to think of nothing but Reubens and pickle spears." I look up, and we are standing right in front of The Deli News. "If we don't get this food back soon, Liz and Shannon are going to go all *The Walking Dead* on any customers that wander in."

I push open the door, and Butter sashays inside, saying, "Lord, I do love a good pickle spear."

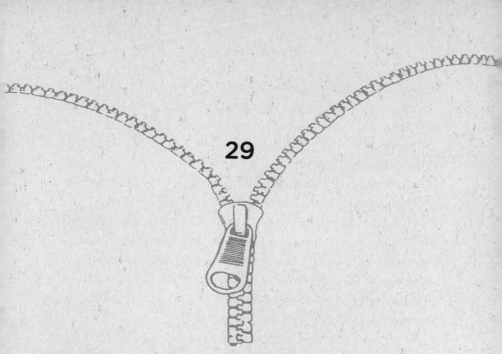

29

I've made no fewer than seven hundred different versions of ravens made out of varying materials. Fondant. Royal icing. Piped buttercream. Those last looked god-awful. Like vaguely bird-shaped poo on a cupcake. Not contract-winning in the slightest.

I did manage to etch out a stencil and created a pretty badass-looking bird in black glitter on top of gold-tinted white chocolate ganache. I might actually be onto something with that one. That went over a dark chocolate cake filled with cherry compote that Butter had spawned sometime past midnight last night. The whole thing is very sexy. It's definitely a contender.

Butter and Shannon have the recipes narrowed down to six different options, of which Shannon will present three to Mr. Peterson and the rest of the committee. I'm trying to perfect the art for each version to make our final picks. It's possible this could get down to the wire as far as actual decision-making goes.

Ben came in for coffee this morning, and even though he

looked fine, and his smiles seemed genuine and forgiving, I still felt a pinch of awkwardness. We were in the middle of the rush, and I didn't have a second to talk with him.

But right now, I'm pushing cupcakes and ravens and deadlines and awkwardness out of my mind. After a twenty-minute ride in Shannon's mommy-mobile, we're all standing in front of The Lenore Theater waiting for the doors to open.

The gals are pumped up. Everyone took turns throughout the day going home to get workout gear so we could all change before we left. It's been so long since I've seen any of them out of shop gear—it's a bit jarring, really. Except for Liz. I could see her in our standard T-shirt and jeans uniform or a wedding dress, apparently, and be fine.

Shannon is decked out in yoga pants and a drapey shirt, and she looks like she's in heaven. Any excuse to not wear real pants always has her bordering nirvana. Butter is rocking sweats and a tank, occasionally grumbling that she couldn't find any shorts to wear and that her legs did indeed get shaved for no reason.

Liz and I both landed in shorts. I'm in a baggy long-sleeved top, and she's in what looks like an elbow-length ballerina shirt. I don't think I've ever appreciated exactly how teeny Miss Liz is until just now. She's amazingly petite. I am struck by the sudden urge to put her in my pocket and take her on adventures.

There's a line forming behind us of other women, all clad for class. Everyone has an air of happy but relaxed excitement.

The door to the theater opens, and a woman in a freaking black lace corset and bright red hot pants stands there grinning at us. "Okay, ladies," she says. "Let's do this."

I don't know why, but the four of us take in a collective gulp.

We file in after Madam Hot Pants and head right into a

dance studio that's all mirrors and mood lighting. There are five other scantily clad dancers standing around the barre that circles the room, chatting away and smiling at those of us coming in.

"All right," Madam Hot Pants says, "drop your stuff off along the wall, everyone take off your shoes, and we'll get started." We do as we're told, and she takes a spot in the front of the room. "Everyone find a space on the floor and make sure to give yourself plenty of room." She stretches her arms out wide to demonstrate. The other instructors join her in a line, and we follow their lead, finding our own little zone on the shiny wood floor. "First off, I'm Robin Monroe, and I'll be leading this class. Second, this is a class for beginners, but it's not a class for quitters. This is a two-hour intensive. We're going to be hitting it hard tonight, ladies. I hope you all came prepared."

Everything Robin says sounds perfectly flirtatious. Like she's grabbing your ass with her words. Her instructions come out as more of a purr than as actual spoken sounds.

Music starts playing, echoing through the room, and Robin and her crew start leading us through stretches. Oh my damn, somehow these women make even stretching look sensual. I catch a glance of myself in the mirror. I appear to make stretching look painful. It's possible I'm slightly out of practice.

There's no time to be self-conscious or get caught up in a moment of regret. These ladies don't mess around. While Robin leads us through the warm-up, her companions walk through the group, assisting us with movements, helping us get the most out of our motions.

After about ten minutes, Robin stands up—quite lithely, considering her ensemble—and announces, "By the end of tonight's class, you'll be able to do not only basic burlesque moves but also a short choreographed dance set to music. And you're going to use muscles you didn't even know you had, ladies." When she says this, she flashes us all a very toothy smile that looks almost wolfish. I don't know whether to be terrified or turned on.

I think I'm both.

They get right into it. Within a few minutes they've got us all bending and twisting and gyrating in ways I wasn't entirely aware I was capable of. At first it takes me by surprise how quickly the class moves along, but after about half an hour, I am completely feeling it.

So are the others. Butter is in the zone. She may not even realize the rest of us are here. Shannon looks to be having a good time, but her perfectionist nature will occasionally stump her, and she insists on repeating the moves until she gets it right.

Little Liz, who I've secretly thought might be a dancer or something based on her attire and physique, is actually adorably uncoordinated. But it hasn't stopped her from trying one damn bit. She is laughing with every misstep and getting right back into it. She's got the air of awkwardness about her, but if she's feeling uncomfortable, I can't see it.

I'm having a blast. I'm sweating like it's my job, because, man, Miss Robin is making us earn our keep, but it's been ages since I've moved like this. Rolling around on the floor, kicking my legs around like they've got somewhere important to be in the air to be, arms writhing around my body in the very best kind of way. It's like taking all the most fun parts of sex and setting them to music, but without the annoyance of having to navigate the politics of dating.

Miss Robin takes a break at the one-hour mark and we, the students, all collapse by the back wall with water bottles and lungs desperate for full breaths. Maybe I should hit the gym now and then. That probably wouldn't hurt.

The Awkward Path to Getting Lucky

During our break, the staff gathers on the floor to show us one of the performances from the shows they do on the weekends. The Lenore Theater is a dance school all week, teaching various forms of dance to all ages, but on the weekends, they light the main stage up with this crew and every pair of fishnet tights in the Midwest.

Oh my god, can these women move. They wriggle and shimmy across the floor in front of us, and it's so impressive I don't even care that I look like an awestruck fish with my jaw on the floor.

And it's *hot*. Like, there's not one of those ladies I don't kind of want to make out with a little bit.

I wonder if I can get my leg all the way over my head like that? I can think of uses for that talent.

The class carries on, and they work us hard. They bring out old-timey wooden chairs and have us straddle them. This is where the first of our choreographed dance moves will start.

As we all get accustomed to our chairs, and the idea of sitting essentially spread-eagle on them in front of a giant mirror, one of the other instructors brings out a giant bin with wheels that is overflowing with sparkling tulle.

"To really bring this home," Robin says, slinking between our chairs, "you ladies need a little bit of flair." She sticks her hand into the bin, pulls out a tutu and hands it to the student closest to her. "These are props in the dance, but they also give your ass a little sass."

They walk around the room and give each of us a tutu. Shannon gets a bright pink one with sequins and gleefully pulls it on over her head. Butter receives turquoise and steps into it like her whole life has built up to this moment. Liz is handed a glittering fiery-red tutu, which I love. She smiles bashfully and tugs it on.

Robin hands me what appears to be black tulle and strips of

pliable tin foil. It's spectacular-looking. These all look hand-made and are very stretchy. I step into my tutu and, without meaning to, catch myself admiring the view in the mirror.

I'd be embarrassed, but all the other women are doing the same. We look awesome. What's not to look at?

Our moment of sparking whimsy passes as the nearly empty bin is wheeled away and Robin snaps her fingers. Asses to chairs, legs in the air.

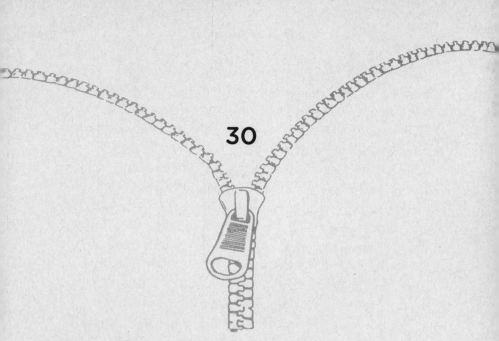

30

My arms feel like gummy worms. My legs are in a state best left unacknowledged.

I don't even care. Last night was the tits.

I'm still shimmying to "Lady Marmalade" in my head.

Plus, we got to keep the tutus. So that was cool.

"I think we should wear them here," Butter says, bagging up some brownies for a customer. "We could make it a thing. Like Tutu Tuesdays or something."

I consider the notion. "I support this."

Shannon hands a coffee across the counter to a customer and winces slightly. There's not a one of us not feeling the burn today. "Thanks for visiting," she says before turning to us. "That would be fun. Tutu Tuesdays. We could have a special cuppie to go with it."

"I just want to wear mine again," Butter says and grins. "I looked good in that thing."

The corner of my mouth pulls up as I pour more grounds in the coffee maker. "Yeah, you did. And I'm not gonna lie, guys. I'm looking forward to breaking mine out, too. As well as any or all of the moves from last night. Or, possibly, should the situation arise, the moves *with* the tutu."

"Good morning, Ben," Shannon says, her voice breaking with laughter. I wheel around, my sore muscles making me regret it instantaneously.

"Naturally," I say, shaking my head. Shannon moves down to help another customer, still laughing. Liz stands beside me at the register, giggling. We are at the end of our morning rush, so this isn't nearly as horrific as it could have been. His presence is familiar, but there's a vibe out of place and it takes me a minute to figure out what it is. "Hey! It's Saturday. You never come in here on Saturdays, and even worse, it's Saturday and you're wearing a *tie*! What fresh hell is this?"

"I'm covering for one of the other managers today." He gives a playful tug of resignation on his tie. "Her daughter's in this statewide debate death match or something."

I click my tongue. "Kids today with their academic blood sports."

"So, tutus, huh?" he says, smiling. "That sounds pretty cool."

"Good morning, Ben." I give him a wink and get back to loading the coffee maker.

"Morning. And to you, ladies," he says.

Butter carefully bounces over to the counter. "Hey, Ben. Do you have any friends?"

I turn around and gape at her. "Butter!"

She shrugs at me. "I mean *single* ones!" Turning back to Ben, she says, "So, do you? Maybe ones that you could set up with me?"

Ben smiles and pulls lightly on his tie. "I can probably think of a few."

Shannon comes back over and sighs at her. "Butter, what—"

"Hey," Butter interrupts and hisses at her. "Look, you. I

232

don't know about you guys, but that class got some things riled up, and I had to go home alone last night, okay? You got to go home to your husband." She turns and points at Liz. "And you have Paul." Then she pokes me in the ribs. "And now you've got that one. So, excuse me, but I've got some needs that have to be met, here." She spins back to Ben and a giant smile appears on her face. "If you can think of any lovely ladies or gentlemen to send my way, I'd appreciate it."

She grabs an empty cookie tray and sashays back into the kitchen. We can do nothing but stare after her.

Eventually, I say, "That was…surreal."

Ben leans across the counter and, with a genuinely worried look, whispers, "What kind of class did she take?"

Liz snort-laughs at the register, and Shannon claps her hand over her mouth.

I grin. "We took a burlesque class last night. You know, as people do."

He blinks at me. "You…you all took a burlesque class? And now you have…tutus?"

One corner of my mouth curls up. "Pretty typical Friday night, I thought."

He steps back and stares at me for a moment. "I honestly can't tell if you're being serious or if you're just trying to see if I'll squirm." Shaking his head, he continues. "Either way, I thought I'd see if you wanted to grab dinner tonight. I know it's a crazy week, so no pressure."

"I am being very serious, and seeing you squirm is just a happy side effect." I give him a little wink. "And sure. I feel like it's been an age since I saw you in a non-mortifying capacity. Dinner sounds nice."

He grins and pushes his thumb between his eyebrows. "Sounds good. Should I come get you after work? If so, can

I be certain there won't be any riots in the lobby? And will you be conscious?"

I reach behind me and pour his regular morning coffee. "Sure on the picking me up," I say, putting the to-go lid on. "I'm almost certain on the consciousness. No promises on the riots. And since I won't have time to change into the tutu before dinner, there's no charge on the coffee."

I hand him the coffee, and he looks suspicious.

Shannon steps in. "Yes, there really is a tutu, and she looks magnificent in it."

I give Shannon the side-eye while Liz giggles hysterically. Ben lets out a slow, deep breath, shakes his head and says, "I'll see you at six." As he's leaving, I'm sure I hear him mutter, "I've got to find a new place for coffee."

Our day trucks on, and all of us seem to have a renewed jaunty feel. Admittedly, Shannon and Liz both appear to have extra jaunt. I'm guessing Butter's theory rings true. She and I had to go home with our post-writhing tension and greet empty beds. The others had outlets for that energy, and they both seem pretty damn chipper about it.

I feel a rejuvenated sense of internal roar that's making me want to throw on something sassy and go dancing, or at the very least invest in a really good push-up bra.

At the same time, there's a buildup of tension that's wearing a bit heavy on me. Last night I had dreams of corsets and sequins and sweatiness. They were some pretty spectacular dreams.

Then they ended, and now I'm awake and alone and elbow-deep in frosting, with aching thigh muscles that hurt like a bastard when I have to squat down and restock the display case. Miss Robin wasn't freaking kidding about using parts we didn't know we had.

At six, I hang up my apron, wave goodbye to my gals, and

head out front to see Ben waiting on the sidewalk by his car, looking very ready to weekend.

"Long week?" I ask as I come through the door.

He smiles at me. "In a few short hours, this tie will be gone and life will be glorious until Monday."

"You could take it off now, you know," I suggest. "I wouldn't report you or anything."

He looks at me as though the thought had genuinely never occurred to him. "See, now I'm wondering what else in my life I'm doing wrong."

Giving him a kind smile, I reach up and loosen his tie. "It's okay," I say, pulling it through his collar. "This whole adult thing is rough. We can't be expected to be on point all the time."

He looks at me and swallows hard. I carefully unbutton the top button of his shirt, working hard not to accidentally choke him. "And it's pretty hot, so if you wanted to take your jacket off, that would be fine," I offer. "I mean, you're off the clock now. This is the wild time."

He nods slightly, so I go ahead and slide his jacket off his shoulders and down his arms.

I drape his jacket and tie over my arm and am standing as close to him as possible without backing him into his car. "And," I continue, "if you wanted to really cut loose, you could even untuck your shirt, Mr. Cleary. Go full rebel."

He clears his throat and jumps out of the way quickly. "No," he says, his hand going to his stomach, where there is no longer a tie to grab. "No, I think we're good where we are. I'm fine."

I grin and open the car door. I carefully set his clothing on the back seat before I climb in the passenger side. It takes him a minute to get into his seat.

We drive in silence for a bit, and I'm a little concerned I

went too far. Maybe on the heels of the morning tutu squirm, he wasn't in the mood.

"Can I ask you something?" he says as he drives.

"Sure."

"Just now, were you teasing me, or flirting with me?"

My head snaps up. "Um. I guess both. Was that not okay?"

"It's fine," he says, although his tone has me thinking maybe that's not entirely true. Guilt settles into my stomach. "No, what's got me confused is how you can be so impossibly confident in every part of your life—including flirting—but so unconfident with sex. I don't get it."

"Whoa!" I turn in my seat so my body is facing him. "For starters, I'm not impossibly confident with every part of my life, but I am *also* certainly not unconfident with sex!"

We are at a stoplight, so he's able to turn and give me a disbelieving look. "Kat."

Bristling, I snap, "Excuse me, I am very confident with sex!" I pull in a breath to form my argument, but all my potential sexual encounters with Ben start flashing through my head. I make a face. "Well, I used to be."

"I didn't mean that as an attack," he says, navigating us through the city. "I know it sounded like one. I'm sorry. But I'm really confused. When you say something to me, I take you at your word—I trust what you're telling me. But you come on very strong like that, and then another minute you're anxious and talking about how important the rules are to you, and I don't understand. I'm trying really hard to keep up."

I wish we weren't driving. I want him to stop so we can look at each other. "Ben, I know I'm…" I pause, trying to find any kind of acceptable word here "…difficult. But I haven't been playing you or something. I swear, I'm not screwing with you on purpose."

"I get that I'm easy to mess with," he says, eyes on the road. "And that's fine, but it gets confusing."

"Ben, pull over," I interrupt. "Please, pull over."

His chest rises, and the muscle in his impressive jaw is working harder than I'd like, but he does as I asked and finds a place to park. I undo my seat belt and pull myself up onto my knees on the seat. He's got his hands resting on his legs, looking down at the steering wheel. I reach out and take his wrist in my hand.

"I'm sorry," I say. "Really, I am sorry. I am sardonic and dry, and I don't always think about how what I'm saying is coming off to other people, and I rarely see how it makes me a jerk."

He breaks his statue pose and says, "You're not a jerk."

"No, I absolutely can be. And I don't mean to be a dick to you. And I will fully admit that I sometimes get caught up in the whole making you squirm thing, because it's supposed to be funny and I don't think about how it's probably not that hilarious to you.

"But, also—" I pull my hand away from his and slide back into my seat, because I'm suddenly feeling very exposed "—I feel like, if we were just…us, you know, without all the rest of the weird stuff happening, these are the things I'd be doing, and it would be okay because there wouldn't *be* the weirdness. I'm sort of out of my depth here."

He leans his head back against his seat, and he slumps down a little. He lifts his hands up and drops them down on the bottom of the steering wheel. He's deep in thought, and I want to know what those thoughts are—desperately—but I don't want to interrupt him.

He's staring at something out of focus, outside the windshield. I stare in the same direction, not finding anything worth that level of attention.

Finally he turns his head to me and says, "This is hard."

I can't deny there's an uncomfortable pang in my chest at his words. "Yeah, it is," I agree. "A lot harder than it should be. And it's okay if you want to walk away. I really would understand."

His head is still tilted against his seat. He looks tired. The corner of his mouth pulls up just enough to ease my discomfort. "And miss out on the tutu? No way. I'm invested."

I laugh, though more out of relief than amusement. It's hard for me, the idea of him reaching his limit. "I'm glad." I reach over and touch his arm, because I want to do something and can't think of anything else I can do that doesn't violate all my own damn rules. "And I am sorry I upset you, Ben. I promise I'll keep the squirming in check. 'Don't be a jerk' is high on my to-do list, okay? You have my word."

He lifts one shoulder and lets it drop. "I don't know. Not all the squirming is so bad."

I consider this. "Can I ask you a question?"

"Of course."

Leaning forward in my seat, I lift an eyebrow at him. "Okay, if you're so awkward all the time, how in the hell are *you* so confident about sex stuff? I mean, the glitter on the neck thing. Dude." I remember the assured way he held me, and how his teeth…

I shudder in a perfectly delightful way.

He looks at me and grins. "We all have our skills."

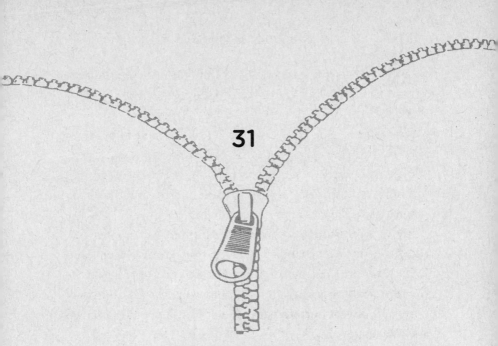

31

Sorting through different shades of glitter pots, I wonder how I became a woman who has an entire drawer of sex toys in her bedroom but can't get laid. How is this my life?

The Coopertown presentation is in two days. The morning show is tomorrow morning. Seven days until my two years of sexless living deadline hits, better known as our anniversary.

I also have no clean socks.

My to-do list is getting out of hand.

Struck by a sudden urge, I pull out my phone and fire off a text to Ben, asking if he'd like to have dinner tonight.

"What are you doing?" Shannon asks, reading over my shoulder.

I gently elbow her in the ribs. "Stop snooping, Maude. In two days, our cupcake gauntlet will be over, and I'm down to a week to get my special in gear, okay? I'm multitasking."

"Oh, no, you don't!" Shannon says, grabbing for my phone. I quickly tuck it into the front pocket of my jeans and stick my tongue out at her. "You have to be up at like four tomorrow to be at the studio, Little Miss. This is not the night for you two to get ten bottles of wine deep in therapy, okay?"

"Rude."

"I'm serious!" She frowns at me. "For the next forty-eight hours, we are all cupcakes, got it? No distractions."

I raise an eyebrow. "The dictator look isn't very becoming, you know. And this isn't about therapy. I just wanted to hang out with him, have dinner or something."

"Aww," says Butter, resuming her piping. "That's sweet."

Rolling my eyes, I head over to the cooling racks and start pulling off the trays of cupcakes I've got resting for the show tomorrow morning. "Chill, Shannon. We are all hyper-focused. We sweat buttercream. We cry little cupcake-shaped tears. We've got this."

"We'd better," she grumbles as she sits at the desk and starts shuffling through invoices.

It's nearing the end of the day, and while we will soon start our nightly teardown, right now my main focus is making sure all my gear is prepped for tomorrow morning. I'll be stopping by before the sun rises to pack everything up for my television debut on Channel 7. I've got little tubs full of sprinkles and decorations all ready to go, prefilled bags of frosting dyed and measured and carefully packed up. Now I will put all of the cooled bare cuppies in boxes, and that should be everything I need to go.

Shannon is going to meet me here at five so I can borrow her van to drive to the studio. Taking all the gear in a cab or on a bus didn't seem like a good idea to anyone.

Maybe that's why she's so grumpy. Shannon isn't much of a morning person.

My phone buzzes in my pocket, and I check it stealthily so as to not draw any further ire from my neurotic friend. A new text from Ben says he's in for dinner tonight, and I feel the edge of my mouth twitch up.

Shannon's right. Tonight is definitely not the night to try anything therapy-related with Ben, but that's not why I sent him the text.

I've done all the prep I can for tomorrow. And every other waking moment of my life here is spent getting ready to send Shannon off to the Coopertown presentation in two days. Sure, a lot of time with Ben is spent freaking out about how we are going to get a thing into another thing, but the rest of the time—the time when we are just us—it's kind of wonderful.

And I need that tonight. I need a break from cupcake madness and the reality that my professional life is hanging in the balance over the next few days.

Plus, I'm still feeling really shitty for the way I acted the other night, and I want to prove to Ben that I can go for extended periods of time without being a monster.

I'm sure I can.

The rest of our day passes, the shop closes and we are all finishing our end-of-day tasks when a shiny blue van pulls up in front of the sidewalk outside.

"Not it," Shannon, Butter and I call in unison. Liz frowns and pouts.

"That's not fair," she says, making her way around the counter.

"Sorry, kiddo," I say as I stuff the mop back into the little broom closet in the front room. "Standard calling rules apply. Therefore, we don't have to tell whoever that is that we're closed, and no, they can't have any damn cupcakes because we locked the doors thirty-seven damn minutes ago."

"What if they yell?"

"Then Kat will punch them in the ear," Butter says as she wipes down the inside of the display case.

I nod. "That seems like something I would do."

"Um, that's not a customer," Liz says, pointing out the window.

We all look up. She's right. By the blue van stands Joe in all his beefy, tattooed beardedness, somehow managing to look like a happy little kid.

Shannon slowly closes the cash register she'd been tallying and heads toward the door. Butter and I shrug together and follow.

Outside, blinking against the evening sun and Joe's megawatt smile, we gather behind Shannon in confusion.

"Surprise!" he says, throwing his arms wide.

We all stare at him. Shannon cocks her head and says, "I like this new festive way we're greeting each other."

For a moment, his joyful stance wavers, and he looks confused. "No, not me. The van," he explains. "Surprise!"

"You've decided to go part-time creeper with a windowless van, and you've come to kidnap us first?" I suggest.

Huffing, Joe finally drops his arms. "Damn it, guys," he says. "Stop killing my moment. No, this van is for you, for the shop!"

Shannon looks at me and narrows her eyes before turning back to her husband. "Wait, what?"

"You know, if you just found it lying around somewhere," I say, "that's actually probably stealing. If I hear sirens, I'm rolling over on ya, big fella."

Joe gives me a hard eye roll. "No, I bought the van for the shop. We've been talking about it for at least a year, and with the contract you guys are going to get, I figured this is the right time, and I got a great deal on it, so, surprise!"

"What!" Shannon's voice has gone ultrasonic. Hand to heart, somewhere in the neighborhood, I hear a dog howl.

Joe's eyes go wide. "I... I bought you a van? You're welcome?"

Butter, Liz and I shrink back against the window of the shop, away from any potential violence that may erupt from Shannon.

"You *financed* a van?" Shannon says, her voice full of acid and daggers. "You bought and financed an expensive vehicle without talking to me about it?"

Joe's eyes go wide, and his giant frame seems to shrink a good six inches right in front of us. "We've talked about this," he replies. "For months! You've been saying how you need a delivery van for the shop, and we've talked about pricing and how you thought you'd do it for sure with the contract! And I found this one, and it was a really good deal, so I jumped on it. You've been so stressed out about the presentation, I thought this would cheer you up."

"We don't have the contract yet!" Shannon bellows, echoing down the street. "And exactly how are we supposed to pay for this thing if we don't get it? You're in banking! You're a goddamn banker, Joe! How could you be this stupid?"

"I thought you'd be happy!" he half yelps. "You've been so mad at me since the Barry thing. I was trying to make it up to you!"

"So because you tried to set my best friend up with a greasy pimp to fix her broken junk, you decide to put our family into debt to make it up to me? Are you serious?"

"Hey," I scoff, "leave me and my broken junk out of this."

Butter clears her throat and offers up, "We really have been talking about getting a delivery van. And, Shannon, a few weeks ago you said we could afford it even without the contract."

Shannon whips around, and her hair looks like a tangled mess of blond snakes and rage. "I will end you, I swear to god."

Looking appropriately terrified, Butter turns to Joe. "You're on your own, man."

Joe starts spluttering out an explanation, and Shannon retaliates with a deluge of shouting and well-versed profanity as a familiar sedan pulls up behind the sky blue van of discontent. Ben gets out of the driver's seat and eyes the situation carefully without actually moving away from his car. He looks to me for guidance. I give him an awkward shrug.

"You go," Butter whispers to me. "I'll finish up inside."

Talking from the side of my mouth, I say, "It feels weird leaving while they're still fighting."

Liz taps my shoulder. "Do we go back inside? I feel like we're intruding."

"Something about their decibel level tells me they aren't super concerned about privacy," I suggest. I turn back to Butter. "You sure you don't mind me cutting out now? If they go all nuclear on each other, I can come right back."

"Pssh." Butter snorts. "I can handle Shannon." Then she glances at our slightly deranged-looking friend still berating her giant husband, and her expression turns a bit unsure. "Okay, maybe don't go too far, though."

"Deal." I give poor Ben—who is still standing practically in traffic—an encouraging look as I step back inside the door to grab my bag off the squashy chair near the entrance. Edging away from the shop window, I tiptoe toward Shannon. "Hon?"

She whips around mid-swear and looks at me with eyes that appear to be vibrating. "What?"

"I'm gonna go, if you're okay here."

She waves her hand through the air casually. "Yeah, I've got this. See you tomorrow."

I give Joe a sympathetic look. "Try not to actually murder him," I suggest. "You'd probably regret it in the morning. And we really do need a delivery van. Just remember you did the numbers, and this is a legitimate expense. I'm sure we'll figure it all out."

Her eyes narrow into bitter slits at me, and I can tell she is in no mood for rational speak at the moment.

I give her a quick pat on the shoulder and scurry away in the direction of Ben's car.

"And you," Shannon shouts. I turn back, and she's pointing at Ben, who has frozen in place. "You two are not having sex tonight, am I clear?"

Ben's mouth falls wordlessly open, and I gasp, "Shannon! What the hell?"

"You think I'm kidding?" she barks at us. "I will see you tomorrow morning, where you will drive—*not* this goddamn van—to the TV studio, and you will be well-rested and ready to kick ass on that show, because you weren't up all night with Mr. Cleary here playing Poke the Special."

"Now, wait just a damn—" I say, stepping back onto the sidewalk. Out of the corner of my eye, I see Joe subtly shaking his head. Behind them, Butter is feverishly waving her arms.

"Girl, run," she hisses. "Just run."

I look at Shannon, her hair twisting into madness in the evening breeze, the bags under her eyes more defined than I'd realized before. Her hands are clenched into death grips at her sides, and she's giving off the exact air of I-can-kill-you-with-my-thoughts. She looks stressed. She looks exhausted. She looks like the next person to cross her is going home in a pastry bag.

I take a long, slow breath, swallowing back the sassy retort and anger at her comment. "Roger that, Boss," I say through my teeth. I turn, yank open the passenger door of Ben's car and find him staring at me, jaw still gaping. "Dude, get in the car and drive like the fucking wind."

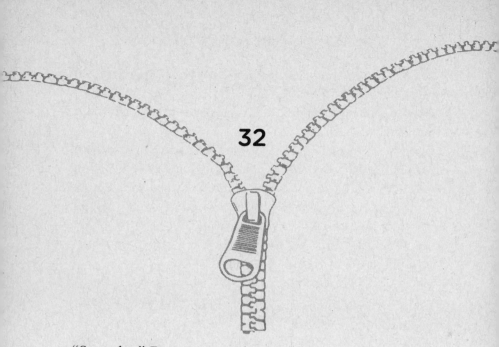

32

"Someday," Ben says over dinner, "I'm going to visit you at the shop, and nothing weird is going to happen. I'll just walk in there, say hi to everyone, and that will be it. No sex toys will fly out of anywhere, no asteroids will fall through the ceiling, no brawls will erupt, nothing."

"It's good that you have these goals," I say.

"What do you think the odds are of that actually happening?"

I consider the chances. "What's important is *you* think it could happen."

He laughs and leans back in his chair. "Be honest with me," he requests. "Is your life always like this?"

"You mean full of excitement and whimsy and colorful characters?" I grin. The waitress comes by with the check, and I hand over my debit card. The subtle wince that crosses Ben's face does not go unnoticed. "Yes. And occasionally exquisitely choreographed dance numbers." He keeps looking at me expectantly, so I answer, "Okay, no. Life isn't generally this animated. This is kind of our Gauntlet o' Stress right now, so I'll admit things are a little high-strung. Lucky you, right?"

He laughs again. "Indeed. It's certainly kept me on my toes the last few weeks."

"You're a trouper. On the plus side, just a couple of days left, and then the Gauntlet will be over. Hopefully we'll be rolling in the new contract, and therapy will be a distant memory for you and me that we will awkwardly refuse to ever talk about."

"It's good that you have these goals," he says with a wink.

My eyebrows rise. "Look at you, all sassy. I'm impressed."

Smiling kindly, he says, "I think you're going to do great tomorrow. And you've all worked so hard that when Shannon goes in for the presentation, she's going to blow it out of the water. And if for some reason they go with another shop, do you want me to hack into their business network and ruin their lives?" Ben asks. "Because I'd do that for you."

I narrow my eyes and grin. "Can you do that?"

He looks up at the ceiling without moving his head. The waitress returns and sets my card and the receipt down on the table. "Probably not. But I'd give it a shot. I'm a good friend like that."

Laughing, I say, "That really is the sign of a pretty good friend."

With one eyebrow raised, he quips, "So you *did* notice?"

"That you're a pretty good friend?" He sits back in his chair and smiles again. "I picked up on it. For example, I saw how it seemed to cause you actual physical pain to let me pay for dinner, and yet you stepped down gracefully."

Groaning, he drops his head. "My grandmother would murder me. I hope you know that. When I see her at Christmas, she's going to smell this on me, and I'll never live it down."

"But I asked you to dinner, so…"

"Nana wouldn't care. These are her facts."

I grin. "Nana. You're really cute." He fidgets with his tie and looks across the restaurant. "That wasn't meant to make you squirm. It was a genuine compliment."

"Well, thank you." Checking his watch, he says, "Should we get you back? Don't you have to get up at dawn?"

I sigh. "Predawn, actually. I have to meet Shannon at the shop at five and then head to the TV station. This week is kicking my ass."

We stand up and make our way out of the restaurant. "And yet you made time for dinner with me," he says. "I'm flattered."

"Well, I still felt bad about being a big jerk to you, and I was feeling very in the mood to see your face tonight."

We hit the sidewalk and head in the direction of his car. We took our sweet time deciding on an actual dinner spot, and then everywhere we tried had tragically long wait times. Thanks to the lovely weather, we decided to walk until we found something we were in the mood for. I'm not sure how far we went, but I know we've got blocks to go.

"I like the sound of that," he says, giving my arm a little poke. "Although please understand that I will have to follow Shannon's orders of no sex tonight, so no funny business."

I snort. "You're afraid of her, aren't you?"

"Yep, and I'm not even ashamed to admit it. Joe looked like he was going to cry, and have you noticed how frickin' huge he is? I wouldn't want to piss Shannon off."

"I think he'll survive, as will you." We walk in silence, enjoying the warm air and light crowds, and I steer my mind away from the chaos of the day. "Can I ask you something?" I say after a few moments.

"Shoot."

"Whatever happened to your ex? Do you guys still talk?"

He shrugs. "Not really. I get a Christmas card from her

folks every year. We're friends on Facebook. But we haven't spoken in a really long time. I did run into her at a gas station back home a few years ago when I was visiting. We are very casually friends, I suppose."

"Where did she land? Did she travel? Become a full-time water purification salesperson?"

He laughs. "No, she went the way we were headed, actually. She got remarried, lives back in our hometown, has three or four kids, I think. She's doing really well. Seems to be very happy."

We walk a few more steps before I ask, "So, does that mean you realized you didn't want those things?"

"No, I still want those things," he says, slowing his pace and putting his hands in his pockets. "I want to get married. I want kids sometime down the road. I just didn't want everything right then. And she wasn't the right person."

"You're awfully Zen about this stuff," I offer. "I'm not sure I could handle that much adulting so smoothly."

"What about you? What's with you and your sort-of-boyfriend?"

I shrug and stare at my feet, watching my flour-dusted sneakers slowly stride along the concrete. "I'm not sure, actually. On paper, we really work."

"On paper?"

I gently push a stick off the sidewalk with my foot without breaking stride. "I mean, he's a good guy. We get along well. We laugh at each other's jokes. We've had this sort of loosely structured plot of getting an apartment in the city, probably getting married someday, doing whatever it is grown-ups do. We've been doing all the right things, I guess. So objectively, it all makes sense. On paper, it's all a solid plan."

"On paper," Ben repeats. "How romantic."

I nudge him with my elbow. "Hey, now. Some of us don't

lead with our hearts, okay? And it's been brought to my attention recently that maybe that's not the most fulfilling way to live, so I'm looking into it."

He pokes me back. "Fair enough."

"Sometimes," I continue, not sure why I'm still speaking, but feeling the need to get the words out, "I wonder if we even really like each other in that relationship way anymore. Which is sad, because we're great as friends. A little listless as a couple, I guess, but great as friends. I think he trusts me and my type A personality to take the reins, but I've been kind of a coward about all of it. When the lady bits drama started, it just made it all a thousand times worse. And I went fulltilt chicken and decided to ignore all my personal life troubles until it all came screaming into focus, and I couldn't do it anymore.

"And we all know how ignoring stuff went for me, so." He's listening intently, and I realize I've just laid a lot out over the last few blocks. Feeling vulnerably exposed, I shift my tone as fast I can without giving myself emotional whiplash. "Basically, what I'm saying is I make super good life choices. In case you weren't getting that."

"It's okay if you don't always get it right," he says.

"Based on the vast evidence that is my life, I'd wager I'm the reigning queen of that," I say with a grin. Desperate for a reprieve, I announce, "Subject change! Do you like dancing?"

The corners of his mouth pull up a bit, but he's eyeing me suspiciously. "As in, do I like watching it or doing it?"

"Doing it. Meaning, do you like to go dancing?"

He chuckles. "No, not particularly."

"Really?" I'm surprised, I'll admit. "I kind of would have had you pegged as a guy who would go dancing. Huh."

"Oh, see, that's not what you asked, though." He's still got his hands in his pockets and one side of his mouth pulled up in a grin, and I'm finding him far more adorable than is probably appropriate.

"So we've moved on to riddles," I say, lifting an eyebrow at him. "Okay. So you don't like dancing. But...?" I point a finger at his chest. "But you'd go if someone asked you to?"

"Probably, yes."

"Why? Why would you go if you don't like it?"

He shrugs. "It depends. If you asked me to go, say, swing dancing or line dancing or something all intense and structured? I'm afraid I'd have to pass. But if you just wanted to go dancing somewhere because it's something you wanted to do and it would make you happy? That I would do."

"But if you don't like it..."

"I don't *not* like it," he clarifies. "I just tend to be a little more introverted, I suppose."

"You? The perpetually uncomfortable man who spends his free time in computer geek heaven? Introverted? The actual hell, you say."

He stops mid-step, clicks his tongue and smirks at me. "Really?"

I close my eyes and shrink down a little. "Sorry. Jerk. See? I don't even know when I'm doing it. Defense mechanism?"

He rolls his eyes, chuckles at me and keeps walking. "And who knows, maybe I'd like it. I like trying new things. I used to hate asparagus, now I love it. You never know."

I consider this for a few steps. "I'm so tempted to ask you to go dancing now, but I wouldn't want you to think I was just trying to make you squirm. I'd be curious to see if you had fun."

"But wouldn't that be an actual date?"

We reach the block where his car is parked, and our pace slows to near glacial. "Yeah, I suppose it would be." A mental mosquito scolds me for feeling disappointed.

When we get to the sidewalk in front of his car, he turns to face me. "It'd be fine with me. In fact, I'd be very happy with that. But I don't want to step on your rules."

I sigh. "I know they're my rules, and I made them up and everything, but sometimes I kind of hate them."

He gives me a soft smile. "I understand. And since we're being so honest, I *would* go dancing with you. I'd be willing to try a lot of new things with you."

My face burns around the edges, and I know I'm stepping out of bounds here. I also know I need to go home. I have a million things to do before I have to get up in a few short hours and shine on the small screen, followed immediately by helping Shannon get ready for the biggest presentation of our professional lives. And I know tonight is absolutely not a night to attempt any sort of therapy with Ben.

But I'm not ready to just pack up and go home. I don't want to see him drive away yet.

"I can take you home," he offers, possibly reading my mind. "At the very least, my car probably smells better than the buses. It does, right?"

I giggle. "Yes. You and your car are both far superior to the buses."

"That's a relief," he says, opening the passenger door. "I mean, you always hope, but you never know."

He stands by the passenger side of his car, and his smile turns a bit awkward as he waits for me to do…anything. He rolls back onto his heels. "So."

"I think we should try again tonight," I blurt out, to our very mutual surprise.

He slowly tilts back onto his heels, swaying slightly. "I'm sorry, what?"

Standing up straight, and feeling a semi-manic grin pull

across my face, I say, "Yes, definitely. We should totally try the therapy tonight. I've got a good feeling about it."

Stunned, but also amused, he argues, "You have to get up before God. Plus, Shannon would kill us both. And I'm pretty sure that's literal."

"What Shannon doesn't know can't hurt us," I offer with an exaggerated wink. Standing in front of his car, I throw my arms up like one of those models on a game show, doing my best to convince the contestant that a lifetime supply of shaving cream is a great prize. "Come on, fella. Are you up for it?"

He tilts his head, looking at me with what I hope is still a twinge of amusement mixed with deep concentration. The spokesmodel pose is making my arms ache.

"Are you absolutely sure you want to do this tonight?" He sighs, grabbing at his tie. "Tomorrow's a big day for you."

I drop my arms and bounce in place a little. "And I can think of no better way to preface it than by going for gold tonight."

He shakes his head ever so slightly, giving his tie a solid yank. "Okay, but if Shannon finds out, I'm fleeing the planet."

"Fair enough," I say, gleefully climbing into the car. Watching him walk around, I'm all but vibrating in my seat.

This is it. I just know it is.

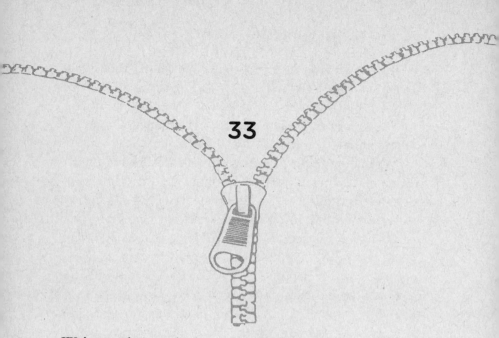

33

We've made it to the key position. After weeks of false starts, we've successfully gotten naked for science.

What an odd set of circumstances that's led to me lying beneath Ben, out on one hell of a limb, in a room illuminated only by stripes of moonlight peeking in through my bedroom blinds.

I'm fueled by near-militant determination, and if I'm being honest, a hefty dose of bravado. While it's a questionable recipe, weeks of obsession and focus and stubbornness have pooled into a level of confidence I've lacked until tonight. There's been no wine, no nethers-targeting anxiety meds, no panic attacks at buttons undone.

I'm ready, and I'm thrilled.

Ben's face is visible amongst the shadows, and he's a picture of quiet concentration. I'm struck by an urge to hug him and thank him for being so amazing with all of this, for the sheer presence of him, but somehow that seems like it would break the moment.

The last few times I attempted this with Ryan, there was

an established feeling of fear that if things didn't work out, there'd be an unspoken sense of awkward failure. Maybe that was all me, but it was there, and I was so very aware of it.

But with Ben, after all the hideous shenanigans we've survived on the quest to get to this moment, I know that no matter what happens, or how it ends, he will be here with me, fully invested in not making me feel like an ass.

Shannon was really onto something with that whole "comfort and trust" sales pitch.

I'm mentally jolted by a surge of affection toward Ben for giving me that security. For being here for me in ways I didn't know I desperately needed someone to be.

He shifts his weight above me, and I know the moment of truth is now.

The bravado and determination trapdoor out from under me, and I'm quite suddenly thrown off course.

The moment I've been desperately counting down to for weeks has arrived, and I'm stuck wondering if I've ever really thought any of this through. I'm seconds from doing something with Ben that I haven't done with Ryan, or anyone at all, in a very long time.

Am I ready to take this step with someone that isn't him?

Am I prepared to fail? Again?

Am I even sort of ready for the potential impending physical pain?

In this moment, lying beneath Ben, clinging to that limb, I realize, I am, in fact, *not*.

And I'm terrified.

The realization catches me so off guard, I lose my breath. Ben senses the shift and freezes. "Are you okay? What happened?"

I look up at him and smile, resisting the urge to quip the fear away, even as amazingly unwelcome tears pool in my eyes. A sense of fight-or-flight kicks in, which is particularly troublesome when you're quite literally lying naked under someone else who is equally unclothed.

"I'm scared," I answer honestly.

"We'll stop, Kat," he says immediately, pulling away. "There's nothing—"

I put both hands on his face and keep him in place. "No, it's okay. I want to keep going. I'm ready. I am very, very ready," I say with a small laugh. "But I'm still scared."

The way he stares down at me, so sincerely, sends a wave of calm through my entire body. "For any reason, if you want to stop, we stop. Okay?" I nod. "I'll be careful, Kat, I promise."

I fight a nearly irresistible urge to tilt my head up and kiss him. Keeping romantic trappings out of sleeping with someone is trickier than I'd anticipated. A decade of riding that bike has conditioned my body to assume a smooching position.

"I believe you."

I know I'm ready. And not just because I'm hell-bent on being so. I've done the therapy. I know that even with the occasionally touch-and-go success of said therapy, I'm physically capable.

Most important, I know Ben is right here with me, and I trust him.

I give him the most confident smile I can muster, nod, and we're off.

I'm trying very hard not to focus on the specifics of what's happening, but my mind is racing. There's been a lot of buildup to this moment, and it's hard to ignore what's riding on it all. Butter's right; I'm doing sex wrong.

Ben moves very, very slowly. For a moment, I'm not even sure what's happening, he's moving with such care. I wonder if maybe I'm so cured that perhaps I'm overly so...

Then I get my answer.

"Stop, stop," I whisper. Ben carefully retreats.

"Are you okay?" he asks quietly.

I shake my head and run my hands through my hair. "It's... not working."

"Do you want to stop?" he asks. He's so calm, and there's no pretense to his question, no personal agenda. My last few bouts with Ryan ended with me either going on with it rather than admit defeat—which did nothing but cause some genuine pain that I didn't need to suffer through—or losing my patience and pushing Ryan away, ignoring the situation entirely.

Shaking my head again, I close my eyes and say, "Just give me a minute."

He leans down and places his head near my shoulder, leaving me in silence. As much as one can in a coital entanglement, I suppose.

I know I can do this, damn it. Sometimes therapy works better than other times, depending on how focused or stressed out I am. I'm not going to rush this. I'm not going to panic and throw a laundry list of rules at the situation.

I'm going to get a grip, and I'm going to try again.

Eyes still closed, I take a deep breath that reaches all the way down to my toes and let it out slowly. Then I take another. And another. By the third breath, Ben is breathing in time with me. I'm not sure if he even realizes he's doing it. Over and over, we pull in slow, comforting, soothing breaths in tandem, then release.

My hands, which until this moment have been resting on Ben's arms, slide carefully up to his shoulders and then down his back.

The sensation is almost alarming, being so aware of the way his skin feels against mine. His weight perched over me. It's been so long since I've been anywhere near this scenario, and I'd definitely forgotten what an inebriating treat it is.

Eyes still shut tight, I tilt my head until my face is resting against his shoulder, and we take in another breath. He smells of something wonderful. Soap, or cologne, or perhaps just essence of Ben. Whatever it is, I breathe it into every inch of my lungs.

I think of the pamphlets and advice I've been given time and time again. Deep breaths, scented candles, taking things slowly. For the first time, if perhaps by accident, I find myself taking all those pointers at their word.

Although in lieu of a Satsuma Dawn candle, I'm gluttoning myself on whatever it is that causes this Benly scent.

He turns his head slightly so our cheeks are nearly touching and whispers, "Is everything okay?"

Smiling against his shoulder, pulling my hands up along the comfortably warm skin of his back, I reply, "Can we try again?"

He puts his forehead against mine and closes his eyes. I do the same and take another breath to my toes.

I feel him moving, but this time, there's progress. My breath catches in my chest and I dig my fingers into his ribs.

"Keep going. I'm okay," I say, both astonished and captivated by the feeling.

My breathing has gone from measured and slow to short and ragged. Ben's is quickly following suit.

The more he moves, the farther my fingers push into the skin of his back. His head drops next to mine, his forehead on the pillow beneath me. With a shuddering whoosh of air, his lips brush past my collarbone. Past the exact spot the glory of edible glitter once resided.

I am one small step away from needing to be physically restrained to keep from kissing him. This habit is not one to go easily into that good night.

There are so many sensations dancing through my entire

body, I couldn't pick one to focus on even if I did have the mental clarity to try. My brain is racing with stimulus over-load as fast as my heart is frolicking around my chest.

The only thought that manages to ring clearly is a small, blissful part of myself reeling in wonderment at how in the damn hell I ever let myself go so long without this.

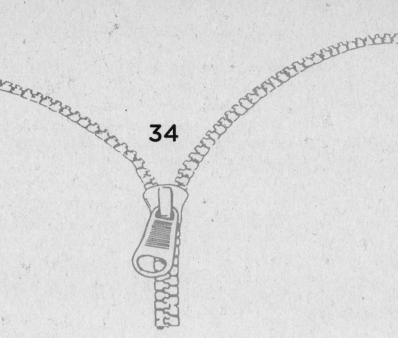

34

"Well," I say, pulling my shirt back on. "That just happened."

Laughing as he ties his shoes, Ben replies, "It certainly did."

I feel weirdly numb and tingly all over. It's not at all an unpleasant sensation.

I had sex. Sex with Ben. Sex with Ben was just had.

I'm not sure what I'd expected, but it was both trickier and somehow also easier than I'd imagined possible.

My mind jumps back to specific moments of the success, and a flush makes its way through my entire body.

"You all right over there?" Ben asks, pushing the end of his belt through the last loop. "You're very quiet."

I turn to him, well aware that the cheesiest grin ever seen by human eyes is plastered on my face, and reply, "I am absolutely all right. How about you?"

Smiling—I'd say sheepishly if I had to pick a descriptor—he carefully rolls up his tie and stuffs it into his suit jacket. "You know," he says, looking bemused, "I honestly don't even know the answer to that."

I sit up straight on the edge of the bed. "In a bad way? Are *you* all right?"

He laughs and pulls his jacket on. "Not in a bad way. It's for sure been an interesting night, but no, not in a bad way."

"That sounds like something we should talk about," I say, back to feeling overly chipper.

Still smiling, he says, "Definitely. But not tonight. You've got to be up in a few short hours for your television debut."

I groan, but—unable to banish the happy from my face—hop up off the bed. "I suppose that's true. And hey," I say, walking over and playfully slapping him on the arm. "Thanks to you, I've got therapy out of the way tonight, so I can head straight to bed."

He rolls his eyes and lets out a small chuckle. "Yes, I'm nothing if not practical."

My mind is catching up with the rest of me, and the reality of the night starts settling in. I did it. I successfully ran the gauntlet, and with days to spare until my deadline, at that. I haven't thought of how I'll approach Ryan with ending our little time-out sooner than anticipated, but I can't wait to tango out of this holding pattern and get back to what life was like before the big *special* bomb went off.

Walking into the living room, we head toward my front door together. In the dorkiest way possible, I bump into him with my shoulder. "Thanks," I say, the full-body flush taking over again. "For, you know, tonight. For everything."

As we step outside onto my tiny porch, the door closes behind us, and he turns and faces me. "I'm really glad things worked out, Kat," he says kindly. "And I'm glad I got to be a part of it."

One corner of my mouth pulls up. "I very literally couldn't have done it without you, fella."

His hand reaches for his tie, coming up empty, and he nervously pats his stomach. "Well," he says, "good luck in the morning. I know you'll do fantastic."

"Thanks," I reply. "And seriously, thank you so much for being here. I know this has been a weird few weeks, and I can't thank you enough for all you've done, Ben."

"My pleasure, Kat."

I reach past him to reopen the front door, but when he shifts to move out of the way, we miscalculate and my fingers trail right across Ben's stomach, just below his ribs. As soon as I realize what I did, my brain prepares to make a joke, to laugh it off.

But the return of the tingling, warm feeling that's shooting through everywhere that's not my brain is what propels me forward.

I kiss him. I don't even know why. Maybe it's the residual tension from our experiment. Maybe it's a leftover urge from feeling his mouth against my neck again. Maybe I'm so grateful to be moving on, my mind chose this as a proper celebratory event.

The only thing I know for certain in this moment is right here, right now, I just really, really need to kiss Ben Cleary.

At first, he's so surprised by my sudden change in direction, he jumps. My hand, my errant, miscalculating hand, finds its way back to that exact spot on his stomach, just below his chest, and my fingers pull against his shirt. My other hand wraps itself around his waist and digs in. The memory of how my fingers felt in this exact spot—without the intrusive fabric of his shirt in the way—just moments ago makes my stomach feel like it's fainted.

For just a moment, I'm kissing nervous Ben. But once his lips catch up to his brain, the Ben I met the night of the edible glitter makes another miraculous appearance.

His hands jump to my face, and oh my god, is he good at kissing. Like, superiorly good.

I realize what a glorious opportunity I'm missing and yank my hand from his waist, making the journey up his chest to his jaw. His perfect, angular, put on this earth possibly just to test my self-restraint jaw.

He's got one hand tangled in my hair, the other arm wrapped around my back, pulling me against him in the most agreeable way possible.

"Woo, yeah!" a random passerby whoops out at us from the sidewalk. The sound jerks me out of my moment, and I pull away with a laugh.

"We just got *woo*ed."

Ben touches his forehead to mine and tries to catch his breath. "Can't say I've ever been *woo*ed before."

I lean back against my door for support and wonder when the feeling will return to my legs. I realize I've got the collar of his shirt clutched in my hand and am trying really hard to remember when I grabbed it.

"We kind of just trampled your rules there."

Pulling in a flimsy breath—doing everything I possibly can to keep the unwelcome thoughts of how amazingly wrong what I just did was at bay—I swallow hard. Why did I kiss him? And more important, why is that at least the third time tonight I've wanted to?

I push those questions and the hundred others on their heels into the abyss, and offer, "Eh. I'm sure Ryan's doing a hell of a lot more." That thought is just as troublesome as the others. I flop my hand through the air and add, "Plus, I'm celebrating the night. We can call it another free pass."

Ben pulls back quickly and stares at me. "Wait, what?"

I reach up and push some hair away from my face. "A free pass. Like we did the other night?" He looks at me incredulously and steps away from our little front door cocoon. "What's wrong?"

He's got one hand on his hip, and the other is roughly pulling through his hair. "Why can't it just be a kiss? Why does it have to be a free pass?"

Standing up, the remainder of my buzz wears off too quickly, and my spine prickles. "Because that's what we agreed to. I don't understand what's happening right now, Ben. Why are you angry?"

"You kissed me," he says, jabbing a finger at the ground. "This whole time, I've respected every rule you've laid out. Even the ones I don't agree with, I've followed them to the letter, Kat. I've been forcing myself not to even *hope* for that first kiss with you for weeks. *Weeks.* And I even let the free pass thing go the other night, because I'm trying really hard to understand what it is you're needing here right now, even though I'm fairly certain you haven't given any thought to how all of this is affecting me. And it might not mean anything to you, but a first kiss with you was important to me. So I never stepped out of bounds. I followed the rules. Then you kiss me, and now you're just waving your hand saying it's a free pass?"

"Ben—"

"Why couldn't it just be a kiss?" he says again, more hurt than angry now. "I get that you're trying to protect yourself. I understand that, I do. And I respect the hell out of it. But you've been sending me every signal from every direction, and I don't have a clue what's going on. I don't know what this is or what we're doing. And what's worse? I think you know exactly how confusing this all is for me, and you don't seem to care. I've let that go because this is your thing, and this should be about you. And I agreed to all of it knowing what your endgame was with Ryan.

"And yeah, I'm not supposed to have feelings for you, but

I do, and I know that's on me. I've kept them separate from this since minute one. But you pull me all over the place. One minute you treat me like we're dating, and a second later you're shouting about the rules, saying over and over how you have to keep them because otherwise, somehow *I'd* get confused, and it would mess everything all up."

He stops and looks at me, his eyes hurt and pleading. "I'm not... I'm not that guy, Kat. I feel like you should know that by now." He takes another step back and looks around, pulling angrily at his shirt where his tie is still absent. "Apparently I *am* the guy who gets his feelings hurt when he gets called a 'free pass,' though, so we both learned something tonight."

"Ben, that's not what I meant," I say, hearing my voice crack. His words—*"I'm not supposed to have feelings for you, but I do"*—are ricocheting through my head so hard I feel dizzy. Stepping away from the door, I move toward him. "I'm sorry."

He holds up his hands to stop me. "No," he says resolutely. "I'm going home."

"Ben, you can't be serious. We have to talk about this."

"I'm very serious," he says, and his expression makes me believe him. "I'm clocking out. I'm tired of working so hard to understand someone who doesn't give a damn about returning that favor. You've got a big day tomorrow. We shouldn't have done any of this tonight. Maybe we shouldn't have done any of this at all."

I scoff, "Okay, fine. If you're 'clocking out,' you can get the hell off my porch." My face is burning in a very different way than before. The cloud of emotional nirvana has dissipated, and I'm left with a thousand feelings I've no hope of untangling in this instant. "I can't believe you're going to unload all of that on me and not even let me have a say."

"I think you've had plenty of say," he snaps. "And quite frankly, I'm too angry to talk about this with you anymore tonight. So maybe just this once, you can let me hold on to a sliver of dignity and leave."

A thousand biting responses flash through my head. If he wants to snark, I'll dance all night. I'll stand here and shout my side of the story for the entire city to hear just because I can. That's how stubborn I can be. That's what makes me The Mouth.

My instinct is to prepare for battle, to dig in my heels to go to the mattresses.

But I don't.

He's wounded.

And I'm the one who wounded him.

"Okay, Ben," I say, swallowing down any barbs, and more importantly, every tear. "That's fine. Good night."

He shakes his head and pulls his keys out of his jacket pocket, and my stomach hurts when I see the edge of his tie poking out. "Wow, thanks for the permission."

I've been thrown completely off my axis. I'm too stunned to cry, too angry to keep shouting, too shaken to stomp into my apartment and slam the door.

Instead I stand with arms crossed tight, watching him turn, head down the sidewalk and climb into his car without breaking stride.

He never looks back. I watch him drive away, and I hold my position on the porch long after the taillights disappear.

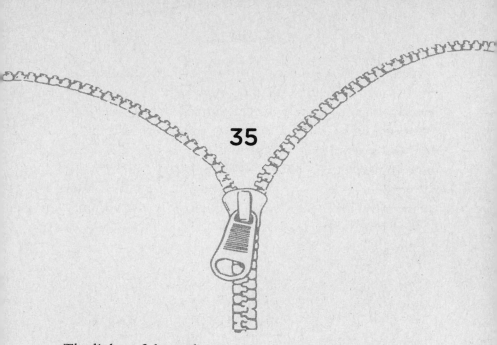

35

The lights of the makeup mirror are so painfully hot, I'm a little worried they'll burn into my skin like a tanning bed. The guy scurrying about with a little ear microphone assures me that isn't the case.

Someone—I don't even know who it was—handed me a giant coffee when I first arrived, and I want to track them down so I can kiss them. Or hug them and cry on their shoulder. That interaction could go either way.

The Channel 7 makeup artist gal comes over, tucks pieces of tissue paper into my Cup My Cakes T-shirt and sticks a straw into my coffee lid. "To keep your lipstick from smudging," she explains when I give her a look.

"I don't wear lipstick," I inform her.

She snickers. "You do today. These are HD cameras, honey. You'll look like a corpse if you don't have something on."

Great. "Can you make it look like I don't have giant bags of sand under my eyes? That'd be a neat trick."

She steps back and assesses my face. "You look like you haven't slept...ever. Nervous about the show?"

Well, yes. That, and the guy I had therapy sex with last night is mad at me because I'm an emotional cadaver, and now I'm supposed to go back to my sort-of-ex-boyfriend with a working special and put an end to this relationship madness, and my entire career is hinging on a single presentation tomorrow, and even though it shouldn't be a priority at the moment—and despite the breakthrough last night—I have enough pent-up sexual frustration to power a small country through what I imagine would be some interesting loin-to-turbine conversion system.

"Yep. Nervous."

"I'll do the best I can," she says kindly. "And I'm sure you'll do great. You know, I've been to your shop! It's really cute. I ordered a cake for my mom's birthday, and she loved it."

"Aww, really? That's so great. Thank you."

So even if everything else is a mess of crap right now, at least I managed to get one thing right.

Except I don't do the cakes and probably had absolutely no hand in that success whatsoever.

"I'm Betsy, by the way," the gal says as she pokes at my face with a goo-covered sponge. "You'll hang here with me until they're ready for you on set."

"Nice to meet you, Betsy," I say, and stick my hand out to shake hers. "I'm Kat."

"I know it's early as balls, so just kick back and relax." She chuckles a bit. "Take a nap if you want. You wouldn't be the first person."

I smile. That's a tempting offer. But if I couldn't sleep in the few hours I tossed and turned in my own bed, I doubt sitting in the chair under the glaring lights of the sun bulbs is going to lull me off to dreamland.

Why did I have to say "free pass"? What in the hell made my brain think that was ever a good idea? It wasn't what I even meant. The whole thing just sort of slipped out. I don't think of Ben as a free pass. I think of him as a beautiful, kind, awkwardly adorable, thoughtful man whom I've grown absurdly attached to over the last few weeks.

He's also someone I'm far more compelled to roll around with in naked ways than I care to admit.

And that's the problem. I'm stubborn as fuck and reluctant to actually admit—even to myself—that I have the tingles for Ben Cleary.

But none of that matters. I'm not supposed to have tingles for Ben Cleary. That wasn't part of the deal.

I sigh inwardly. I'm such an idiot. Me and my control-freak boundaries. I should never have done any of this. The whole point was to get back to Ryan so we can try to ignite *our* tingles, for sobbing out loud.

Ben's right; this never should have happened. Sex shouldn't have happened. Kissing. Glittery necks.

The memory of our sparkly moment races through my brain, and I want to cry. Ryan would never in a million years have participated in glittery times. He'd feel self-conscious and think it was stupid, which would make me feel self-conscious and stupid.

When we'd been together six months or so, way before the rut, I remember we were having dessert at a restaurant and I accidentally got some whipped cream on my wrist. I was going for coy—or whatever passes for sexy in my attempts—and I held it out to him, thinking he'd maybe lick it off, or at the very least, semi-sensually pull his finger across it to banish the cream.

But no. He didn't even seem to notice the loaded-lust gaze I was giving him and just handed me a napkin without looking up from his lava cake.

He's never been one for PDA.

If I'd never gotten into this fiasco with Ben, I'd never know about the *fantastic* ways to remove edible glitter from a neck.

Maybe that would be better. I wouldn't have known what I've been missing.

I just... I don't think I want to miss that anymore.

"Are you okay?" Betsy asks. "Your whole body just sort of...clenched."

I slump in the chair. "I'm fine. Just sitting here regretting all my life choices. It's cool."

Betsy breaks out a calm and casual smile, and I get the feeling she's had her fair share of crazy in this chair. I assume the makeup artist for a morning show is like the psychotherapist to the barely conscious before dawn.

Time passes, and I sit quietly, watching her work as I finish my coffee, which is super weird through a straw. I have to admit, she does a very impressive job of making me look passably human. Eventually the stage manager comes to take me over to the main stage. The hosts are already on camera, chatting away about morning traffic with some poor schmuck out on the streets with a remote camera and a crowd of flailing douche-monkeys behind him.

During a commercial break, the three hosts hop offstage and come over to say hi as another makeup person touches them up.

The station manager introduces us. "Kat, this is Sandra Wen, Don Collins and Rachel Hollowell. They'll be doing your segment this morning. Guys, this is Kat Carmichael from Cup My Cakes bakery."

"Pleasure to meet you all. I'm a big fan," I fib as I shake their hands. Although if I ever had time to watch a morning show, I would probably watch theirs. I hate the Channel 4 team. Their meteorologist inspires a blind irritation that borders on rage as soon as he speaks. I don't even really know why.

"So great to have you here," Don says in a very loud news-caster voice. I wonder if it's possible for him to turn it off, or if that's a full-time sound. "My son Connor's birthday is this weekend, and I thought it would be fun to have you come on and do a demonstration for us," he explains.

"That's what your station manager said," I reply, smiling.

Don laughs what seems to be a perfectly rehearsed laugh. Gosh. I bet that doesn't get annoying to be around on the regular at all. "I think they just like to see how much I can embarrass myself."

Rachel rolls her eyes. "The segment was your idea, Don."

I immediately like Rachel.

"Well, I'll try not to let you look too foolish," I say with a disgustingly coquettish chuckle. I hate myself a little.

Someone with a microphone runs up to us. "After this seg-ment, we go to commercial, and then it's over to you guys. Three minutes."

My stomach flops a little. I bet the gals are back at the shop watching this right now on the TV in the lobby, waiting for the show to start while they wrangle the morning rush. The stagehands are taking all my equipment onto the kitchen part of the stage. All my piping bags are being laid out, so I go up to help out and give a quick rundown of my gear to the hosts before the weather segment is over. I brought my very best apron with me—a blue one covered with little mischievous foxes frolicking with umbrellas—and tie it on. The hosts stand beside me, and I set out a piping bag and batch of naked cup-cakes for each of them, plus some small bowls of decorations.

Another one of the equipment guys whose name I didn't catch comes over and starts placing a tiny microphone under my apron, clipping it to the neck strap. I give him an incred-ulous look as he essentially heads to second base, sticking his hand up my shirt, but I assume this is something he does fifty times a morning. I wipe the incredulity off my face and try to focus.

I turn back to the hosts. "When we start, I'll demonstrate how to do a few different animals for the audience, but then I'll walk you guys through how to do elephants on the cupcakes, okay? They're pretty easy."

"Sounds great," Don says, eyeing his piping bag with a big, shiny grin.

"Don't be nervous," Sandra says kindly. "These are fun segments. They're mostly so we can look like idiots and you can have some free advertisement. Don't feel pressured."

"Thanks," I say, smiling gratefully. Sandra seems like she's been at this for an age. Don, on the other hand, closely resembles a sentient Ken doll.

A stagehand on the floor waves wildly in our direction and counts down with his fingers, finally pointing at Rachel. She looks at the camera and says, "We'll be right back after this with Kat Carmichael from Cup My Cakes bakery, so stay tuned!"

After a second, the stagehand waves his arm again and everyone goes back to what they were doing. I look at Sandra. "Were—were we just on air?"

She nods. "Yep."

"One minute, guys!" the stagehand yells.

Oh, shit. Okay. Things move fast here. All right. One minute. I can totally do this. I've decorated thousands upon thousands of cupcakes. And it's entirely possibly the decision-makers from Coopertown are watching this right now. Even if they aren't, the good press from this show could help out a lot. Shannon is going to rock things tomorrow, but every little bit helps. I can totally do this.

God, what if Ben is watching?

What if Ryan is watching?

What if Mr. Peterson is watching?

Why are the studio lights so goddamn hot?

The stagehand pops in front of the camera and points at all of us. "Fifteen," he announces.

Fuck.

It's time to put my money where The Mouth is. I suck in a deep breath and take my spot up by the counter.

Rachel, Sandra and Don line up beside me, each doing their last-minute preening rituals before the cameras go live. It must be exhausting to be on TV.

The stagehand counts down on his fingers. Five, four, three, two, one. He points at us. Here we go.

"Welcome back," Sandra says brightly. "We are joined by Kat Carmichael from the adorable bakery Cup My Cakes, located on the corner of Eighth and Central. Good morning, Kat!"

I smile. "Good morning, Sandra. Everyone. Thanks for having me."

Don chimes in. "All right, Kat, now, my boy Connor's birthday is Saturday, and my wife and I thought it might be fun to give decorating some cupcakes for his party a shot ourselves this year, but we don't have a clue what we're doing. We went onto Pinterest, and apparently you need a master's in cake decorating to even attempt any of those!"

I shake my head and grin. "Yeah, don't go to Pinterest for ideas unless you want to feel really bad about yourself."

They all laugh. "So, do you think you can help us out?" Don asks, grinning his best broadcaster smile.

"Well, I can absolutely show you some basics," I say, gesturing to a tray of unfrosted cuppies. "Mostly it takes a little practice and remembering that you're a busy parent, so don't beat yourself up too much about making perfectly decorated cupcakes. Your kid will be happy you gave it the effort. Even better, get the kids involved in the process, and everyone has a fun, messy time." I pause and give the hosts a pointed look. "Of course, if you *do* want perfectly decorated cakes, I highly recommend ordering from Cup My Cakes. I hear their staff is top drawer all the way."

That gets a big laugh. "I see what you did there," Don says, still chuckling. "All right, so Connor wants a zoo-themed party. Can you make anything zoo-ish on cupcakes?"

The other hosts are watching intently, and I appreciate them as an audience. The edge of my mouth curls up in a mischievous little grin. Shannon always says it's good to show off a little when there's a crowd.

"I think I could probably manage a few things," I say casually.

There's a row of all different colors of frosting bags laid out, and I set to work. I've been practicing this for days to get it done as efficiently as possible, and it's paid off. First I pipe out a zebra. It's simple enough, but it looks impressive on the chocolate cake.

I've only got a couple of minutes, so I quickly pipe out a lion's face that covers an entire cake, followed quickly by monkeys that have very chubby cheeks and look perfect for a toddler's birthday party.

Finally I go for a giraffe. I brought along a little grass fondant topper to place him on since his long neck is slightly problematic, but he looks very cool when he's finished, so I knew it'd be worth the trouble.

The hosts circle around, oohing and aahing appropriately. "These are incredible!" Rachel says.

"Thanks, Rachel."

"I don't think Don is going to be able to pull these off," Sandra says with a laugh.

We all chuckle. The banter laughter is strenuous. I should

have stretched first. "Oh, I don't know. I think Don is probably better equipped than he thinks!"

Don looks worried. "Can I just place my order with you now?" Everyone laughs again. He picks up the zebra cuppie. "Also, can I eat this? It looks amazing!"

"Nope!" I say, pulling it from his hands just as it reaches his mouth. "You've got work to do, fella. You can eat the cakes you decorate."

"She runs a tight ship!" Rachel says approvingly as she moves over to the spot with her cakes and frosting. "Okay, Kat. Walk us through it."

Sandra goes to stand beside Rachel and picks up a bag, surreptitiously nibbling on a few sprinkles. Don stands next to me.

"I'm going to show you guys how to do some elephants. Who doesn't love a good elephant? Plus, they are relatively foolproof." I raise an eyebrow at Don, and he gives an exaggerated sheepish look.

Picking up a bag of gray frosting, I indicate that everyone should follow me. "All right, so, don't worry if you don't get it right at first—the best part of baking is when you mess up and get to eat the evidence.

"First we are going to pipe out two big ears." I bend down and squeeze out two globs. "Then we will come down the middle, and that will work as the face and the trunk. Then we can add the fine details of the face. You guys try."

The hosts get started, and it's as hilarious as you might expect. Don puts a little too much force into it and a giant sploosh of icing covers his first cupcake. "I get to eat that one, right?" he asks.

"Yep," I say, patting him on the shoulder. "Let's try again."

They set to work and roll back into their usual cheerful chatter, and I stand here piping elephant after elephant. Ear,

ear, trunk. In a moment, I'll show them where to put the eyes and extra flairs.

This is going okay. This is fine. We've got maybe a minute and a half left, I think.

The hosts are getting a little carried away with their frosting rivalry and are poking at each other like children with sticky fingers. I shake my head and take in a breath to scold them, but I look up and see one of the screens behind the stage manager that's got an up close shot of my undetailed elephants.

Just as I see it, the stage manager spots it, too, and his face registers a level of shock that will haunt me for the rest of my days. He starts hissing into his microphone. The hosts must hear it in their earpieces, because they all look down at the countertops at the same time. Sandra's eyes go wide. Rachel coughs. Don starts to giggle. An actual man-giggle.

I look down at the cupcakes. I've got at least a dozen in front of me. The two ears and long trunk have taken an unfortunately Freudian turn, and now it's all I can see. I didn't so much draw elephants as I drew a bunch of gray frosting penises.

Frosting penises on parade.

My jaw flops open, and a little squeak escapes me.

"We can't go to commercial yet," the stage manager whisper-shouts off camera. "Get them out of the shot!"

I can see the screen behind the cameras flashing, trying to find an angle in which the hosts are visible but the elephant penises are not, but they are just everywhere. Oh, Jesus.

In a panic, I reach down, grab a bowl of sprinkles, and dump them all over the cakes, hoping to hide the very visible mistake.

Now we have fancy sprinkled penises. Outstanding.

Don's giggles are getting louder, the station manager is flailing wildly off camera and the lights above the stage are melting away what little sanity I have left. In a surge of frantic desperation, I lift my arms up high and slam them down on the cupcakes.

Chocolate cake, gray frosting and sprinkles splatter in every direction, including all over me. I have dessert carnage stuck up to my elbows.

I drop my head down into my boobs.

"Shit." I say a split second before I remember I have a microphone clipped to my apron. Yanking my head up away from the mic, I reflexively clap my hand over my mouth, successfully covering half my face with icing, cake and sprinkles.

"Wrap it up!" the stage manager moans into his microphone.

Don has completely devolved into laughter and steps off to the side, covering his mouth. Rachel is trying her best not to giggle and is turning her head away from the camera. Sandra steps up beside me and says, "Thank you so much for the demonstration, Kat. It was...surprisingly educational."

I'm going to shrivel up and die right here on television.

"Once again, check out Cup My Cakes, located at the corner of Eighth and Central." Sandra turns to me and smiles her most professional smile. "Thanks for coming in, Miss Carmichael."

The stage manager waves his hand, throws his clipboard down on the chair beside him and shakes his head as I attempt to nonchalantly lick smooshed cake off the side of my mouth.

We're off the air.

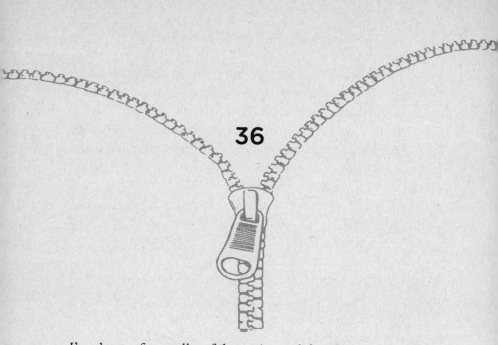

36

I've done a few walks of shame in my life. The worst was with
a guy I'd been casually seeing right before I met Ryan. He had
a puppy that had a real taste for anything that had been worn
on a human body. In the heat of the moment at his place, he
forgot to mention that clothes absolutely could not be left on
the floor or they would meet an edible fate.

The jerk never even offered to pay for his puppy's feast.
Dude obviously didn't understand how expensive a good bra
actually is.

He also didn't have a car, so I took a cab home wearing
nothing but one of his button-up shirts and one and a half
Chuck Taylors. Literally nothing else.

Even that was less humiliating than this.

Betsy the makeup guru did the best she could to help me
clean off before I headed out of the studio. I washed bits of
elephant penis cake out of my hair in the bathroom sink, but
there are still tiny streaks of buttercream up in there. She gave
me a Channel 7 T-shirt to change into and wear out. My poor
mischievous fox apron is tucked away in my supply bags, hid-

ing from my shame. There are giant swaths of gray frosting smudged all over my pants.

I open the back door of the shop and slowly trudge inside.

Liz is at her station, closest to the door, working on a giant *Harry Potter*–themed birthday cake. She is drawing details on the Sorting Hat topper when she sees me, stands straight up and stares, jaw open.

Butter sets down her piping bag, suddenly ignoring the large batch of lavender cuppies in front of her. I can't read her expression. Maybe it's pity? Maybe she's about to burst out laughing? It's a hard one to call.

I hear Shannon close the cash drawer on the register, and seconds later, she appears in the doorway from the front of the shop.

No one says a word. I don't know what else to do, so after many awkward seconds of unbearable silence, I shuffle over to my station and drop my prep bag on the floor before sitting down on the rickety old stool—the stool I always thought was good luck. We bought it from a thrift shop when we first started the business out of Shannon's garage years ago. Even though I will likely fall to my death one day when the wood finally gives out, I love this stool.

Though I kind of feel like even it's judging me right now.

I place my hands on my station, waiting for the shouting to start, but there's nothing. They stare. That's it.

I notice there's still gray frosting caked underneath some of my fingernails.

How long we stay here like this, I don't know. Minutes. Months. Millennia?

I do know the silence is genuinely harshing my will to live.

"Oh my god!" I shout. "Someone say *something*!"

The phone rings, and Shannon disappears to answer it. My stomach is currently located somewhere around my ankles.

Finally, it's Butter who breaks the silence.

"Girl."

I slam my head down onto the station. "Oh my damn."

Liz pipes up. "What *happened*?"

Lifting my head just enough so I can see them, I whine, "How bad is it?"

Butter looks up at the ceiling. "Well, the clip of the show has already hit YouTube, and last I checked, it had over seventy thousand views."

"Ninety thousand," Liz corrects her, staring at her phone.

Butter shrugs. "Hey," she says in a chipper voice, "you've gone viral! That's pretty cool, right?"

"Oh, sweet Jesus." I drop my head back onto my station. "How is that even possible!? It's only been, like, two hours!"

Shannon pokes her head in through the door. "Guys. The Horwitz order, they called to say they don't want any art. Just go with plain buttercream. Did we start those yet?"

"Fuck," I moan into my hands.

"Nope," Butter says, looking at the racks. "They're out, but we haven't put anything on them yet."

"They're wanting a more, erm, classic look, they said," Shannon clarifies. "They'll be here at five." Her head disappears.

"Everyone saw it," I groan. "I drew penises on kid cupcakes on television and then smashed them. I smashed elephant penises."

Shannon starts to appear in the doorway again, but the phone rings and she heads back up to the counter.

"The phone has been ringing nonstop," Liz says quietly as she goes back to painting on the fine details of the Sorting Hat.

I groan louder. "Okay, seriously, how bad is it?"

Butter shrugs and resumes piping out lavender frosting. The

smell is delightful and would be soothing were it not for the horrors of the day prancing around in my head.

"It's not the worst thing," she offers. "We've had three orders cancel, but that's not that bad."

I choke on a panicked, nervous laugh. "I can't believe this."

Shannon reappears and quickly reaches for her coffee mug. I wonder if that is regular coffee, or whether my antics this morning have caused her to drink something slightly more flammable.

"So," she says to me before taking another sip. "I may have some notes about the show, Pumpkin."

I stand up and can't physically decide whether I should throw myself at Shannon's feet and beg for forgiveness, or run away and lock myself in the supply closet so she can't murder me.

Instead I just start pacing in front of my station.

"I am so, so sorry," I blurt out. "To all of you. I can't believe how badly I screwed this up."

"Look, I saw you practicing those elephants for a week," Butter says. She takes a tray of cuppies out of the oven and puts them on the cooling rack. "I never saw that until it was on-screen. I would have told you. That was a freak accident, hon, it could have happened to anyone."

I groan. "No. No, it really could have only happened to me."

Shannon considers this. "You're right. Only you."

The phone, now tucked in her apron pocket, rings again. Her head drops with a sigh, and she sets down her mug before taking the phone back into the front room.

The day doesn't improve from there.

We stop talking about the morning show altogether, but its presence hangs in the air, making it hard to breathe without choking on the stench of my incredible fuckup.

Shannon has to field calls all day, alternating between accepting canceled orders or trying to assure a customer I won't be the one decorating the cupcakes for their gram's eightieth lest I somehow cause the buttercream swirls to become indelicate. Even worse, she isn't discussing it with any of us. I'm not sure if she's trying to spare my feelings or if she's just that pissed about the situation. I know she's trying to stay on task on today, but the guilt is eating me alive.

What should have been a boost to our good reputation became a pornographic display of incompetence, and I know I let everyone down.

My viral humiliation notwithstanding, I still have to get my shit together for Coopertown. In addition to the handful of orders I currently have from people who either haven't seen the video or maybe don't care if I penis up their cuppies, I have to focus on every intricate detail of the presentation.

I might be banned from attempting anything related to zoo animals ever again, but I will not mess up this raven.

The awkward silence in the back room while we work is forcing me to stay inside my head, which is not a great place right now.

Ben.

What did I do?

I hurt him. My brain can't shake the image of his pained expression, the anger in his voice, the weight in my stomach as he left. Those things and more are trapped inside my mind, ricocheting off the edges of my concentration, tangoing with the flashes of disgrace from the studio.

This should have been a day of absolute triumph. I mean, I successfully slept with Ben last night. I planned to flounce in here after the morning show with the confidence of someone who kicked the ass of my TV debut, promoted the hell out of the shop and got to announce the miraculous night of special success. There should have been celebration. Fireworks. Songs written about these magical accomplishments.

Instead, I'm drowning in shame.

Ben hasn't responded to a single text I've sent. I even tried calling after I left the studio, and no answer.

I can't even talk to the girls about what happened last night. I don't want Shannon breaking off and stabbing me with a palette knife.

In retrospect, she might have had a point when she banned us from giving it a go last night.

This feels like a new personal low.

Coopertown is tomorrow. I refuse to go into that with this horrible anti-mojo hanging over me. The cakes I prepare have to be in top form. There is exactly no room for error here.

I need to find a way to turn things around. I need the strut I was sure I would have after I beat my deadline.

And then I remember.

Ryan.

That was the whole point, wasn't it? Going through all these dramatics and toils with Ben so I could get back to Ryan? So we could restart what was good and get to where we definitely should be now.

I look down at my worktop and realize I've made a huge mess on the cupcake I was stenciling. A practice cake for Coopertown. Instead of an intricate design, I've got a shapeless blob of edible glitter.

Oh, how I miss the *fantastic* aspects of edible glitter.

Ack. No. I definitely should not be thinking about that right now.

I'm so crazed with all of the *everything*, I have no focus.

I look up at my industrious coworkers, and all I see are successful endeavors. How is no one else cracking under the pressure like I am?

I can't carry this into Coopertown. I just can't. I won't cost my friends, my *family*, this contract. I refuse to screw that up the way I've completely messed up every other little thing over the last twenty-four hours. I have to find a way to turn this all around. My trajectory for failure here can't continue.

No. I need a win.

I need *the* win.

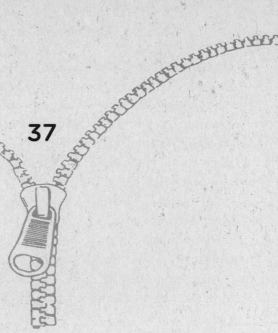

37

Standing at a door I've stood in front of hundreds of times before, I'm struck motionless. Do I knock?

I've never had to knock on this door before. I have my own key to this door. Are you ever supposed to knock on a door you have a key to?

It's all different now. This is Ryan's place. Not Ryan-who-has-a-steady-girlfriend-with-a-key's place.

Tonight that uncertainty is going to change, by god.

I reach up and knock. There's a shuffling sound on the other side, and a moment later, Ryan opens the door.

"Kat, hey!" he says, and my shoulders relax a little when I see his expression reads as glad to see me. "What's up?"

He motions for me to come in, and I do, hands wringing. I'm a solid step above high-strung, and it's not just the weight of the task that brought me here that's got me on edge.

Stepping into his living room, I look around. His place looks exactly as it did the last time I was here. Lots of light, but in that way that feels like he bought bulbs with a higher wattage than the room calls for. He likes to keep a bright room. I tend to prefer more natural light.

I feel completely out of place. I realize that this is the first time in weeks we've seen each other. It's an unsettling thought.

However, as uncomfortable as I am, he seems to be totally calm. There's no air of awkwardness. There are no jittery vibes. He's laid-back Ryan, as always.

"I have some news," I say, turning back to face him as he shuts his door.

He has a pleasant look about him. He's recently buzzed his hair down even shorter than normal, and he's dressed in a pale green button-up shirt and chocolate-colored slacks. This is far beyond his usual work attire. I can only assume he had a manager meeting today. "Oh, yeah?"

I had myself all pumped up on my way over to cut the proverbial ribbon, here. To bring him into the loop. My junk is no longer fritzing, and the time has come to put all of this insanity behind us. It's time to move forward.

But now that I'm here, I'm finding it difficult to get those words out.

"I've been here all of thirty seconds, and you haven't brought up the newscast," I say with a pathetic chuckle, chickening out of the subject at hand. "You've got more self-restraint than I do."

He tilts his head. "What newscast?"

"The newscast I was on."

"You were on a newscast?"

I blink at him, feeling like I've been sucked into an Abbott and Costello act, but then I remember. "Oh yeah. We haven't talked in four weeks."

Realizing we are uncomfortably standing by the door, he walks over to his ancient and well-loved couch and flops down. "So, what was the newscast thing, anyway?"

Images of sugary gray edible penises flash through my brain, and I shudder. "Actually, it wasn't important. Just some shop promotion."

"Is that the news?"

I squint at him. "Well, I mean, it's a news show, so technically?"

He smiles and rolls his eyes a little. "No, you said you had news. Is that it?"

My hands resume wringing. "Uh, no, actually." I take in a big gulp of air and clear my throat. "The news is, well, I'm ready to have sex."

His expression is indescribable. It's both blank and full of implications, and I can't make out a one of them. My declaration hangs in his overly lit living room while we stare at each other.

I suddenly hate his light bulbs. I feel exposed and vulnerable. There are no dark corners, no soft shadows to hide in.

"So, you're..." he says, starting a sentence that's never finished.

"Ready to have sex," I repeat. "I've fixed everything below the belt, and six days before our anniversary, even."

"That's...great?" I don't think he meant for that to come out as a question.

My hands are starting to sweat. "I figured it would be good to start things over," I explain. "Why wait, you know? I figured we can get moving now, and then have a great, non-dramatic anniversary without this hanging over us."

"Uh, you mean you want to have sex right...now?"

I shrug. "Yeah."

Leaning forward on the couch, he clasps his hands. "Isn't that a little, er, sudden?"

My eyes feel as though they've spontaneously grown three sizes. "Nothing about this situation feels sudden. This is all the exact opposite of sudden, Ryan. It's been two years of bullshit, and I'm ready to be done with it. Aren't you?"

His jaw goes a little slack. "I mean, yeah. Sure."

I stretch my neck out like I'm about to go into battle and do my best to sound confident. "Well, then. Let's do this."

Without further discussion, I traipse through his living room and head right into the bedroom.

I've not been here in an age and a half. We usually meet up at my place, and at the moment, I can't remember why. His apartment is so sparse; he's never been one for tchotchkes. Whereas my apartment has random little trinkets I've picked up over time, his is mostly basic furniture and visible electronics cords. Even his comforter is a solid brown color.

He seems so Zen here, and I suppose I always have been, too, but I'm suddenly very aware of how stark his place is.

Maybe it's the light bulbs.

I don't realize how long I've been standing alone in his bedroom until he shuffles in behind me.

What. The hell. Am I doing.

My body feels like my blood's been replaced by club soda, and not in a fun, tingly way. More like there's pressure building up from the bubbles and there's not enough room in my body to sustain a life of carbonation.

My head is racing with sound bites that have never been spoken but definitely would be if everyone in my life knew what I was doing at the moment.

"*Girl.*" That'd be Butter, spoken with disbelief.

"*Oh my gosh, are you sure this is a good idea?*" Liz.

"*Are you out of your fucking mind?*" Shannon, never mincing words, even in my hallucinations.

Then, a voice I don't expect.

You have to apologize to Ben.

The voice is mine.

"So," Ryan says, walking around me and standing at the foot of his bed. "What's happening here?"

I rush forward and kiss him. I don't know what else to do. There's a feeling of mania guiding me, and I can't sort through any of it.

This has to happen. I can't let myself keep free-falling down this rabbit hole of Ben and tingles and deadlines and this situation that's entirely my fault. I can't stay here. I won't. I don't want to feel this way anymore, and the only way out is to dive off that proverbial cliff and hope the water below is welcoming.

Ryan and I have to get back to where we belong.

He kisses me back, his hands landing on my hips, and I can't help but acknowledge how weird this feels. I'm back in Ryan's arms, kissing him, working toward a very specific goal that's been guiding me for some time now, and it all feels…off.

It's been so long since we've held each other like this. Since we've stepped anywhere inside the circle of things passionate couples do.

Once upon a time, this was an easy thing for us. We were never ridiculous about our displays of affection, but we had our own vibe, and it came naturally.

It's been two years since anything in this arena felt natural, and that ends tonight.

Of course this feels odd. Following the whole bicycle thing, you never forget, but if you haven't been on two wheels for a few years, hopping on that seat is damn sure going to feel wobbly at first.

I throw myself back into the moment and run my hands up his back, trying to lose myself in the sensation. It's the nicest I've seen him dressed in years, and while I know it has nothing to do with me, I try to imagine his wardrobe selection was meant for this night together. I grip his shirt in clenched fists that are currently powered by nerves, but I'm hell-bent and beyond to switch that power to need.

I feel like I'm on display with the lights so bright in the room, so I reach behind me and flail blindly, hoping to hit the switch. After an awkward moment, my fingers pass over it, and it's slightly less like standing directly on the sun.

Putting my hand back into play, I gently push against him, and we sort of tumble over onto his bed.

It's still so bright in here. I peek through one eye and see his bedside lamp on. It's got one of those horrible white light bulbs, and I feel like I'm stuck making out under the fluorescent lights of a discount store.

We've hit a stride that feels familiar, and I relax a little. I'd honestly forgotten what it felt like to be in a horizontal position with Ryan, but now that we're here, there's a twinge of soothing calm I've been searching for with him for I can't remember how long.

I grab onto his shirt again, but this time, I tug until it's no longer tucked into his pants.

I remember this. I can do this. This is what I've been fighting for.

There's a buzzing against my leg, and it tickles. I pull away and grin. "Is that your phone, or are you like, *really* happy to see me?"

He gives a little laugh, and I admire the slight puffiness of his lips. It's been too long since I've seen his lips swollen from kissing. His pocket buzzes again.

Looking amused and only slightly annoyed, he takes his phone out and reaches over to set it on his nightstand. Before he sets it down, I see him glance at the message presented on the lock screen.

"Something important?" I ask, feeling a bit off about lying

underneath someone who just checked their phone, albeit subtly.

"A friend I've got plans with later," he says, resuming his position, both beside and over me. "I messaged to say I'd be late."

I gently slap my forehead. "I'm such an idiot. I didn't even think to ask if you had plans tonight." I sigh. "Is it some work thing?" I playfully poke his chest and add, "Although if you can blow it off, I kinda have plans to keep you busy tonight."

One side of his mouth crooks up, and he pokes me back. "It's no big deal. I just told her we'd meet up later."

Mildly disappointed, but well aware of how I stormed his gates without asking if he had real-life stuff going on first, I reach up to kiss him again. Just as my hands drag through his hair, though, a single word he said burns inside my brain in bright flashing neon letters. Almost as bright as this light bulb. I pull away.

"Wait. Her?" I ask, pushing myself down into the mattress so I can take a better look at him. "Are you...do you have a date tonight?"

He looks down at me, appearing to be genuinely unaware of how this could be taken as something that would cause my blood pressure to spike, and mightily so.

"Yeah," he answers. "I didn't know you wanted to get together tonight."

I suddenly feel eleven kinds of icky, and I wriggle out from under him. Standing up, I turn my back to his ungodly bright lamp and ask, "But you said you messaged her? When?"

He sits up and shrugs. "Before I came in here."

"And you messaged her to say you'd be late, not that you couldn't come?"

He shrinks the tiniest amount, and with a hint of compunction says, "Well, yeah."

"Ew!" I erupt. "You were going to sleep with me and then go on a date!? What the hell, Ryan!"

He whips up straight, looking both contrite and annoyed. "It's not like I had a lot of time to process things and think it through! You just showed up, and I wasn't thinking. But it felt rude to just suddenly cancel over text, so I said I'd meet her later."

I shudder, but then quickly remember that not even twenty-four hours ago, I had therapy sex with Ben. I realize that maybe, *possibly*, I have zero room to talk.

Well, that's not all I did with Ben.

I can't let myself think about any of that right now. I just can't.

I raise my hands in front of my chest, clenching them into fists as I breathe in deep, stretching my fingers wide as I slowly whoosh the air back out.

"Okay," I say slowly. "This may possibly be the most awkward situation that has ever happened. And that's coming from someone who made a dozen frosting penises on live television today."

"You did what?"

I wave my hand through the air. "It's not important. But what are we going to do about this, dude? This is some soap opera shit."

As he runs his hand over his shorn head, I feel that pang of loss for the curls again. He says, "I can call Alice and cancel. I'm sure she'll understand."

I'm gaping at him, I can feel it. "Alice?"

He nods. "Yeah. You remember her, right? She said she stopped by the bakery to see you a few weeks ago."

"You've been seeing Alice since we took our break?"

"I guess so?" His face is not at all registering the level of horror that I assume mine is. "But she knows all about what's happening with you and me. I told her everything."

"But you didn't think to mention it to me?"

He shrugs again. "Honestly, I didn't think you'd want to know."

"One-night stands, I wouldn't want to know." I feel like squinking out harder than anyone has ever squinked. "I think." I don't actually know the answer to that potential question. "But this isn't you going out and hooking up with random people. You're actually, like, dating her. Seeing someone for almost a month straight is a relationship."

Finally, at long last, he looks stunned. "I… I mean, I guess it is."

"It is!" I insist. "If you guys are seeing each other regularly and, I have to assume, sleeping together, that is definitely a—"

I'm frozen, mid-rant, as all the words I'm shrieking fall upon my own ears.

Oh god. I'm in a relationship with Ben.

Oh my good goddamn and hell.

I may actually vomit.

"I didn't think it would be bad," Ryan explains, but his voice sounds hollow and a thousand miles away. "I didn't even intend to do the whole sleeping with other people thing, but she asked me out, and I like her, and I sort of figured it would be better to stay with one person than be with more than one, or someone I didn't know. I wasn't thinking beyond that, really."

I look up at him, and he doesn't appear to register the blatant horror in my eyes.

"You know what?" I say, sounding completely detached. "It's okay. I completely understand. It's a thing that happens. No one plans for something like that, you know?" My limbs are all numb. "Tell you what," I say as I walk robotically out of his bedroom and back into his blindingly bright living room. He scrambles to follow me. "I'm actually going to go now. You go ahead and keep your plans with Alice. It was really rude of me to just spring this all on you, anyway."

"You're serious?"

"Absolutely," I say blankly, grabbing the doorknob. "Tell Alice I said hey, will you?"

I don't even wait for him to answer; I just step out into the hall and pull the door shut behind me.

My boyfriend and I accidentally started having relationships with other people.

I need a drink.

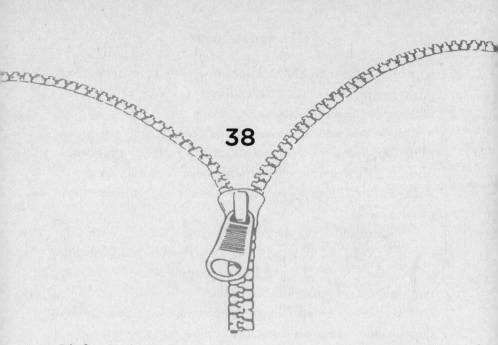

38

It's five in the morning and we are all here, wired and ready to go. I doubt any of us got any sleep last night at all.

This makes several nights in a row I've had zero sleep. This bodes well for the day.

Shannon leaves in three hours for the presentation. We've already begun baking the final batches of cakes for her to take with her. I worked on art all day yesterday before the nightmare evening at Ryan's place and have the best picks set aside, plus numerous extras ready just in case.

Liz is off to the side, offering moral support and getting a head start on her cakes for the day.

Butter is making extra batches of cuppies, because we are crazed women and don't know what else to do as the show-quality batches bake. We decided we'd do slight variations of the Coopertown offerings as our featured cakes today. At least if the Ravens don't like them, maybe our usual customers will.

Shannon and I are over at the stove making second and third batches of compotes and liquid fudge. We decided on a dark chocolate cake with cherry compote, covered with a golden white chocolate ganache and accented with a finely detailed raven made from black edible glitter. It's very impressive-looking and quite delicious.

Our second cake is a golden butter cake filled with liquid fudge, topped with crimson buttercream. It has the team's initials, CR, made from royal icing angled on top. This one is a favorite because it's got that lava cake yumminess without the mess.

The third and final cake is Butter's finest version of red velvet ever, topped with a dark chocolate buttercream frosting and dusted with gold glitter. This one is classic and elegant, but looks just as gorgeous as it tastes.

The cakes are beautiful when assembled, look outstanding side-by-side on the presentation display, and taste even better. After the weeks of struggling and pulling our hair out, I think we've got a winning offering.

Shannon is in game mode and barely talking. I've known her long enough to know she is running through our pitch in her head over and over. She used to do this in college for big assignments. If I watch her closely enough, I can see her lips moving ever so slightly.

I can't tell if Butter is nervous, determined or too exhausted to be her usual bubbly self.

I feel like an exposed nerve. I'm focused on our cakes, but I can't help the images swimming through my mind. Ryan at the exact moment he realized he's been officially involved with Alice. Ben's hurt expression and his anger with me. The fleeting but glorious feeling of joy after our successful therapy romp. Ryan's friggin' light bulbs from hell. The equally irritating and bright Channel 7 studio lights. Phallic cupcakes that will almost certainly be on the minds of everyone at Coopertown when Shannon arrives.

But I can't focus on that right now. I have to get this right. I can't screw *this* up, too.

All I can do is try to keep my shit together long enough for Shannon to ride off into the sunrise and bring it all home.

The morning passes way too quickly, and before we're ready, the shop opens for the day. Butter is done with the baking, so she and Liz man the front of the store. I carefully decorate all of the cupcakes, making four times the amount Shannon will need for the presentation. There are all sorts of situations that could arise in which extras might be needed, and I'll be damned if we're taking any chances.

Shannon is meticulously filling the cuppies that have middles, piping in the fudge and the compote and then placing them on trays for me to decorate, when Butter comes running into the kitchen with a beautiful vase of flowers and a completely cheesed-out smile.

"You guys," she squeals. "Look what just came!"

Shannon pokes her head up. "Where did those come from?"

"They were just delivered! Look at the card!" She hands a small white card to Shannon and goes to set the flowers on the desk.

Shannon reads the card, breaks loose a very impressive grin considering her stress level and hands it to me.

Good luck today, everyone. The other shops won't know what hit them.
    (Literally, with you all. You keep weird things in your kitchen.)
Ben

I stare at the card and feel my stomach curl into an uncomfortable position. Like it's trying to do advanced yoga without warming up first or, you know, without having any knowledge of yoga whatsoever. Why would he send flowers after what happened? He hasn't called or sent me any texts since he left the other night. He didn't even come in for coffee yesterday and now he sends flowers? What is that supposed to mean?

"You have to marry him," Shannon says, returning her attention to her work. "I've been married nine years and Joe never sends any friggin' flowers."

"He sent you flowers!" Butter squeals, prancing around the prep area.

"He sent *us* flowers," I mutter, putting the card down next to the flowers.

"You're acting really weird," Shannon says, carefully piping fudge into a cuppie. "Did you guys have a fight or something?"

I poke at the petals on a daisy. "Sort of."

Butter looks up at me, the glazed-over look of focus in her eyes disappearing in a blink, replaced by a fervent sparkle.

"You had sex!" she yelps.

Shannon's head snaps up at once, and Liz peeks in from the front, looking shocked.

"What?" I gasp, sounding as though I'm being strangled.

Butter points at me. "You had sex!"

"How could you possibly know that!?"

"Oh my god!" Shannon says. "Are you serious? I don't know whether to be happy for you or kill you! Boy, am I gonna have a word with Ben."

I turn back to my station and pick up a bag of frosting. "Yeah, well, maybe you'll have better luck getting him to talk to you than I'm having."

Liz jumps into the conversation. "Wait, you slept together, but you're not talking now?"

Squeezing out a perfect topper onto the cuppie, I say, "Basically."

"What the hell happened?" Shannon demands.

I slam the bag down on the counter so hard we all jump. Even me. "Well, let's see. I went against your decree and dragged Ben home and we had therapy sex. It went amazingly well, actually. Then I kissed him. Why? Couldn't fucking say. Then he got pissed at me for it and stormed off and I haven't heard from him since.

"And," I continue, laying all my matzo balls out in the open, "last night, after I completely fucked up the newscast and any hope for good shop promotion, I went over to Ryan's because, hey, my special is off the bench, and tried to sleep with him, too, but that didn't happen because he told me he had a date with that Alice chick, who he's been seeing for the last month, by the by, and felt weird about rescheduling on the fly like that, and it kind of killed my hard-on, if I'm being honest.

"Which is fine, because apparently I'm dating Ben Cleary." I throw my hands in the air and slam them down on the metal station top. The sound echoes through the kitchen. "At least, I was, because I demonstrably messed that up real nice."

Jaws are on the floor. I've never seen these women in a state of frozen silence for this long.

"Look," I huff, picking the frosting back up. "It doesn't matter. None of that matters today, because we have to get Shannon ready."

"But—" Butter interjects.

"No," I say, putting my proverbial foot down as hard as I can. "This isn't the time. We need to get back to work."

Shannon, sensing my tone and knowing how right I am about the tasks at hand, nods. "She's right. We can talk about this later. And we *will* talk about it." She gives me her best mom stare, and as much as I usually consider myself immune to those motherly wiles, I feel myself shrink down a solid inch.

I bend over my station to finish the cupcakes and push every thought I'm having about Ryan and Ben and the Vagina that Ruins Lives as far into the back of my head as I can cram them for now.

At seven forty-five, an alarm goes off on Shannon's phone, and her face goes into serious mode. It's time to load the shiny new van. I stick my head out front and let Butter and Liz know I'll be back, then start packing everything up.

"Okay, everything is separated by box," I remind her. She knows this, I know this, but I'm nervous and it helps calm me. "You've got three extra boxes of each, but drive really carefully anyway. No Shannon-on-her-way-to-Little-League road-rage stop-and-go, promise?" I give her a wink. She smiles.

"Got it." We carefully put the boxes in the cargo area of the van. All afternoon yesterday, she rambled in tangents about refusing to use the new van to make this trip, but eventually saw reason in the fact that we own the damn thing, so we might as well use it.

"You're going to do great," I say, stepping away. "You look professional, you know your shit and you've got this."

She nods. And suddenly she's nodding a little too fast. "Yes." Then her head starts to shake, and her lip trembles. "No. No, I don't. Kat, I can't do this."

"I'm sorry?"

"I can't do this!" She doubles over, a swirl of curly blond hair whooshing past my face, and she begins to hyperventilate. "I'm going to fuck it up! I'm not ready! Mr. Peterson scares the crap out of me! You saw what happened when he was here the other day! I panicked! I completely froze up. We can't afford for me to do that here. What if I cost us this contract, Kat? What if I walk in and drop all the cupcakes on the floor? What if I forget all of the ingredients? Or the pricing margins? Or the bid numbers? I can't do this!"

I put my hand on her back and pat. "Honey, you aren't

going to screw anything up. You're awesome. You can totally do this."

She whips up so fast that if I'd been standing a few inches closer, she'd have knocked me out. "You have to come with me. You have to be The Mouth."

My eyes go big. "You're not serious."

"I'm deadly serious. Kat, you're better at this. And I need you there. We'll be a united front. A team. We always do better as a team."

I splutter, "Are you freaking kidding me? Did you not see the morning show? It's up to three hundred and fifty thousand views, if you're curious. Have you been watching my *life*? If you want a guaranteed fuckup, you'll bring me."

"Oh, come on. That was a freak accident. We all know that!" she insists. "And, well, we can sort out that life stuff later. Come on! I need you! You'll do great!"

"But I—"

"Butter!" Shannon yelps. Butter comes running into the kitchen from the front room. "I'm taking Kat with me for the presentation. You and Liz can watch the shop until we get back, right?"

Butter looks stricken. "Sure? Of course. Is everything okay?"

"No!" I say desperately. "Shannon is freaking out and thinks she can't handle the presentation on her own, which she absolutely can." I turn back to my hysterical friend. "Look, I have every confidence in you, sweetie. You're a pro. But if you truly feel like you need me to go with you, I will."

"I need you to go with me," she says without missing a beat.

I throw my hands in the air. "Jesus." Hissing, I turn to Butter. "We have to be on the road in about three minutes. Do we have any clean shirts around? I've got to make myself at least sort of presentable."

"I'll look," Butter says, scurrying around to the storage closet.

Shannon is standing by the back door, looking at the stock in the van, making sure we've got everything we need while pulling at her fingernails and chewing on her lip. It's very unnerving to see her this far from chill.

I scamper into the bathroom and whimper. I've got flour in my hair, which I'm pretty sure I forgot to brush this morning; my apron is covered with smears of fudge; and I don't have a drop of makeup on.

I wipe the residue out of my hair as best I can, splash some water on my face, and pledge to steal some mascara out of Shannon's purse in the car.

I meet Butter back in the kitchen and she's holding out a clean black Cup My Cakes T-shirt. With no time to spare, I tug my apron off, then my shirt, and pull the new one on as fast as humanly possible.

"Well, thankfully Ben didn't walk back here for this one," I mutter, searching for a clean apron.

"We have to go," Shannon says, looking at the time on her phone. Her eyes look manic. "We've got everything we need, and we can go over the presentation in the car to practice."

Butter runs up and throws her arms around us both as tightly as she can, and I cling to her a second longer than I mean to.

"All the luck, ladies," she says as we climb into the van.

Shannon turns the key, the engine roars to life, and while balancing her presentation notes on my lap, I start digging in her purse for any goddamn makeup I can find.

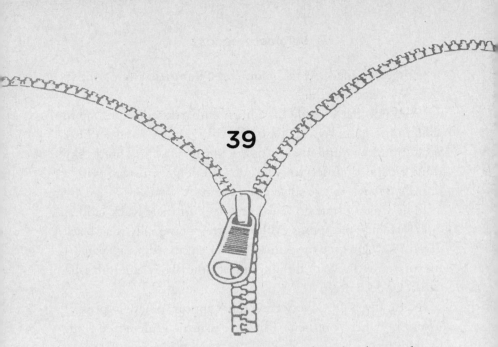

39

The drive to the Coopertown stadium doesn't take nearly as long as I need it to. I'm still rehearsing Shannon's speech and slicking on a coat of her lip gloss when we pull into a parking spot.

Shannon is compulsively repeating facts about our shop, our sales, and our cakes to herself and appears to have forgotten I'm with her, other than the occasional glance at me in which she alternates between uninhibited gratefulness and abject terror.

My stomach is in my throat, but I'm here for support, so I manage to keep it all calm and collected on the outside.

"Brings back memories, yeah?" I say as we unload boxes from the van. "College days? Maybe we can party-crash a kegger after the presentation and blow off some steam. I'm sure we could pass for some Alpha Something-or-Other girls."

Shannon almost laughs, but her gaze is caught by another van about thirty yards away. The Cakery. With their posh company van. Stupid official decal.

Joe told Shannon he had planned to get the van decorated with our shop's logo, but she put the kibosh on any plans until her rage subsided. At this moment, I am officially on Team Joe. We need a decal.

And not that I would have been embarrassed to pull up in Shannon's mommy-mobile or anything, but I do feel a little grateful to be climbing out of our shiny, new and pretty sky blue ride as opposed to a decade-old beige minivan with a family of stick figure stickers on the back window.

The Cakery staff do look very sleek in their black clothes and matching red aprons. Although we occasionally wear black T-shirts, I don't see the point of a black uniform at a bakery. I mean, honestly. With the amount of flour we wield, it doesn't make good sense.

Naturally, The Cakery crew don't appear to have a speck of flour anywhere on them. I have to assume gluten-free flour is invisible.

I try to smooth my hair back and hope I got all the visible caking evidence out.

Loaded up with our bounty, we head into the stadium. Shannon seems to know where we're meant to be, so I quietly follow her lead, occasionally throwing her a reassuring smile or silly face, hoping to lighten her mood.

After passing through an absolute labyrinth of corridors, we are led by a staff member to a large meeting room. There's a large mahogany conference table surrounded by fancy, squishy chairs. There are already several bakeries set up at the table, eyeing us as we come in and find a spot. The Cakery hits the room a few minutes behind us.

Shannon is side-eyeing the competition just as much as they are us, but I'm trying to keep her focused.

"Okay," I say quietly, hoping no one can hear us over the quiet sounds of chatter. "Which cake are we presenting first?"

She seems to have a hard time prying her gaze away from the other boxes at the table, even though none of them are opened yet. "I think we should save the dark chocolate for last. It's the prettiest."

"Agreed," I say, making a little note on the papers in front of me.

"Oh my god," Shannon whispers as her eyes narrow. "That blonde woman from Odessa? She came into the shop a few weeks ago and bought a cuppie sampler. They were freaking spying on us!"

I look up at the blonde woman and definitely recognize her. "Well, that just shows how little confidence they have in their own shit."

"We should have let Butter go Olga on their asses."

"Shannon, stop paying attention to them. It doesn't matter what they've brought. We have our best work in these boxes. They have theirs. Nothing is going to change what we've made. Let's focus."

We decide to open with the red velvet, move to the butter cake with liquid dark chocolate and end with the glitter ravens for an impressive visual finish. No one else in the room is daring to show a hint of their work until the last minute. Who knew cupcakes could be so cutthroat?

After what feels like half of my life, but in reality is about eight minutes, the Coopertown committee makes their way in, taking seats at the head of the conference table.

"Good morning, everyone!" Mr. Peterson says jovially. This man really does get jazzed about cupcakes. "We are very excited to see what you've all brought for us today, so let's go ahead and get started."

He introduces the three other members of the committee, and I'm sure I should be listening, but I'm not. I'm watching each person, checking to see how they react to what's happening in the room around them. The woman in her forties on the far left seems to be very serious, or maybe just not a morning person. Possibly she doesn't give two fucks about cupcakes, and this just happens to be a part of her job she doesn't care about. I'm guessing the whole audition is something born out of Peterson's enthusiasm more than an actual concessionary need.

Next to her is Mr. Peterson, who we know is all about the cuppies.

Then there's a man I'm guessing to be in his fifties who looks friendly enough and seems to genuinely want to greet all of us.

The final member is another woman, who appears to be more interested in her coffee than anything happening in the room, until she looks up and spots me and Shannon. Her java focus shifts into what I'm reading as a snarky smirk, and my stomach clenches.

"Shannon," I whisper out of the corner of my mouth. "Why is that lady giving us the eye daggers of death?"

Shannon pretends to be studying the papers in front of her and replies so quietly I almost can't hear her. "I have no idea, but she doesn't look happy to see us at all. Do we know her?"

"I don't think so?" I say uncertainly, just as Mr. Peterson launches into a very enthusiastic description of the audition process. Tuning him out, I try to nonchalantly place the dagger woman who is still very much hate-staring at us.

She's a well-put-together woman and certainly has a higher level of dignity about her than I do. I'd love to blame this on my minivan makeover, but my guess is this gal hasn't ever found fudge in her hair at midnight, a full six hours after she got off work.

Her blazer looks perfectly pressed and tailored, and just as she taps the screen of her phone with a perfectly polished finger, it hits me. The Burberry phone case.

"Oh my god," I quietly yelp to Shannon as Mr. Peterson

carries on with his introduction. "It's the horrid sprinkle lady, Shannon. The chick who counted sprinkles at her son's birthday party. The one I got sassy with."

Shannon's eyes uncomfortably bulge as the memory hits her. "You've got to be fucking joking."

Our terror must be readily apparent, because Sprinkle Lady raises an eyebrow and sits back in her seat, looking satisfied. A tiny whimper escapes Shannon as she fidgets with the folder on the table.

"This is fine," I mutter. "This is still super fine."

"Oh, shut up," she hisses. "I'm going to have a stroke."

Before my partner can spontaneously combust, Mr. Peterson goes around the table and calls each group up to present one at a time. I can't tell if our placement is good or bad. If he keeps going in order, we will be next to last, right before The Cakery.

I recognize the first shop from the wedding cake circuit. Jan's. They tend to do a lot with edible flowers. Their cakes are simple, possibly too simple. Though they run a shop out of a remodeled garage attached to Jan's house, so their cost of production is far lower than the rest of ours, I assume.

Odessa goes next. Odessa is actually a great shop located on the far side of town. They were featured on the Food Network for one of those architectural cake-decorating shows a few years back. Visually, their items are always impressive, but their flavors and textures aren't anywhere near as good. The three cupcakes they present look amazing, but when the committee members bite into them, no one seems ready to fall off their seats from flavor explosions, so I'm crossing my fingers. I'm also sending violent thought-vibes to the blonde one for her shoddy spy work.

Tarts is a fine shop that I think would have more going for it were it not located next to a Laundromat. Their cakes look nice enough, and their flavors sound good, but when they walk past us, I get a strong whiff of dryer sheets, and I can't help but wonder if that saturates the cakes, as well.

Finally it's our turn.

Shannon and I walk up together, smiling even at Sprinkles Lady, who is giving us the sneer to end all sneers, and we present plates with three cakes on them to each committee member. Shannon launches into the business side of things, doing what she does best. She's performing very well, but her nerves are visible to me. Maybe it's just because I know her so well. I'm hoping no one else is picking up on the gentle shaking of her hands.

When it's time to present the cakes, she turns to me, and I take over. I'm calm, I'm collected, I'm on point.

I've studied these cakes inside and out, I've put everything I have into them, and I sell the hell out of our products. I watch the faces of all the committee members as they taste, and even Sprinkles Lady on the end seems to loosen up when she gets to the liquid dark chocolate. So far, just visually, our cakes are the clear front-runners. Odessa is close, but ours are even more impressive in a boardroom than they were in our kitchen.

I say that in a completely unbiased way, of course.

Shannon looks ten pounds lighter as we retake our seats. Just as my ass hits the leather, I hear a light scoffing sound. I look up and see one of the guys from The Cakery smirking at me as he unboxes their cupcakes.

"Holy shit," Shannon breathes in my ear.

I'm not proud of the expression on my face. I'm really not. But I can't help it. One of their cupcakes is topped with fresh strawberries that have been brûléed. Which looks outlandishly impressive, and will likely taste even more so, but is completely absurd for a wintertime cupcake. Strawberries will be out of season, and even worse, who the hell is going to brûlée straw-berries for over one thousand cupcakes per game?

One of their other cupcakes is even worse. I know Shannon sees it, because she makes a quiet choking sound and her hand jumps out into a death grip on my knee.

The cupcake is topped with what appears to be hand-spun sugar formed into the shape of tiny basketball hoops.

Are they kidding?

The whole table is leaning forward for a better look. All sense of competition has been lost, and everyone is mesmer-ized. Apparently no one realizes this just makes The Cakery look all the more impressive.

I grab Shannon's hand and squeeze back. Mr. Peterson emits an echoing "Ooh!" as his plate is placed in front of him.

"Oh, come on! There is no way you could make hand-spun sugar hoops for a thousand cakes per game!" The words are out of my mouth before I even know I'm speaking. Shannon clenches her hand on my leg tighter, and the blood supply to my foot cuts off.

"Is there something wrong, Miss Carmichael?" Mr. Peter-son asks. Even Sprinkles Lady perks up. I get the impression she has a taste for drama, no matter where it's coming from.

"I am so sorry," I say, truly abashed, putting my hand over my mouth. "I didn't mean to say that. Really, I apologize."

The scoffing man from The Cakery looks down at me with the snootiest expression I've ever been on the receiving end of and says, "Just because your shop couldn't handle that kind of intricate workload doesn't mean other shops can't, honey. We get by just fine."

My eyebrows shoot up, and a pair of sassypants magically appears on my body. "Excuse me?"

Cakery Man continues, "Look, sweetie, your cakes are cute and everything, but don't hate because you aren't up at our level, okay?" Sprinkles Lady is leaning forward on the edge of her seat. "I think we should all just be grateful the Coopertown mascot isn't an elephant, am I right?" He gives a little snort at his own joke, and I swear I can feel Shannon's blood pressure rising beside me.

I calmly stand up and smooth down my apron. "Listen, *sweetie*. First, our products are magnificent, so you can swallow that little scoff of yours down with a big bite of shut-the-fuck-up cake. Second, this contract is for cakes to be sold during basketball season, as in during winter. When strawberries are not in season. Who is going to take the hit on the cost of bringing in all those fresh strawberries you intend to top all those lovely cuppies there with? You? Or are you going to upcharge Coopertown later on, citing market costs?

"And let's just be real here. There's no way you're going to be able to brûlée strawberries and make spun sugar hoops for thousands of cakes for every single game. So either you're trying to impress them now to land the contract and hope you can wriggle out of these specific items later on, or you're going to go with it and likely serve subpar product when the time actually comes. Either way, you need to calm your tits and settle your brassy ass down."

Without breaking eye contact, I return to my seat, lean back in my chair and motion for him to continue. "Again. My apologies. I didn't mean to crush your moment. Do carry on."

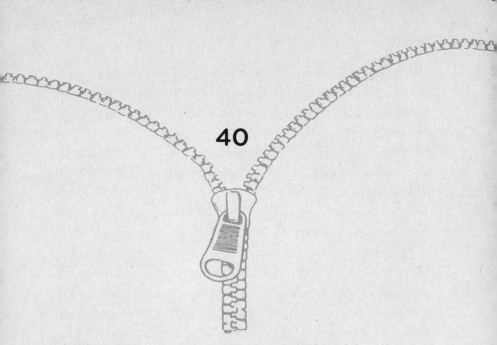

40

I held my composure through the remainder of the presenta-
tions. I managed to smile politely and shake Sprinkle Lady's
hand as we all said our goodbyes. I even kept calm and professional as we made our way out of the Freudian tunnels of
the stadium and back into the daylight-filled parking lot. And
while my goal was not to flip my shit until we were safely
buckled in and back on the freeway, I am nevertheless rage-
slamming our gear into the back of the shop's van.

I'd feel worse about my lack of self-control, but Shannon is
matching my aggression and upping me with barked profanity.

"I mean, who the *fuck* do they think they're kidding?" she
growls as she shoves the boxes of leftover cuppies into the
cargo bay with significantly less care than she loaded them
with earlier this morning. "Sugar hoops. Peterson has to know
that isn't a remotely feasible decoration to serve on a consis-
tent basis, right?"

I make an unintelligible grumbling sound as I try to untie
my apron. "I don't know. They'll be the ones getting screwed
if they fall for it. The Cakery can't possibly keep their costs

low enough to make a viable profit with those cakes. They'd either be losing money on the deal or jacking up expenses for Coopertown, and somehow The Cakery doesn't seem like the giving type to me."

"Ugh!" Shannon yells, throwing the binder with all her meticulously calculated reports for the presentation as hard as she can into the van with the rest of our stuff. "And that horrible woman! That's why she asked if we knew who she was! She was trying to blackmail us into refunding her order!"

"I wouldn't have done it even if I had known," I grumble, but I'm pretty sure Shannon would have given her the refund and her firstborn to land this contract. My frustration has caused the bow on my apron strings to form a knot, and I seem to be trapped. This does nothing for my sanity. "This is not how this week was supposed to go!" I shout. "This was supposed to be us kicking ass here and wowing on the morning show, and not me learning Ryan is part of a couple that isn't with me and getting Ben super pissed at me. Forty-eight hours ago, we had all this hope. And now it's penis elephants and douchey sugar hoops, and lives ruined by vaginas, and what the hell, Shannon?"

She whirls around and snaps, "Look, the penis thing wasn't your fault, and I'm not mad, but I'm standing here looking at a van my stupid-ass husband bought and wondering how the hell we are going to keep it after losing this contract and everything else. So, Kat, I love you, but right now, I'm not real concerned with your quest to get laid."

My hands freeze in my now completely knotted apron tie, and I flutter my eyelids at her. "Excuse me?"

"I'm sorry your deadline stuff didn't work out the way you wanted it to and all," she says, not sounding sorry in the slightest, "and that the last month has been all about you and your vagina, but right now I'm more worried about us not losing our business, so maybe we could big-picture for a minute."

"Jesus," I say, throwing my hands up. "You're being a little overly dramatic about this. We haven't even lost the contract yet. Just because you were able to fix your own damn vagina like it was no big deal doesn't mean you get to be all high-and-mighty about mine, lady. And okay, yes, I quite literally cocked up the morning show yesterday, but we don't know how much business we're going to lose yet."

"No, you know what? Of course this all blew up in your face! In what world would Ryan sleeping with other people be a good plan? Oh, and therapy sex? God, yeah, there's something that couldn't possibly go wrong in every conceivable way. And it's not that my vagina wasn't a big deal. It's that no one's vagina could ever possibly be as big a deal as yours! We get it! Your junk is broken! And yet the world continues to spin on, Kat!"

"What the fuck, Shannon?" I yell. My shock is compounded by the burning coals of embarrassment stoking the flames of my rage.

"You know, you're not the first person to go through this. And just because the rest of us went to therapy instead of control-freaking our way through it on our own doesn't make us weak, and it doesn't make you stronger than us!"

"I never said either of those things!" I start struggling with my friggin' apron knot again. "Don't put your insecurity shit on me, man. I know you're worried about the shop, but you don't get to dive into overdramatics and start taking shots at me! Yeah, we've had a rough week, but I think it's a bit premature to hang up the going-out-of-business signs already!"

"What if we can't pay for this van?" she shrieks, waving her hands through the air with a manic look in her eyes.

"Who told your husband to buy the goddamn van in the first place?" I shriek right back.

"Well, now," a scoffing voice interrupts. "This isn't behavior becoming of a reputable bakery." The ass-knuckle from The Cakery strolls past with his associates, smirking at us.

"There is no freaking way you can make those strawberries and sugar hoops for a thousand cupcakes every game," Shannon says, turning her anger on Scoffy. "We could have brought in a bunch of fancy bullshit to rope them in, too, but you know it's not possible to financially sustain those cakes. *We* chose to present honest products to them."

The Cakery crew Scoffer stops and turns back around to face us. His minions follow suit. At least one of the women beside him has the decency to look mildly uncomfortable. I resolve to hate her the least. "Like I said before, you can't hang with the big kids, ladies."

I take in a deep breath and try to regain some balance to my heart rate. "Just admit you're hosing them, for god's sake. You're playing a game. Don't act like you've got bionic staff, because that just makes you sound like a twat."

He rolls his eyes. "Sometimes ingredients change, and the final product changes. So?" Snorting, he says this as though it's not a completely dishonest and manipulative thing to do.

"So you'd rather get the contract by lying to them instead of just presenting a good product. You have that much faith in your own work, huh?" Shannon shakes her head.

Scoffy shrugs. "Does it really matter? The point is, *we'll* be the ones with the contract. But I'm sure you'll feel much better about yourselves on that moral high ground or whatever. We'll just have to soothe our blackened souls with those big checks we're gonna get."

Shannon shakes her head and starts walking forward, and I

recognize the gait as her "Hold my earrings" walk. "No, no, no!" I yelp, grabbing onto her arm.

"I'm going to knock the smug out of you, you little shit," Shannon says in a voice that is oddly calm. I've only seen her in an actual fight once in our many years together. It was in college, many Miller Lites were involved, and a guy who had taken the virginity of her friend Patrice from world lit and then never called the poor girl again showed up at a party. Shannon had this exact tone to her voice right before she kicked his ass across the front lawn of that fraternity house.

We were never allowed to return to Theta Omega Chi. I think they still have her picture on the wall.

"You can't seriously beat him up for being a prick," I squeal, pushing her back toward the van. I will throw her ass in there and lock her in if I have to. "I'm pretty sure there are laws against it, hon."

Scoffy bursts out laughing, and his minions awkwardly join in. "At least have the sense to lose with a little dignity," he says. Shaking his head, he turns and starts walking back to his fancy van. All sleek and black and decaled, with no looming threat of losing that van due to frosted penis elephants.

I can't articulate the thought process that leads me to let go of Shannon, reach behind her into the van, tear open one of the boxes of leftover cupcakes and grab one. All I can see in my head are flashes of bright soundstage lights, Alice's stupid red hair, Ben's hurt face, spun sugar hoops, Mr. Peterson's Colonel Sanders–looking mug, Sprinkle Lady's sneer, Ryan's clueless expression illuminated by his horrible choice in light bulbs, blonde Odessa spies and a sudden burst of rage.

Without thinking, I wheel around and lob a liquid dark chocolate cuppie right at Scoffy as hard as I physically can.

It lands with a squishy thud between his shoulder blades, and he emits a frightened squeal, dropping the trays he's carrying. His minions gasp, looking in horror as the gooey chocolate drips down his shirt and onto his apron strings.

For the briefest of moments, it occurs to me to be mortified by what I've done, but my guilty reverie is halted by a feral noise ripping through Shannon as cupcakes go flying from her own hand-cannons.

Terrified screams from the minion I hate the least resonate through the parking lot as she dives for their van. Scoffy and his other minion scramble for the trays he let fall to the pavement, and a clump of brûléed strawberries goes whizzing by my face.

Shannon takes a blast of berries to the head, and the red streaking through her blond curls gives her the look of someone in the midst of a blood-soaked massacre. I hurl a red velvet, and the gold frosting explodes satisfyingly all over the minion's red apron.

Somewhat maniacal noises are emanating from my friend, and she's firing off cakes with both hands, landing them on Scoffy, the minion, the van. She's a woman on a mission, or possibly possessed by a confectionary demon.

Scoffy, now with crimson and gold buttercream in his hair, has one of my painstakingly conceived royal icing CRs dangling from his left cheek. His eyes are wide, debatably crazy, but the squeaky yelling sounds he's making are equal parts anger and fear and blatant astonishment.

He gets a good shot off, and a sugar hoop-topped cupcake hits me in the neck. "Ow! Those are pointy, you dick!" Shannon and I both aim for him at the same time, and three cupcakes land in rapid succession, all hitting him around the head. The only visible part of his face is panicked eyes, surrounded by a mosaic of gold, fudge, red and edible glitter.

Least-Hated Minion starts their van up and begs the others to get in, and they gratefully obey. We keep heaving cakes.

Shannon nails Scoffy on the ass as he climbs into the passenger seat, and I find this particularly satisfying.

Their windshield wipers fly, smearing frosting all over the glass as they pull out of their spot, and I catch the buttercream-covered face of Scoffy glaring hard at us as they drive away. Shannon lobs one final cuppie, and it lands right on the *a* of The Cakery decal.

We watch the van pull out of the parking lot, tires softly squealing as they pull out onto the main street.

Panting, I look over at Shannon. Her hair is a wild mess of frosting and fruit and broken spun sugar. She looks animalistic and a bit worse for wear.

Our van is in similar shape. I silently hope those godforsaken hoops didn't scratch the paint.

I reach over and pull a particularly large chunk of strawberry off her hairline. "I think we handled that really well."

She nods. "Yeah, we did good." She calmly scrapes a wad of frosting off my shoulder. "Hey, I'm sorry I said I didn't care about you getting laid. That wasn't fair. And I didn't actually mean what I said about you and Ryan and Ben. I was being a bitch, and I really do want you to get some and be happy."

Pulling a sugar-hoop fragment from the collar of her shirt, I say, "And I'm sorry I keep making everything about my vagina. Me and my junk have been monopolizing the conversation a lot lately. I'm so grateful you've been here to support me, especially with you having gone through this yourself. I shouldn't have been so stupidly stubborn. I should have leaned on your experience more. My not going to therapy is based entirely on my being a straight-up coward. And I hope I never made you feel like you aren't the strongest motherfucker I know, because you are."

Shrugging, she uses her pinky finger to scrape frosting out of her ear. "You didn't. I should have been less know-it-all about how I thought you should be doing things. And my vagina and I are both here for you, always. This month has made me very aware of my personal and professional limits, and I was projecting your shit onto myself."

Carefully trying to pull edible glitter off my eyelashes, I say, "I love your stupid face."

"Love your idiot guts." She wipes a smear of frosting off her eyelid. "Think we should get back to the shop now? Liz and Butter probably want to know how things went."

I shrug, digging a chunk of chocolate cake out of my bra. "Probably. And also, we should maybe get out of here before we get arrested."

I start reloading the back of the van as well as I can, and she carefully unknots the strings of my apron for me. Peeling it off, I set it on the now-empty cupcake boxes and close up the doors. We climb into our seats, thanking the gods Joe insisted on the leather seats, because I don't think crimson frosting would ever come out of cloth upholstery.

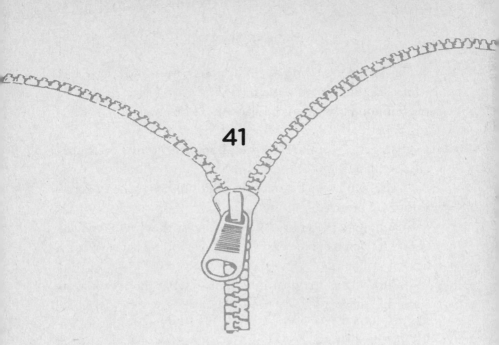

41

While Shannon and I were off at Coopertown, having a bitch-cuppie turf war in the parking lot, Butter and Liz have been continuing to deal with Penisgate fallout.

The video now has over seven hundred thousand hits, and I officially hate YouTube.

My own damn mother shared it on Facebook. Thanksgiving is going to be awkward as fuck.

I was wrong; this is my new personal low.

I'm curled up in the rolling desk chair, huddled under a blanket of shame, willing the world to forget I ever existed within it.

The phone rings in the front room—*again*. I drop my head back and let out a whining sound, but cut it short when my hair brushes against the flowers Ben sent. My heart sinks, and my focus shifts to a particularly painful dagger in my stomach.

"Why the hell did he send us flowers when he's pissed at me, Butter? What does that even mean? He hasn't contacted me at all, won't reply to any of my messages, but he sends flowers?"

She shrugs, buckling down to pour batter into a new tray. "That's a good thing, though, right?"

Shannon pokes her head back in. "Um, Kat?"

"What?"

"I've got a customer on the phone, and they have a specific request."

"Tell them I won't turn their child's birthday into a Penispalooza, I promise."

Shannon makes a face. "Well, actually, they were wondering if you'd make some cakes for a bachelorette party. With... intentional penises."

I blink at her a few times. "That's what they took away from that newscast?"

"Evidently."

I shake my head. "Sure. Why not. With all the business I probably just cost us, we can't be picky. Ask her if she has any specific penis preferences, because this isn't like the boobcake where I can just look down, you know. Does she want them uncircumcised, any length or girth preferences, that sort of thing?"

Shannon gives me an odd look, puts the phone back to her ear and disappears again.

"Okay, see? This is what happens when someone doesn't have sex for two years," I say to Butter. "Their brain becomes completely debilitated by sexual frustration, so they snap and draw penises on cupcakes. This is a nightmare. I've completely cocked up my whole life in the last forty-eight hours."

Butter raises an eyebrow. "Interesting choice of words."

"I'm serious!" I shout. "Ryan is off dating some scarlet-haired home wrecker, Ben is so pissed he won't even talk to me, I completely humiliated the shop and probably ruined our chance with Coopertown, Shannon and I still have fucking frosting in our hair and—real talk here—sure, the therapy sex worked, but I'm not any closer to getting properly laid than I was a month ago, and I'm reaching critical levels of chaos here, man."

Standing up straight, Butter looks at me. "Okay, you know what? You need to deal with some shit here, lady."

"Excuse me?"

She puts her hands on her hips and gives me a rare serious face. "Kat, I love you like family, but you are being pretty damn ridiculous about a lot of stuff right now. You told Ryan to date other people. So he did. What did you think was going to happen? And of course Ben is pissed at you. You've been treating him like an inflatable doll for the last few weeks."

I blanch. "What? Is this Yell at Kat Day or something? What does that even mean?"

Butter throws her arms up. "Those rules? Are you kidding? I've watched you swoon over Ben more than I've ever seen you like that with Ryan in the entire time I've known you. Ben likes you! You like him! And you guys can't date or touch or be intimate, but you wanted to have sex with him? Then you kiss him, and obviously it meant a lot to him, and you try to blow it off like it didn't really count? And have you ever stopped to think about how all of this has to feel for him? Sure, he signed on to be your under-the-table therapist or whatever, but he's not a sentient dick that you can just snap to attention. He's a pretty sensitive dude, you know? This has to be really scary for him, and I haven't seen you give a shit about his perspective once.

"And while we're on the subject, you always do this. Look, you know I like Ryan. He's a fine dude. But you act like your relationship with him is this hallowed thing you have to get back to, and yes, I know you love the guy, like, really and truly love him, and I'm sure it hurts, but honestly, do you really, actually care that he's with someone else? Sure, he never called you on your break, but you never called him, either. And have you ever stopped and talked with him about how you both feel about the relationship? Can you even tell me why you're with him? Have you asked if he wants to get back with you? No! You just order everyone around and then act so shocked when it backfires! You're always talking about how all this is messing with you, but you never once talked about how he felt about everything. Do you even know? Did you ever ask him? Or is he just another man-shaped game piece you move around when you're trying to level up?

"You've been acting like Ben's a freaking piece of therapy equipment while he's been strolling around falling in love with you. And you aren't even paying attention to that because you're so focused on getting a piece. I swear, sometimes you sound like a douchey dude-bro trying to score."

I'm gaping at her. "What the hell, Butter?"

"I'm sorry, hon, I mean, I've been trying to let you do this your way, but I don't think even you know what you're doing anymore! This isn't you. You're not this thoughtless and inconsiderate person who would completely ignore the fact that you've been trampling that boy's feelings this whole time."

Stricken, I cling to the arms of the chair. "I... I didn't mean to trample his feelings. Or Ryan's."

Butter softens her stance. "Kat, I know that. And I think they do, too. You're the real you most of the time. Otherwise they wouldn't have stayed around. But this has all gotten way out of hand. Not only are you completely bypassing their feelings, but I also don't think you've ever stopped to think about yours. Ignoring how you feel about everything doesn't seem like a healthy way to live. And it's spilling over into everything. You're strung out and unhappy. I'm worried about you."

I blink away the burning behind my eyes. "Look, it's not like I'm some kind of sexual robot or something, but I'm not used to this. Sex was always a casual, easygoing thing. And now it's this huge, scary big deal with all this pressure, and it's been built up into this giant monolith that's blocking out everything else.

"And with every other guy I've been with, I get a crush, then comes the sex, and then maybe we'd fall for each other. That's how it was with Ryan. And yes, I do love Ryan. I just…" My head twitches to the side, and I will tears to stay behind my lids where they belong. "It's just been easier for me not to think about it. He's always waiting for me to make the decisions, you know? But I don't know what decisions I'm supposed to be making here. Objectively, all the facts say we should be a perfect couple, you know? But it doesn't feel perfect. It doesn't even feel right. And I kept thinking if I could fix the sex stuff, it would all fall into place."

She shakes her head. "Is that really how you want to be in your relationship? Trying to force it to live up to some bogus idea of perfection?"

I'm horrified when I feel my lip wibble. "No. I just never thought of it like that before." Willing my mouth to behave, I add, "And as for Ben, I don't know how to deal with feelings for someone I am definitely not supposed to be having. Especially after sleeping with him, albeit therapeutically. Everything is so backward." I lightly kick the desk drawer. "I say that like I could ever have a shot to be with him. I really screwed this up. He was so angry with me, Butter."

"Have you told him any of that? About being scared and how you're all up to your ears in feelings for him? Or told Ryan that the fire died out a long time ago?"

"Not exactly."

"Then Ben should be angry with you. Ryan put you in the place of decision maker, and maybe that's not fair, but Ben's been looking to you to lead the way because you flat-out told him you needed everything to be this and that way with your rules. And then what? You expect him to read your mind? Or worse, you think he can do all the right things with only half the information? You're setting the whole operation up to fail, Kat. Damn right he's mad."

I look down at my hands, fidgeting uncomfortably. "I don't know what to do, Butter. Fixing stuff is what I do, it's my thing. But I don't know how to fix any of this."

Butter shrugs again. "Maybe it's time to swerve your approach, baby. Because what you've been doing sure as hell isn't working."

Bashfully tugging at the seam down the leg of my jeans, I ask, "Have you felt this way the whole time? Why didn't you say something?"

She grabs her glitter brush and starts twirling it between her fingers. "For a while, yeah. And sweetie, have you ever tried telling you anything? You're stubborn as hell."

I tilt my head. "I get that a lot."

"Now," she says, pocketing her brush, "while you're thinking of that spectacular new approach, get your ass out of that chair and help me out. We are way behind, and it sounds like we are going to have to learn how to make fondant penises."

I grin at her. "Never a dull day at work."

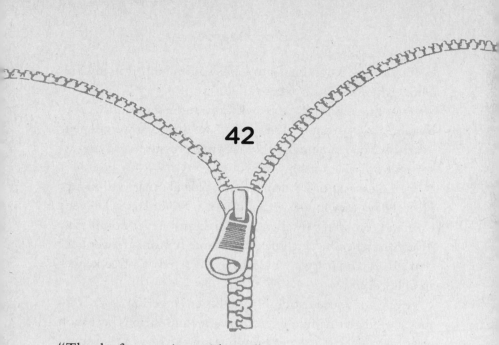

42

"Thanks for meeting with me," I say, awkwardly adjusting my glass of wine on its coaster.

"No problem at all," Ryan says with a calm smile. "I'm glad you called. Things were really weird last night."

After everything Shannon and Butter said to me earlier, I've realized this is the closure I should have made a priority ages ago.

It's time to get to the bottom of the mess.

It's taking every fiber of my being not to pick up this glass of wine, unhinge my jaw and swallow the contents whole. And then follow suit with the rest of the bottle.

He looks nice. Like himself. He's come straight from work, clad in a T-shirt under an open flannel shirt and jeans. It suits him.

I managed to sneak out of the shop in time to grab a shower before we met up. There was a moment of dismay when I realized it was the second time in two days I had to shower pieces of cake and frosting out of my hair.

If that's not a sign I need to make some changes in my life, I honestly don't know what is.

Sitting here with Ryan is awkward, but it's a weirdly comfortable awkwardness. This is the same groove we've spent years in, but I can't deny the nagging pressure of trying to sort out our relationship woes.

He takes a sip of his drink, some pale ale that was on tap. He's always very low-key about booze. He orders whatever's on hand, or what's listed as a special, and never complains. Not even when he gets stuck with some bottom-drawer beer that's beyond what we would have tolerated at a free kegger in college.

A year into our relationship, all his engineering work buddies started getting into microbreweries and various beer snob activities. They'd attempt brewing fancy beers in their own garages, have weekly tastings and stand around talking hoppiness and undertones, but Ryan couldn't take it all seriously. He went when invited, was polite and enthusiastic about their pursuits, but as soon as he came home, he'd laugh with me about how not a one of those home brews tasted like anything other than spoiled, wet bread.

It was endearing.

I'd forgotten he could be endearing.

When did I forget that?

"So," I say, trying to coolly take a sip of wine. "How's Alice?"

He smiles. "We don't have to talk about her, babes. I figured you wouldn't want to know."

"I miss your hair," I blurt out, still clutching my wineglass.

"What?"

I slump down against the table. "I miss your curls. I never said anything because I knew that whole Cumberbatch thing bothered you, but I really miss them."

He absentmindedly reaches up and tries to tug at the tiny strands of hair. "Huh. I kind of like not having them."

"You look really great either way," I offer truthfully. "I just always loved the curls."

With a gentle smile, he takes a drink. "Look, I am really sorry about the last night. That was a bizarre situation."

"Honestly, that was all on me. I should've called first."

"Do you want to go for it again?" he asks. "I don't have any other plans tonight."

My stomach feels heavy. I know the answer to that question, and it's not what I ever would have expected.

"No." I sigh. "I don't want to try again."

"That's cool," he says, so casually that I know he doesn't understand what I mean. "We can wait until Monday for our anniversary like we planned."

I try to pull in a deep breath, but there's no room for air in my tension-filled body. "No, I mean I don't want to try again at all, Ryan."

He's mid-sip as I say this and freezes for a moment, his eyes locking with mine over the pint glass. Finishing the swallow, he sets the beer down.

"Well, that's fine. I always said the sex stuff didn't bother me, anyway."

I take an extraordinarily long pull on my wine before placing my glass back on the table. I twist the stem around with my fingers and stare at the dark crimson liquid lightly sloshing around inside.

"Ryan," I say, knowing this is the beginning of the end. "Tell me some bad things about our relationship. What do you think doesn't work with us?"

He narrows his gaze, obviously confused, but lifts a shoulder and drops it quickly. "I don't think there's anything *bad* about us."

"You don't think there's anything that doesn't work about you and me?"

He truly considers this. "No, I don't. I think we get along fine with everything. I mean, the last few weeks have been kind of weird, but I wouldn't call it bad. We get by fine."

I take another sip of my pinot noir. "'Fine.' I think that's the whole problem right there."

He is starting to look annoyed. "What problem?"

"Are you even happy?" I ask, feeling years of frustration building up behind my tongue. "I am seriously asking."

"Sure!" he says too quickly. No time taken to think about the answer. "Well, I'm not unhappy, anyway."

"That's not how relationships are supposed to be!" I insist, trying to convince myself as much as him. "Caring a lot about the other person but feeling completely neutral about everything else isn't romance, hon. It's friendship."

He taps his glass with his fingernail while he thinks. I hate how genuinely perplexed he looks. Part of me wonders if I've put off acknowledging the details of this mess for so long because of just how much it pains me to see him look this way. "Isn't that good, though? A relationship where two people are best friends?"

My chest is aching. Not because I know what's coming, but because I'm certain he doesn't, and I don't want to hurt him, ever.

"It is," I agree. "But there has to be more, you know? A spark."

"We don't have a spark?"

There's a burning flash of resentment I can't keep inside. I've always appreciated his go-with-the-flow approach to life, but sometimes people have to adult, whether they want to or not. And right now, I need him to get with the program of honestly searching that soul of his.

"I don't want to give you my last dumpling!" I snap at him. He blinks at me. "Is that a euphemism?"

I roll my eyes so hard I see gray matter. "No. And I'm serious. I haven't wanted to offer you the last dumpling for a long damn time, Ryan. That's not good."

It's his turn to sound resentful. "I don't have a fucking clue what that means, Kat."

I take a slow, unsteady breath. It's not his fault he isn't following along. I'm barely making sense to myself. Reaching over, I set my hand on his. "Ryan, I genuinely wouldn't mind hearing about you and Alice."

He squints at me. "That's a weird segue."

I smile as I sigh and give his hand a squeeze. "I mean it. It should absolutely bother me that you've been seriously dating someone else when that wasn't part of our break agreement. But it doesn't. When I think about it, I just wonder if she makes you happy—like, spark happy—and it makes me want to hear all about how great she might be.

"And that's great from a best friend, but it's really, really bad from someone who is supposed to be your girlfriend."

"What does that mean?"

My breaths are becoming shallow, and I want to be damn sure I say this right. "Do you know we never talked about what brought on the vaginismus?"

He sits back in his seat, pulling his hand out from under mine. "I thought we did. It was just a thing that happens sometimes, right?"

I feel really, really sad. Because he's right, in a way. At the time, I had no idea why my business went on strike.

But I'd figured it out after a few months, even though I'd refused to admit it to myself until now.

"I love you a lot. I loved you back when this started. But I don't think we were ever as good a fit as the pro and con lists made us look." I can't help it when my eyes drop to the table. I'm ashamed I let myself ignore all the blatant signs of us heading south for this long. I'm ashamed I let us both waste this much time when things should have gone so differently.

"If I'd been paying attention, I would have known that things started to end for me when you made it very clear how stupid you thought something like role-playing is. I was only sort of serious about it, but that you'd blow something off and mock it without even stopping to think that it might be important to me was such a bad sign."

I see it in his eyes, the indignation that comes with being called out on a mistake. I know that feeling all too well. It's disconcerting at best to see it play across his face. And even more unsettling to see the remorse that replaces it.

If I stop to focus on how pained he looks, I'll lose my nerve trying to undo it. Grasping at resolve, I continue, "And then, when I was having trouble, you snarked about how weird the couples therapy stuff was. Your reactions made me feel guilty and embarrassed for needing or wanting things you didn't. And since feeling exposed isn't my favorite thing, I felt like I couldn't trust you with the vulnerability of being honest with you."

I can't read his expression properly, but if I had to guess, I'd pick anger. "Are you seriously trying to blame your broken... stuff on me because I didn't want to dress up like Captain fucking America?"

I feel like jumping out of my skin, cracking a joke and fleeing from this bar. My feet are twisting over each other under the table, and I feel uncomfortably hot despite the normal temperature of the room. "Not at all! I take full responsibility for not being more honest with you about how everything was making me feel. Hell, I wasn't even honest with myself at the time."

"Are you breaking up with me?"

There it is. The question. The bomb that's been hovering in the air, defying gravity and waiting to crash down to earth for far too long.

The explosion is real, but less damaging than I'd feared.

I close my eyes and try to conjure up the air I need. "Do you remember when we started staying in more, and we'd find some awesome new show on Netflix, completely fall for it and spend an entire weekend devouring every episode we could squeeze in because it was so perfect and gave us all the feelings?"

He nods, and I continue. "But after four or five seasons, the shows would start sucking. They'd lose all the good stuff that made them great originally. The quippy side character left to star in some other show that only lasted a season. The head writer quit because of contract issues. The show runner got so popular that they had three shows going and their attention was spread too thin. The chemistry that reeled us in was gone because the original story line was all played out.

"We kept watching out of loyalty, you know? It made us so happy once, so we kept going, thinking maybe it would get awesome again, the way it was during those first few seasons. But it never did. And one day, when that stupid, judgmental Netflix question popped up—'Are you still watching?'—we couldn't bring ourselves to click Yes.

"But we didn't have the stones to click No, either. We just let that question sit on our screen, because we knew the next season would suck the life out of us, but we felt too guilty, too loyal to something that once brought us so much happiness to just walk away."

He looks sad as he flattens out the edges of the napkin under his glass against the table. "So you're saying our show is over?"

My stomach is in knots hearing him say that. But I know

it's because I can't bear to see him hurt, not because I'm sad to see us end.

"I'm saying that I'm afraid if we don't hit No now, and we try to keep watching, we're going to end up hating the show, resenting every part of it for dragging things on and ruining the memories we have of when it was wonderful and we loved every part of it.

"Because I do love you, Ryan," I say, truly meaning it. "But I'm already starting to resent you."

Slumping back in his seat, he sighs. "I think I already resent you, too."

I relax a little, almost happy he's starting to read the page we're on. "I don't blame you at all. I've been a thoughtless jerk. I'm dead inside. I'm emotionally distant. And not just to you. And you've never once called me on it. You deserve to tell me the wrong things I've done, because I know I've done a lot of them. And quite frankly, I need to hear them."

He's gaping at me, and the look in his eyes is a slot machine of emotions, spinning through anger and fear and confusion and pain and shock. I want to leap across the table and hug the hell out of him.

"You seriously want to hear this stuff?"

"Desperately."

He shrugs. "I mean, yeah. You've always been emotionally distant."

"Really? How so?" I lean forward, rapt attention given.

His brow furrows a bit, but there's a hint of a smile as he takes a drink. I'm still pressed against the table, secretly wishing I had a straw to plop in my wineglass so I could work on getting good and drunk without having to move.

"Well, like the clock on the stove," he begins, and it takes me a moment to follow his line of thinking. "Every time the power goes out, the clock resets, and I have to fix it because you don't know how. I love doing that. It's one of the few things you let me help you with. I love how independent you are, but at the same time, it never really feels like we're partners. You do your thing, I do mine, but there isn't anything you ever need from me. I guess I kind of sometimes feel like you keep me around for show, or because you don't want to be alone."

It is definitely my nature to want to slam my hands on the table and argue the shit against what he's just said, but I don't. I take a long, slow breath and say, "I'm sorry I ever let you feel that way. But this is good. What else?"

"Honestly," he continues, "I still can't believe you told me to go sleep with other people."

"Wait, really? I thought that was, like, being the best girlfriend ever. Just because I couldn't have sex didn't mean you shouldn't."

He shakes his head, and a wave of freshly realized frustration wafts over him. "I didn't acknowledge it or anything, but it kind of hurt me. I wasn't having sex with you just because I wanted to have sex and you were the closest chick. We're a couple. I wanted to sleep with *you.*

"I admit I didn't go too crazy insisting you let me help out with all that couples therapy stuff your doctor gave you. That's definitely something I put in the 'Kat's got this' category. But at the same time, it kind of sucked that you cut me out of the process entirely after that. You wouldn't even talk to me about it."

I'm stunned. My face is set in an unflattering trout-like expression, and I can't seem to form words anymore.

"I'm sorry. I didn't mean to hurt your feelings," he says, tilting his beer on the table. "But you asked, and it's how I feel."

A manic, hysterical noise tears out of my throat, and I pick up my wineglass, draining every last drop of pinot noir in three giant gulps.

"Are you okay?" he asks, appropriately terrified.

"I am so, so sorry I ever made you feel like that," I insist, wiping a drop of wine off my chin with my wrist. "I'm a monster."

"You're not—"

"But I am!" I interrupt. "Jesus, I had no idea I was acting like this. Like that." I shake my head as the haze of wine settles in. "When I suggested you sleep with other people, I think a big part of me was a lot less concerned with your sexual needs being met than with wanting to not have to think about them. To not constantly worry about how my action, or inability to get action, was affecting you.

"But the rest of me felt so goddamn guilty about not being able to fix things immediately, and I was feeling so pressured to get it right. I mean, if we're laying it all out here, I've been bitter as hell with you for that. It was crazy hard for me to ask you to do that couples therapy with me, and when you blew it all off, I felt so stupid for letting myself rely on someone else for a minute. I knew I wasn't going to just magically be able to have sex again, but you didn't seem to have any motivation to fix us, and I felt like I was drowning in responsibilities. But you never said anything about feeling hurt when I suggested the break!" I slump in my chair, feeling a bit defeated and a little tipsy, not at all related to the wine. "I'm such an asshole."

"I'm an asshole, too," he says with an exaggerated wink. "I should never have made you feel bad for asking for help. I should have stepped up. I thought it was all weird, but I never stopped to put myself in your shoes and get over myself enough to help out." I almost want to smile at hearing the thing I've suspected for two years confirmed, but it's all too depressing. "I guess it's good we figured all this out, right? I actually feel a lot better right now." He reaches across the table and taps my hand, grinning. "I'm sad that we aren't 'us' anymore, but it's not like we hate each other, and we both made it out alive."

I look up at him and feel a horrible pinch in my stomach. Part of that is chugged wine on an empty stomach, but mostly, it's guilt. So much bitter, choking guilt. I've learned nothing. I'm doing to Ben exactly what I did to Ryan.

I'm on a history-repeating loop, and all it's getting me is a trail of hurt feelings and perpetually broken nethers.

I'm stuck in a circle of selfishness and denial.

Ryan's expression is kind. He's not holding on to his pain, and bless him for that. I hate myself so hard for ever having given him pain to let go.

I'm almost thirty. How do I have exactly no self-awareness of how I make other people feel?

"So," I say, using everything I've got to push a genuine smile onto my face. "Tell me about Alice?"

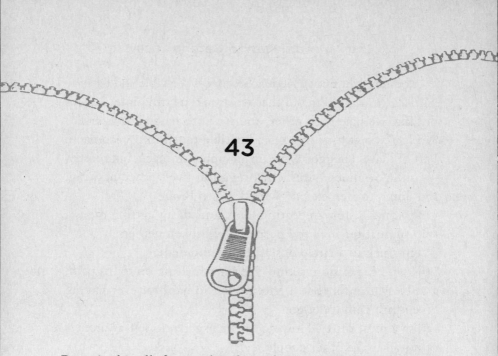

43

Ryan and I talk for another forty-five minutes about life and letting go. I tell him all about Ben and what had happened with the therapy sex, and my own stupidity. Ryan is amazingly understanding about everything, and impressively happy that I've managed to break the sexless streak, even if it was without him. He tells me about Alice and how he doesn't know where their relationship is going, but he really does enjoy being with her.

He even admits near the end that he does feel a spark with her that he hasn't felt with us in ages, but has been ignoring due to feeling like the worst kind of human.

I assure him I am beyond familiar with that feeling.

I think his good thing with Alice definitely contributes to his understanding of Ben.

Or it's just the final confirmation that Ryan and I were done a hell of a long time ago without either of us acknowledging it.

By the time we've finished our official parting of ways and our second round of drinks, he seems like he is in a really good place. And while hearing the reality of my behavior stings in a way I didn't know souls could be wounded, I'm grateful to have the pain as a reminder to do better.

I leave the bar and walk through the city. And keep walking.

I walk and walk until my feet hurt, my brain swirling with the events of the last month. The last two years. The last decade or so.

Somehow, as though my body is magnetized to the North Star that is Cup My Cakes, I find myself standing in the kitchen, all dark and quiet and locked down for the night. Cakes for tomorrow's orders lie on the racks, waiting to be festooned with delicious decorations.

I want to make something better. I want to make an improvement somewhere. Giving the kitchen a deep cleaning seems like a good place to start, but even after grabbing a roll of paper towels and spray cleaner, I can't find anything that isn't already pristine.

We run a tight and notably hygienic ship here.

I sit down at the desk, and when I set the cleaner bottle down, my elbow bumps into the laptop, jostling it out of sleep mode.

I'm suddenly struck by inspiration, and before I even realize what I'm doing, the printer is screeching out an invoice. I grab it, the paper still warm, and race back outside, arms flailing to hail a cab.

Fifteen minutes later, I'm not entirely sure I have the right apartment, but I knock anyway. I listen carefully and hear padding footsteps. A moment later, the door opens and a visibly surprised Ben stands on the other side.

"Kat? Wh-what are you doing here?"

I shift my weight awkwardly. "Are you still too angry to talk?"

"I…no," he stammers. "No, come in." He moves out of

the way, and I walk in past him. "Um, how did you know where I live?"

My eyes go a bit shifty. "Um, you put your address on your cupcake orders. I kind of hoped that wasn't creepy to do, since you've been to my place a few times."

He looks amused, so I let out a relieved breath. "I admire the detective skills."

"I like your place," I say, and I mean it. It's got a geeky man cave vibe to it. It's small but comfortable. The far wall is a giant window that overlooks the city. It's a hell of a view. His living room is divided into two sections. One half has a small couch aimed at a wall-mounted television, the other half a desk with three computer monitors set up on it. There's a small fish tank on a bookshelf by the desk, which I find tremendously charming. The adjacent wall has framed posters. A pop art Iron Man, and the "I want to believe" poster famous from *The X-Files*, but with a TARDIS flying in the background instead of a UFO. I smile.

He looks a little embarrassed. "I, uh, well. Thanks."

"You're not wearing a suit," I point out. He is, in fact, wearing a T-shirt with what appears to be his hospital's logo on it, a pair of jeans and no shoes.

"I'm at home. No suits at home."

This is impossibly awkward. He seems just as aware of it as I am.

"We got your flowers at the shop," I say. "They were lovely, thank you. And everyone else says thanks, too."

He shifts his weight from foot to foot and looks down at the floor. "You're welcome."

My goal to move things away from awkward isn't working, so I go with it. "Why did you send flowers if you're mad at me?"

He looks confused. "I can be mad at you and still care about you."

"So you *are* still mad at me?"

He sighs. "A bit."

"You should be," I admit.

His head tilts uncomfortably. "Again, thank you for your permission."

Resisting the instinct to bristle, I say, "I broke up with Ryan. Officially this time."

Ben looks torn about his response. Shifting slightly on his feet, he finally says, "Oh. I'm sorry about that."

I shrug. "I'm not. I'm sorry I let it drag on so long that people got hurt, but I'm not sorry we both finally realized we weren't the right fit."

He nods—it looks almost involuntary—and offers, "Well, then I'm happy for you."

"Butter yelled at me," I divulge.

"You're really making the rounds. Why'd she yell at you?"

"She said I've been treating you like a sex doll."

His expression freezes for a moment, and he blinks a few times. "That's...that's not quite how I would have put it, but she's got a point."

A nervous gust of air whooshes out of me. "Ben, I'm sorry. Truly, genuinely sorry. I didn't mean to hurt you, and I'm so unbelievably horrified that I did. I've been selfish and awful, and I regret every part of it.

"This whole thing was my fault. From staying in a dying relationship for four years without stopping to ask why it was dying, to pretending like that hasn't been completely messing with me this entire time—I did all this to myself. And I tried to ignore the stupid disorder, and then it came up and punched me in the face, and now here I am. All of this could have been avoided. Literally, years of emotional bullshit could have been avoided by me just accepting that I don't have all the answers. But nope. I made rules. I thought they'd protect me from my own stupidity.

"But I'm broken. A big part of me is broken, and that terrifies me—and I don't just mean my vagina, by the way. I've known it for two years and have been doing everything I could to just avoid it. I'm sorry it felt like I was using you, because that's absolutely not what I intended to do. There were so many times when I was with you and wanted to *be* with you—like, *really* be with you—and feeling that way scared me to death. And yes, it's stupid, I get that. And yes, I understand now that I've been self-sabotaging this entire time because I've got no clue what I'm doing, but I'm a big ol' control freak, and this was easier than admitting that.

"I swear, you're not just a dick to me, Ben. And if I've ever made you feel like that, I am so, so sorry." I take a deep, shuddering breath. "And now I'm crying, god. I don't cry. And yet this is twice now. I'm not a crier, Ben."

He moves a little closer to me and quietly asks, "Can I hug you?" I sniffle and nod, feeling just about as low as I've ever felt. I could be standing here naked and I don't think I'd feel this exposed. He very carefully wraps his arms around me and pulls me in close.

"Is this a hug because I'm crying and you feel uncomfortable and don't know what else to do, or because you're maybe forgiving me a little?"

He rests his chin in my hair. "Probably a bit of both."

My fingers pull on his shirt. "I appreciate the honesty."

He sighs. "I knew all of that stuff, Kat. Believe it or not, I've been paying attention. And I didn't always agree with your methods, but I understood. You were dealing with things in your own way."

I pull away and stare at him. "So I didn't have to spill all that out and turn into a blubbering mess?"

He's still got his arms around my shoulders when he says, "Actually, it's nice to see you open up."

"If you knew all of that, then why are you angry with me?"

His arms drop, and he sighs again. It bothers me how cold and lonely my shoulders feel without his arms there. "Because I've spent the last month paying attention and you haven't. And I get it—you've had a hell of a lot going on. But like I said the other night, at some point, Kat, I kind of feel like you should have picked up on who I am, too."

"But I did!" I argue, feeling tears well up again. I angrily brush them away. "I did, okay? I absolutely saw who you are the entire time! I've spent the last few weeks falling ass over ankles for you, and the whole time I've told myself that I couldn't, that I wasn't supposed to, because it was against the rules, or I wasn't ready. Or at least, I thought I wasn't ready." A frustrated sound escapes me. "I was afraid to be ready. Whatever. But I was paying attention, too, Ben. I might not have let either of us know that, but I was."

His hand jumps to his stomach where his tie should be and comes up empty. He tugs at his shirt instead. "And now?"

I swallow hard. "Now I'm ready. I'm ready to try, anyway."

Shaking his head, he steps back and says, "No, that's not what I want, Kat. I don't want you to think you have to push yourself into something because I got angry with you."

"Ugh," I growl. "You're not listening to me! I'm not pushing myself into anything, Ben. I've been pulling myself back for weeks, and I'm tired of that. After our night together, I tried to tell myself it was time to go to Ryan, and I actually went over there the next day. But you know what? Instead of being excited that I was done with the deadline crap and about to start fresh with him, all I could think about was you, and how it all meant I wouldn't get to see you or be with you the same way, and I couldn't do it. I didn't want to do it. All I was thinking about when I was there was how I wanted to see you and apologize and fix things. And maybe that makes me a horrible person for even going over there in the first place, but I think we've established I'm not exactly in line for sainthood.

"And when I say 'be with you,' I'm not just talking about sex. I'm not saying I want to run and go get it on. I'm saying I want to try *being* with you. Whatever that entails." My eyes burn, and I close them for a moment. "Look, this is all really difficult for me, okay? I know I come off all sassy and like I'm not invested in things, but this is all manner of scary. This is me realizing that I've been willing to trust you this entire time with my physical well-being, which was this huge deal to begin with, and now I'm trusting you with my stupid emotions. That's something I haven't done with anyone since— well, maybe forever. I'm feeling vulnerable as fuck here, Ben. It's a big moment, personal growth–wise." I stand up straight, realizing how much I've just laid out there. "I don't want you to feel pressured by all of that, either. I understand I've made a pretty solid mess of things, but I wanted to be honest with you. I should have been more open with you and everyone, including myself, from the start.

"For the first time, I'm leading with my heart. I'm told there's something to that."

His hand is back at his shirt, pinching the fabric between his finger and thumb as he stares at me. I purse my lips together and try my best to keep eye contact with him. My reputation as The Mouth is crumbling under the weight of this conversation.

After what feels like forever, he finally says, "I'd like to try being with you, too."

A gust of air rushes out of me, and my shoulders deflate a little. "Well, then," I say, my voice shaking some. "Look at us making progress here."

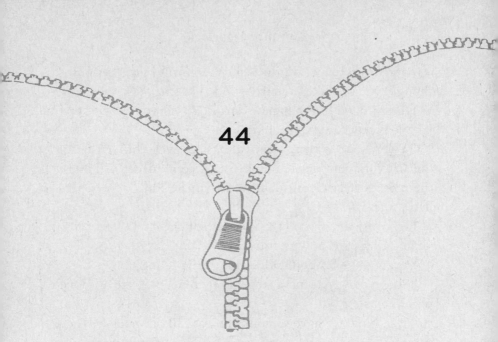

44

"This is awkward progress," I say, swinging my arms at my sides.

"Yeah, I'm not really sure what to do from here," he says, squinting at the wall.

I tilt my head to the side and I stare into space for a moment. Eventually I snap out of it and say, "Okay, look, I know I made this very complicated and bizarre, but if we do this, do you think maybe we could just abandon all precedent?"

"What do you mean?"

"No rules, no deadline, none of that stuff. It's all gone. It's just you and me, and whatever happens. Like what I assume normal people do in relationships."

The corner of his mouth pulls up. "I'd like it very much if we could do that."

"Again," I say, poking his carpet with the toe of my shoe, "I'm sorry for how I made you feel the other night. And I'm really sorry about ruining our first kiss. It was a damn fine kiss."

"I would have rated it up there pretty high."

Forgetting our awkwardness for a moment, I say, "Seriously, though, you are, like, unfairly good at kissing. What is that?"

He grins and runs a hand over his jaw nervously. Oh, that jaw. "I accept the rave review."

"You know, with my confidence in every other part of life and your confidence in sexy times combined, we'd make the most perfectly confident human ever. They'd be superhero caliber."

He considers this. "Or it'd get all the awkward, self-deprecating parts and go full supervillain."

I frown. "Good point. Best not to risk it."

"So," he says, taking a step closer to me. "We're all done with the rules?"

"Yep. Now we have to communicate all our issues as they come, like real grown-ups." A small flush of embarrassment washes over me. "That's more for me, but yeah."

"And we are talking *done*, done, right? No takesies backsies?" He takes another step closer to me, and my stomach does a little flop.

I nod. "Totally done."

He moves right in front of me and stops. "You're saying if I were to kiss you right now, it would be acceptable and not violate any codes or doctrines, and would officially count as a kiss in a court of law?"

"Exactly that," I breathe out. "In fact, it would be strongly encouraged."

His hands grasp my waist as he leans his forehead against mine. I want to reach out and touch him. No, I want to reach out and grab him and throw him down on the couch, but I'm slightly worried that it would spook him. So I stand here patiently as he tilts his head down, and I move only at the last second to raise my lips to his.

Kissing Ben is quickly becoming my favorite activity. While

I certainly sullied the memory of our magnificent kiss the other night with my little outburst, this is a fine—and perhaps superior—follow-up.

His hands travel from my waist. One rests between my shoulders, the other on my lower back, both encouraging my body to curve perfectly against his. I reach up and feel his chest through the worn-out fabric of his T-shirt and dig my fingers in a little rougher than I mean to.

I wait for him to pull away, but he doesn't. His breathing picks up, and I pull myself closer still against him. I run my thumb along the length of his jaw, and it's almost more than I can take. He twists his head and turns the attention of his lips onto my neck, working his way down to my collarbone again. I quite literally almost bite him as a reflex.

"Ben." I gulp, still clinging to him. "I fully respect wherever you may be at on this, but for what it's worth, I'd like to go on record saying that I'd really, really like to try again."

His right hand, holding tight on my lower back, clasps shut on a fistful of my shirt. He pulls back to look at me, and his eyes are dark and clear. His breathing is level but fast. "Kat..."

His voice is a little lower than usual, and it's possibly the sexiest sound I've ever heard. I make my case. "Look, if you're not up for it, I understand, and that's fine. And I'm trying to be dignified about this right now, but I'm about two seconds from throwing you down on this carpet and doing very bad things to you, Mr. Cleary. And yes, stuff's complicated, and I get that. If it works, it works. If it doesn't, it doesn't. But Ben, I'd *really* like to give it a shot."

"Kat, look," he says, pulling away from me just enough that the wind whooshes out of my sails. "I do want to start over with you, and I'm glad we made your deadline."

"Ben—"

"But at the same time," he continues, "I was mad at you

for making the situation what it was." I hang my head a little, embarrassed. "I want to be with you. That's all I've wanted this entire time, which was admittedly stupid of me, know-ing the circumstances. But I don't want the deadline or your therapy or any of this to be a regret. More than that, I don't want you to push yourself into something because you're afraid of that regret."

A flash of a smile hits my face as I recall our night together. Pulling away the sheer madness of therapy sex and all it en-tailed, I haven't been able to get the magnificent feelings of the two of us together out of my head. The repeated urges to kiss him. The way his skin felt under my fingers. The glori-ous scent as I breathed him in over and over until I reached a state of total body joy.

I reach out and put my hands on his arms, resisting the urge to fling them around me again. "Ben, I wish I could take back the whole idea of therapy sex, but honestly, I'm so glad it was with you. But I'm not talking about therapy sex now. I meant what I said in the shop that day. I wanted to have a wild, jawline-biting romp with you then, and, well, I'm far beyond that now. I want to have real sex with you. Not because of deadlines or rules or any of that, but because I've wanted to for a very long time and you're giving me the *fantastic* feelings."

"Oh." He pulls at his shirt again. "Would that...even work?"

"I assume there have been studies done to support the the-ory," I say with a shrug. "Although I kind of feel like we're back to setting up rules, here. It's taking a little bit of the ro-mance out of the situation."

He smiles a confused smile, and returns his hands to my waist. "It really is, isn't it?"

"Bit clinical."

"So, no more therapy sex at all?"

"It's not even a thing. Completely off the table."

"And you're sure?" he says finally. "Really sure?"

"Very super sure," I concede.

He kisses me again, and it takes a hell of a lot of control not to start ripping clothes off him right where we stand.

Eventually he pulls away, and takes my hand from his chest and holds it in his for a moment. "Let me give you the tour, then."

He leads me through his living room and through a doorway near the back. I have to stop myself from bouncing with glee the entire way.

We reach his bedroom, and I can't even be bothered to look around. My focal point is demonstrably more interesting.

He turns to me and takes my face in his hands. I'm not sure I've ever swooned, but I assume this is what it feels like.

"Kat, when we—"

I shake my head. "I don't want to worry about any of it," I say, running my hands up his arms and joyously appreciating the feeling. "I just want to be here with you. Is that okay?"

Apparently it is. I can't even keep track of the course of events that move us from standing in that spot to lying on his bed, but somehow we get there. At some point I peel off his shirt and absolutely marvel at the feeling of his skin against mine again. This is far preferable to getting naked for science. Further along in the unclothing process, I uncage weeks of self-restraint and flat-out have my way with his jawline. I feel like it was put on this earth for the sole purpose of making me feel an unfathomable tingling.

After what I can only describe as the longest session of foreplay in the history of sexual record, I'm beyond ready for what's next.

It takes quite a bit of time, but after much effort and a lot of breathing, we're there. It's everything that was superb about the other night, with none of the stifling restraints. My entire body feels like it's going to fracture from the tension that's built up.

Ben's breathing is fractured and the muscles in his back are coiled tight. "Are you all right?" he asks, sounding ragged. I bury my face into the spot where his neck meets his shoulder and place my lips against his skin. Breathing in as deeply as my lungs will allow, I smile, savoring everything about the moment.

"I'm *fantastic*," I say, and mean it.

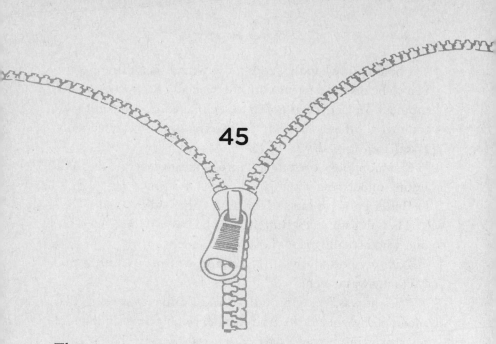

45

The morning rush has ended, and we're standing in the kitchen, awaiting our daily instructions from Shannon, who is cradling her coffee mug like a newborn.

"In a weird little twist," she says, "we've had an outrageous number of orders for naughty novelty cakes in the last twenty-four hours. I think we all know who to thank for that."

I grin. "Hey, man, everybody needs a niche."

She smiles at me. "Business is business. And no one canceled orders yesterday. So far, other than those three orders the first day, that broadcast has gotten us nothing but new business. I'm not even mad."

"I have to make a penis cake, don't I?" Liz asks wearily.

Shannon checks her notebook. "Three, actually. By next Saturday." I snort. She looks up at me, and her expression is positively wicked. "And you've got seventy-five vagina cup-cakes and two hundred boob-cuppies due by next Friday. So. Good luck with that."

Butter bursts out laughing so hard, she has to lean on her station for support. Liz giggles into her apron.

I hold up my hands. "You know what? That's fine. I happen to be on good terms with the specials of the world at the moment. In fact, I was going to see if anyone minds if I take tomorrow off as a vacation day. Seeing as I've never actually taken a vacation day."

Shannon looks confused. "Sure, you can take the day. But I don't understand what…"

Butter points at me and screams, "She had sex again!"

They all gasp. Even Butter. Which is weird, since she is the one who actually made the announcement.

"Oh my god, did you?" Shannon whisper-shouts at me. "Was it…was it Ben?"

"Yes, it was," I say proudly. "And I'd like to revel in that accomplishment a little. And maybe, *possibly* have some more sex that is in no way a part of physical therapy. The regular kind is far superior. So, vacation day?"

Shannon slaps her notebook down on the metal countertop. "Hell yes, you can have a vacation day. Girl. No wonder you look so damn happy. Good for you."

"How was it?" Butter asks, bending forward, hanging on the potential for a story.

Liz makes a noise. "If she's taking a day off work to do it again, I'm thinking it was probably pretty good."

"I've always said you were the smartest in the group," I say, taking a sip of my own coffee.

"Oh my god, you had sex with Ben," Butter purrs loudly. "He's so pretty."

"He's so good at it," I say in a giddy, hushed tone in spite of myself. "Sorry, but I don't see how someone that socially uncomfortable can have that kind of inherent mastery. I'm just saying."

Shannon sits down on a stool and puts a hand over her heart. "It's always the quiet ones."

"But everything went okay? Your special played nice with... everything? And you guys are good now?" Butter asks.

Without my permission, my face erupts with a giant smile. "Well, Ryan and I officially parted ways—on amazingly good terms, I might add—and after copious amounts of groveling on my part, Ben forgave me for being a huge ass. Thank you for calling me out on that, Butter, and you, too, Shannon. But yeah, we got it sorted out. And the sex, well, it took some time, and it was kind of like an alternate universe of losing my virginity, but once we got there, it was pretty damn magnificent. I won't ever be going anywhere near a two-year dry spell again, thank you very much."

A ding sounds out from the front room, and Butter almost chokes on her laughter. I shake my head as Liz squeaks. Shannon pokes her head through the door and sighs.

"Come on back, Ben," she says in her mommiest voice.

A moment later, he appears in our kitchen, and Butter can barely contain her glee.

"I'm going to put a bell on you, fella," I say with a giggle.

"I've been in locker rooms that have more wholesome conversations going. I hope you know that," he says, pulling at his tie.

"I'm pretty sure we had a deal," I say. "Did you accidentally leave your mom here?"

He throws his head back and lets out a laugh. "I thought we'd abandoned precedent."

"Damn." Smiling, I lightly punch the air. "Foiled again."

Ben looks around the room and nods. "Good morning, ladies."

Liz and Shannon say hello back like normal people. Butter stares at him silently, grinning like a hyena until it gets uncomfortable, and then she finally says, "You guys totally had sex. Good on ya."

I close my eyes. "Butter. What the fuck."

Ben reaches up and rubs his eyes with his fingers. "I forget why I came here."

Shannon shakes her head and stifles her giggle. "Butter, don't you have an order to be prepping?"

"Yes, I do," she says. "Kat, you better not have lost your naughty cake mojo now that you're getting some. We've got about fifty loin cakes going out this week."

"I think I can manage."

"Oh, one more thing," Butter says, sashaying over to me and unscrewing the lid off a little pot. In a flash, she has her glitter brush out and flicks a cloud of sparkles at my cleavage. "You're welcome."

I have a moment of déjà vu as I stare down at my bedazzled chest, and Ben chokes trying to hold in a laugh. Shaking my head, I look up at my friend. "Goddamn it, Butter."

Shannon turns to Ben and says, "You can hang out as long as you'd like, at your own peril. You've become sort of a mascot, I think." She heads back into the front room, and Ben moves over to my station.

"And how are you this morning?" he asks, still fighting back laughter.

I reach over and straighten his tie. "I am quite good, sir. And I also have tomorrow off. I have some ideas about what we might want to do with that free time."

The edge of his mouth pulls up. "Aside from just wanting to see how you were doing, that's why I stopped by. I wanted to see if you'd like to have dinner tonight. We could start the event off properly."

"Sold." I run my fingers down his tie and find that I'm pulling on it nervously the way he does. I almost laugh, but I've got something to say. "I think we should talk about the actual activities we've got planned. I'm all on board for this, but since I just got back in that saddle, I'm not sure how it's all going to work, you know?"

He leans over and gives me a very quick kiss. "Trust me, now that we're past the confines of the rules, I can think of plenty of other activities to keep us busy. Plenty."

I grin as genuine tingles spread all the way down to my toes. "I bet you can."

He leans in and very quietly says, "Here you were, celebrating mastery, when we've barely scratched the surface. I've got more *fantastic* plans for you, Kat Carmichael."

I swear to god, my knees almost buckle.

Shannon comes running into the back room, hissing, "Shh!" loudly at us all, even though none of us were making a sound louder than a whisper. We all turn and stare at her. "Yes, Mr. Peterson," she says pointedly into the phone, "thank you for getting back with us so quickly." She scurries into the front room again.

I grab Ben's arm and squeeze. "Oh, shit."

Butter looks gutted. "I thought we had until next week," she whispers.

Liz stands up straight and puts down her spreading spatula. "We all did our best, remember?"

I nod. "We did. Even without that contract, we're an amazing shop. And we have great customers who love us. And there will be other contracts, okay? We did a great job."

Liz reaches over and takes Butter's hand, and Ben takes mine. We stand there silently, hoping to hear anything from Shannon's end of the call. The shop is deafeningly quiet.

A moment later, she walks into the back room looking completely stricken, still clutching the phone in her hand.

I pull in a deep breath and let it out. "Okay. This is fine. What did he say, Shannon?"

She looks up at us, tears falling down her cheeks, and shakes her head. "We got it."

"I'm sorry, what?" I say, my hand locking into a vise grip on Ben's.

Shannon erupts with a huge sob that rebounds off the stainless steel and reverberates through the entire kitchen. "We got the contract. They thought the spun sugar basketball hoops weren't sensible and that the strawberries would just end up costing the concessions department more overall since they would be out of season during the games. The committee thought our cakes were well-thought-out and matched up with the branding of the university."

"We…" Butter stammers, still clutching Liz. "We got the contract?"

Shannon is sobbing harder. "We got it. It's ours."

Butter unleashes an unholy bellowing cheer that will echo across the universe until the end of time. It's so loud Ben actually jumps. She yanks Liz into a bear hug, jumping up and down, ignoring whether Liz wants to participate or not.

Shannon leans against her station and ugly-cries in the way only a woman who has been holding on to a life's dream and just witnessed it come to pass could. I walk forward and hug my best friend as tightly as I can, letting her sniffle all over my shoulder, and try to decipher the incoherent excited babble she's letting fly.

"We did a great job," I say again, patting her on the back.

She squeezes me tight, sucking in shuddering gasps of air, and I think of her telling Joe the news. And the kids' faces when she tells them they get to go to Walt Disney World sometime this year.

Butter and Liz come over and jump into the hug. Well, Butter comes over, and she's still dragging Liz, so.

"I get to go see my Noni," Butter squeals.

"Have you picked a honeymoon spot?" I ask Liz, who is looking pretty red in the face.

She gasps for air but clings to us anyway. "We hadn't because we didn't want to get our hopes up. I can't believe we get to take one now!"

"And we'll have a new employee to cover for all of us when we go places!" Shannon hiccups through her sobs. She dissolves into hysterics again, and I can't really make out what she says next. But it's a happy babble.

I move out of the way and let the group smooshing continue as I step back to admire my people. I don't think I've ever seen Shannon this emotional.

Turning around, I see Ben standing quietly by the desk, enjoying the moment.

"Congratulations," he says, smiling. "I never doubted you guys."

"Why, thank you." I'm beaming. "You know, this is a pretty good day." I walk over and wrap my arms around his waist.

"I'd like to think it's going to get even better. I could take you dancing tonight," he offers, the corner of his mouth pulled up slightly. "I did promise, after all. Perfect for celebrating your contract, and it would be a very official date activity."

He pulls his finger down the front of my apron, and I'm once again compelled to throw him down on my station and have at it, health codes be damned.

Ben without the constraints of rules is delightfully touchy. Oh, the weeks I've wasted.

I smooth down the lapels of his jacket. "While that sounds magnificent, honestly, everything has been so go, go, go lately. What sounds more wonderful right now is a weekend of you and me spending an entire day in bed, binge-watching something on Netflix and eating takeout, all while theoretically naked. Would it be okay if we kept things low-key?"

His face lights up like a little kid on Christmas morning, his eyes genuinely gleeful and sparkling. "Is it too soon to propose? Because I'm deeply considering it at the moment."

I grin. "Maybe a tad. But in the meantime, tell me more about what's under this *just-scratched surface*. I'm intrigued."

He leans down and kisses me on the forehead. "I'll go into great detail tonight, I promise. In the meantime, I think we both have a few more hours of work to survive."

I sigh and lean against his chest. "That's cruel, really."

"Indeed." After a beat, he asks, "I'm curious, though. Do you really have to make a penis cake?"

"Several. And seventy-five vagina cupcakes."

My head bounces when he laughs. "You have the best job."

He's not wrong.

★ ★ ★ ★ ★

THE AWKWARD PATH TO GETTING LUCKY

SUMMER HEACOCK

Recipes

The Best of Cup My Cakes

Shannon says it's always good to show off our baking skills to customers, but alas, I've not yet mastered how to jump through these pages to deliver fresh batches of cuppies to you, dear reader. Though honestly, with my newfound penchant for perving up confections, you might consider yourself lucky.

However, as Butter's creations aren't to be missed, I've included a few of her very best recipes here. Set your tit-cannons to stun and dive in.

May your buttercreams always be fluffy and your necks perpetually glittered.

Coconut Cuppies with Pineapple Curd and Candied Bacon

Ingredients (makes 24)

Pineapple Curd
4 large egg yolks
½ cup pineapple juice
½ cup granulated sugar
⅛ teaspoon salt
4 tablespoons unsalted butter, cut into pieces

Cuppies
1 cup all-purpose flour
¾ cup coconut flour*
1 teaspoon baking powder
½ teaspoon salt
½ cup butter, melted
1 cup sugar
4 eggs
¾ cup coconut milk

Meringue Buttercream
2 cups sugar, divided
⅔ cup water
5 large egg whites
pinch salt (optional)
pinch cream of tartar (optional)
2 cups butter (4 sticks), cubed, room temperature
2 teaspoons vanilla extract
Candy thermometer

Candied Bacon
1 lb. bacon
1½ teaspoons ground black pepper
⅓ cup packed light brown sugar

Coconut flour is just unsweetened, finely ground coconut. If you can't find any, or it's absurdly expensive, definitely grind up your own!

Instructions

For Curd:

1. In a large, stainless steel or heatproof bowl, combine the egg yolks, juice, sugar and salt. Whisk until well combined. Set the bowl over a saucepan of simmering water and cook, stirring constantly, until the mixture thickens. (Watch out for scrambled eggs!) It should be the consistency of regular (not Greek) yogurt. This can take up to ten minutes, depending on how hot your simmering water is.

2. Remove from heat. If necessary, strain the curd through a fine mesh sieve. Stir in the butter until it is fully melted and mixed in. Cover with plastic wrap, pressing down on the surface of the curd to prevent a skin from forming. Refrigerate until cold. The curd will thicken as it cools.

3. The curd will keep for up to ten days stored in an airtight container in the refrigerator and can be made in advance.

For Cuppies:

1. Preheat oven to 350°F. Line two twelve-muffin tins with liners.

2. In a medium bowl, whisk together the flour, coconut flour*, baking powder and salt. Set aside.

3. Using a hand mixer or stand mixer fitted with the paddle attachment, beat together the butter and sugar

on medium-high speed until thick and paler in color, approximately 2–3 minutes. Add the eggs one at a time, beating well after each addition.

4. Alternately add the flour and coconut milk, mixing on low speed. Add the next addition when your batter is streaky; if you wait too long, you will overmix by the time you've added the remaining ingredients. Try folding in the last bit of flour with a spatula to avoid overbeating.

5. Divide batter among lined muffin cups, filling each cup about ⅔ full.

6. Bake in preheated oven for 15–20 minutes. Start checking around 12 minutes to keep from drying out!

7. Immediately remove from tins to a wire rack to cool completely.

For Meringue Buttercream:

1. Timing is everything here, so premeasure your ingredients and have them ready to go. Make sure your mixing bowl is clean and free of any residual fat, or your meringue won't whip up, and you will cry Kat's real Jesus tears.

2. Mix half of the sugar with the water in a medium saucepan over medium heat. Stir just until the sugar dissolves. When the pan heats up, brush around the sides of the pot with a clean pastry brush or folded paper towel dipped in water to dissolve any sugar crystals stuck to the sides of the pot.

3. When your sugar starts to bubble, begin whipping your egg whites in the bowl of a stand mixer with the whisk attachment. You can add a pinch of salt and/or cream of

tartar for stability if desired. When your eggs begin to look frothy, slowly begin adding the second half of the sugar, whipping constantly on medium-high.

4. Continue whipping your egg whites until they form stiff peaks. Ideally, your meringue should reach stiff peaks at the same time that your sugar syrup reaches 235°F.

5. Turn your mixer up to high and very slowly pour the sugar syrup down the side of the bowl. Do not hit the whisk, and try to pour it all down in the same spot, as it will solidify as soon as it touches the bowl.

6. Keep whipping the meringue on high until it forms stiff peaks.

7. When the bowl feels just slightly warm, switch to the paddle attachment and begin adding your room-temperature butter one cube at a time.

8. Continue to beat the butter in on medium-high speed until the buttercream is smooth and there are no remaining chunks of butter. Add the vanilla and (if desired) switch back to the whisk attachment for extra fluffiness!

For Candied Bacon:

1. Preheat oven to 350°F. Line two baking sheets with parchment paper. Place a wire rack on top of each sheet.

2. Combine black pepper and brown sugar in a shallow dish.

3. Dredge bacon on both sides with brown sugar mixture.

4. Place bacon in a single layer on the two racks.

5. Bake in preheated oven until bacon is crisp and browned, about 25–30 minutes, flipping bacon halfway through for even cooking. (Start checking around the 12-minute mark on each side to avoid overcooking.)

6. Cut/break into cuppie-topper sizes, about 1½ inches each.

For the Assembly:

1. Cut a hole in the top of each cupcake with a paring knife and fill each with about 2 teaspoons of pineapple curd. (The more you can cram in there, the better.)

2. Fit a piping bag with a tip of your choosing, fill with frosting and pipe on the desired amount of buttercream. (Less is more with this frosting, unlike the pineapple curd.)

3. Top each filled and frosted cuppie with a piece of candied bacon.

Butter's Legendary
Crème Brûlée Cuppies

Ingredients (makes 12)

Pastry Cream
1 cup heavy cream
⅔ cup milk
½ cup granulated sugar, divided
⅛ tsp salt
½ vanilla bean
4 large egg yolks
3 tablespoons cornstarch
1 tablespoon unsalted butter

Cuppies
1½ cups all-purpose flour
1 teaspoon baking powder
¼ teaspoon salt
½ cup unsalted butter (1 stick), room temperature
¾ cup plus 2 tablespoons granulated sugar
1 large egg, room temperature
2 large egg whites, room temperature
1½ teaspoons vanilla extract
½ cup whole milk

Topping
Granulated sugar, approximately ½ cup
Butane torch
Whipped cream (optional)
24 fresh raspberries or strawberry slices (optional)

Instructions

For Pastry Cream:

1. In a medium saucepan, heat heavy cream, milk, 6 tablespoons sugar, salt and the seeds from half a vanilla

bean (along with the vanilla bean pod) over medium heat. Bring mixture just to a gentle simmer, stirring occasionally (watch closely to prevent vigorous boiling).

2. In a mixing bowl, whisk together egg yolks and 2 tablespoons sugar until blended. Add cornstarch to egg yolk mixture and mix until well combined and slightly pale and fluffy. Take about ½ cup of the hot cream mixture from the pan, and while vigorously whisking, temper the egg yolk mixture (watch out for scrambled eggs!) by slowly pouring in hot cream mixture about 1 tablespoon at a time.

3. Reduce burner temperature to medium-low. While whisking hot cream mixture in saucepan, slowly add in egg yolk mixture. Cook mixture, whisking constantly, until thickened (allow it to boil for approximately 30 seconds to cook out any starchy flavor). Immediately force mixture through a fine mesh strainer into a bowl. Mix in 1 tablespoon butter.

4. Cover with plastic wrap, pressing directly against surface of pastry cream to prevent skin from forming. Chill thoroughly, at least 2 hours. (Can be made up to 24 hours in advance.)

For Cuppies:

1. Preheat oven to 350°F. Line twelve-muffin tin with liners.

2. In a medium bowl, whisk together flour, baking powder and salt. Set aside.

3. In the bowl of an electric stand mixer fitted with the paddle attachment, whip butter and granulated sugar until pale and fluffy. Mix in egg, followed by egg whites, and vanilla.

4. Alternately add the flour and milk, mixing on low speed. Add the next addition when your batter is streaky; if you wait too long, you will overmix by the time you've added the remaining ingredients. Try folding in the last bit of flour with a spatula to avoid overbeating.

5. Divide batter among lined muffin cups, filling each cup about ⅔ full.

6. Bake in preheated oven for 21–24 minutes until toothpick inserted into center of cupcake comes out clean.

7. Immediately remove from tins to a wire rack to cool completely.

For the Assembly:

1. Pipe or spread chilled pastry cream evenly over cooled cupcakes.

2. Working with one cupcake at a time, sprinkle entirety of pastry cream with sugar, approximately 2 teaspoons of sugar per cupcake. Or gently press custard side of cuppie onto a plate of sugar. (Kind of like salting a margarita glass, but cover the entire surface of the custard.)

3. Using a kitchen torch, carefully heat sugar until it begins to melt and caramelize.

4. Once completely cooled, garnish with a dollop of whipped cream and a raspberry or strawberry slice, if desired. Serve immediately.

Coopertown Ravens Red Velvet Cuppies

Ingredients (makes 24)

Cuppies
3 eggs, room temperature
¾ cups unsalted butter (1½ sticks), room temperature
3 cups flour
2 teaspoons unsweetened cocoa powder
¾ teaspoon salt
2¼ cups sugar
1½ teaspoons vanilla
2 tablespoons red food coloring
1½ cups buttermilk
1½ teaspoons baking soda
1½ teaspoons vinegar

Dark Chocolate Fudge Frosting
1 cup unsalted butter (2 sticks), room temperature
4 tablespoons cream cheese
½ cup dark chocolate cocoa
½ cup regular unsweetened cocoa
5 cups confectioner's sugar
½ teaspoon salt
2 teaspoons vanilla
¾ cup heavy cream

Topping
Gold edible glitter

Instructions

For Cuppies:

1. Preheat oven to 350°F. Line two twelve-muffin tins with liners.

2. In medium bowl, whisk together the flour, cocoa powder and salt. Set aside.

3. Place butter in a separate mixing bowl and beat with an electric or stand mixer on medium speed for 30 seconds. Add sugar and vanilla and continue to beat until all the ingredients are incorporated together.

4. Add eggs one at a time, beating after each egg addition until fully incorporated.

5. Add the food coloring and beat on low speed until combined.

6. Alternately add the flour and buttermilk, mixing on low speed. Add the next addition when your batter is streaky; if you wait too long, you will overmix by the time you've added the remaining ingredients. Try folding in the last bit of flour with a spatula to avoid overbeating.

7. Place the baking soda in a small bowl and stir in the vinegar.

8. Add the mixture to the batter and beat on low speed until just combined.

9. Divide batter among lined muffin cups, filling each cup about ⅔ full.

10. Bake in preheated oven for 15 minutes or until a toothpick inserted in the middle comes out clean.

11. Immediately remove from tins to a wire rack to cool completely. Fit a piping bag with tip of your choosing, fill with frosting and pipe on the desired amount of dark chocolate fudge frosting. Finish with a Butter-sized sprinkling of gold edible glitter on each cuppie.

For Dark Chocolate Fudge Frosting:

1. In a medium bowl, whisk together the confectioner's sugar and both types of cocoa powder. Set aside.

2. Beat together butter and cream cheese until smooth.

3. Add the confectioner's sugar mixture and salt to the butter mixture and beat until combined.

4. Add the heavy cream and beat until light and fluffy. Once the frosting is at desired consistency, add in vanilla and mix until combined.

Chocolate and Peanut Butter Cuppies

Ingredients (makes 24)

Cuppies
1¾ cups flour
⅓ cup unsweetened cocoa powder
⅓ cup dark unsweetened cocoa powder
½ tablespoon baking soda
½ teaspoon salt
¾ cup unsalted butter (1½ sticks), room temperature
⅔ cup brown sugar
⅔ cup white sugar
1 teaspoon vanilla
3 eggs, room temperature
1½ cups buttermilk

Peanut Butter Frosting
½ cup unsalted butter (1 stick), room temperature
1½ cups peanut butter
2¼ cups confectioner's sugar
2 teaspoons vanilla
½ cup milk

Instructions

For Cuppies:

1. Preheat oven to 350°F. Line two twelve-muffin tins with liners.

2. In a medium bowl, whisk together the flour, cocoa powders, baking powder and salt. Set aside.

3. Place butter in a separate mixing bowl and beat with an electric or stand mixer on medium speed for 30 seconds. Add the two sugars and the vanilla and continue to beat until all the ingredients are incorporated together.

4. Add eggs one at a time, beating after each egg addition until fully incorporated.

5. Alternately add the flour and buttermilk, mixing on low speed. Add the next addition when your batter is streaky; if you wait too long, you will overmix by the time you've added the remaining ingredients. Try folding in the last bit of flour with a spatula to avoid overbeating.

6. Divide batter among lined muffin cups, filling each cup about ⅔ full.

7. Bake in preheated oven for 15 minutes or until a toothpick inserted in the middle come out clean.

8. Immediately remove from tins to a wire rack to cool completely. Fit a piping bag with tip of your choosing, fill with frosting and pipe on the desired amount of peanut butter frosting.

For Peanut Butter Frosting:

1. Beat together the butter and peanut butter until smooth.

2. Add the confectioner's sugar and vanilla to the butter mixture and beat until combined.

3. Add the milk and beat until light and fluffy. You may add more milk or sugar if needed to achieve the desired consistency.

Strawberry Short-Cuppies

Ingredients (makes 24)

Strawberry Compote
⅓ cup sugar
¼ cup water
1 teaspoon cornstarch
4 cups strawberries (fresh or frozen), tops removed

Stabilized Whipped Cream "Frosting"
1½ teaspoons unflavored gelatin
6 teaspoons cold water
1½ cups heavy cream
¾ cup confectioner's sugar
¾ teaspoon vanilla

Cuppies
3 cups flour
2 teaspoons baking powder
¾ teaspoon salt
6 ounces unsalted butter (1½ sticks), room temperature
1½ cups sugar
2 teaspoons vanilla
4 eggs, room temperature
1½ cups whole milk

Topping
Red or clear edible glitter, optional
Sliced strawberries, optional

Instructions

For Strawberry Compote:

1. In a medium-sized saucepan, whisk the cornstarch into the water until dissolved.

2. Set saucepan over medium heat and add sugar, stirring until sugar dissolves.

3. Add strawberries to saucepan and heat until simmering, then reduce heat to low.

4. Mash strawberry chunks with a potato masher until the mixture is relatively smooth, like the texture of jam.

5. Continue simmering until the compote thickens, about 10 minutes. Remove from heat and cool completely before filling cuppies.

For Stabilized Whipped Cream "Frosting":

1. Place the cold water into a small bowl and sprinkle gelatin over it. Let mixture set for five minutes.

2. While the gelatin is setting, place the heavy cream, sugar and vanilla in the bowl of a stand mixer with a whisk attachment.

3. Place gelatin in the microwave and heat for 10 seconds or until the gelatin turns to liquid.

4. Beat the cream mixture on high speed for about 1 minute, then pour in the melted gelatin in a slow, steady stream.

5. Continue beating the cream until stiff, then refrigerate until it's time to top the cuppies.

For Cuppies:

1. Preheat oven to 350°F. Line two twelve-muffin tins with liners.

2. In a medium bowl, whisk together the flour, baking powder and salt. Set aside.

3. Place butter in a separate mixing bowl and beat with an electric or stand mixer on medium speed for 30 seconds. Add the sugar and vanilla and continue to beat until all the ingredients are incorporated together.

4. Add eggs one at a time, beating after each egg addition until fully incorporated.

5. Alternately add the flour and milk, mixing on low speed. Add the next addition when your batter is streaky; if you wait too long, you will overmix by the time you've added the remaining ingredients. Try folding in the last bit of flour with a spatula to avoid overbeating.

6. Divide batter among lined muffin cups, filling each cup about ⅔ full.

7. Bake in preheated oven for 15 minutes or until a toothpick inserted in the middle come out clean.

8. Immediately remove from tins to a wire rack to cool completely.

For the Assembly:

1. Cut a hole in the top of each cupcake with a paring knife and fill each with about 2 teaspoons of strawberry compote. (The more you can cram in there, the better.)

2. Fit a piping bag with a tip of your choosing, fill with stabilized whipped cream and pipe on the desired amount of cream.

3. Sprinkle with a Butter-sized sprinkling of glitter and add a slice of strawberry, if desired.

Acknowledgments

When I was twelve and first decided I wanted to do the words, I would fantasize about this section and all the grateful drops of unicorn spit I'd fling at the page in glee. Now I'm afraid I'll forget someone impossibly important and get punched in the face.

To my glorious, magical, perfect editor, Lauren Smulski: My darling Ketchup. I SQUEE. You are all the things a writer dreams about when they imagine putting a book baby into the world. I gladly cashed in all my karmic brownie points to end up with you, madam. Your majesty will be honored by a marble fountain I'm having commissioned to stand proudly in my front yard. My HOA can fight me.

Brent Taylor and Uwe Stender. My fellas. My guys who plucked a query about broken vaginas out of the slush and found that book a home. Which is really the best part of all of this—that I will forever be able to say that you two dudes pulled this off. HashtagTeamVagina. You're both incredible and everything I needed in agents that I worried didn't exist.

Extra shout-out to Brent for somehow being able to sense

my neurotic combustions across state lines. Telepathy is always appreciated in an agent.

All the love and snuggles to my HarperCollins/Harlequin/MIRA family. What an incredible team of people to whom I will forever be indebted for your efforts and brilliance. Emily, you are glorious. Shara, you're a gem and a half. Meghann, you're a goddess, and your book is friggin' hilarious. Jennifer, thank you for your talent and for laughing through 360+ pages of vagina euphemisms.

T.S. Ferguson, my soul twin. I am utterly grateful for you.

Huge thanks and love to my Midwest Writers Workshop family. Forever and ever.

Getting to know and love Dee Romito has been the best part of the writing world.

Special love to Dee and Christa Desir for their literary matchmaking skills. I owe you ladies many fruit baskets, and I'm honored to call you friends.

Thank you to Brenda Drake, who will appear in ten thousand acknowledgments sections, and it still won't be thanks enough for all she does.

Triona, my grammar guide. We will always have the red-faced septuagenarian at our table, and bless you for that. Adriana Cloud, you are a goddamn editing genius, and I am so grateful for you. Amy Reichert, I will eternally aspire to be even a fraction as badass as you. Sarah Cannon, for your chats and support and existence. Katie Glover, for being so very Buttery, and for being the fastest reader in all of time and space. Thank you, ladies. Thank you from the bottom of my fizzy little heart for all you've done and all you are.

Mr. S, I thank you for your friendship and Yodaing. You are forever appreciated, sir.

Shannon Teague and the Cake, Hope, and Love crew: Thank you for letting me prance around your shop and for the technical assist and for letting me borrow your name for a particularly awesome character. From a MySpace blog to this, Shannon. What even.

To the handful of cartoon villains who've passed through my life over the past thirty-six years: SUCK IT. (If that sentence makes it past my editing team, Twitter owes me $15.)

My soon-to-be sister-in-law, Angela Durall, thank you for all you do, and for periodically keeping my kids alive during deadlines and doctor's appointments. You absolute angel, you.

To my mother, my sweet Mommy: You were right. You always said there was something there with my writing. Thank you for decades of support and love and for driving me to my first RWA conference when I was twelve. I'm super sorry my first book is about vaginas. I promise the next one will be about puppies or similar so you can tell your friends. Well, puppies or prostitutes. Either/or.

My darling children. My precious babies. I'm sorry you had so many nights of pancakes and mac and cheese when I had wording to do. Thank you for never blowing up the garage or sacrificing your father to our critter overlords while I was talking to myself at the laptop. If you're reading this book… it had better be the year 2030 or later, or you're bloody well grounded. Mommy loves you.

Behind many a writer is a spouse wondering WTF they married into. Drew, thank you for being mine. The house only caught on fire once during your watch. (That toaster was shifty anyway.) Thank you forever for the endless support and for doing your best to keep up when I'm freaking about the imaginary people in my head not being accommodating, and for rubbing the migraines out of my neck after fifteen-hour sessions curled up at my desk. Thank you for loving roller coasters so much it makes me happy to go with you, even though they terrify me. And also for finding it hilarious when

I scream, "YOU'RE DEAD TO MEEEEEEEEEEEEE!" at you on said rollercoasters. You are loved. You are valued. You are cherished. (We've gotta get out of here, baby!)

And finally, a round of applause to my vagina. Thanks for the inspiration, lady. We make a good team.